TREE-HOUSE COMIX PROUDLY PRESENTS

DOG MAN
MOTHERING HEIGHTS

WRITTEN AND ILLUSTRATED BY DAV PILKEY

AS GEORGE BEARD AND HAROLD HUTCHINS

WITH COLOR BY JOSE GARIBALDI

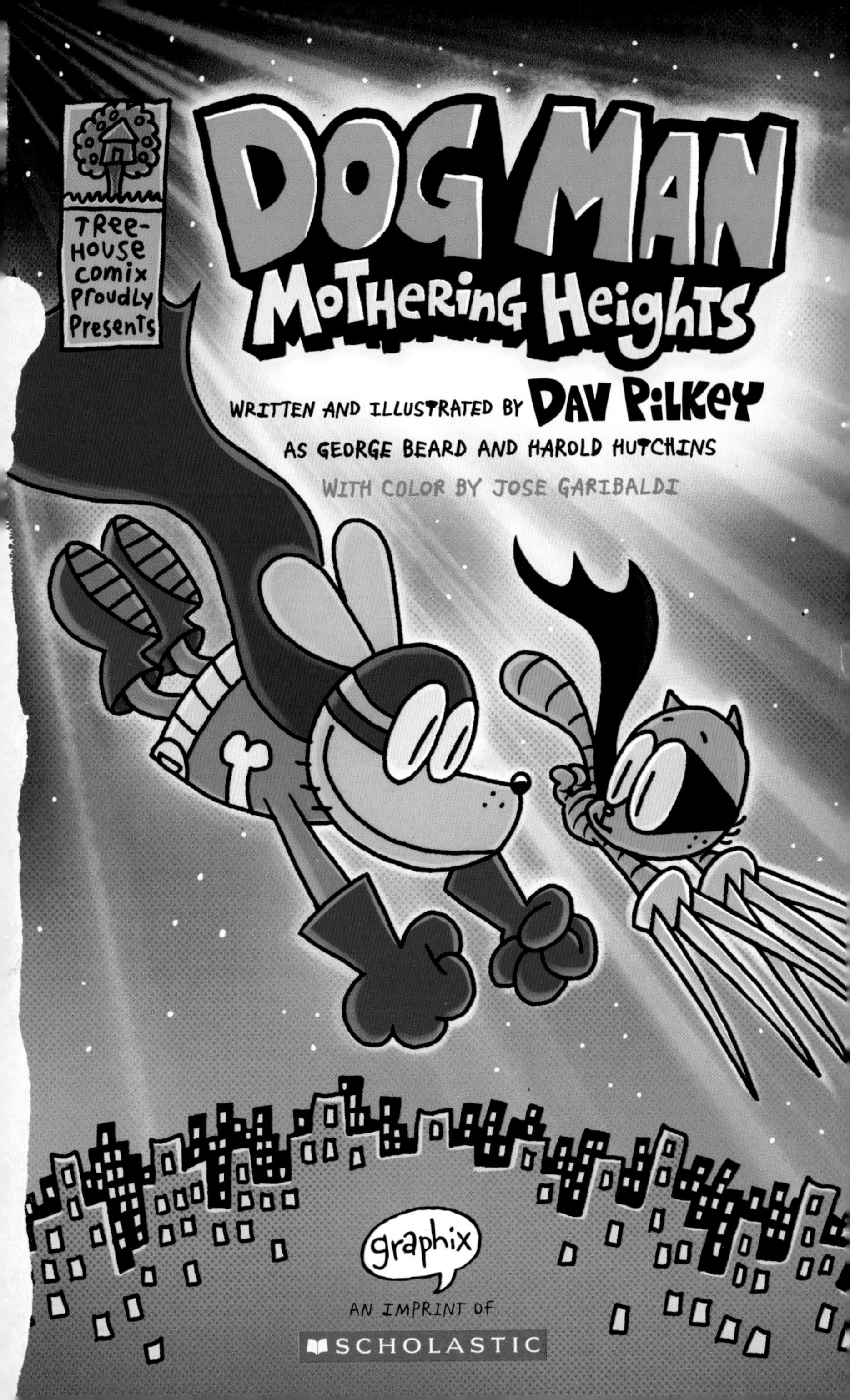

graphix

AN IMPRINT OF

SCHOLASTIC

Library of Congress Control Number 2020949707

978-1-338-68045-4 (POB)
978-1-338-68046-1 (Library)

10 9 8 7 6 5 4 3 2 1 21 22 23 24 25

Printed in China 62
First edition, April 2021

Edited by Ken Geist
Book design by Dav Pilkey and Phil Falco
Color by Jose Garibaldi
Color flatting by Aaron Polk and Corey Barba
Creative Director: Phil Falco
Publisher: David Saylor

CHAPTERS

MEET THE CAST

DOG MAN: He has the head of a dog, the body of a man, and the heart of a HERO!!! He's lovable, brave, and enjoys chasing squirrels.

STRENGTH: Kindness   WEAKNESS: Easily Distracted

PETEY: Once known as the World's Most Evilest Cat, Petey is now working on becoming a better version of himself.

STRENGTH: Intelligence   WEAKNESS: Easily Annoyed

LI'L PETEY: Petey's son. He's a force for Goodness and Kindness, who lives with Petey during the week and Dog Man on weekends.

STRENGTH: Optimism   WEAKNESS: Can Be Annoying

MOLLY: An amphibious kid with a heart of gold and a propensity for silliness. She can fly and can move stuff with her brain.

STRENGTH: Psychokinesis   WEAKNESS: Stubbornness

SARAH HATOFF: An Investigative journalist/blogger who fights injustice wherever it lurks. She's an immigrant from Australia and has a pet poodle.

STRENGTHS: Bravery & Brains   WEAKNESS: Impatience

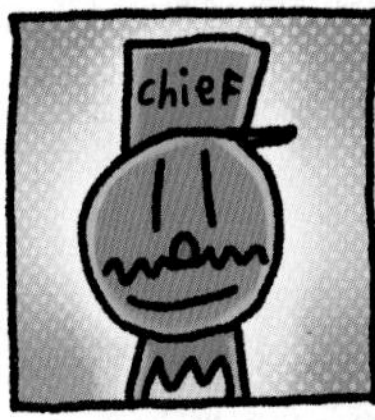
chief

CHIEF: The fearless boss of the local police department. He's got the bravery of a warrior, and the heart of a kid.

STRENGTH: Loyalty WEAKNESS: Impulsiveness

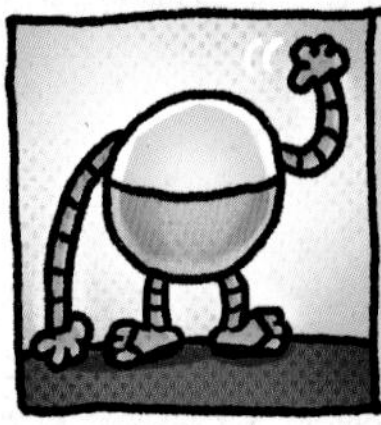

80-HD: A friendly sentient transforming robot who is a loyal friend to Li'l Petey. 80-HD sometimes gets destroyed, but he always comes back for more!

STRENGTH: Creativity WEAKNESS: Malic Acid

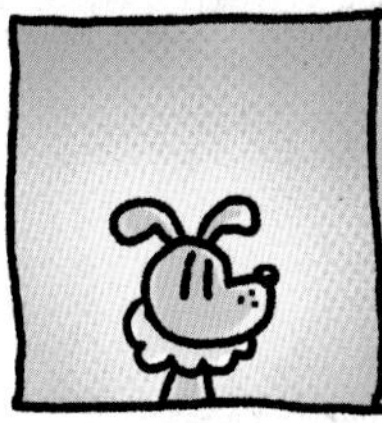

ZUZU: Sarah Hatoff's feisty Poodle who bites first and asks questions later. Actually, she doesn't really ask questions. She's a dog.

STRENGTH: Tenacity WEAKNESS: Holds Grudges

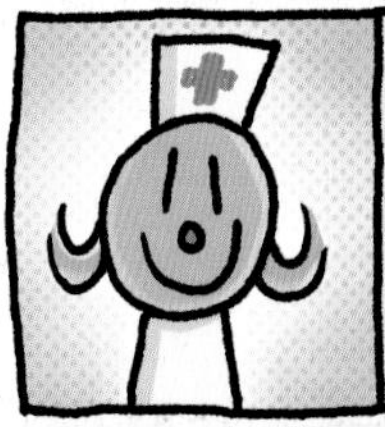

NURSE LADY (a.k.a. Genie S. Lady, RN, BSN): Her genius ideas and caring bedside manner are world renowned. Her quick thinking saved Dog Man's life.

STRENGTH: Moxie WEAKNESS: Chutzpah

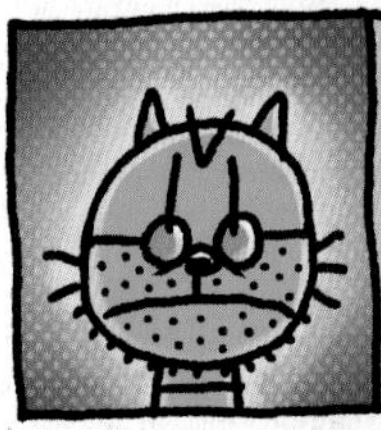

GRAMPA: Petey's dad. He's a selfish, egotistical meanie who currently resides in cat jail. Petey and Li'l Petey no longer associate with him.

STRENGTH: Intelligence WEAKNESS: Arrogance

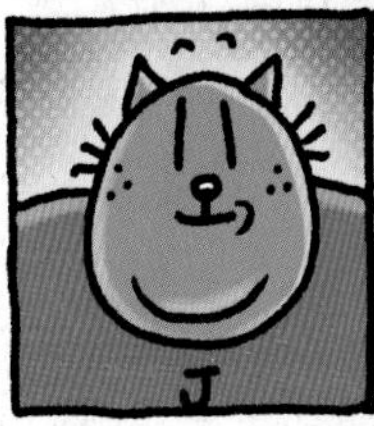
J

BIG JIM: Grampa's pure-hearted cellmate in cat jail. Sometimes he moonlights as a superhero named Commander Cupcake.

STRENGTH: Cupcakes WEAKNESS: Cupcakes

Thank You,
Randy Kessler

"...love is something eternal.
It may change in aspect,
but not in essence."

-Vincent van Gogh

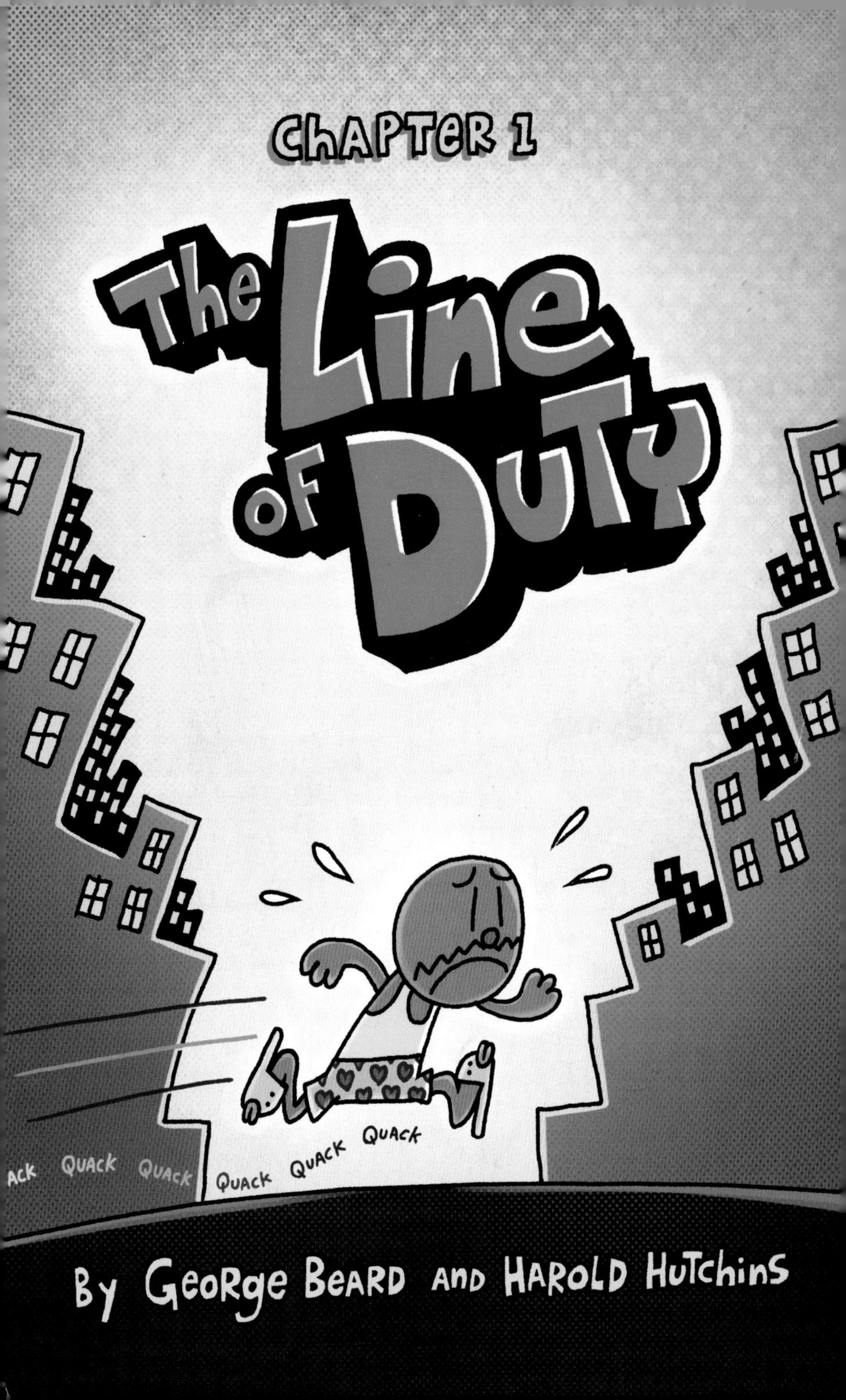
CHAPTER 1
The Line of Duty
ACK QUACK QUACK QUACK QUACK QUACK
By George Beard and Harold Hutchins

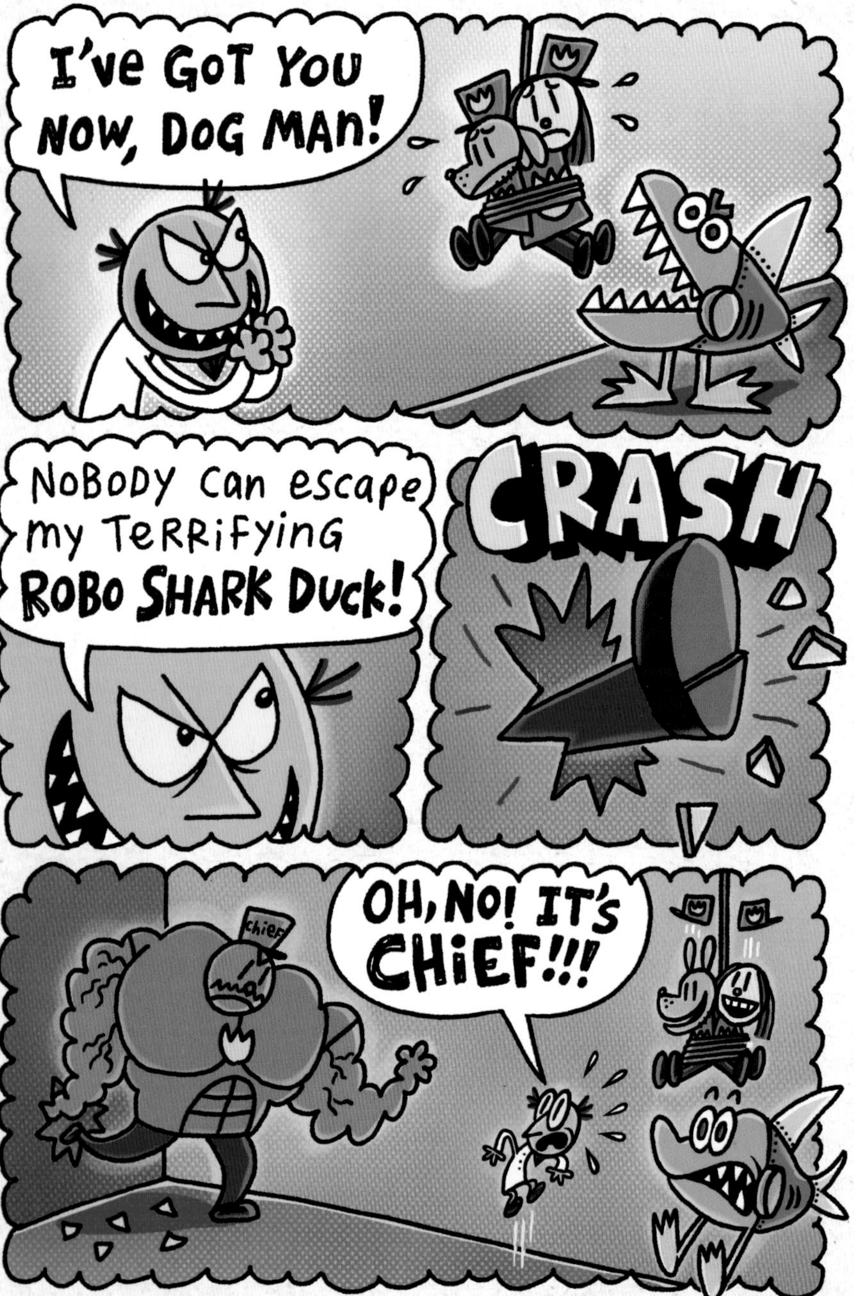
I've GoT YOU NOW, DOG MAN!
NoBoDY Can escape my TeRRiFying ROBO SHARK DUcK!
CRASH
OH, NO! IT'S CHiEF!!!

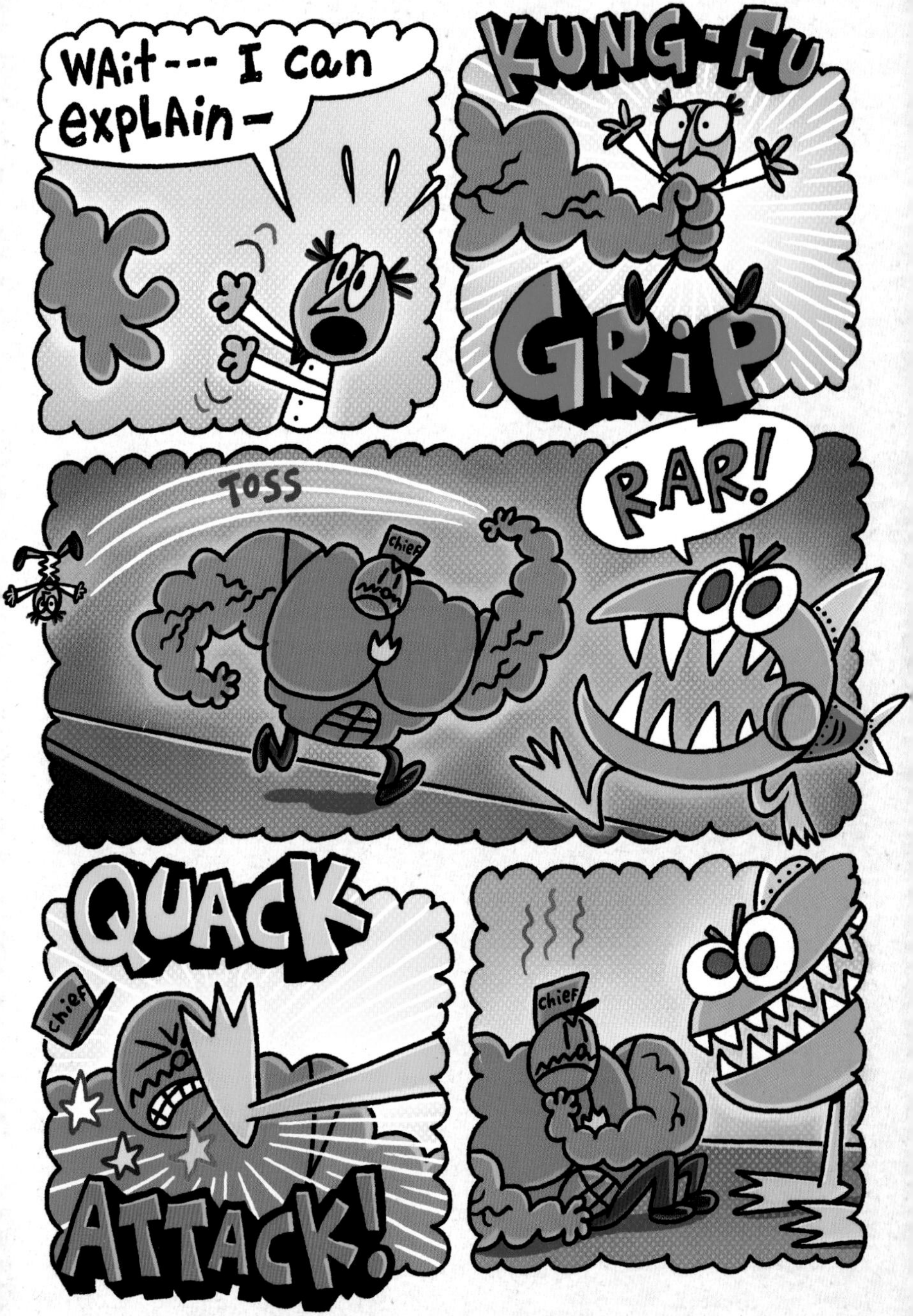
WAit--- I can explAin-
KUNG-FU
GRiP
TOSS
chief
RAR!
QUACK
chief
ATTACK!
chief

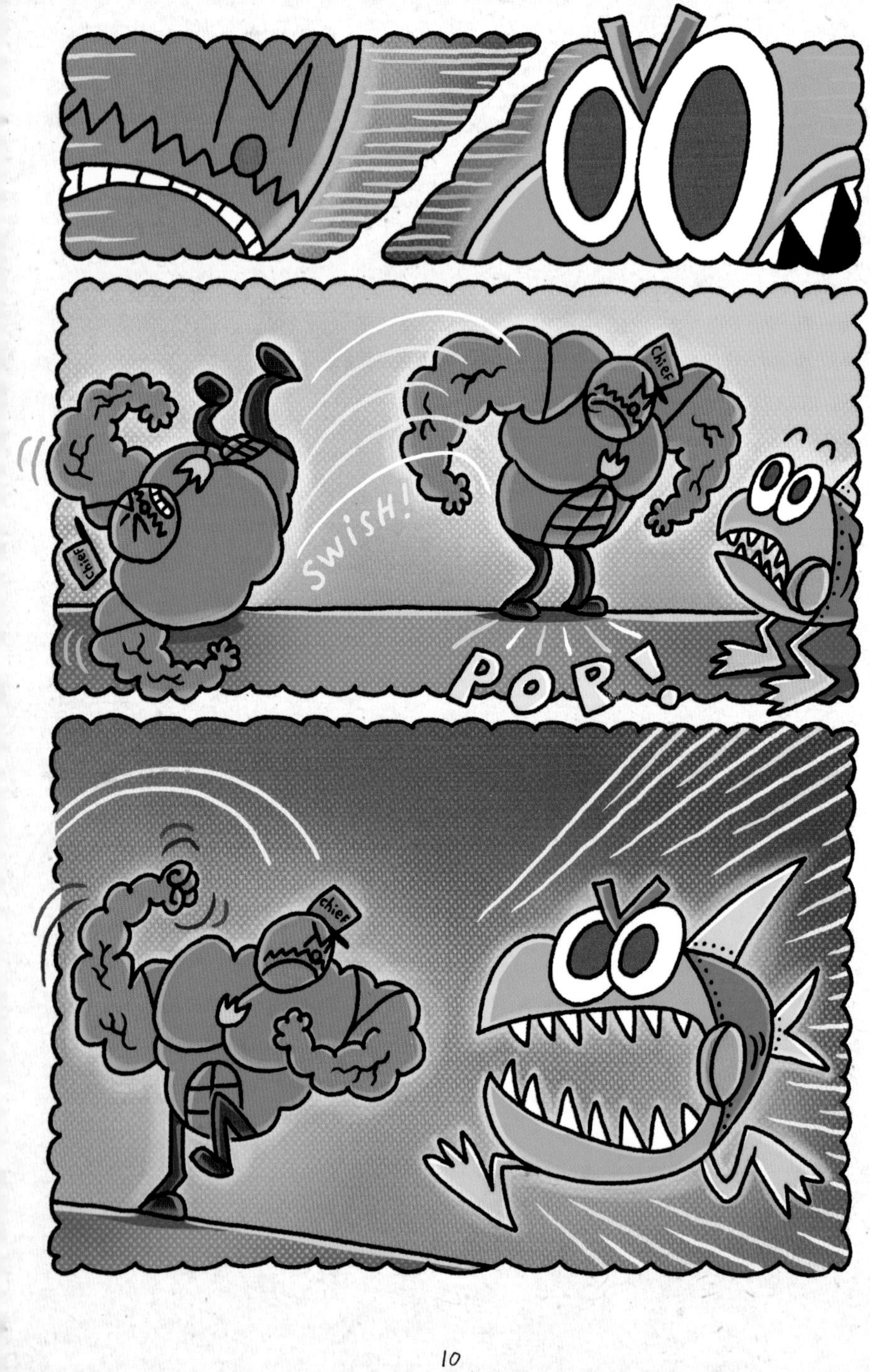

chief
chief
SWISH!
POP!
chief

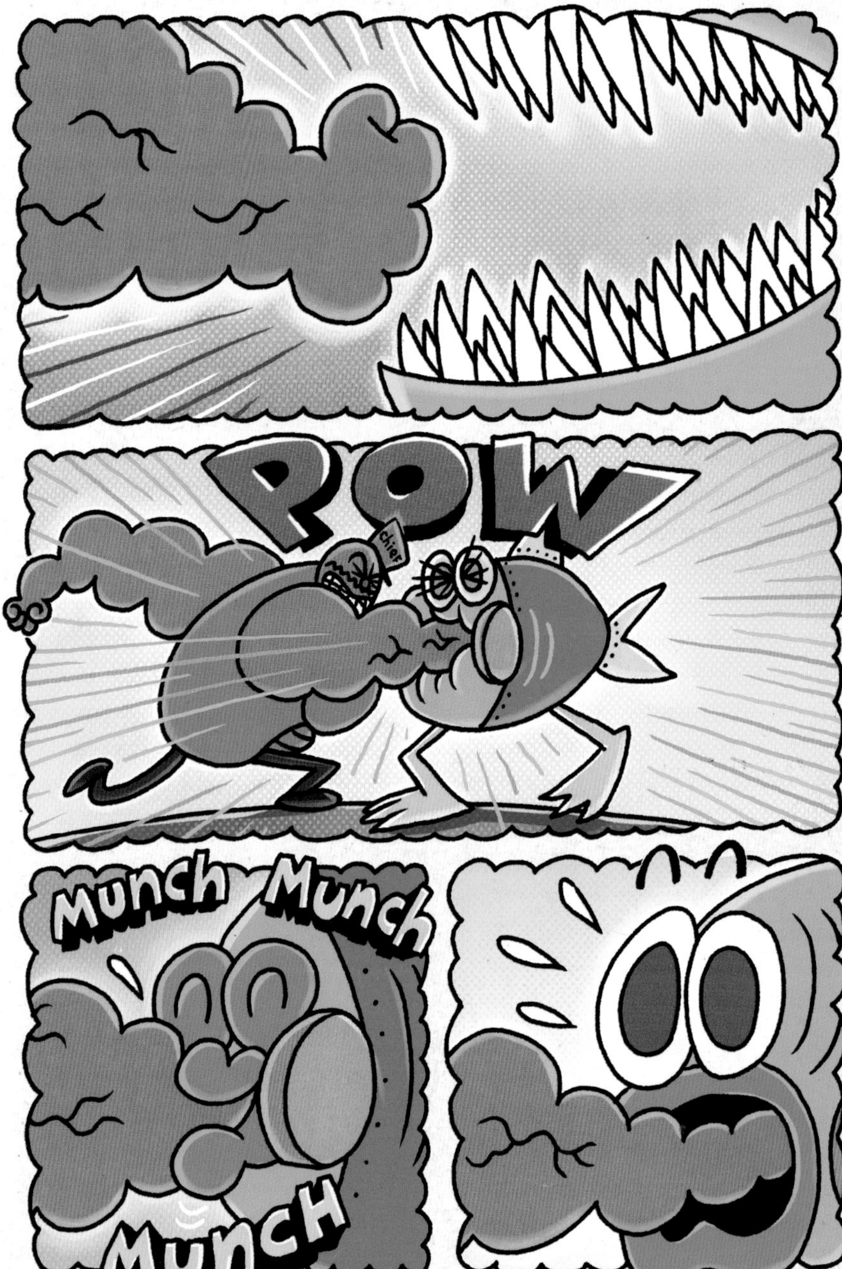
POW
Chief
Munch Munch
Munch

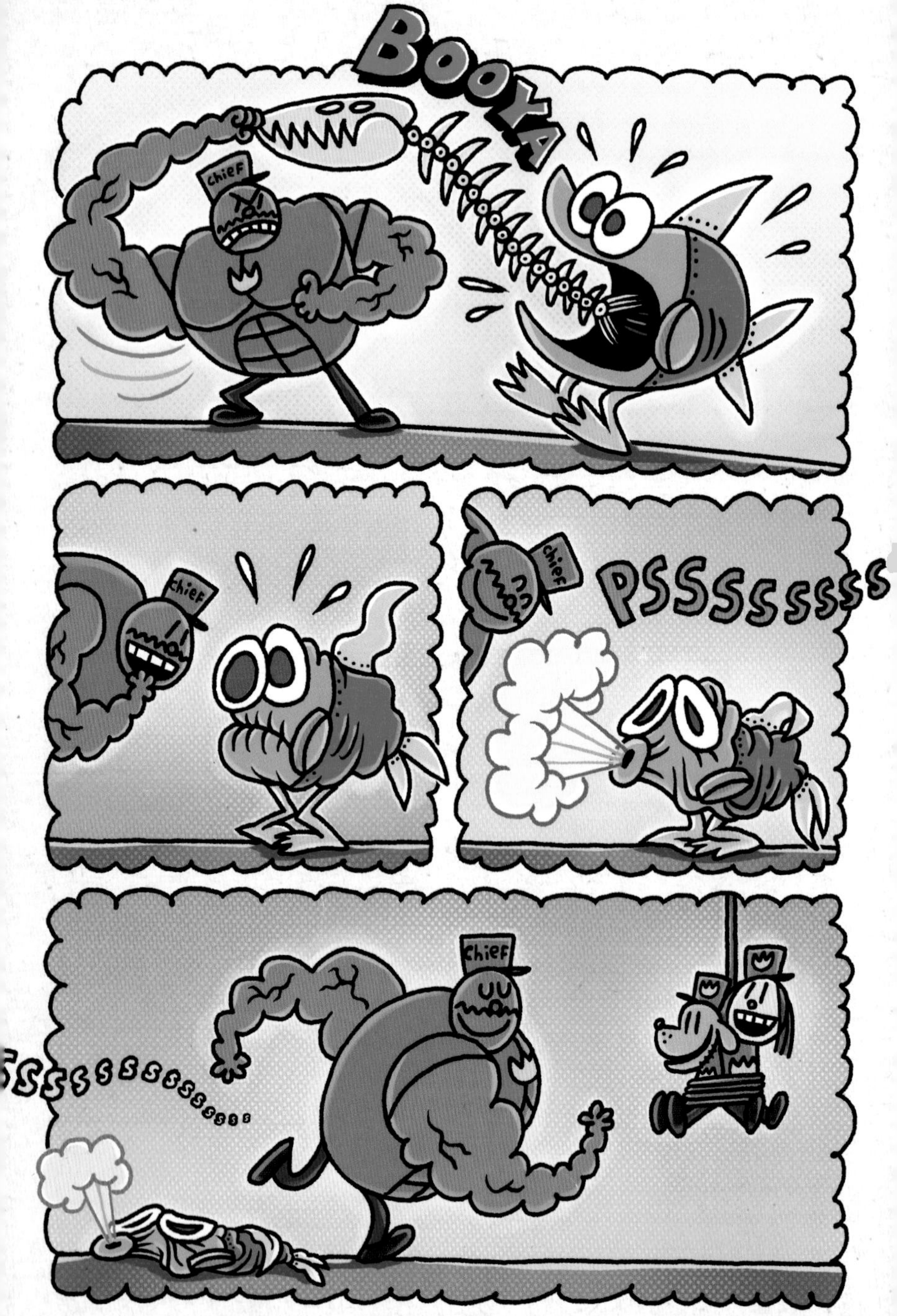
BOOYA
CHIEF
CHIEF
CHIEF
PSSSSSSSSS
CHIEF
SSSSSSSSSSSSSSS

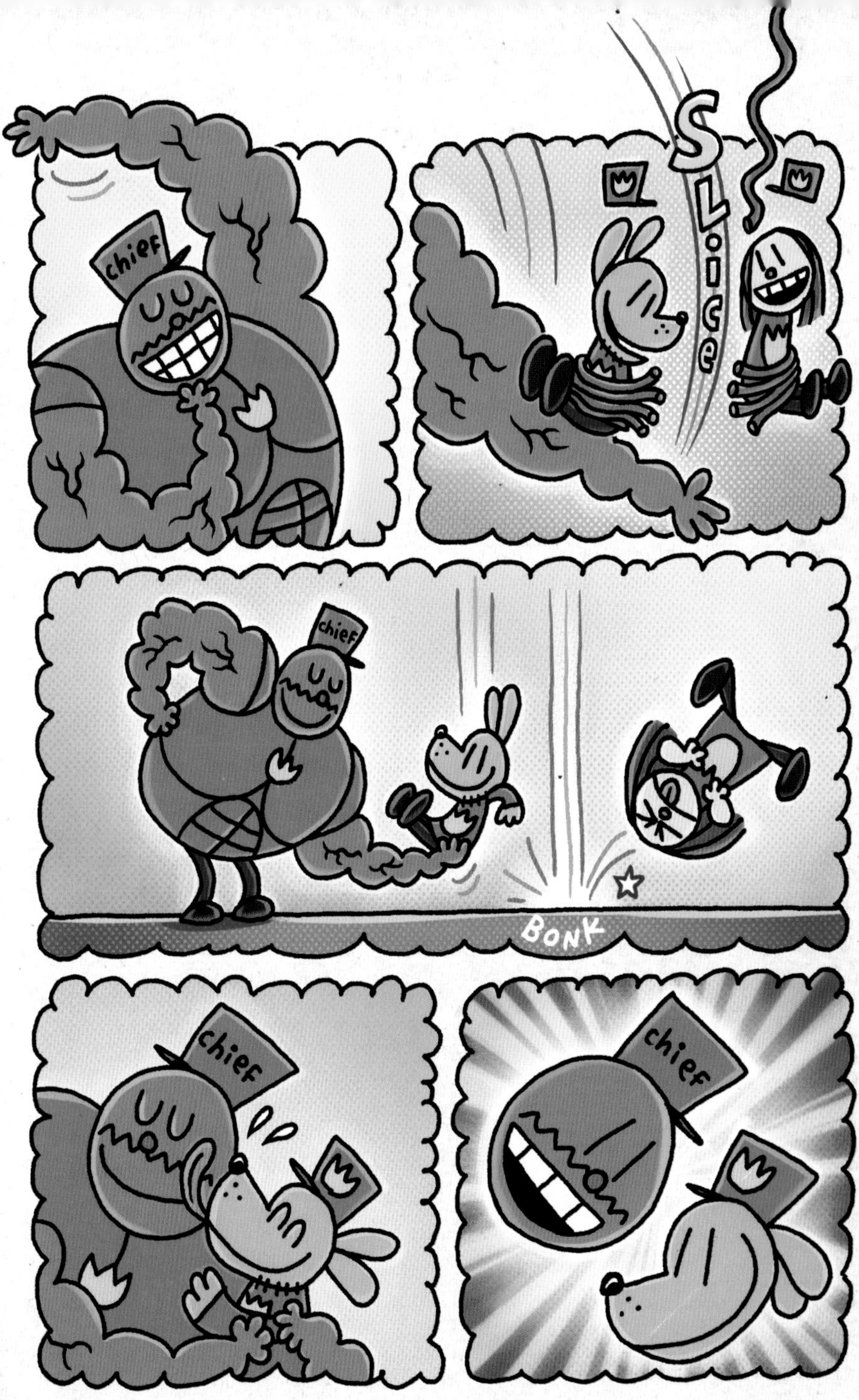
chief
SLICE
chief
BONK
chief
chief

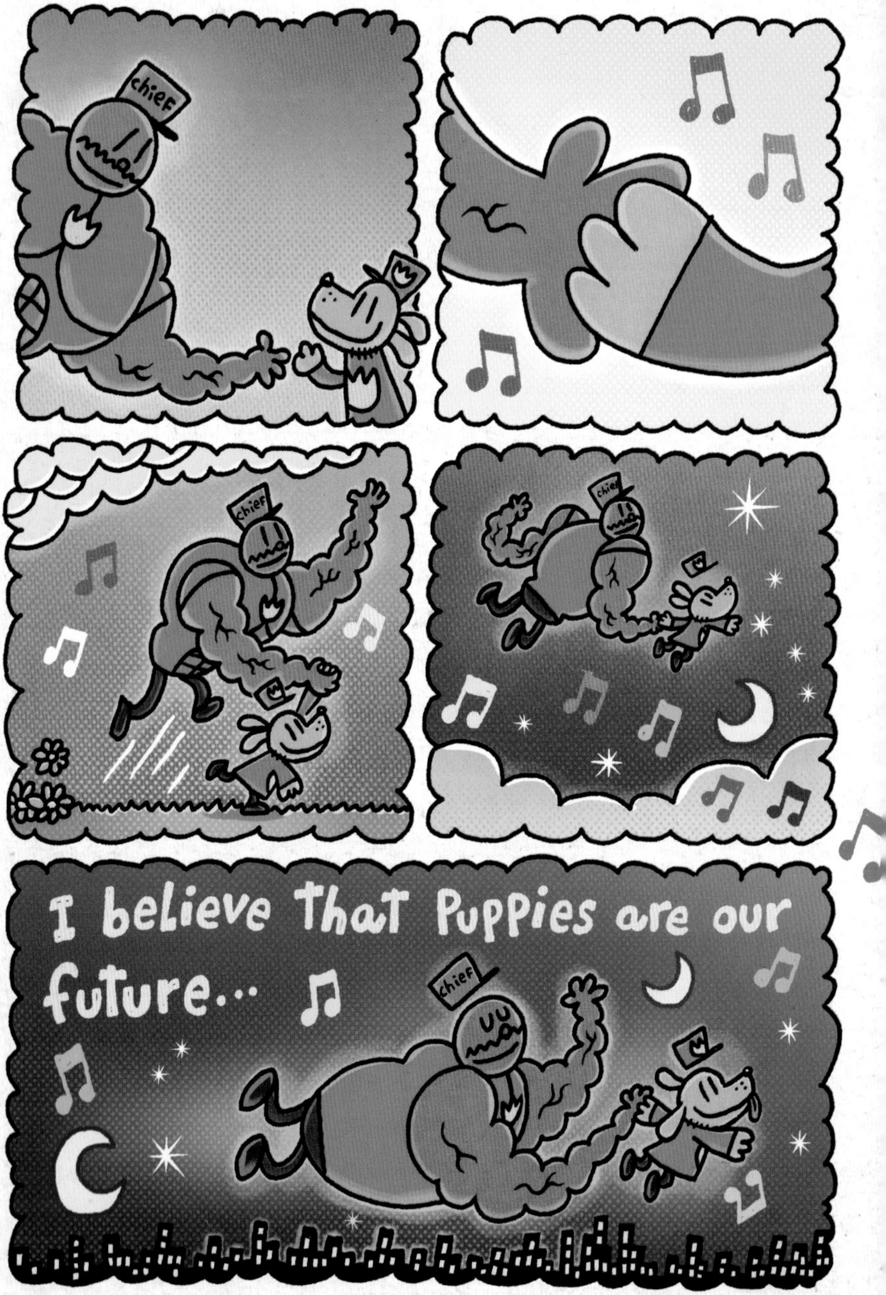
chief
chief
chief
I believe that puppies are our future...
chief

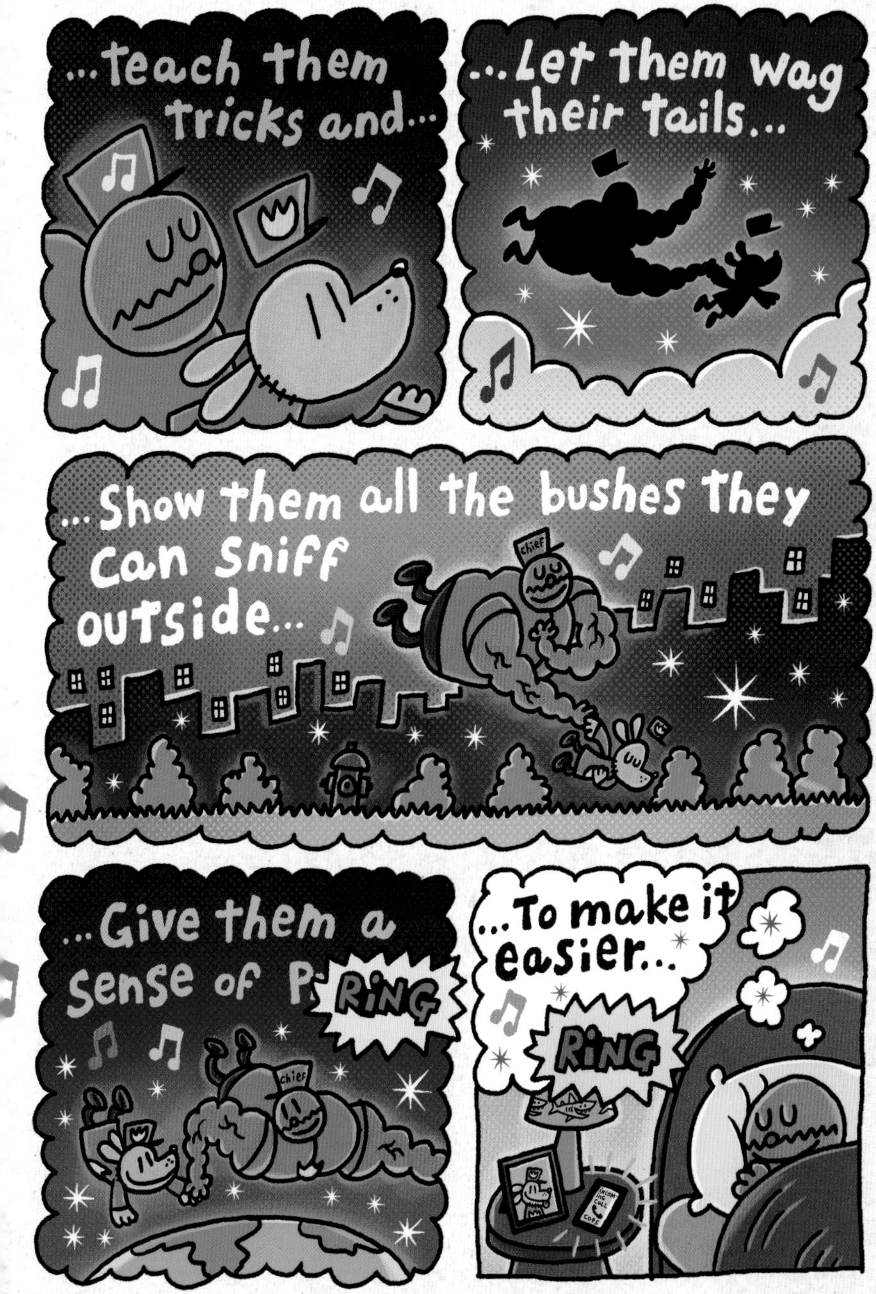

...teach them tricks and...
...Let them wag their tails...
...Show them all the bushes they can sniff outside...
chief
...Give them a sense of P
RING
chief
...To make it easier...
RING

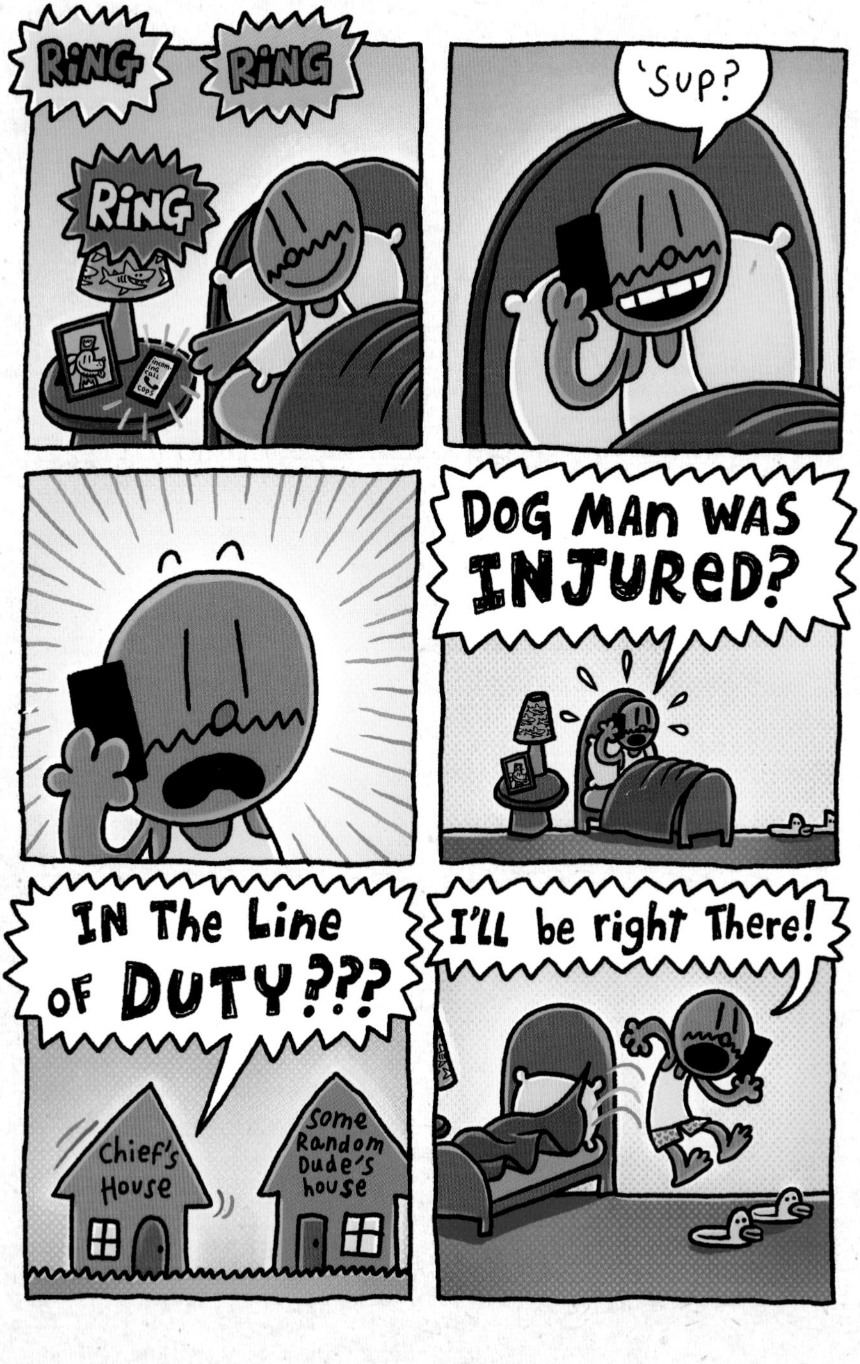
RING
RING
RING
incoming call
cops
'SUP?
DOG MAN WAS INJURED?
IN The Line of DUTY???
Chief's House
Some Random Dude's house
I'LL be right There!

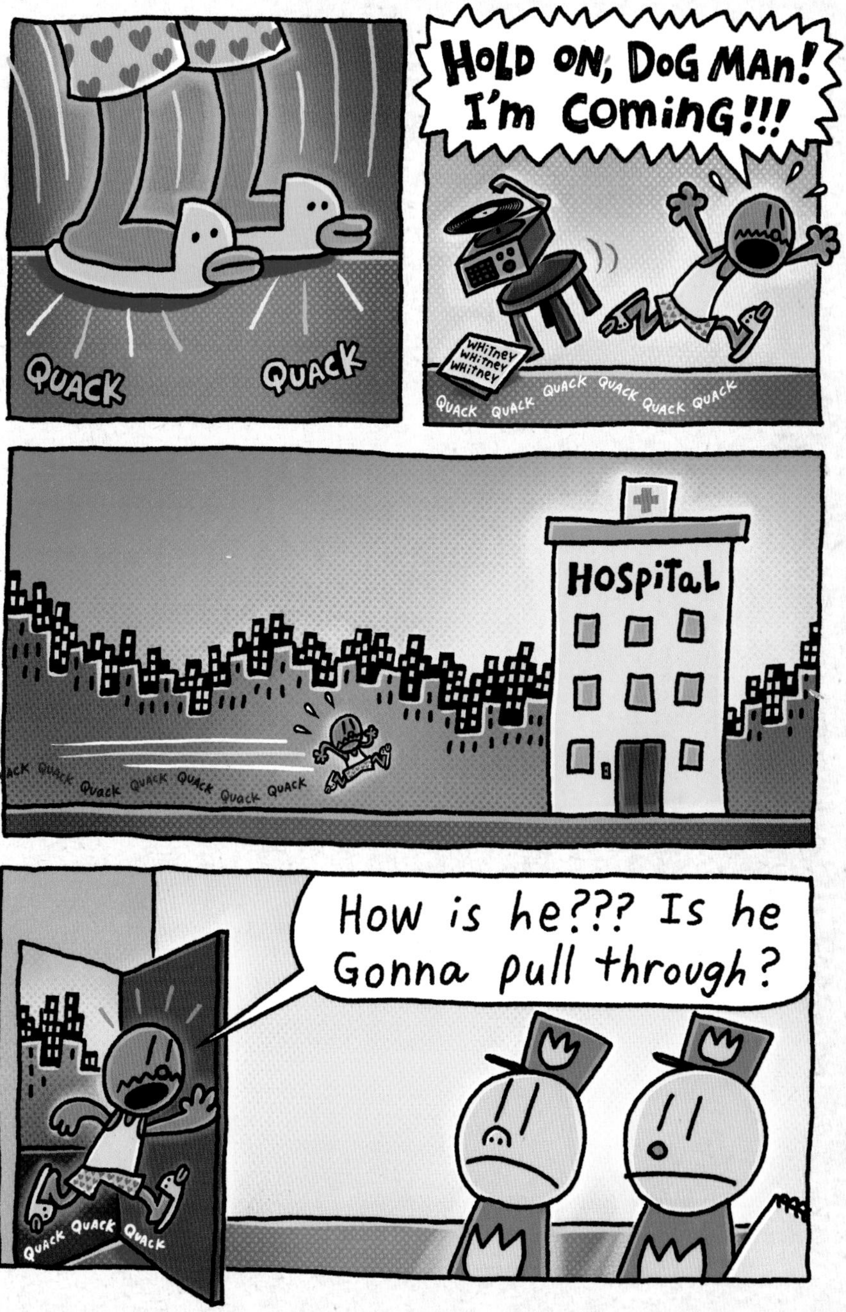

QUACK
QUACK
HOLD ON, DOG MAN! I'M COMING!!!
WHITNEY WHITNEY WHITNEY
QUACK QUACK QUACK QUACK QUACK QUACK
HOSPITAL
QUACK QUACK Quack QUACK QUACK Quack QUACK
How is he??? Is he
Gonna pull through?
QUACK QUACK QUACK

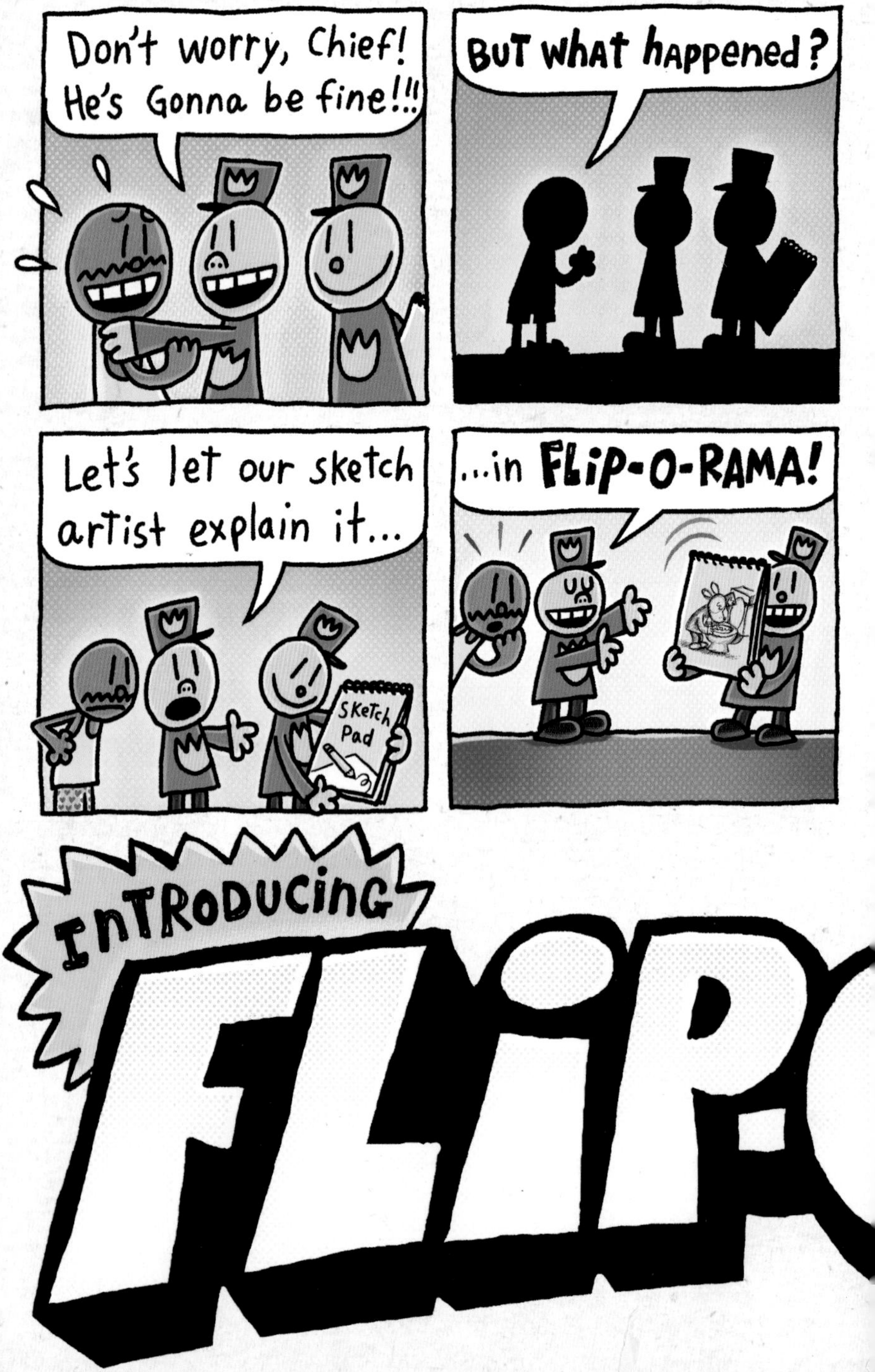

Don't worry, Chief! He's Gonna be fine!!!
BUT WHAT happened?
Let's let our sketch artist explain it...
SKetch Pad
...in FLiP-O-RAMA!
InTRODUCinG
FLiP

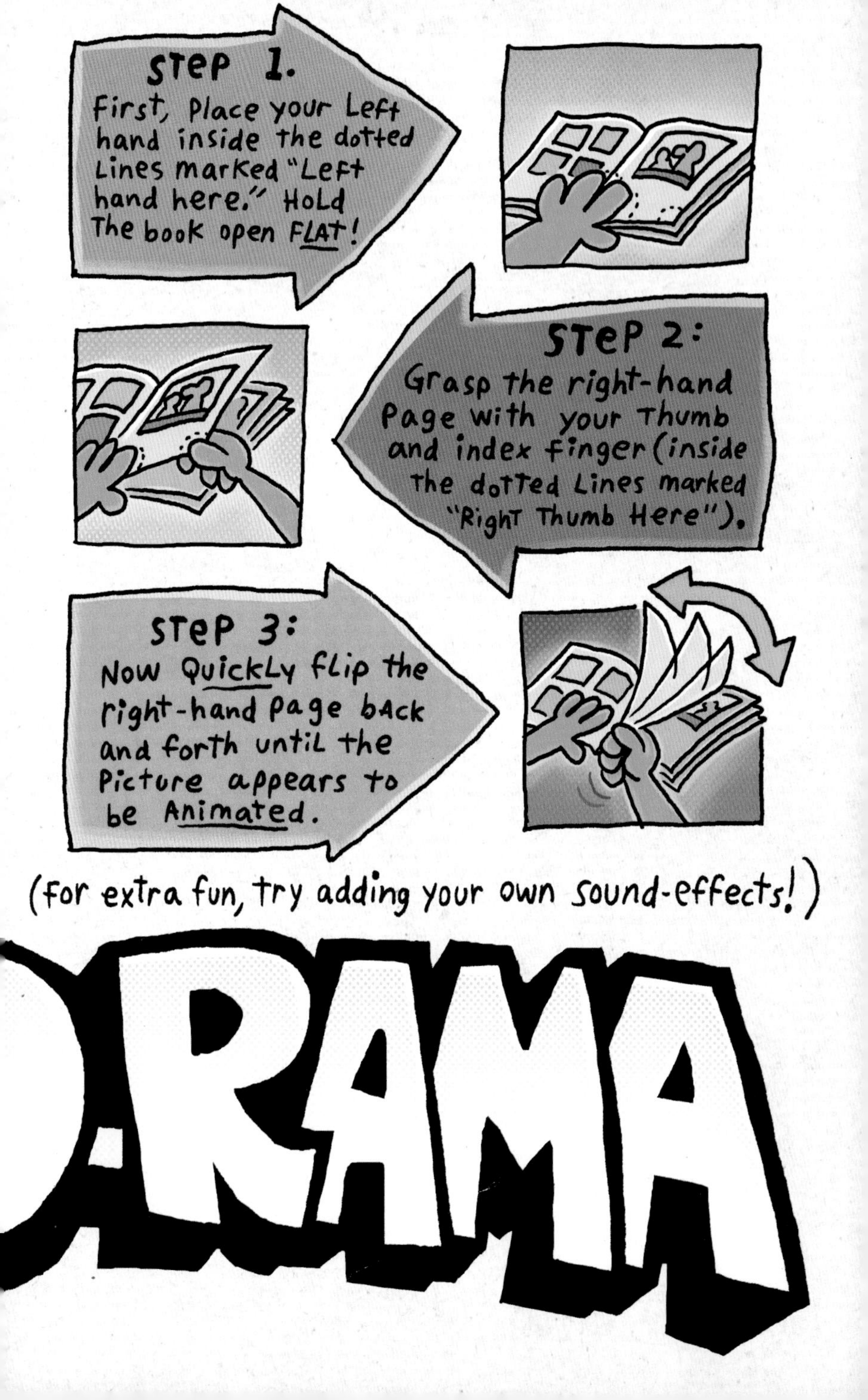
STEP 1.
First, Place your Left hand inside the dotted Lines marked "Left hand here." Hold The book open FLAT!
STEP 2:
Grasp the right-hand Page with your Thumb and index finger (inside the dotted Lines marked "Right Thumb Here").
STEP 3:
Now QUICKLY flip the right-hand page back and forth until the Picture appears to be Animated.
(for extra fun, try adding your own sound-effects!)
RAMA

ReMeMBeR,

While you are flipping, be sure you can see the image on page **21** **AND** the image on page **23**.

If you flip quickly, the two pictures will start to look like **ONE** **ANIMATED** cartoon.

Don't forget to add your own sound-effects!!!

Left hand here.

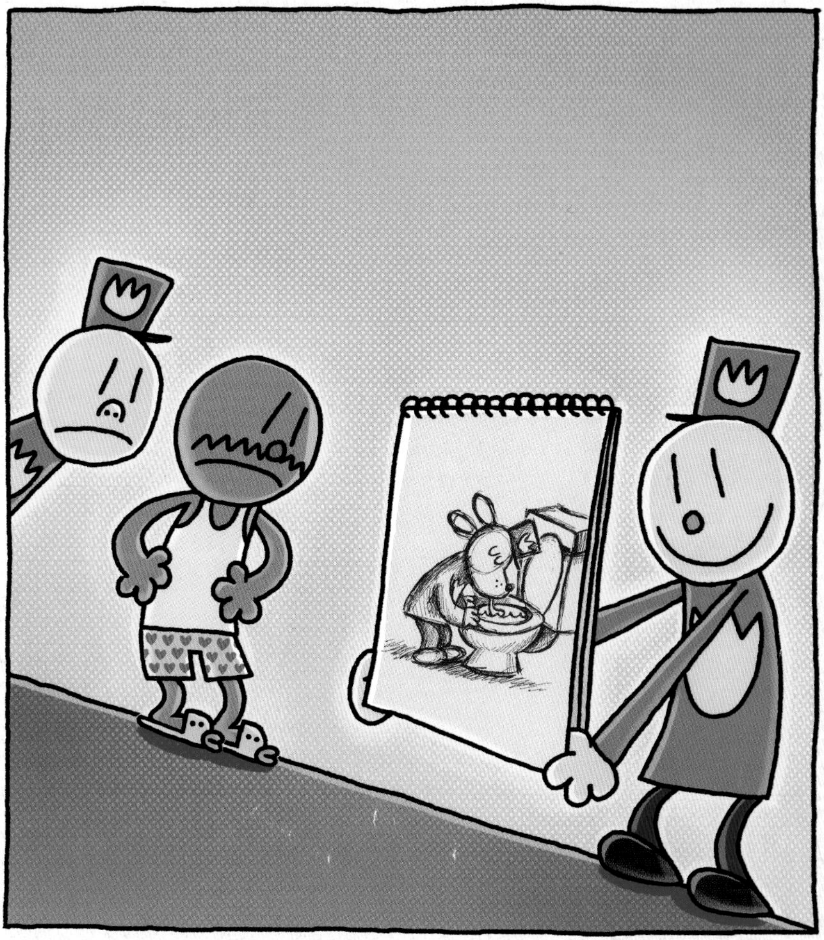

Right Thumb here.

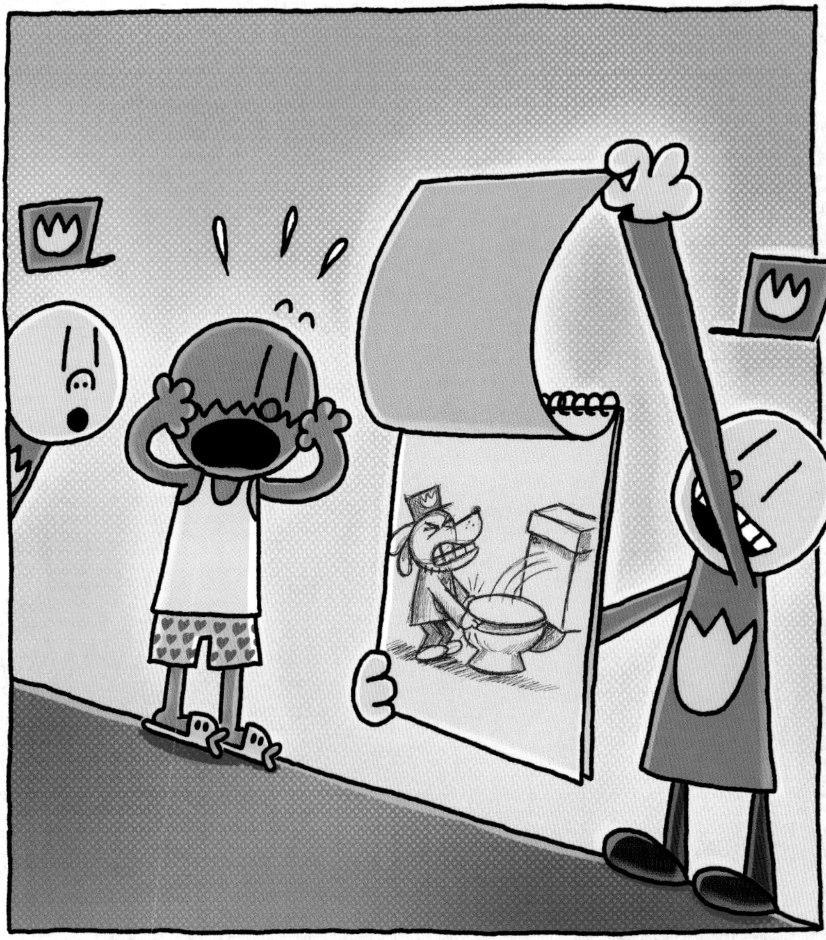

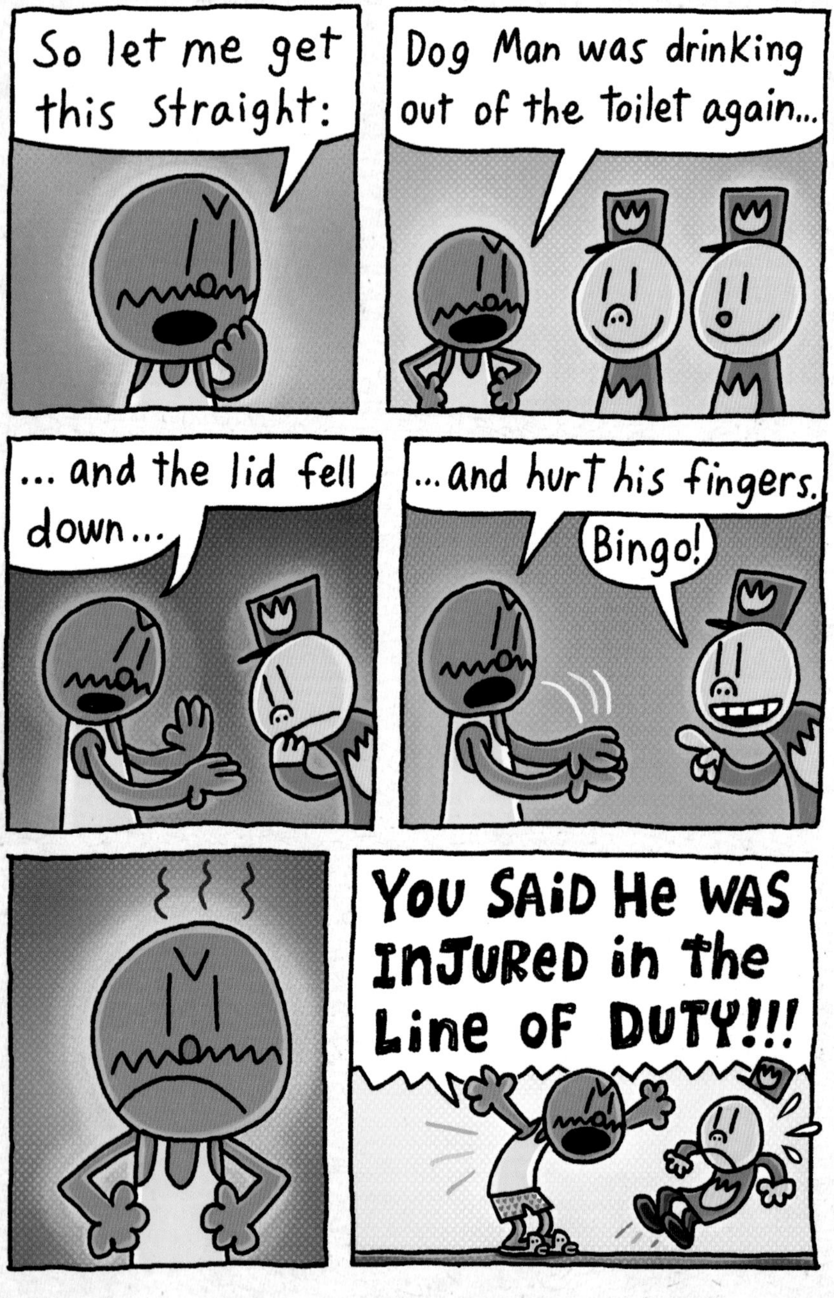
So let me get this straight:
Dog Man was drinking out of the toilet again...
... and the lid fell down...
... and hurt his fingers.
Bingo!
YOU SAID He WAS INJURED in the Line OF DUTY!!!

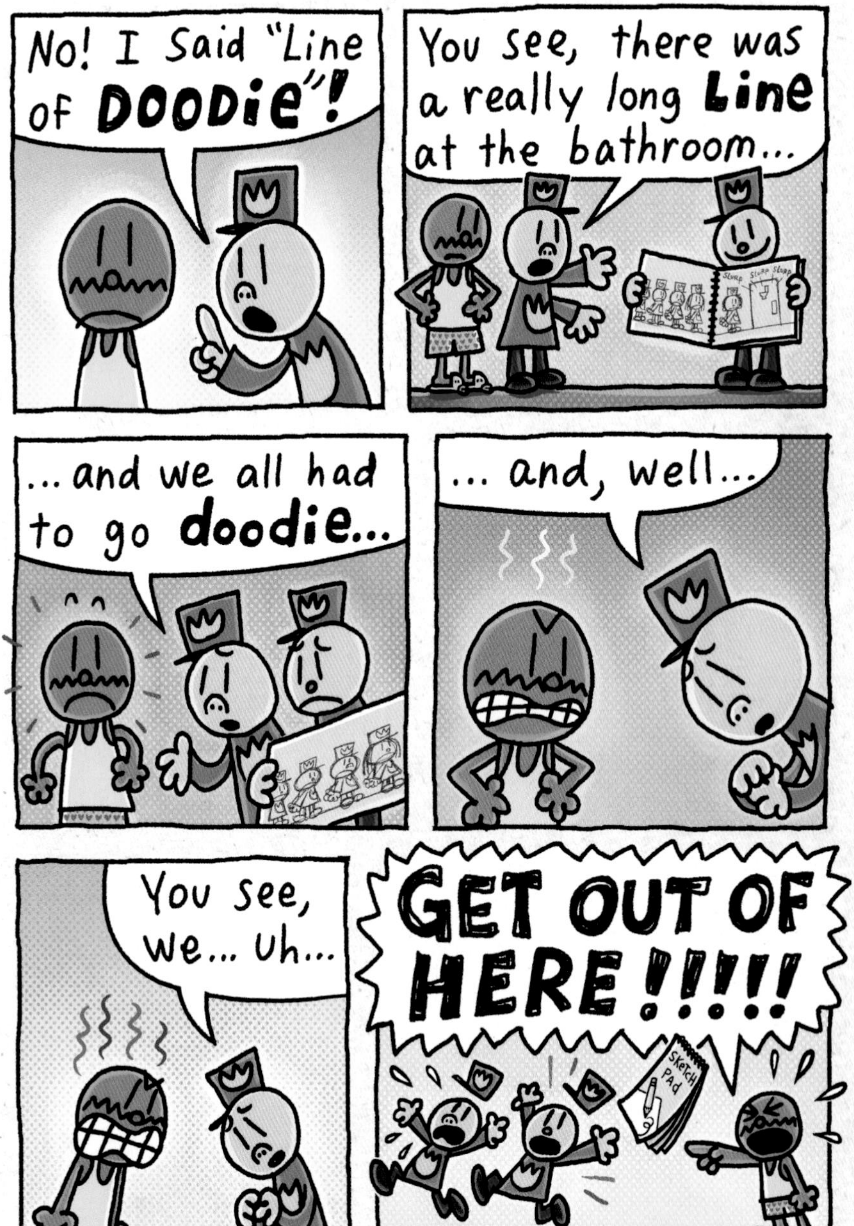
No! I Said "Line of DOODIE"!
You see, there was a really long Line at the bathroom...
...and we all had to go doodie...
... and, well...
You see, we... uh...
GET OUT OF HERE!!!!!
SKETCH PAD

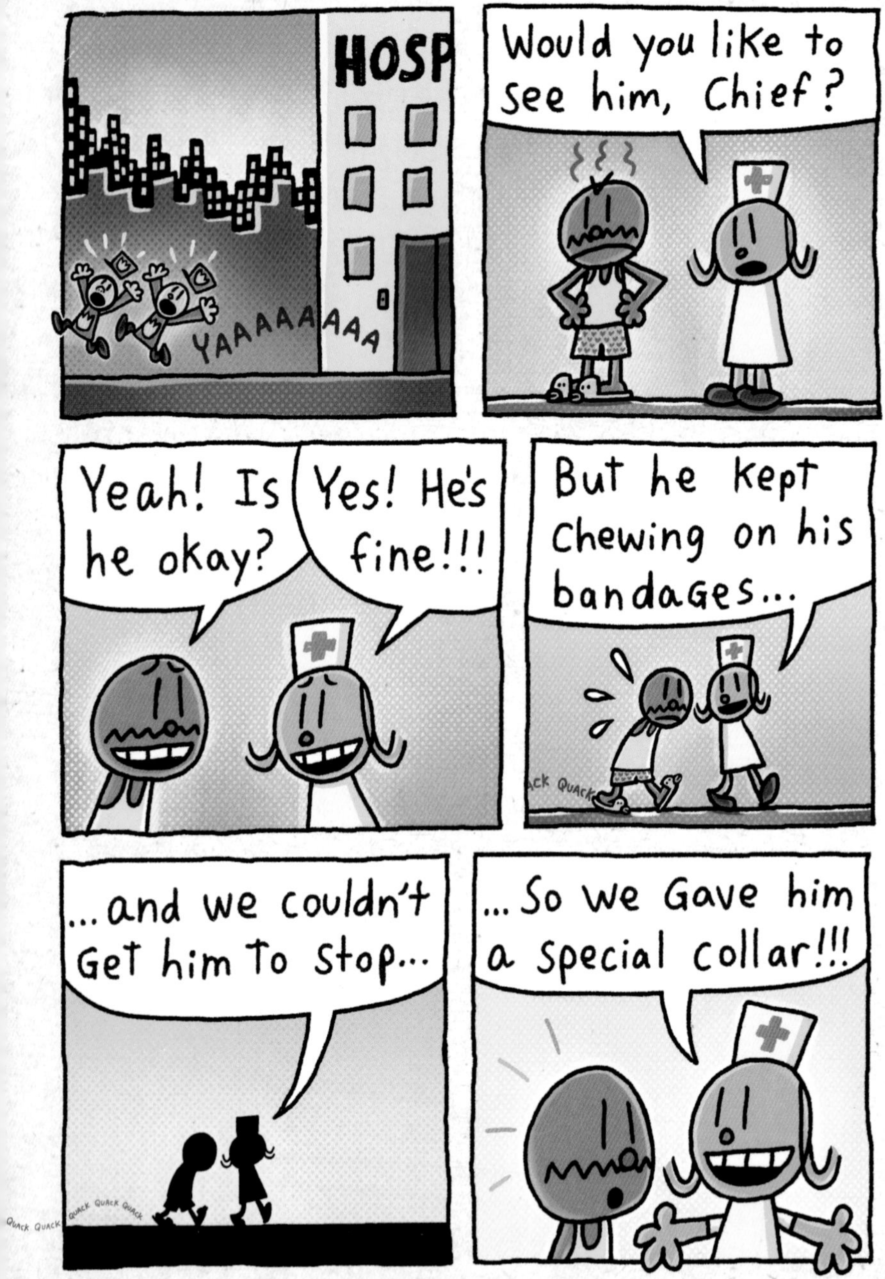
HOSP
YAAAAAAAA
Would you like to see him, Chief?
Yeah! Is he okay?
Yes! He's fine!!!
But he kept chewing on his bandages...
QUACK QUACK
...and we couldn't get him to stop...
QUACK QUACK QUACK QUACK QUACK
...So we gave him a special collar!!!

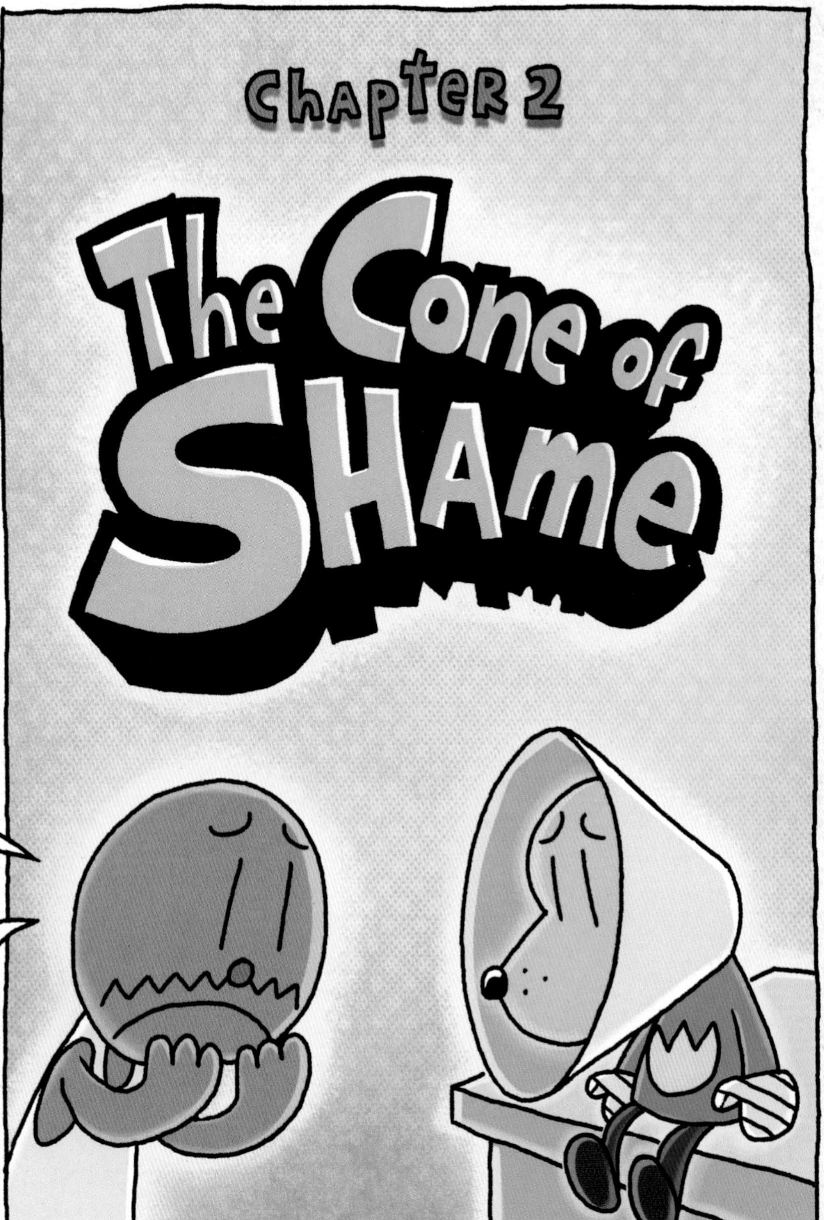
Chapter 2
The Cone of Shame

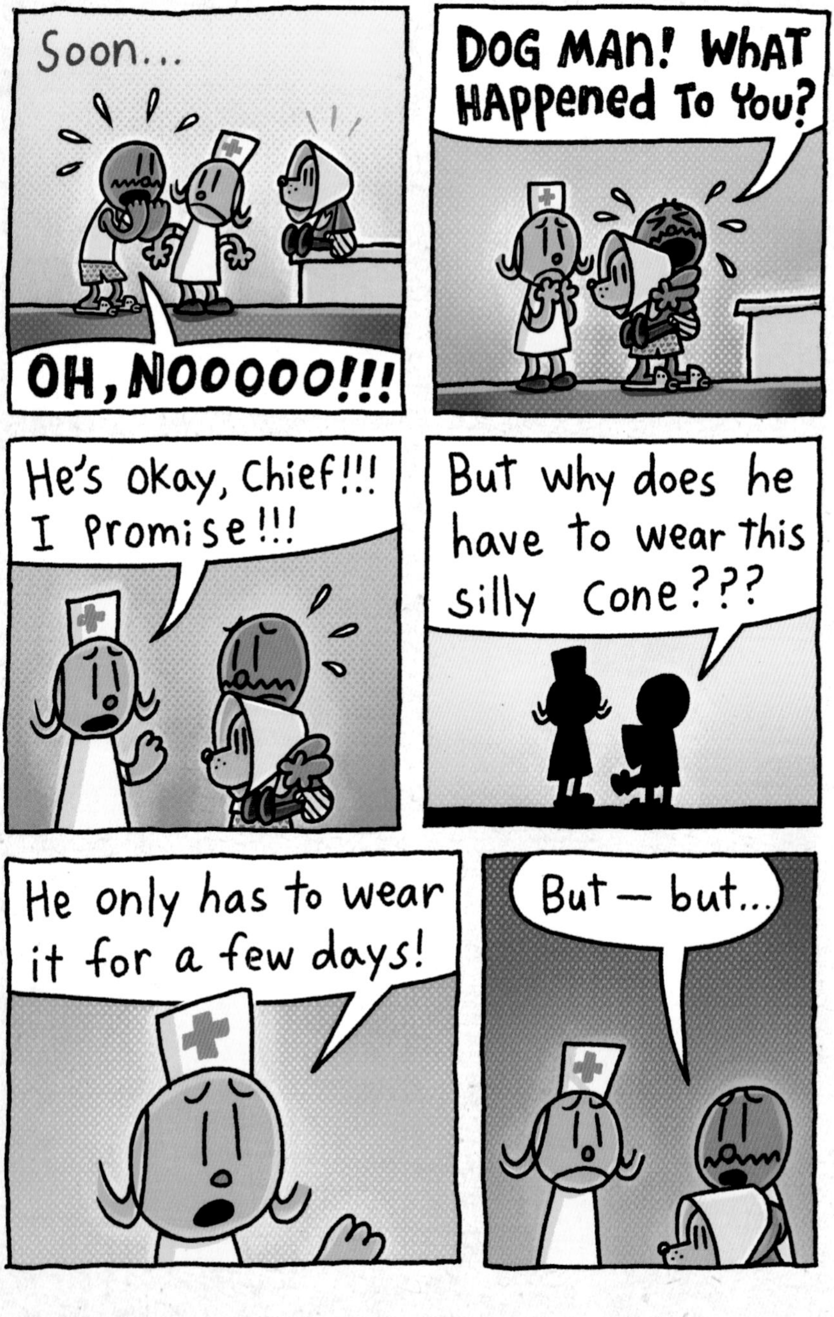
Soon...
OH, NOOOOO!!!
DOG MAN! WHAT HAPPENED TO YOU?
He's okay, Chief!!! I Promise!!!
But why does he have to wear this silly cone???
He only has to wear it for a few days!
But— but...

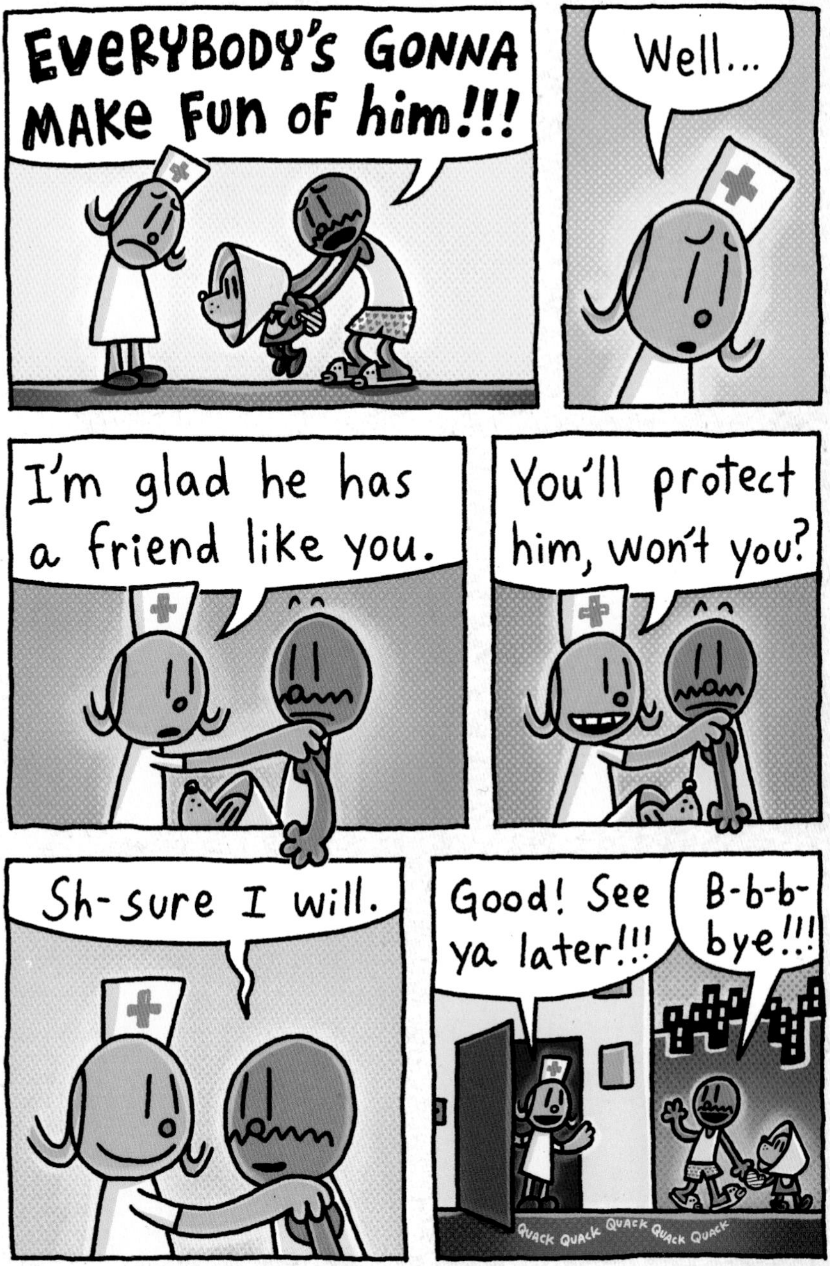
EVERYBODY'S GONNA MAKE FUN OF him!!!
Well...
I'm glad he has a friend like you.
You'll protect him, won't you?
Sh-sure I will.
Good! See ya later!!!
B-b-b-bye!!!
QUACK QUACK QUACK QUACK QUACK

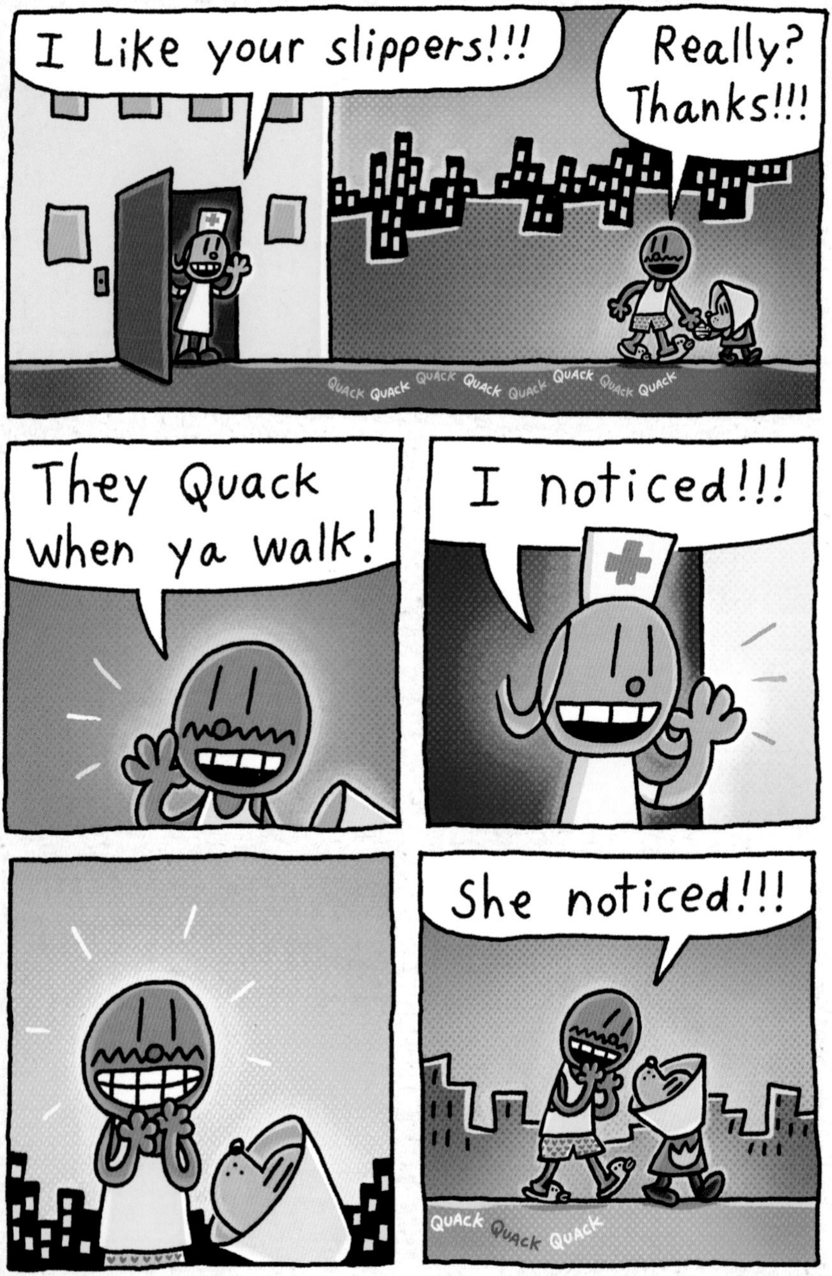
I Like your slippers!!!
Really? Thanks!!!
QUACK QUACK QUACK QUACK QUACK QUACK QUACK QUACK
They Quack when ya walk!
I noticed!!!
She noticed!!!
QUACK QUACK QUACK

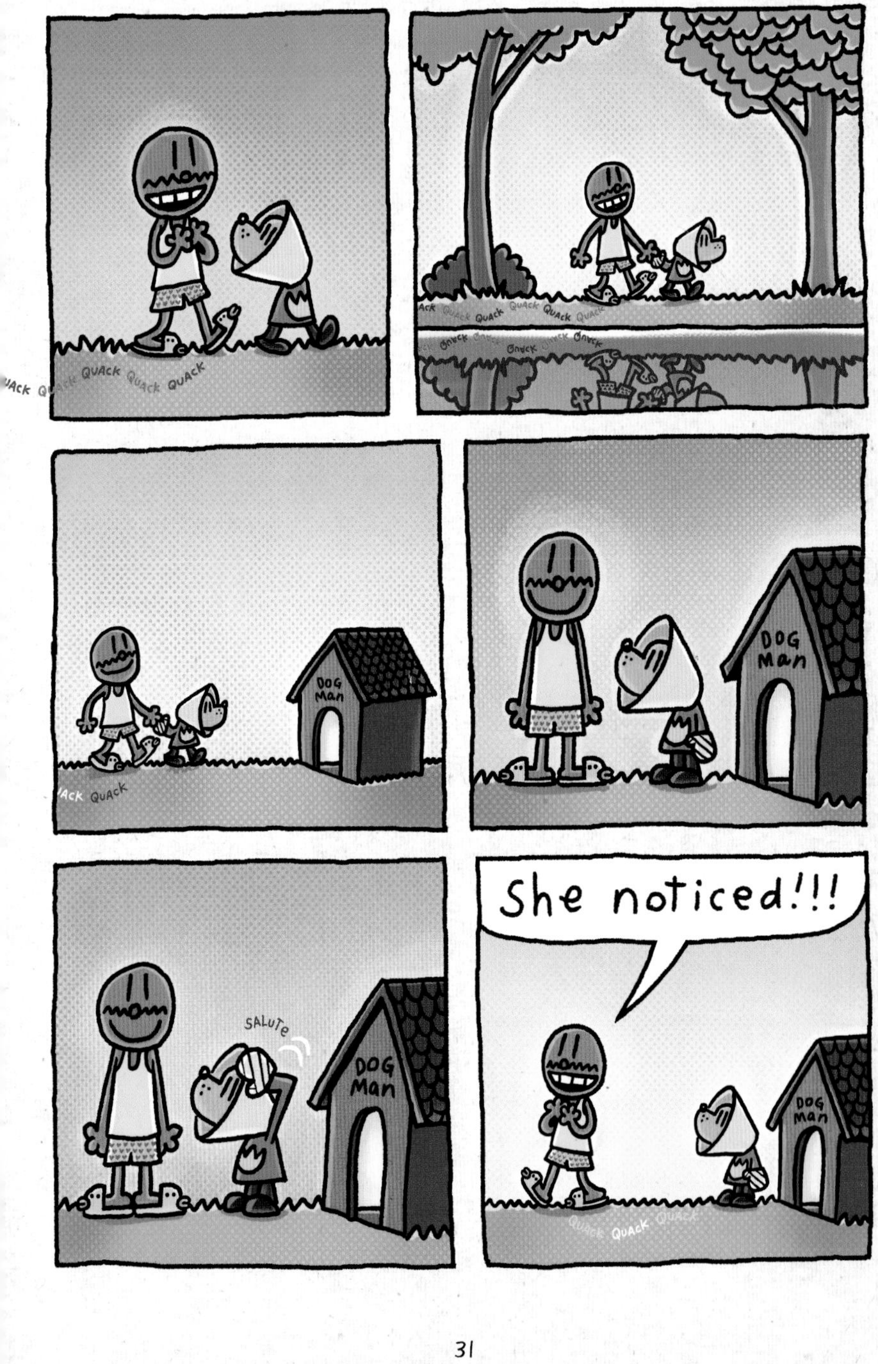
QUACK QUACK QUACK
QUACK QUACK QUACK
DOG Man
QUACK
DOG Man
SALUTE
DOG Man
She noticed!!!
DOG Man
QUACK QUACK QUACK

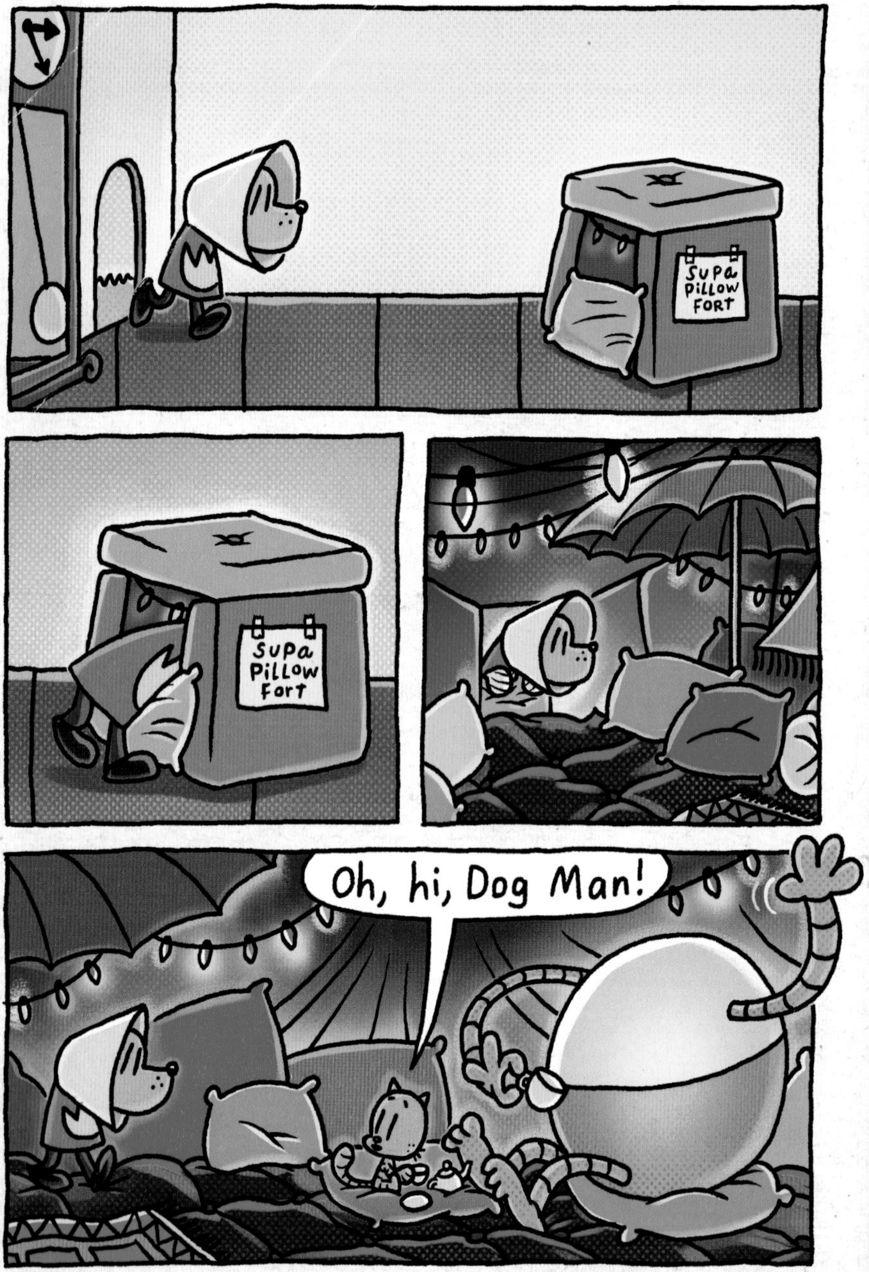
SUPA PILLOW FORT
SUPA PILLOW FORT
Oh, hi, Dog Man!

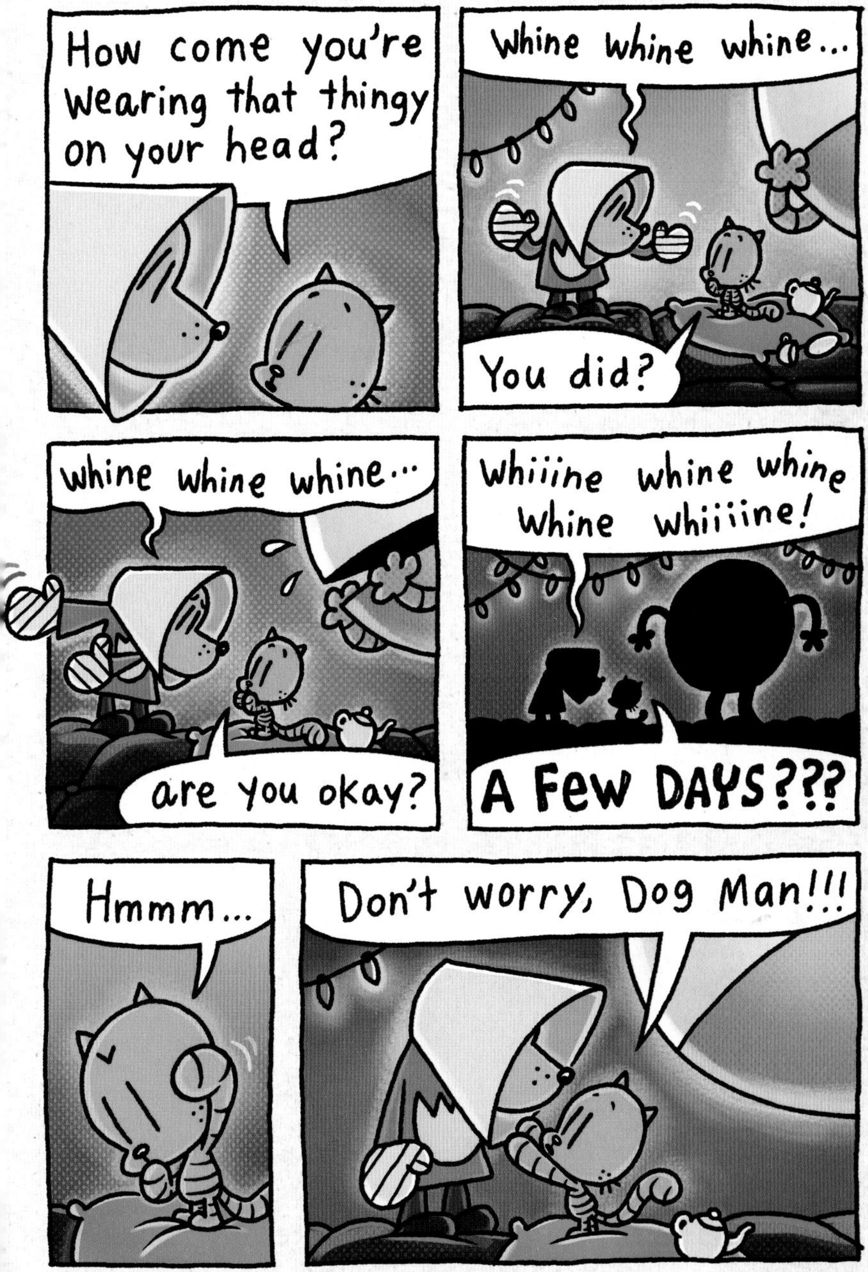
How come you're wearing that thingy on your head?
Whine whine whine...
You did?
whine whine whine...
are you okay?
Whiiine whine whine whine whiiiine!
A FEW DAYS???
Hmmm...
Don't worry, Dog Man!!!

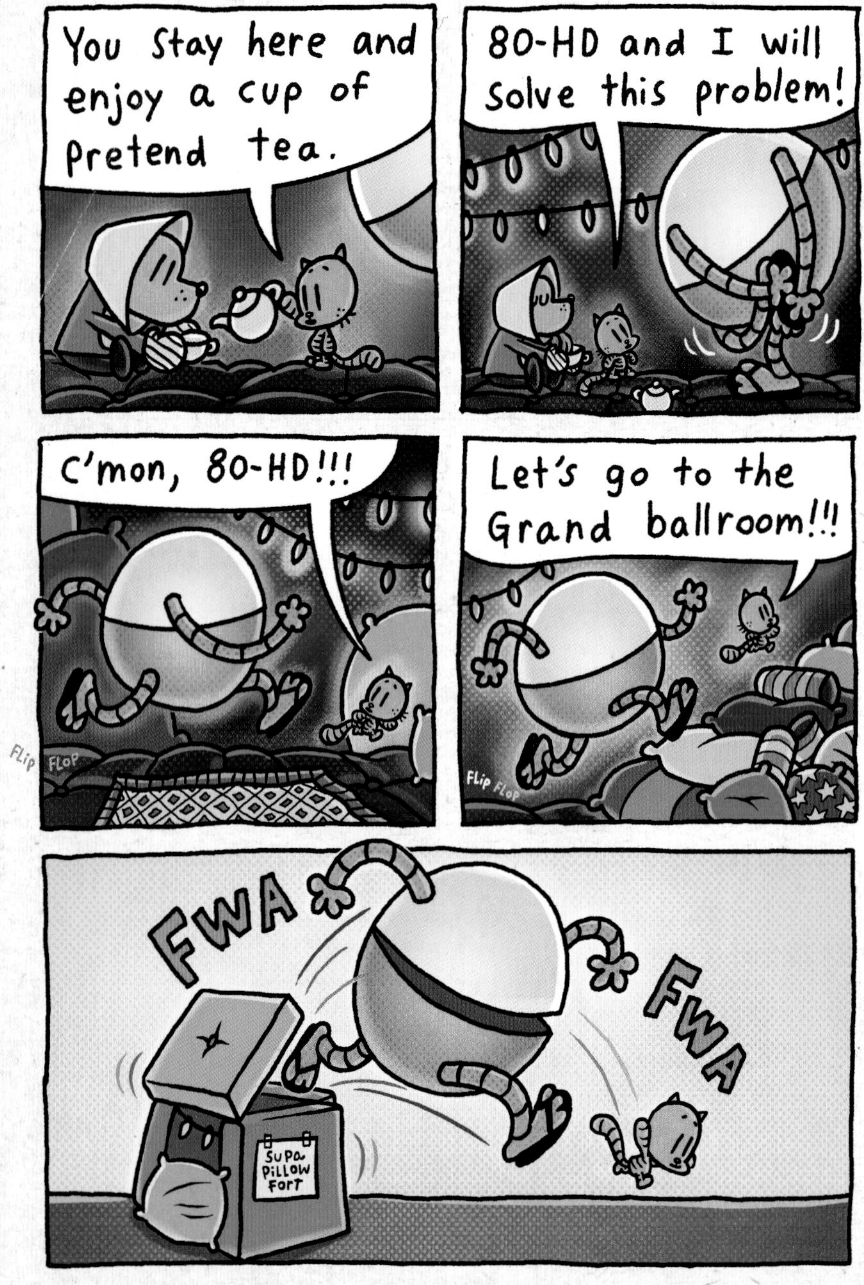
You stay here and enjoy a cup of pretend tea.
80-HD and I will solve this problem!
C'mon, 80-HD!!!
FLIP FLOP
Let's go to the Grand ballroom!!!
FLIP FLOP
FWA
FWA
SUPA PILLOW FORT

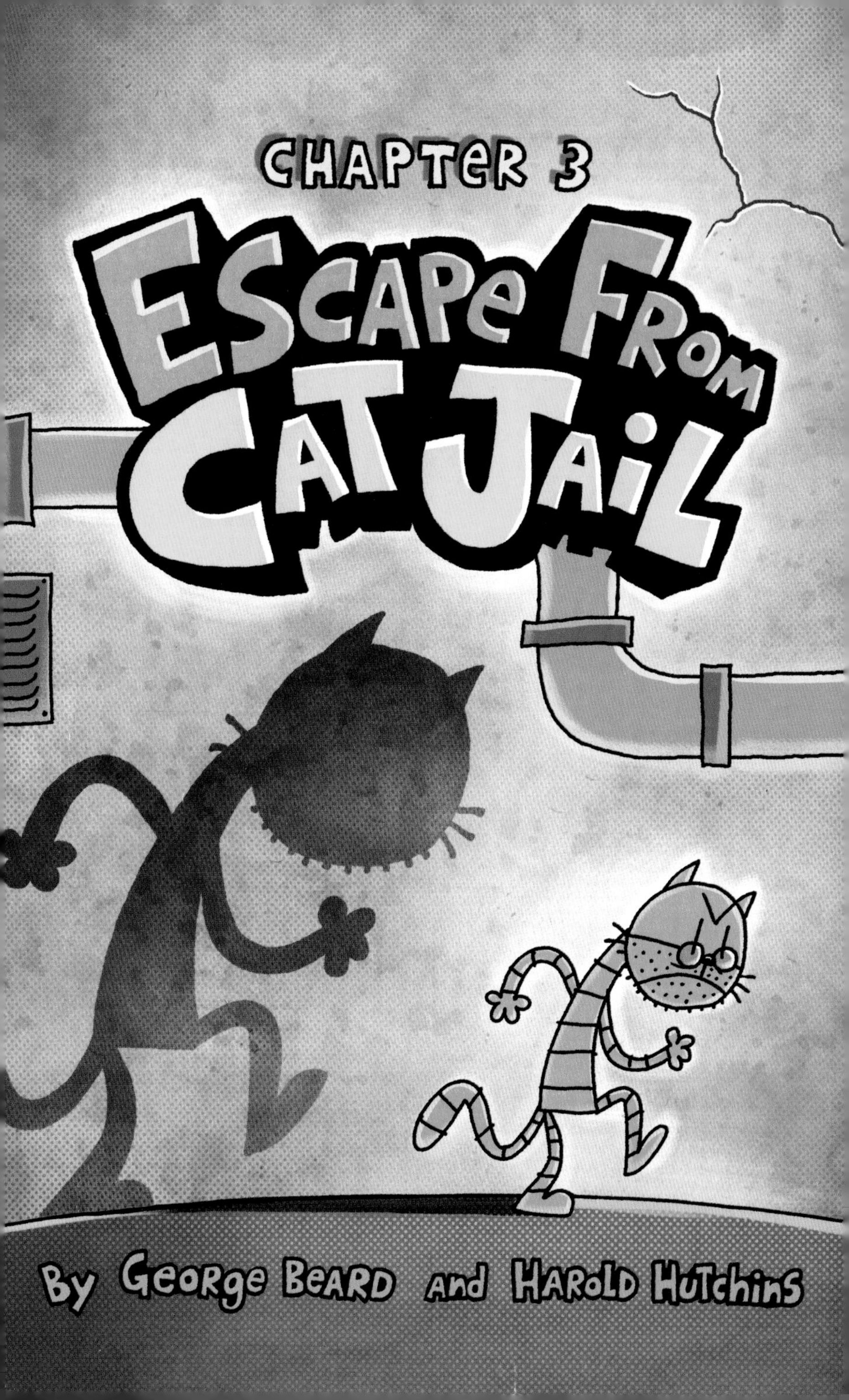
CHAPTER 3
ESCAPE FROM CAT JAIL
By George Beard and Harold Hutchins

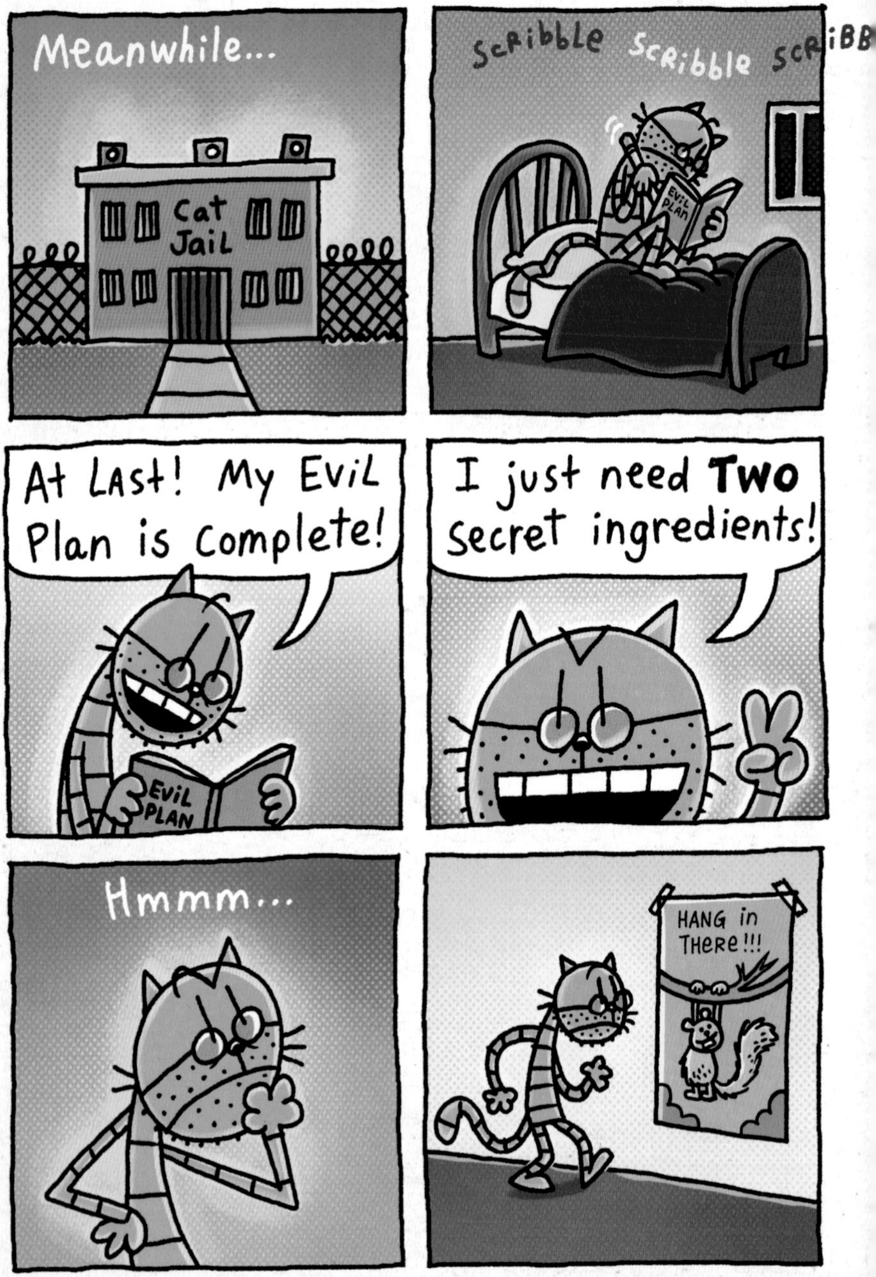
Meanwhile...
Cat Jail
SCRIBBLE SCRIBBLE SCRIBB
EVIL PLAN
At LAST! My EVIL Plan is complete!
EVIL PLAN
I just need **TWO** secret ingredients!
Hmmm...
HANG in THERE!!!

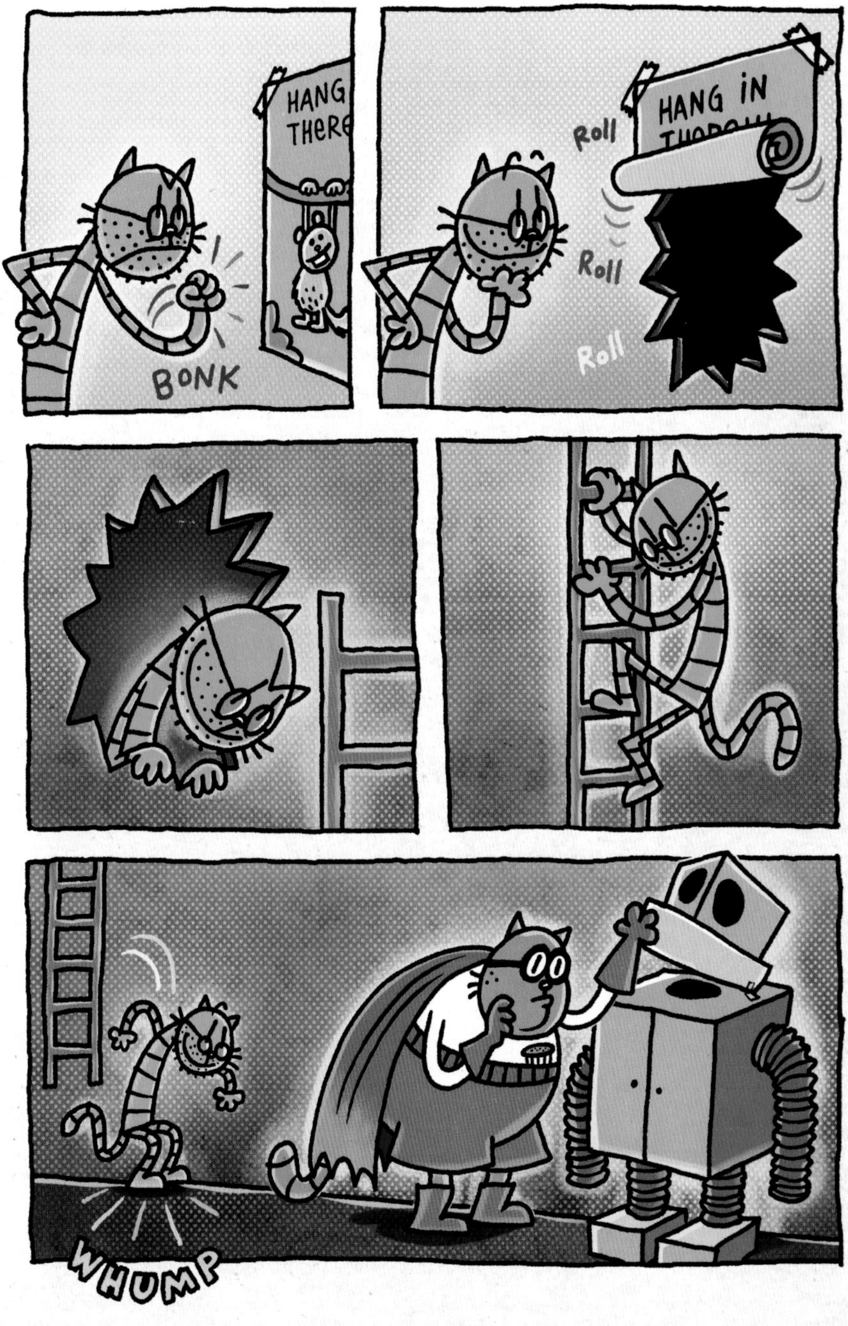
HANG
THERE
BONK
HANG IN
Roll
Roll
Roll
WHUMP

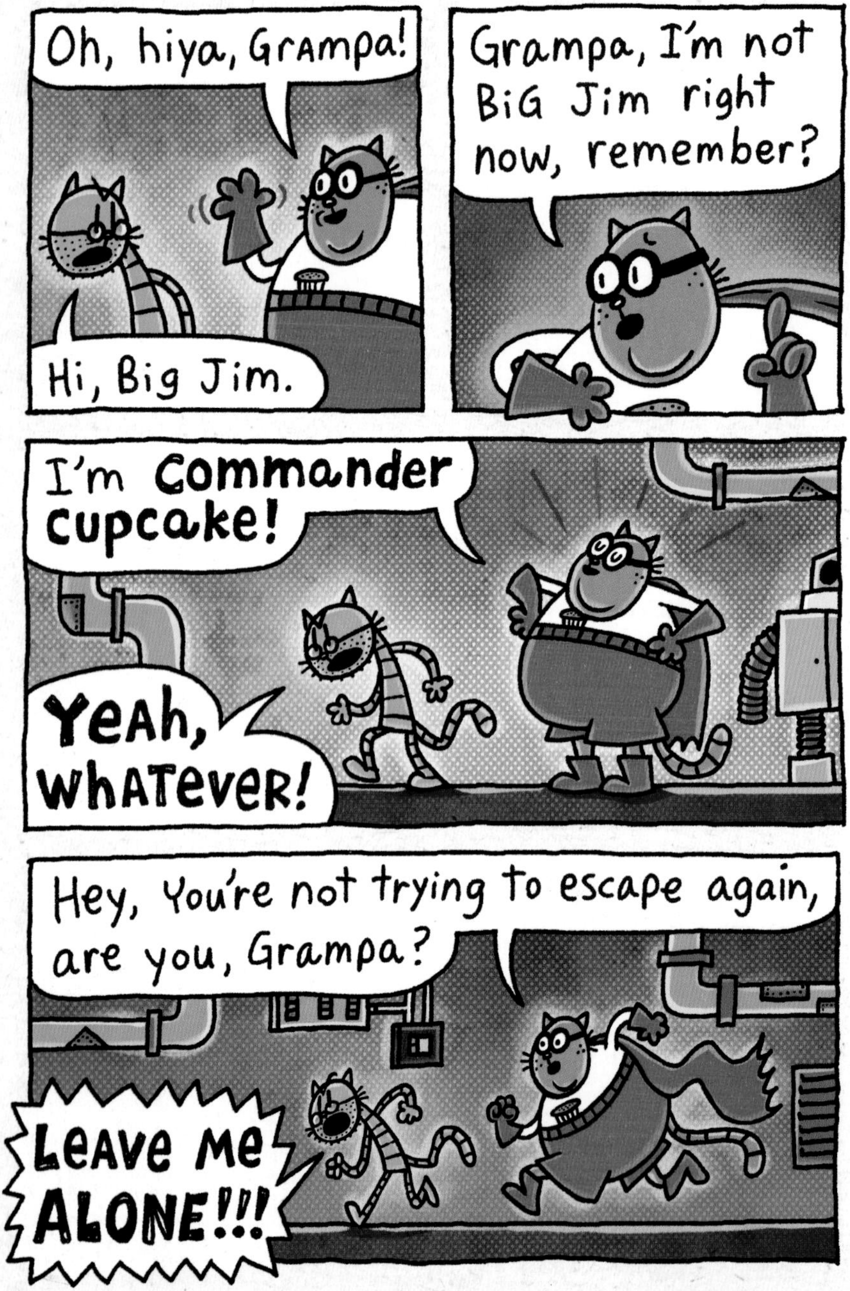
Oh, hiya, Grampa!
Hi, Big Jim.
Grampa, I'm not BiG Jim right now, remember?
I'm Commander cupcake!
YeAh, WhATeveR!
Hey, You're not trying to escape again, are you, Grampa?
LeAve Me ALONE!!!

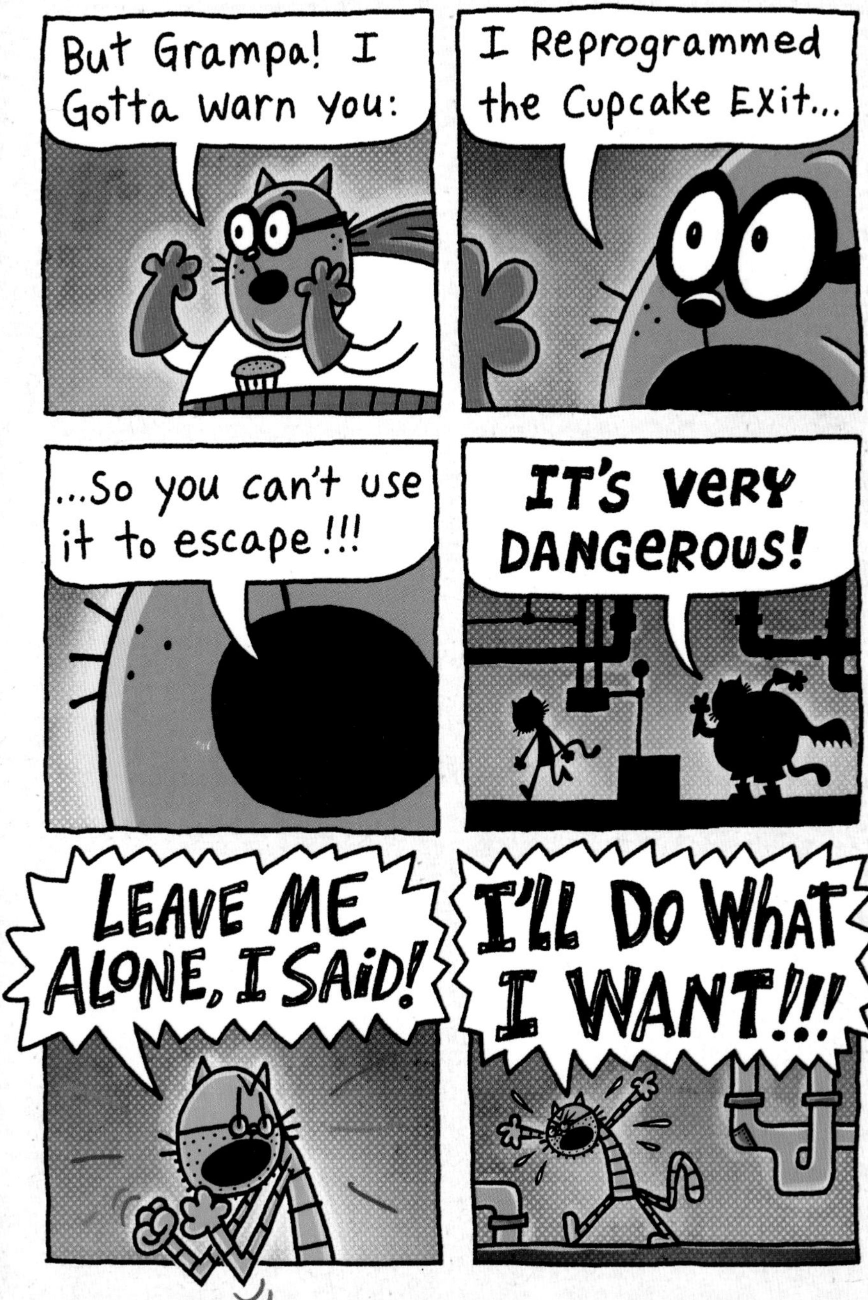
But Grampa! I Gotta warn you:
I Reprogrammed the Cupcake Exit...
...So you can't use it to escape!!!
IT'S VERY DANGEROUS!
LEAVE ME ALONE, I SAID!
I'LL DO WHAT I WANT!!!

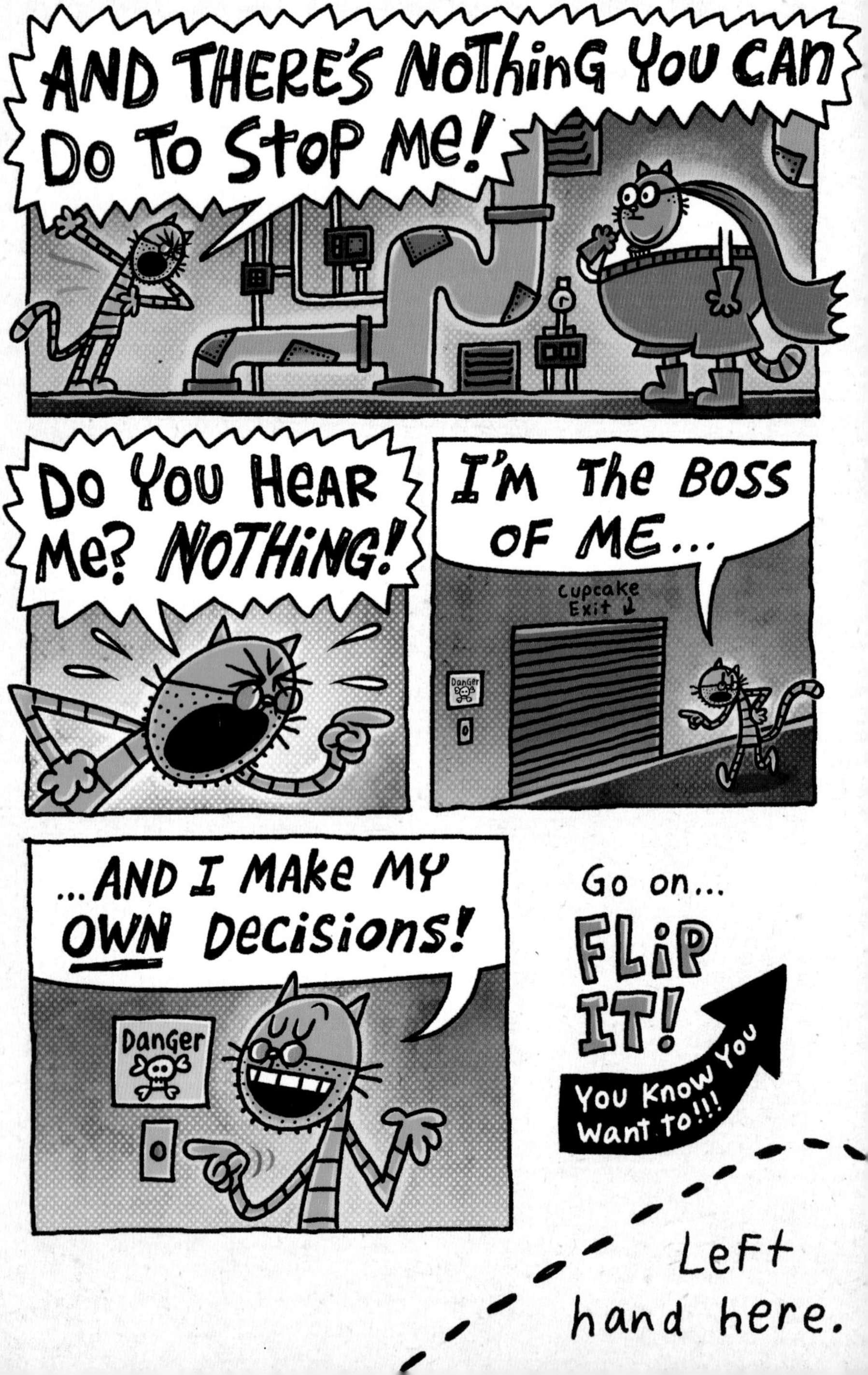
AND THERE'S NOTHING YOU CAN DO TO STOP ME!
DO YOU HEAR ME? NOTHING!
I'M THE BOSS OF ME...
Cupcake Exit
Danger
...AND I MAKE MY OWN DECISIONS!
Danger
Go on...
FLIP IT!
You Know You Want to!!!
Left hand here.

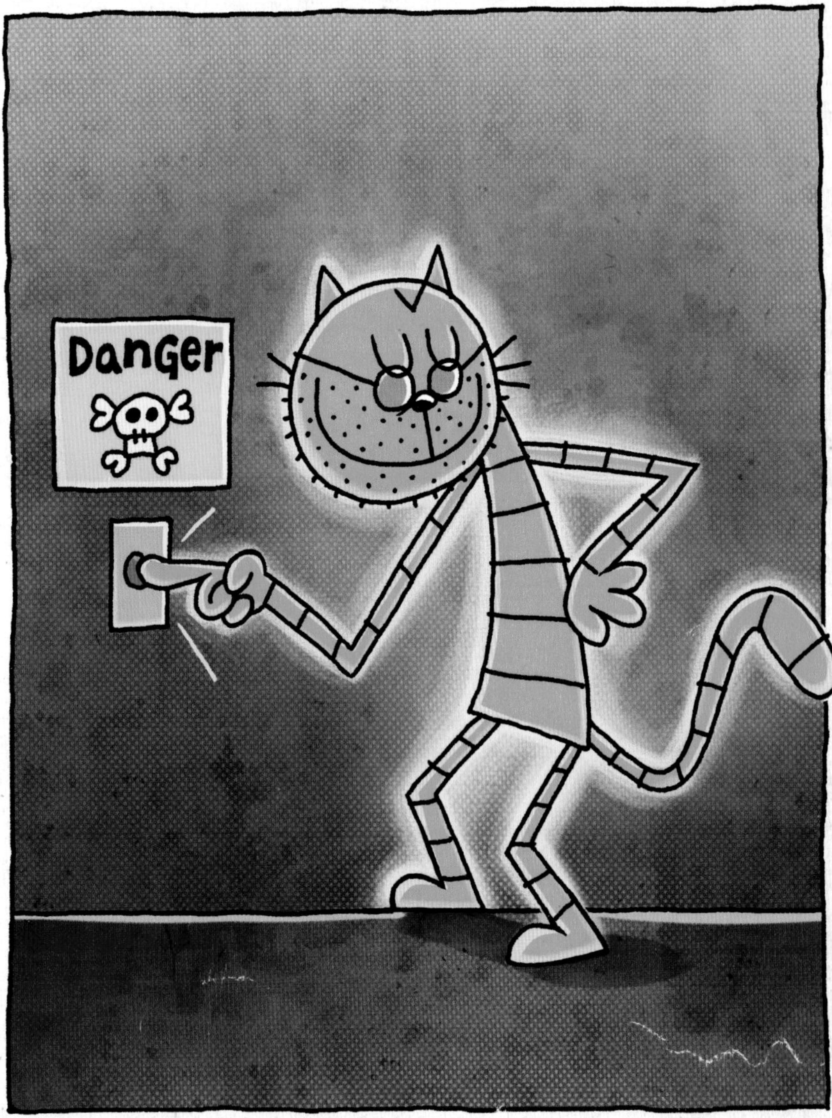
Danger

Right
Thumb
here.

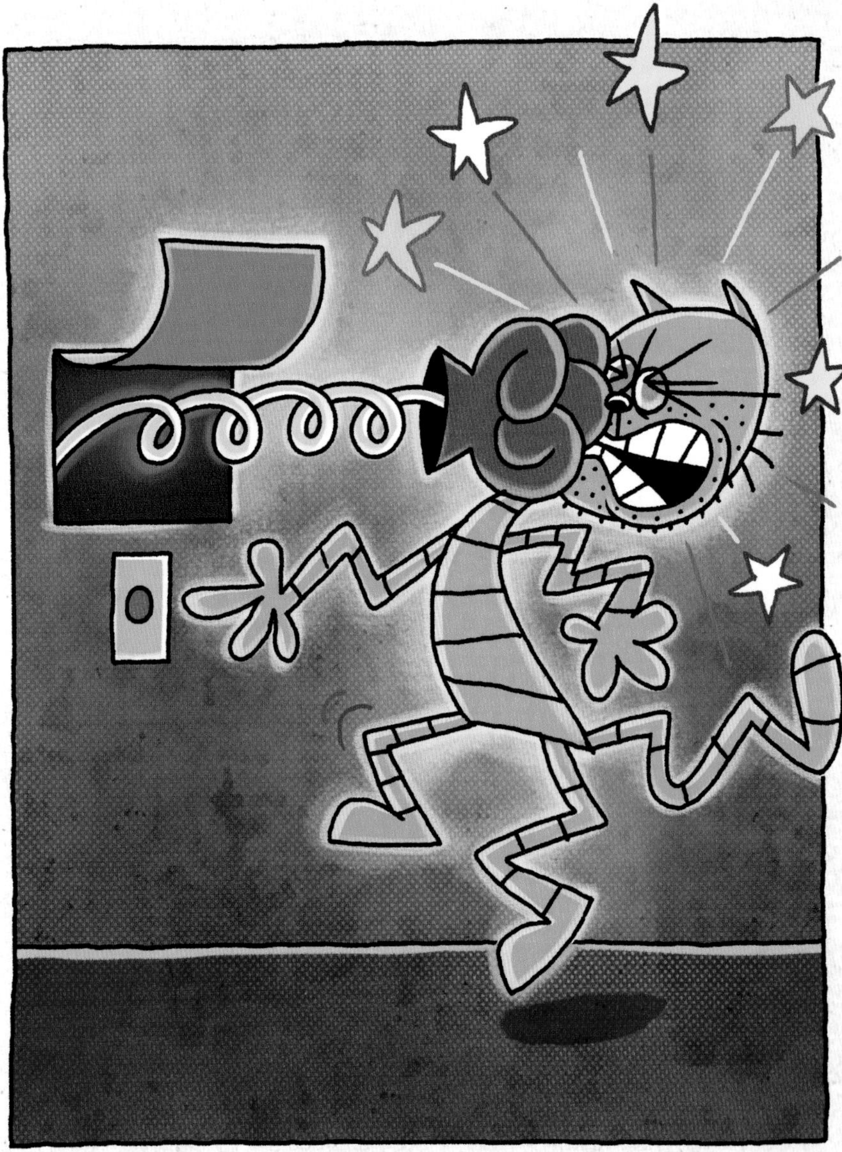

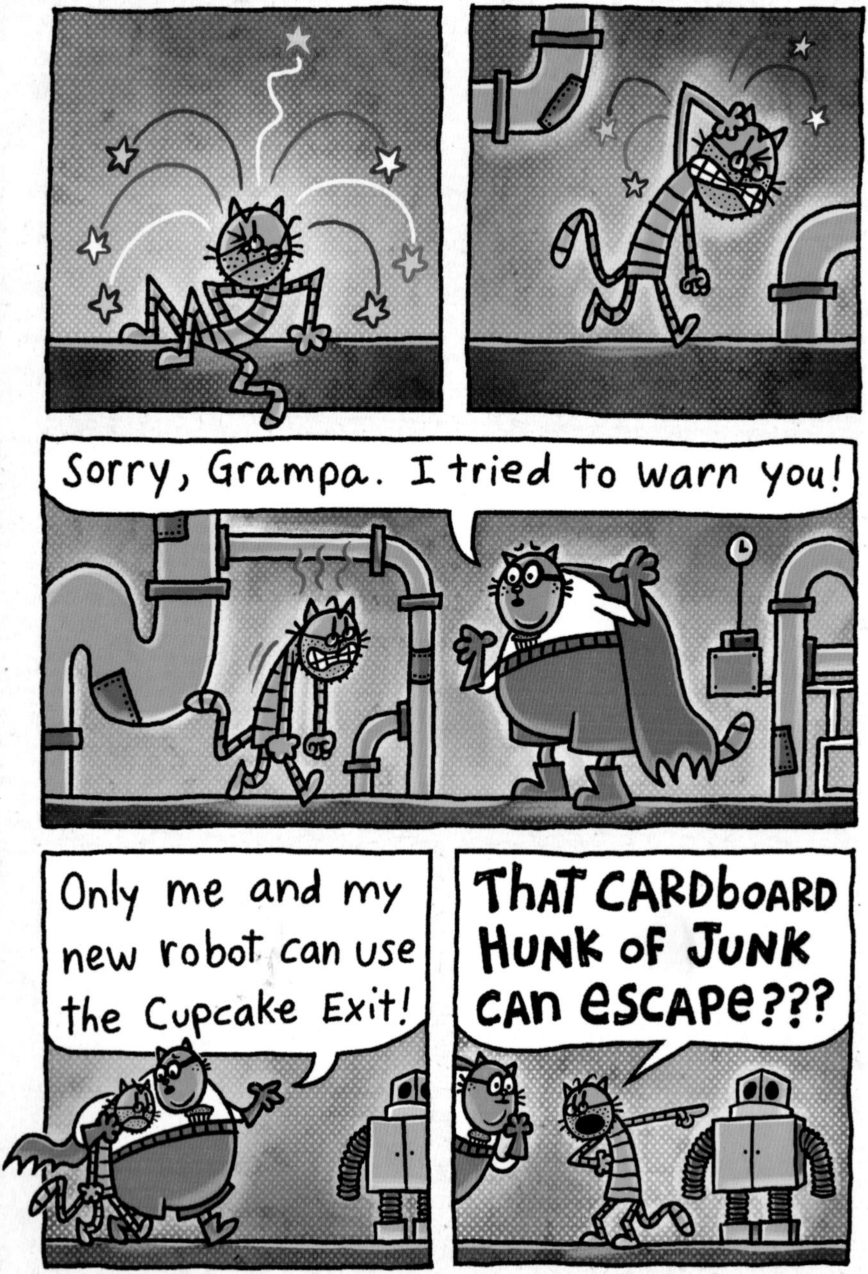
Sorry, Grampa. I tried to warn you!
Only me and my new robot can use the Cupcake Exit!
THAT CARDBOARD HUNK OF JUNK CAN ESCAPE???

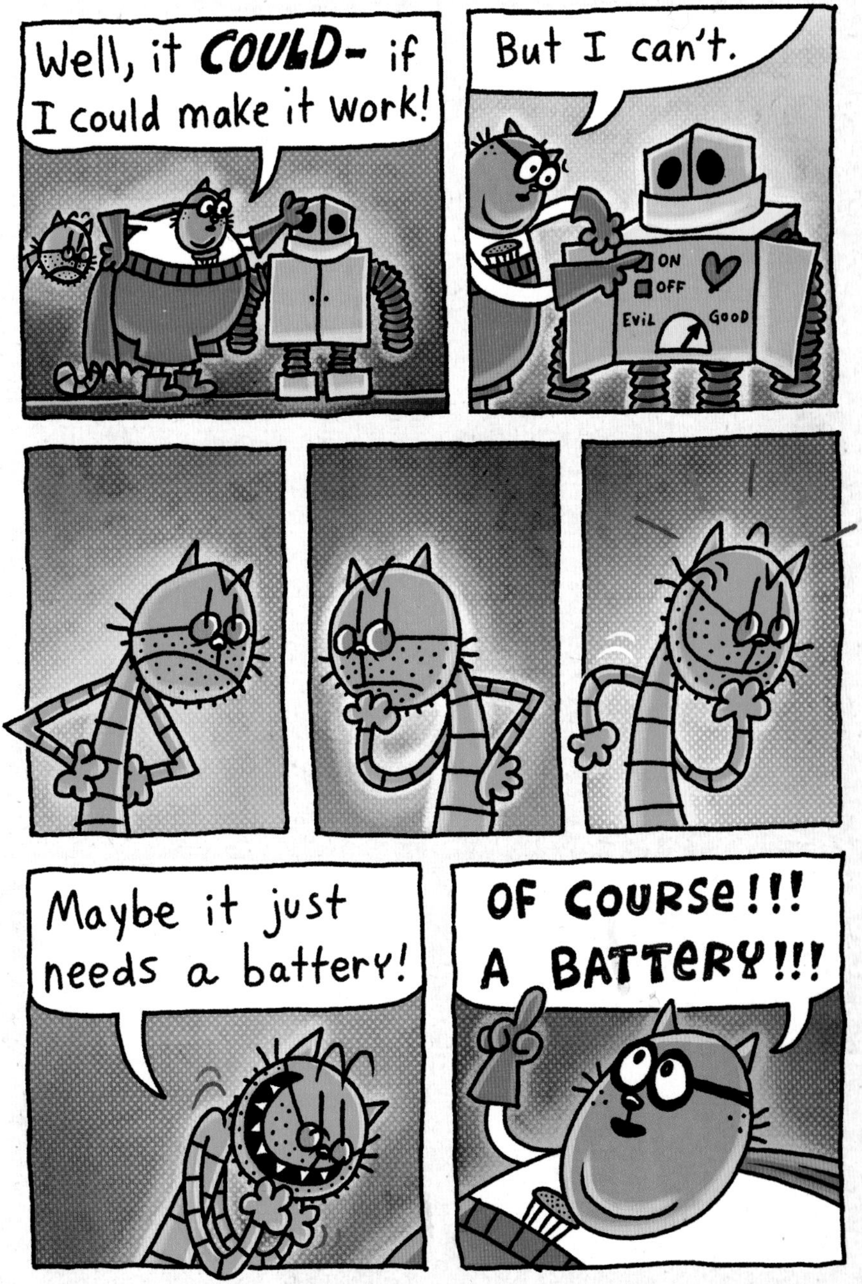
Well, it COULD- if I could make it work!
But I can't.
ON
OFF
EVIL
GOOD
Maybe it just needs a battery!
OF COURSE!!! A BATTERY!!!

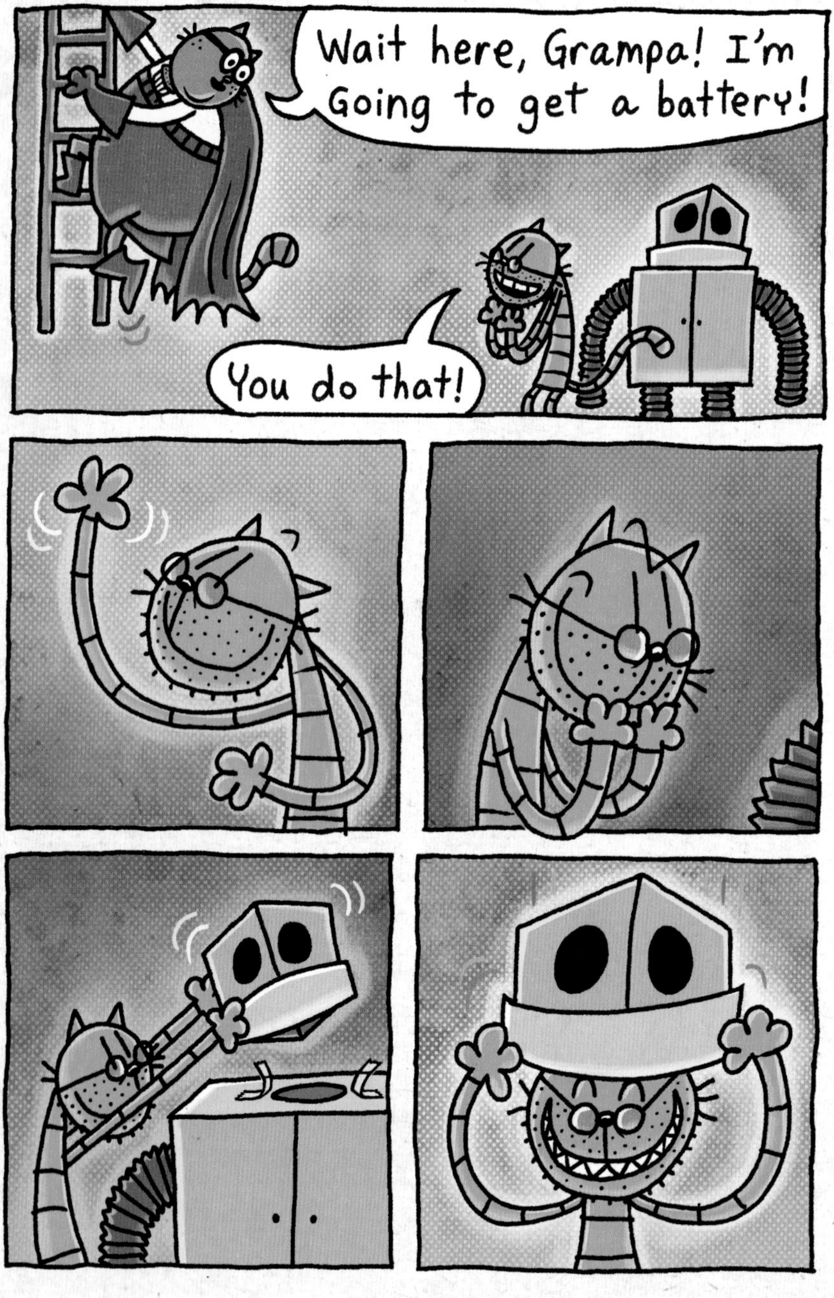
Wait here, Grampa! I'm Going to get a battery!
You do that!

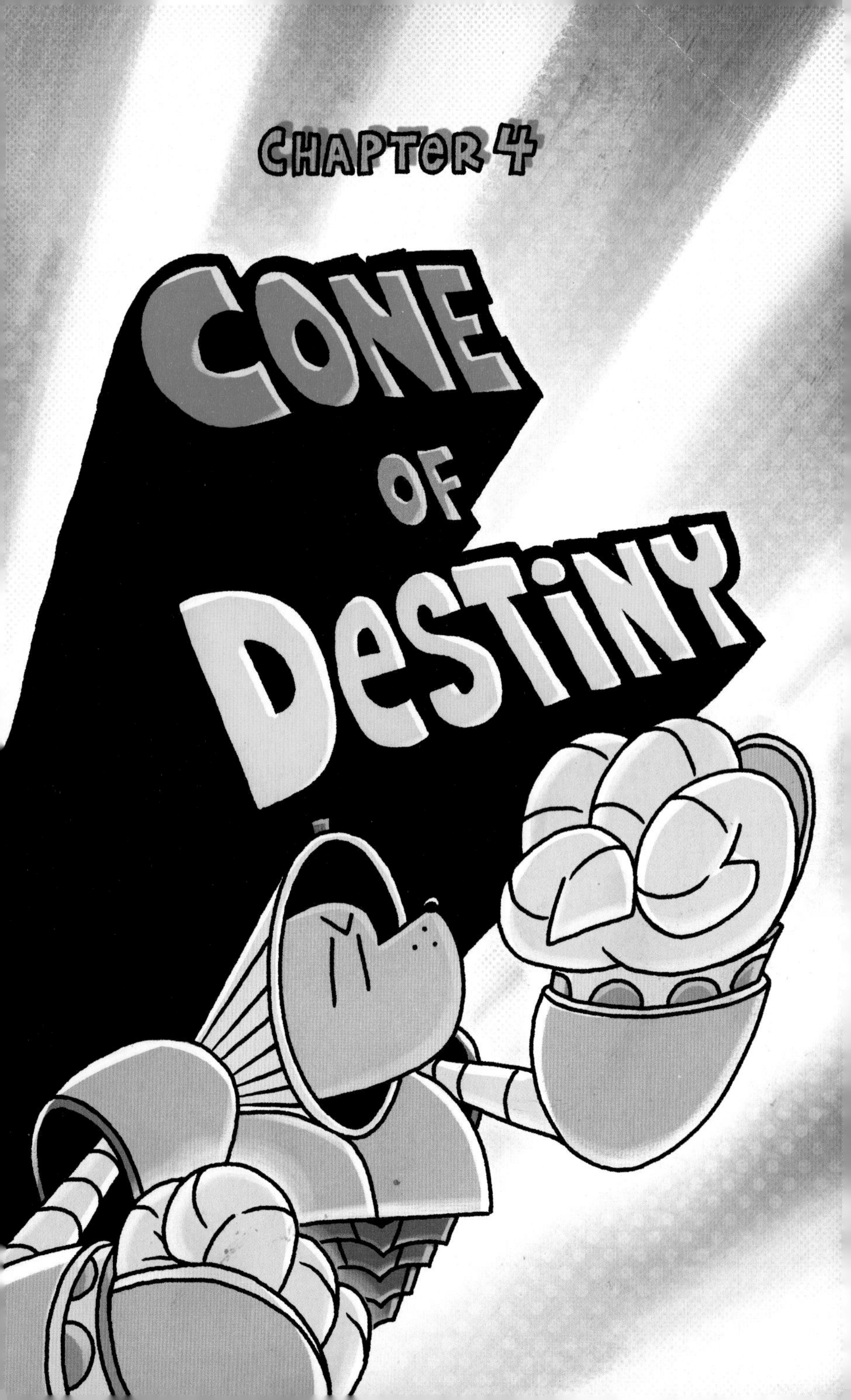
CHAPTER 4
CONE OF DESTINY

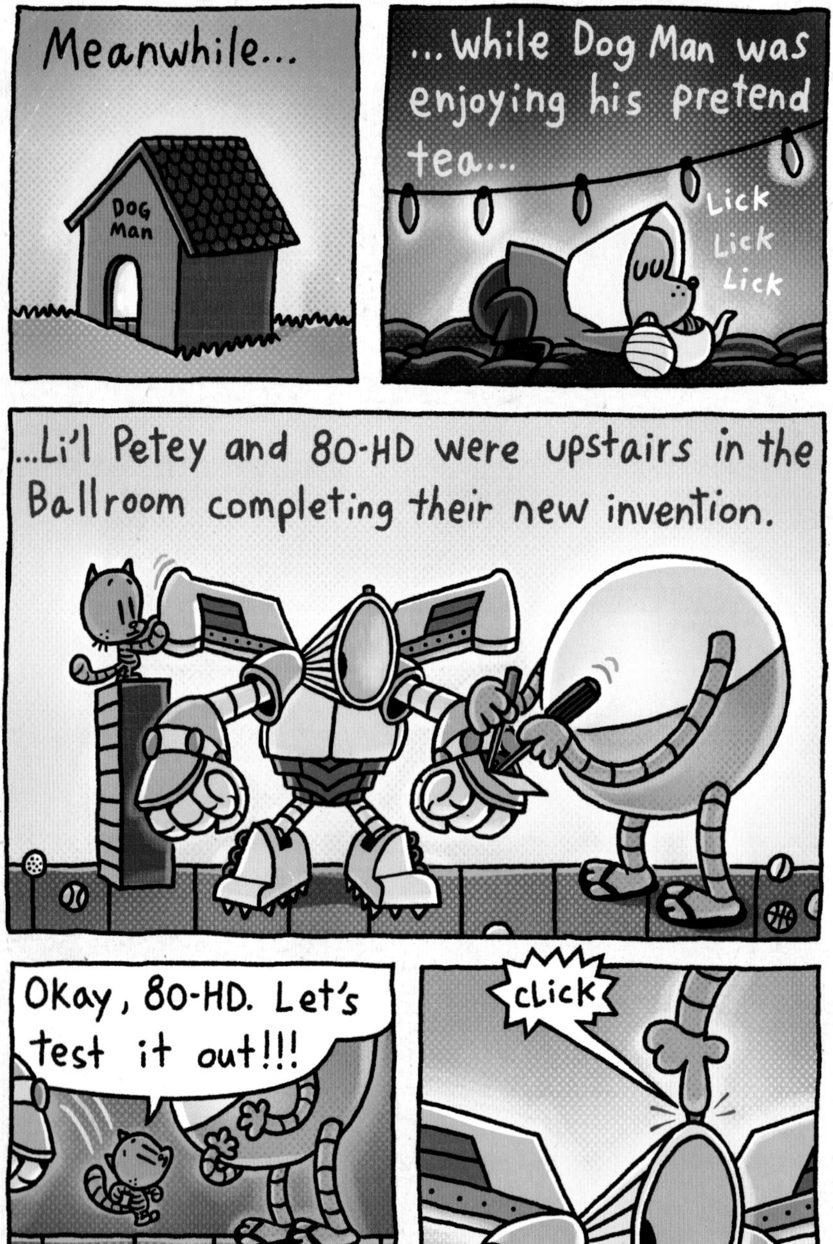
Meanwhile...
DOG Man
...While Dog Man was enjoying his pretend tea...
Lick
Lick
Lick
...Li'l Petey and 80-HD were upstairs in the Ballroom completing their new invention.
Okay, 80-HD. Let's test it out!!!
CLick

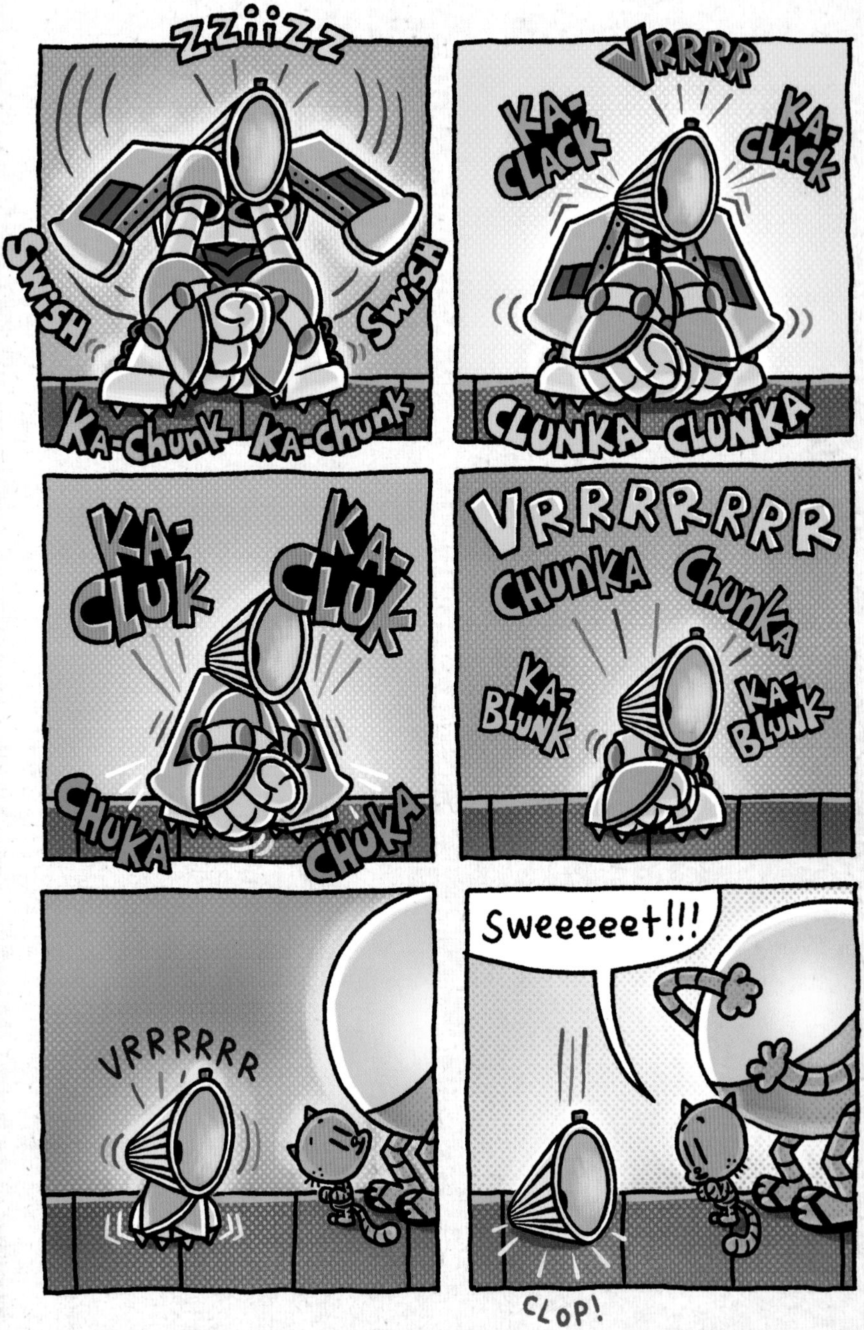
ZZiiiZZ
SWISH
SWISH
KA-Chunk KA-Chunk
VRRRR
KA-CLACK
KA-CLACK
CLUNKA CLUNKA
KA-CLUK
KA-CLUK
CHUKA
CHUKA
VRRRRRRRR
CHUNKA Chunka
KA-BLUNK
KA-BLUNK
VRRRRRR
Sweeeeet!!!
CLOP!

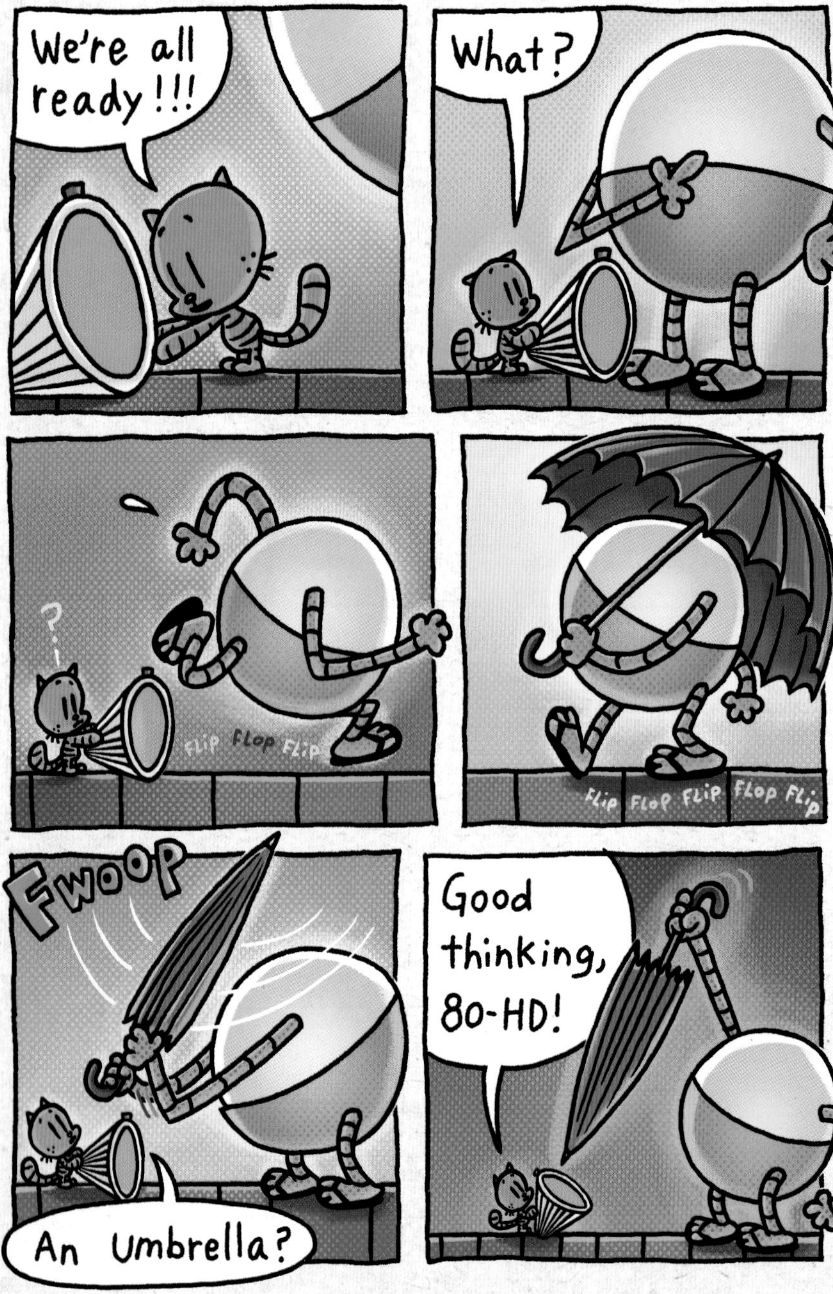
We're all ready!!!
What?
FLIP FLOP FLIP
FLIP FLOP FLIP FLOP FLIP
FWOOP
An Umbrella?
Good thinking, 80-HD!

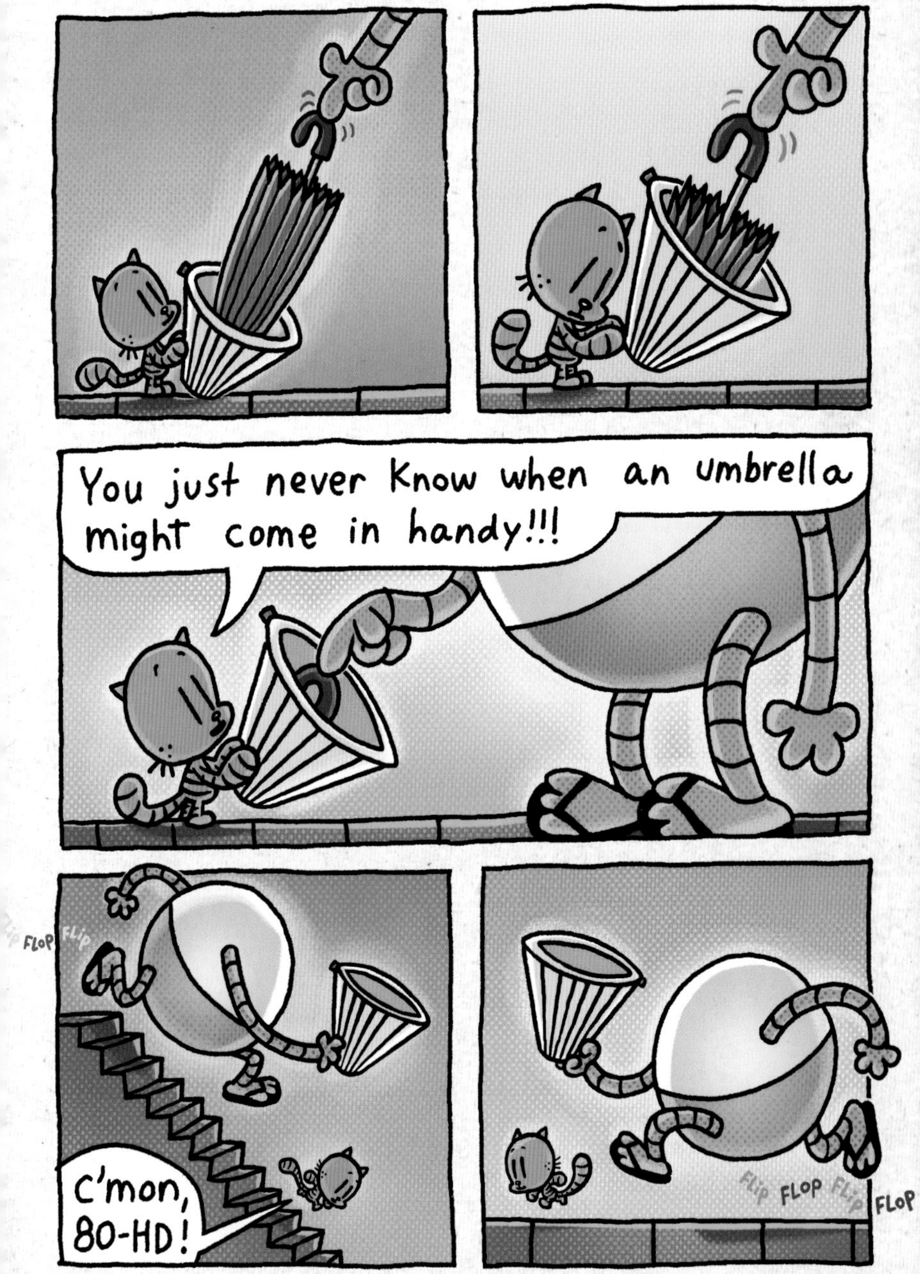

You just never know when an umbrella might come in handy!!!
FLOP FLIP
C'mon, 80-HD!
FLIP FLOP FLIP FLOP

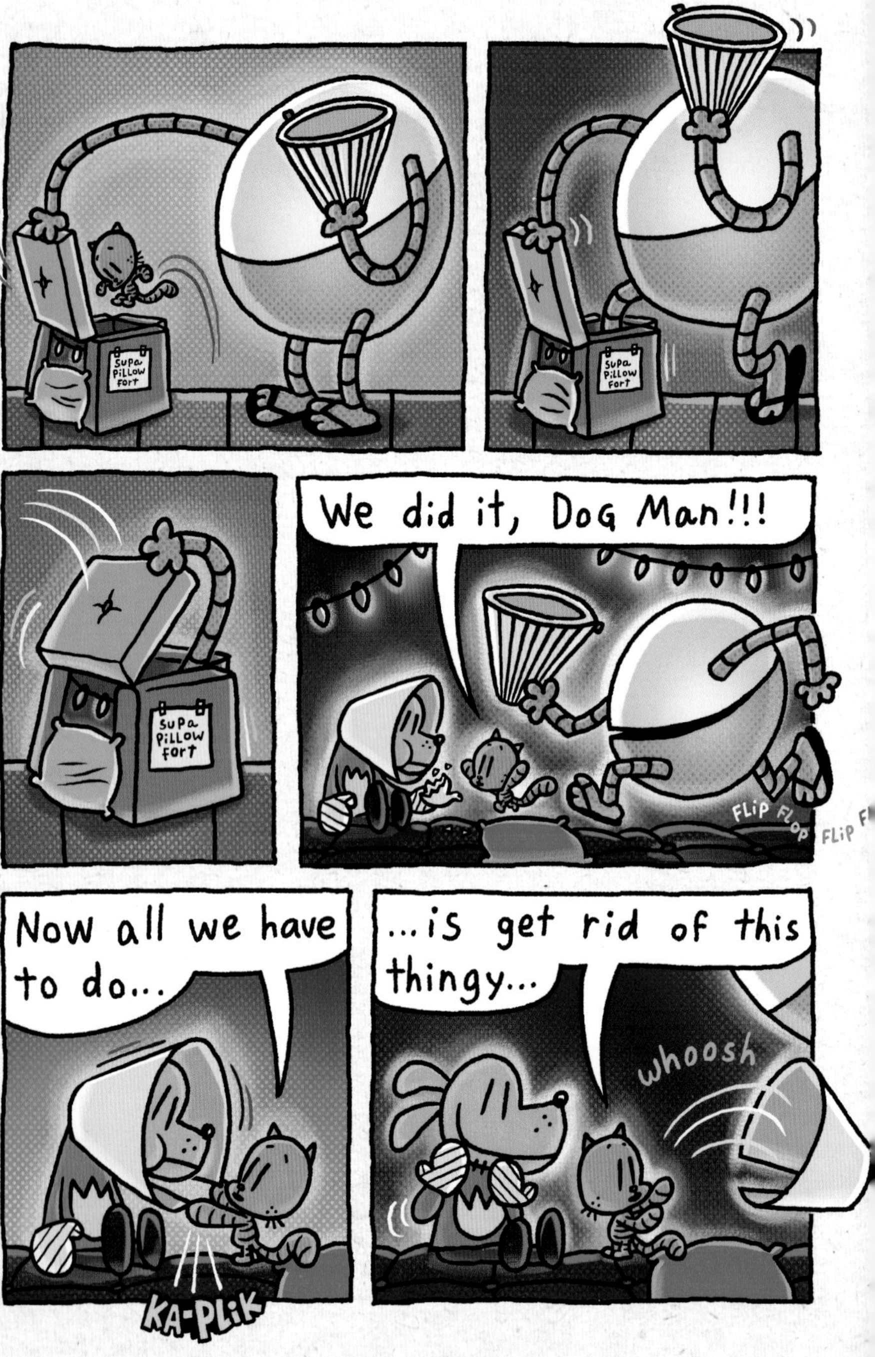
SUPA PiLLOW FORT
SUPA PiLLOW FORT
SUPA PiLLOW FORT
We did it, DoG Man!!!
FLiP FLOP FLiP
Now all we have to do...
KA-PLiK
...is get rid of this thingy...
whoosh

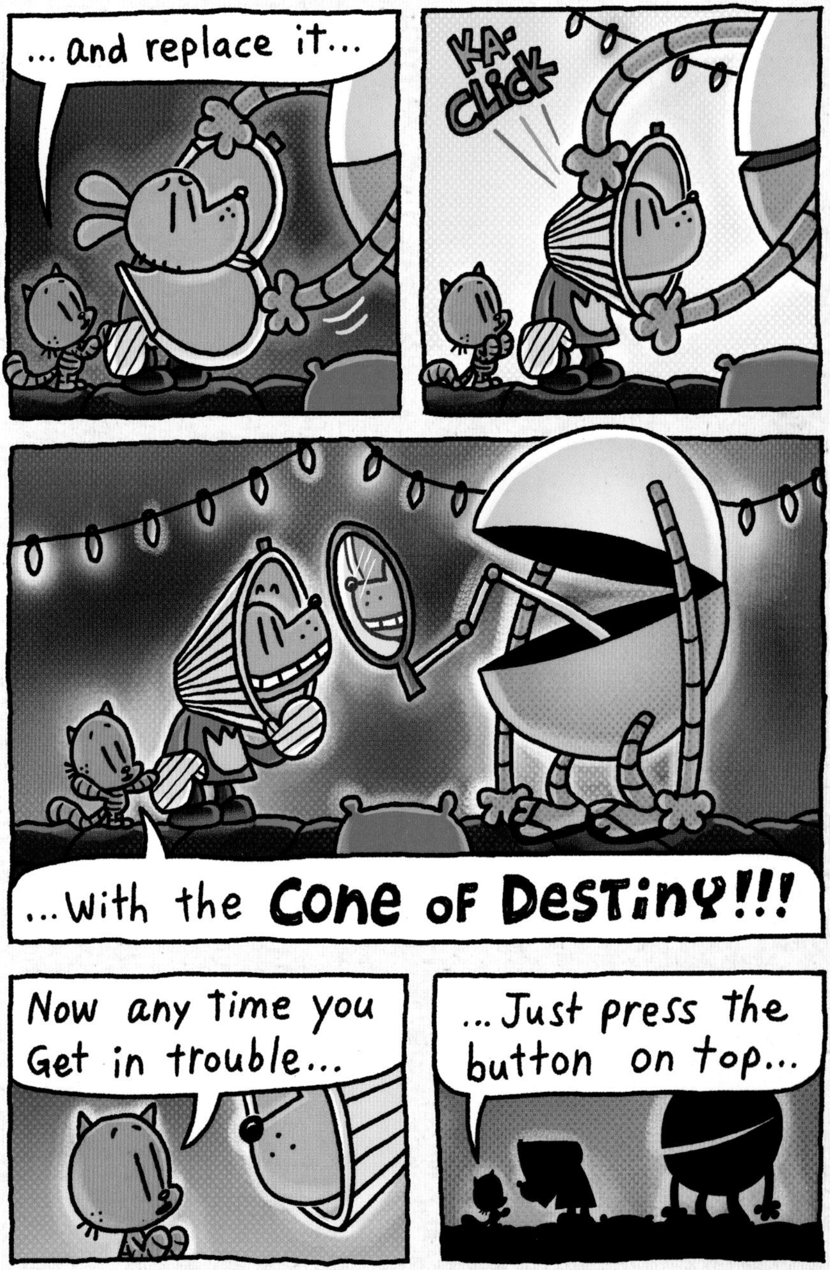

... and replace it...
KA-CLICK
...with the CONE OF DESTINY!!!
Now any time you Get in trouble...
...Just press the button on top...

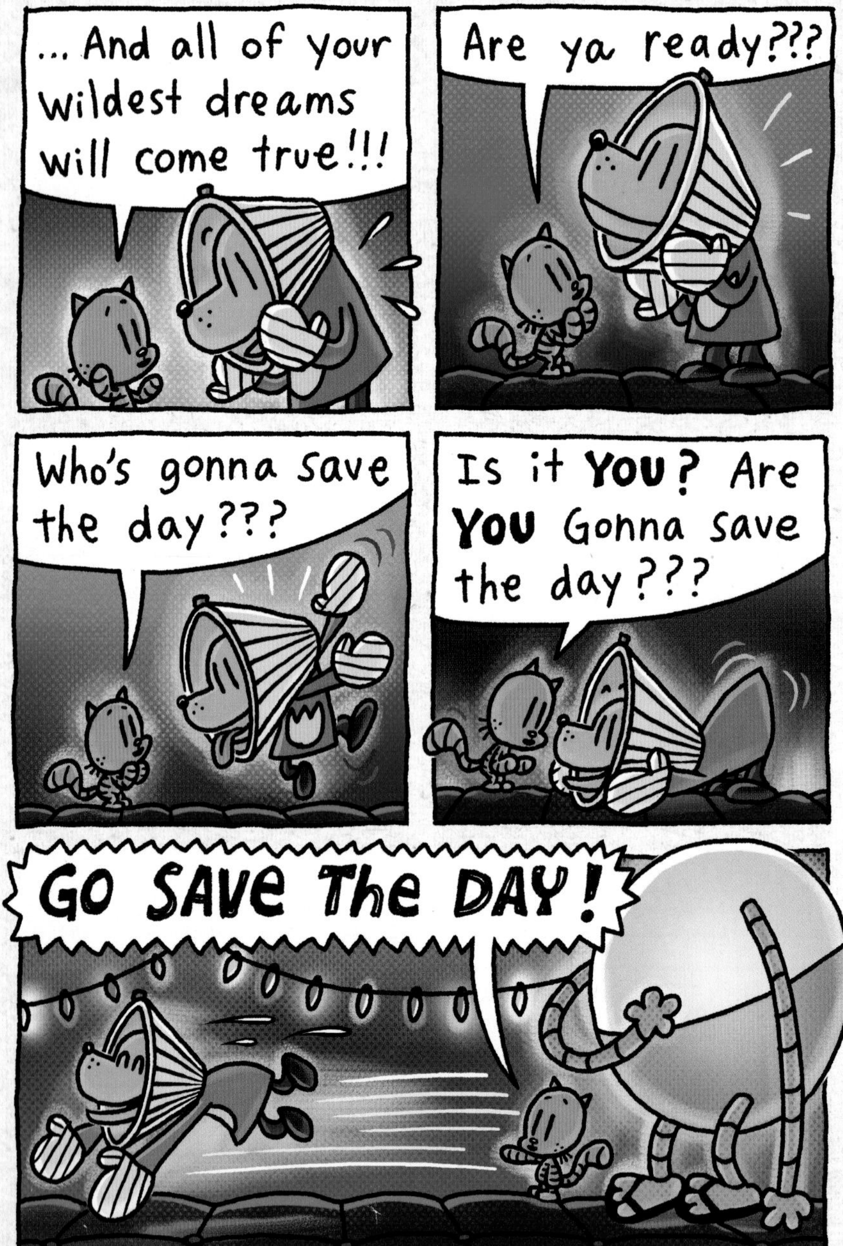
... And all of your wildest dreams will come true!!!
Are ya ready???
Who's gonna save the day???
Is it **YOU**? Are **YOU** Gonna save the day???
GO SAVE THE DAY!

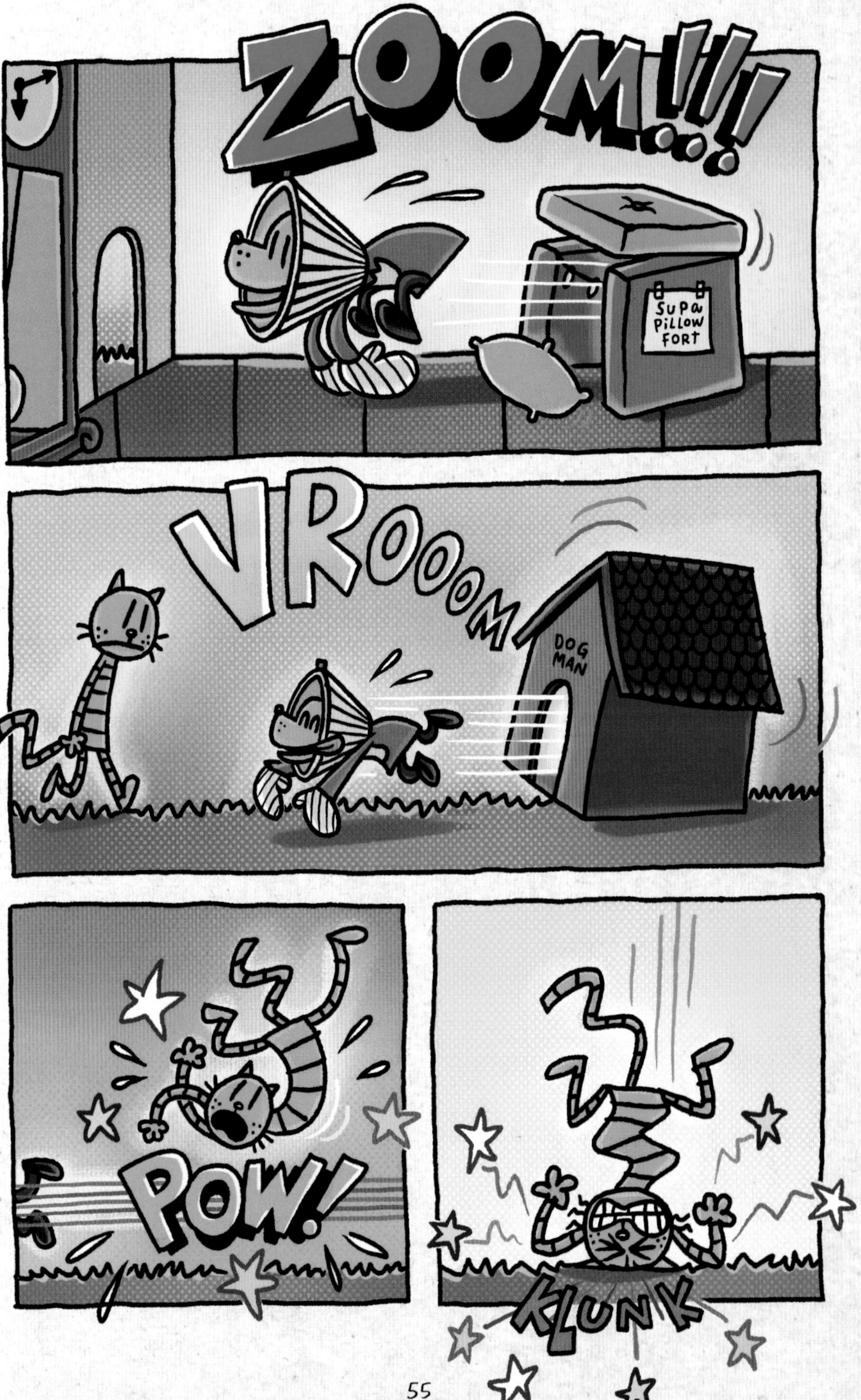
ZOOM!!!!
SUPA PILLOW FORT
VROOOM
DOG MAN
POW!
KLUNK

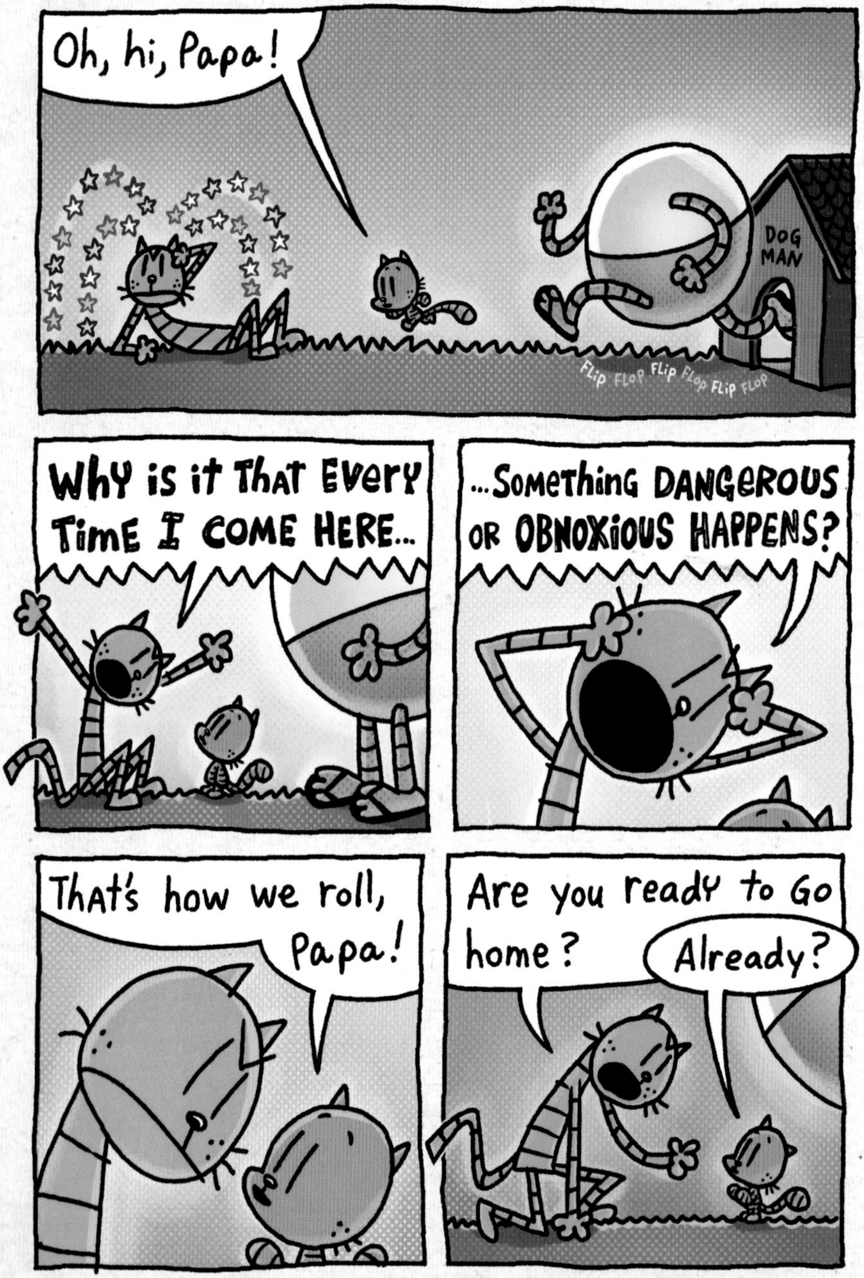
Oh, hi, Papa!
DOG MAN
FLiP FLOP FLiP FLOP FLiP FLOP
WHY is it THAT EVERY TIME I COME HERE...
...SOMETHING DANGEROUS OR OBNOXIOUS HAPPENS?
THAT'S how we roll, Papa!
Are you ready to Go home?
Already?

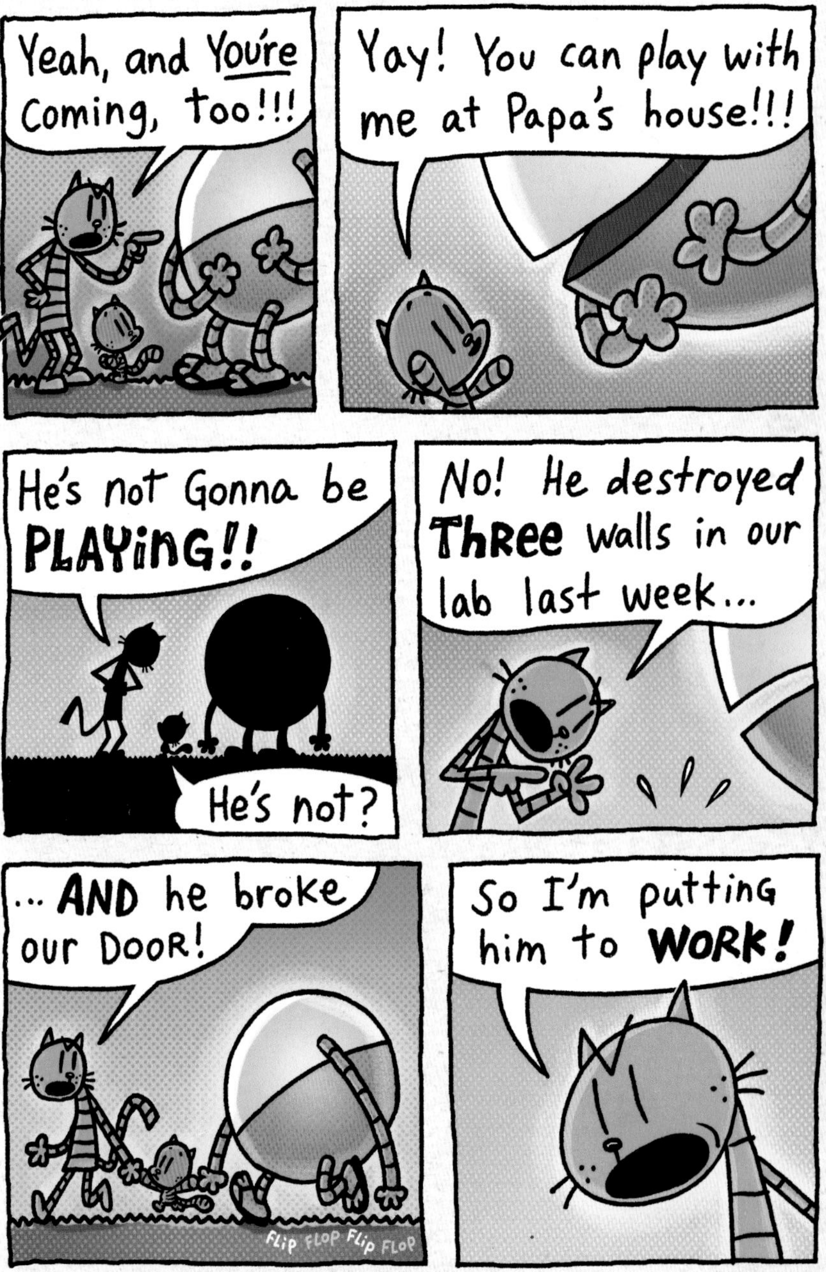
Yeah, and You're Coming, too!!!
Yay! You can play with me at Papa's house!!!
He's not Gonna be PLAYinG!!
He's not?
No! He destroyed THREE walls in our lab last week...
... AND he broke our DOOR!
FLip FLOP FLip FLOP
So I'm putting him to WORK!

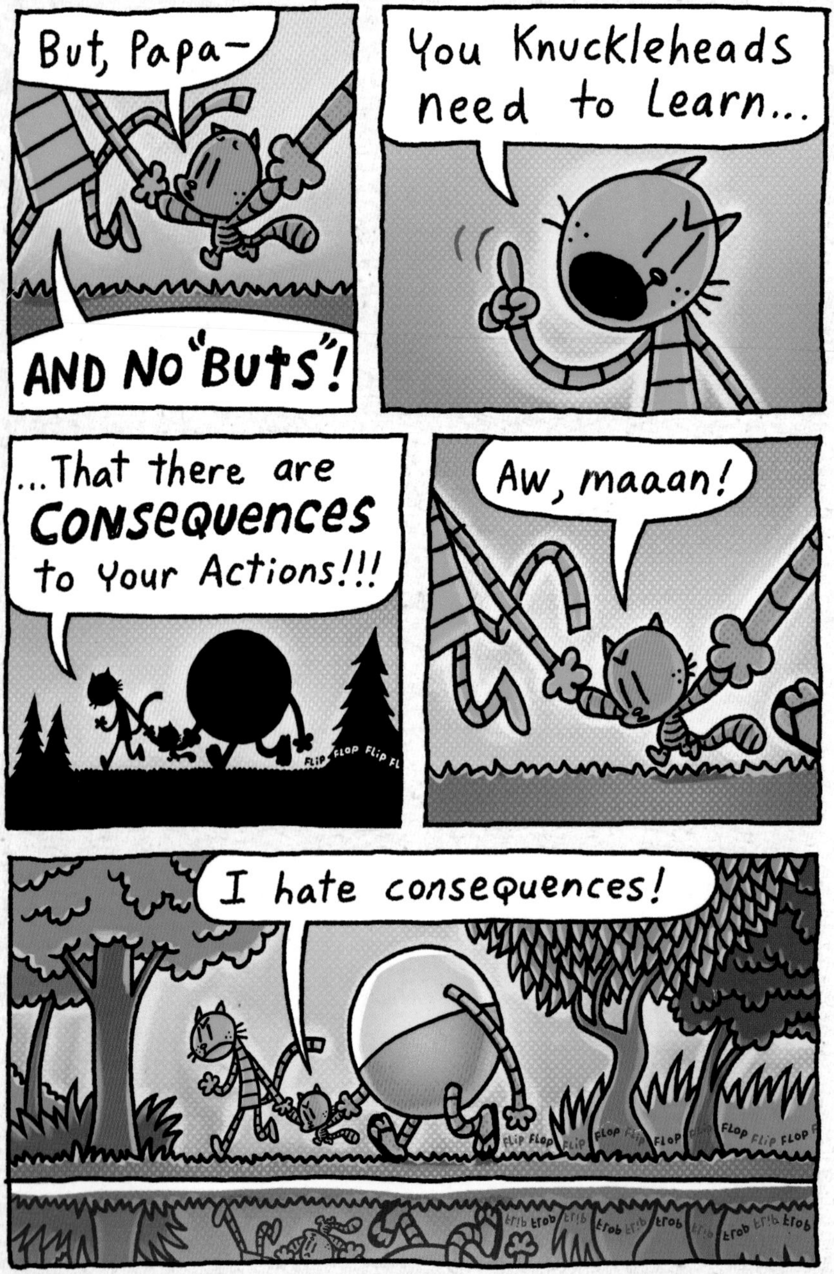
But, Papa—
AND NO "BUTS"!
You Knuckleheads need to Learn...
...That there are CONSEQUENCES to Your Actions!!!
FLIP FLOP FLIP FL
Aw, maaan!
I hate consequences!
FLIP FLOP FLIP FLOP FLIP FLOP FLIP FLOP FLIP FLOP
trib trob trib trob trib trob trib trob trib trob

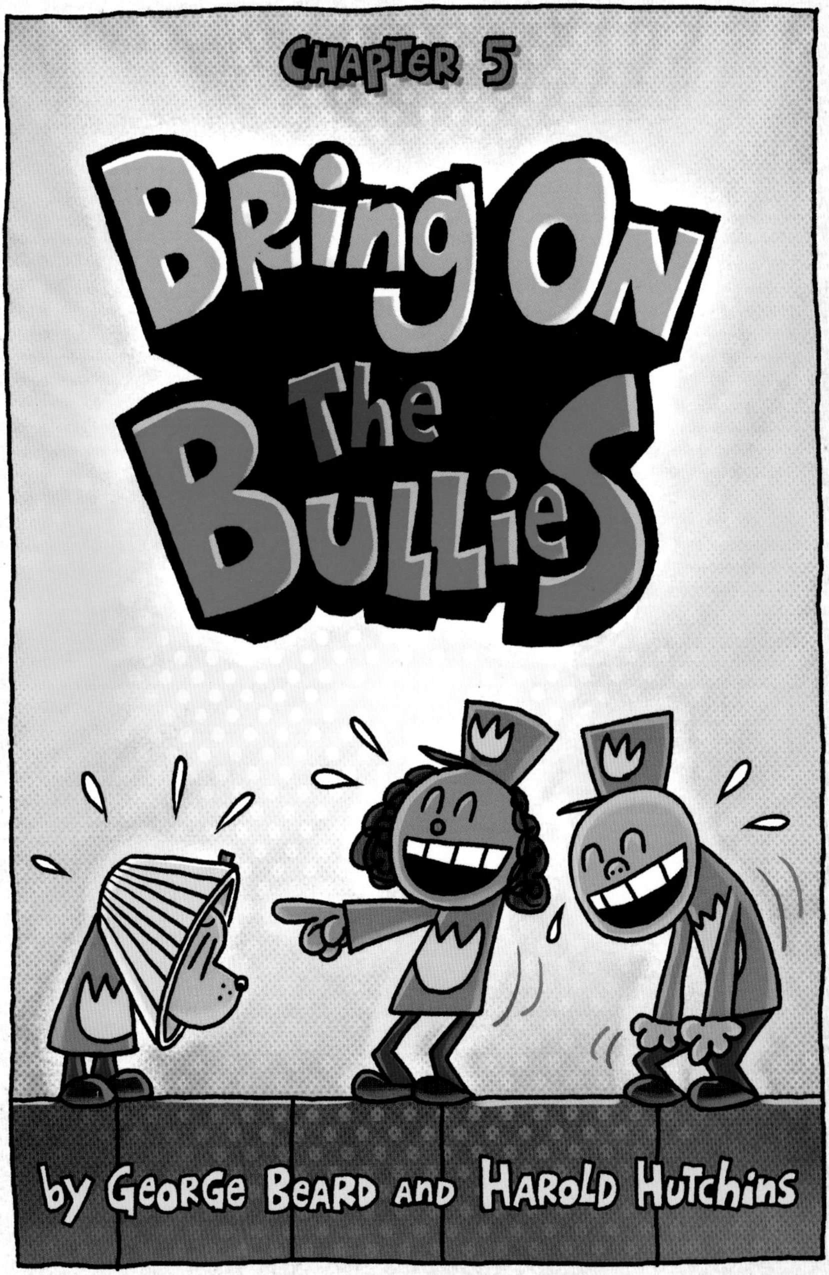
CHAPTER 5
Bring On The Bullies
by George Beard and Harold Hutchins

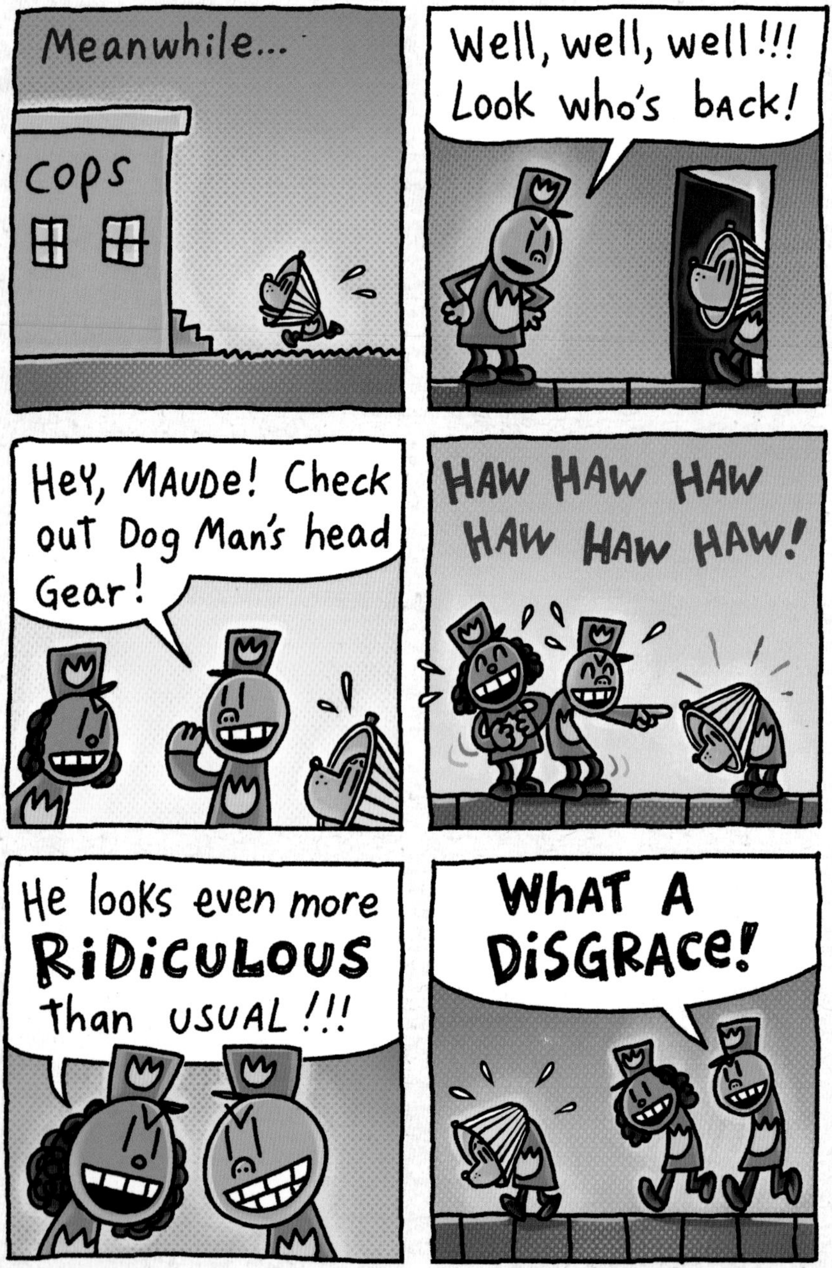
Meanwhile...
COPS
Well, well, well!!! Look who's back!
Hey, Maude! Check out Dog Man's head Gear!
HAW HAW HAW HAW HAW HAW!
He looks even more RIDICULOUS than USUAL!!!
WHAT A DISGRACE!

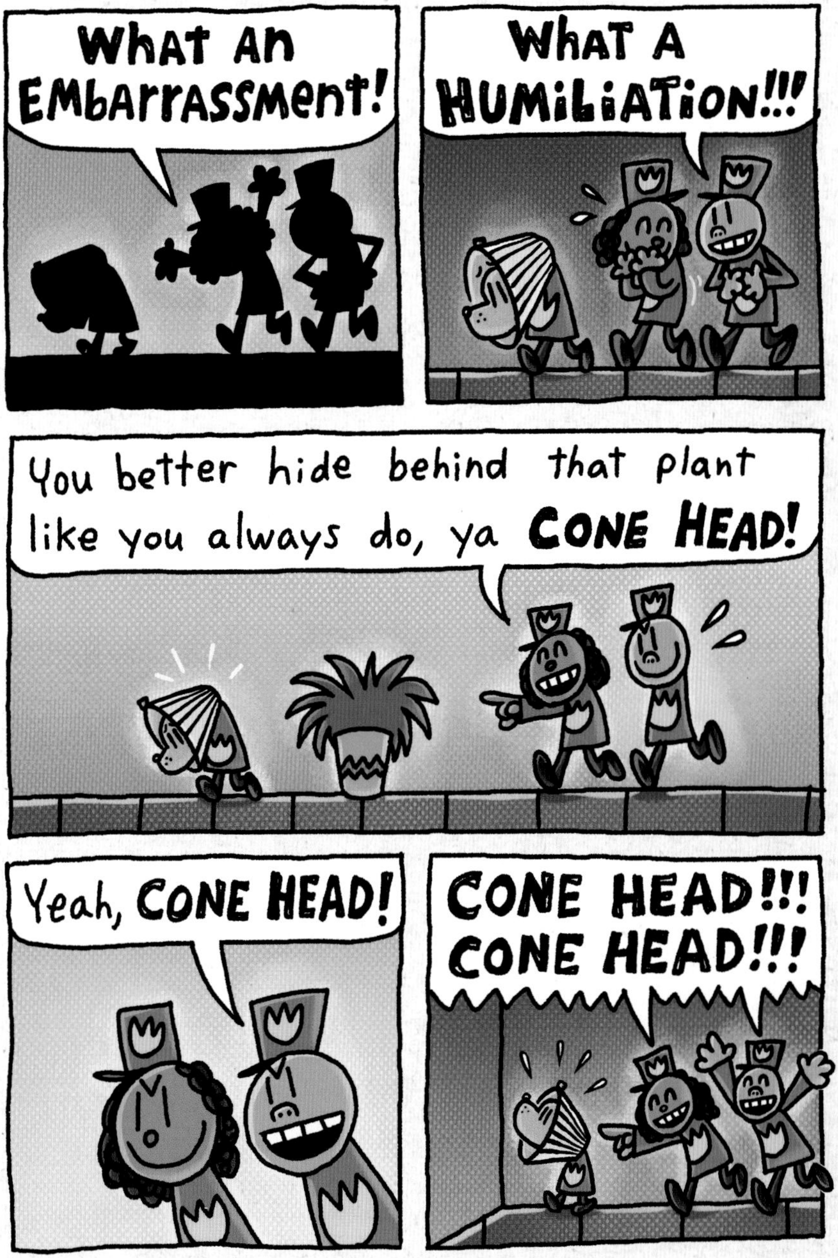
WHAT AN EMBARRASSMENT!
WHAT A HUMILIATION!!!
You better hide behind that plant like you always do, ya CONE HEAD!
Yeah, CONE HEAD!
CONE HEAD!!! CONE HEAD!!!

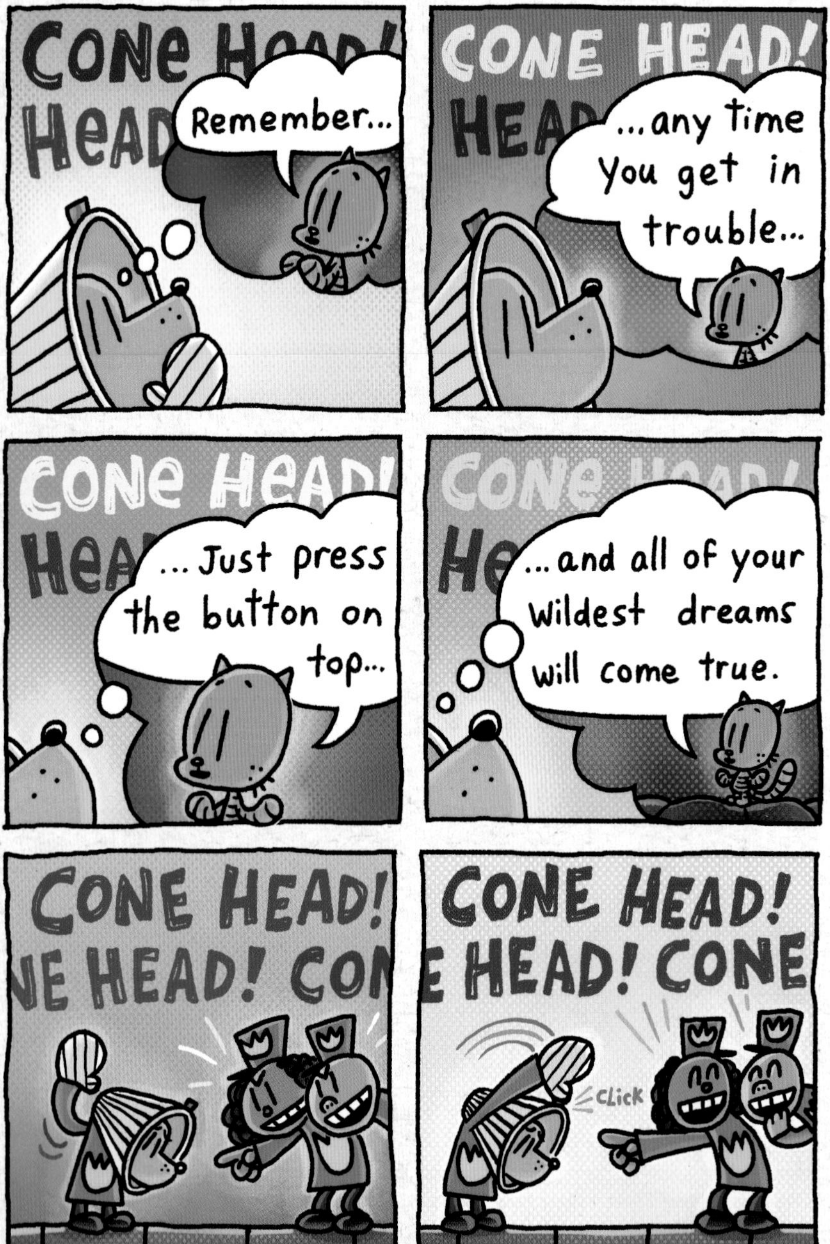
CONE HEAD! HEAD
Remember...
CONE HEAD! HEAD
...any time you get in trouble...
CONE HEAD! HEAD
...Just press the button on top...
CONE HEAD! HE
...and all of your wildest dreams will come true.
CONE HEAD! NE HEAD! CON
CONE HEAD! E HEAD! CONE
CLICK

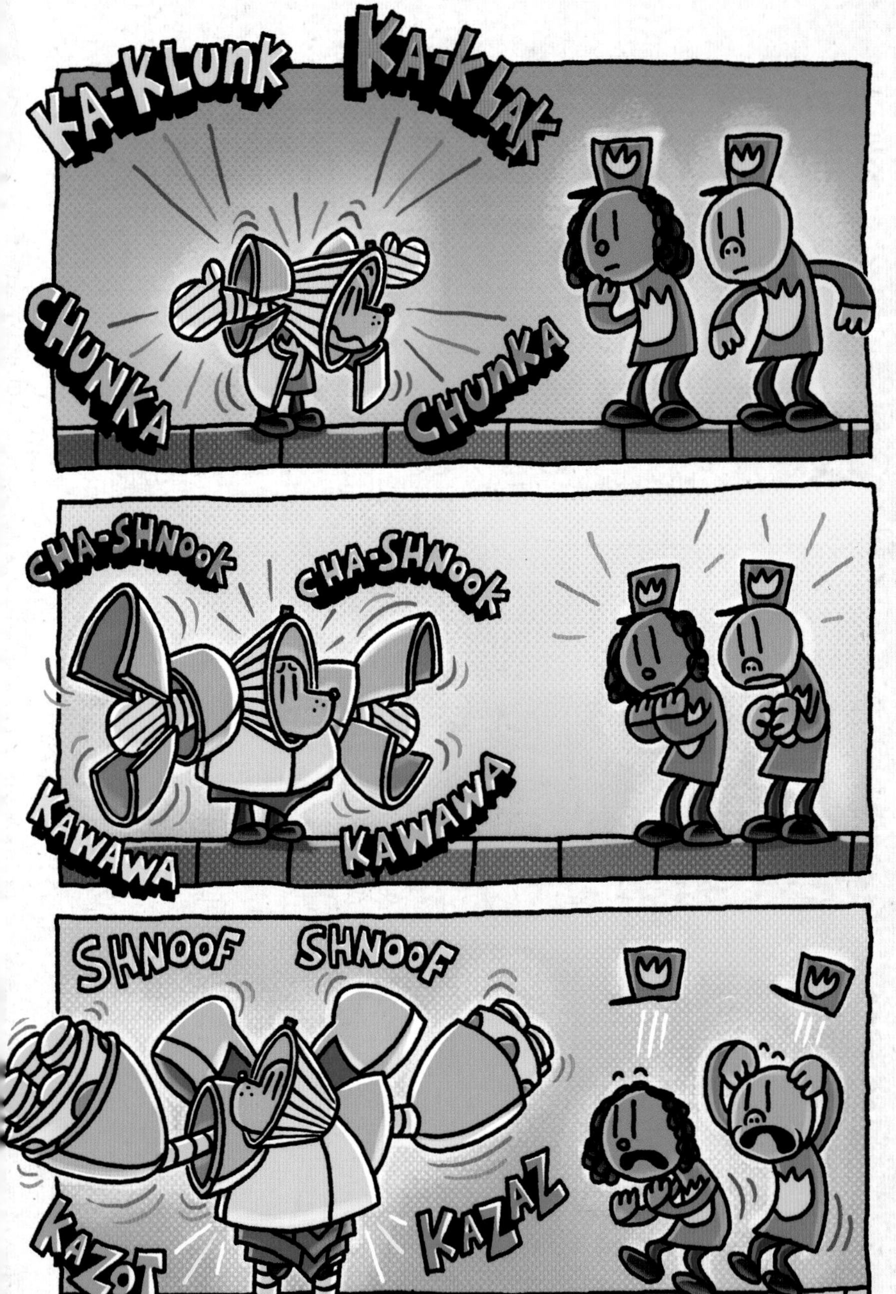
KA-KLUNK
KA-KLAK
CHUNKA
CHUNKA
CHA-SHNOOK
CHA-SHNOOK
KAWAWA
KAWAWA
SHNOOF
SHNOOF
KAZOT
KAZAZ

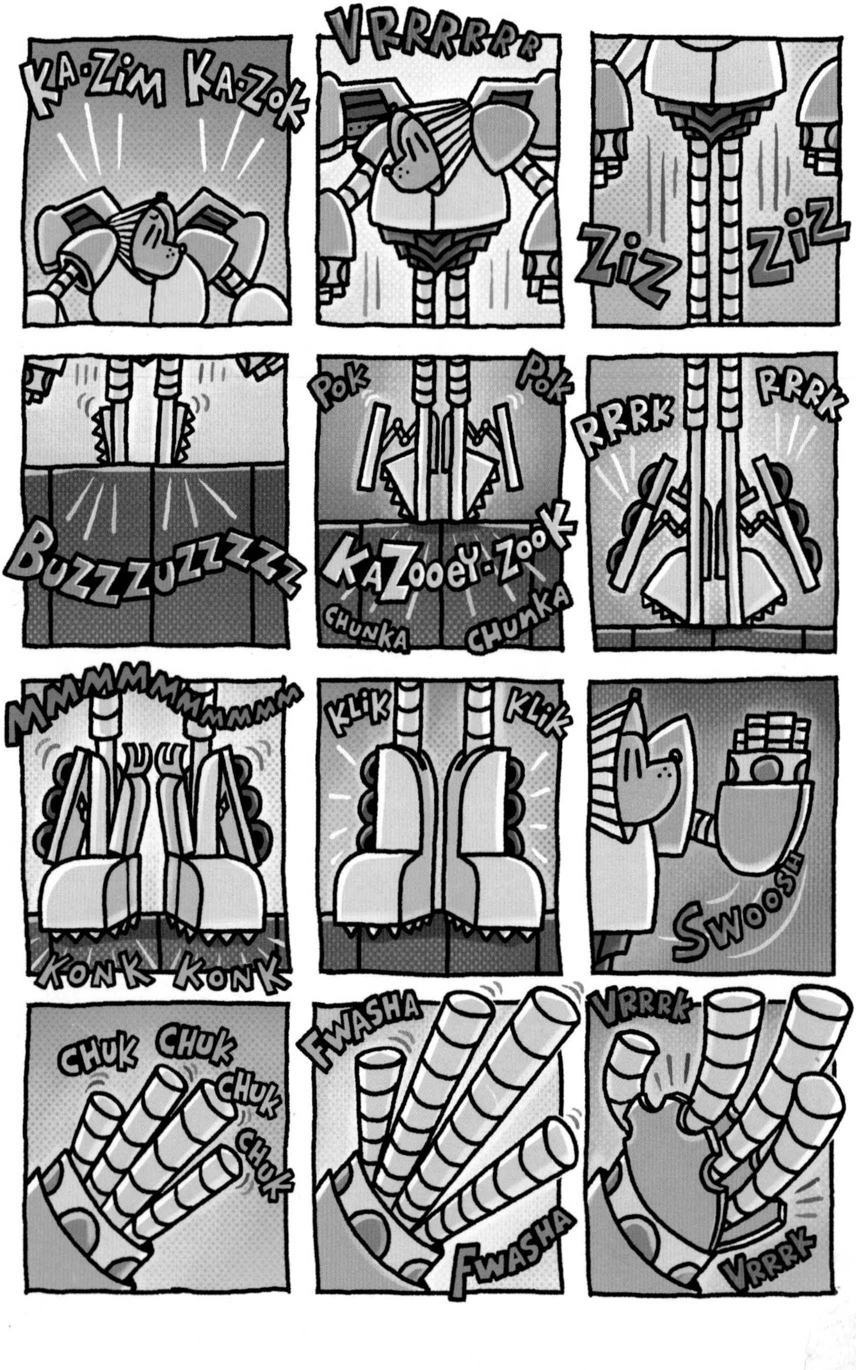
KA-ZIM KA-ZOK
VRRRRRRR
ZIZ ZIZ
BUZZZUZZZZZ
POK POK
KAZOOEY-ZOOK
CHUNKA CHUNKA
RRRK RRRK
MMMMMMMMMMMM
KONK KONK
KLIK KLIK
SWOOSH
CHUK CHUK CHUK CHUK
FWASHA
FWASHA
VRRRK
VRRRK

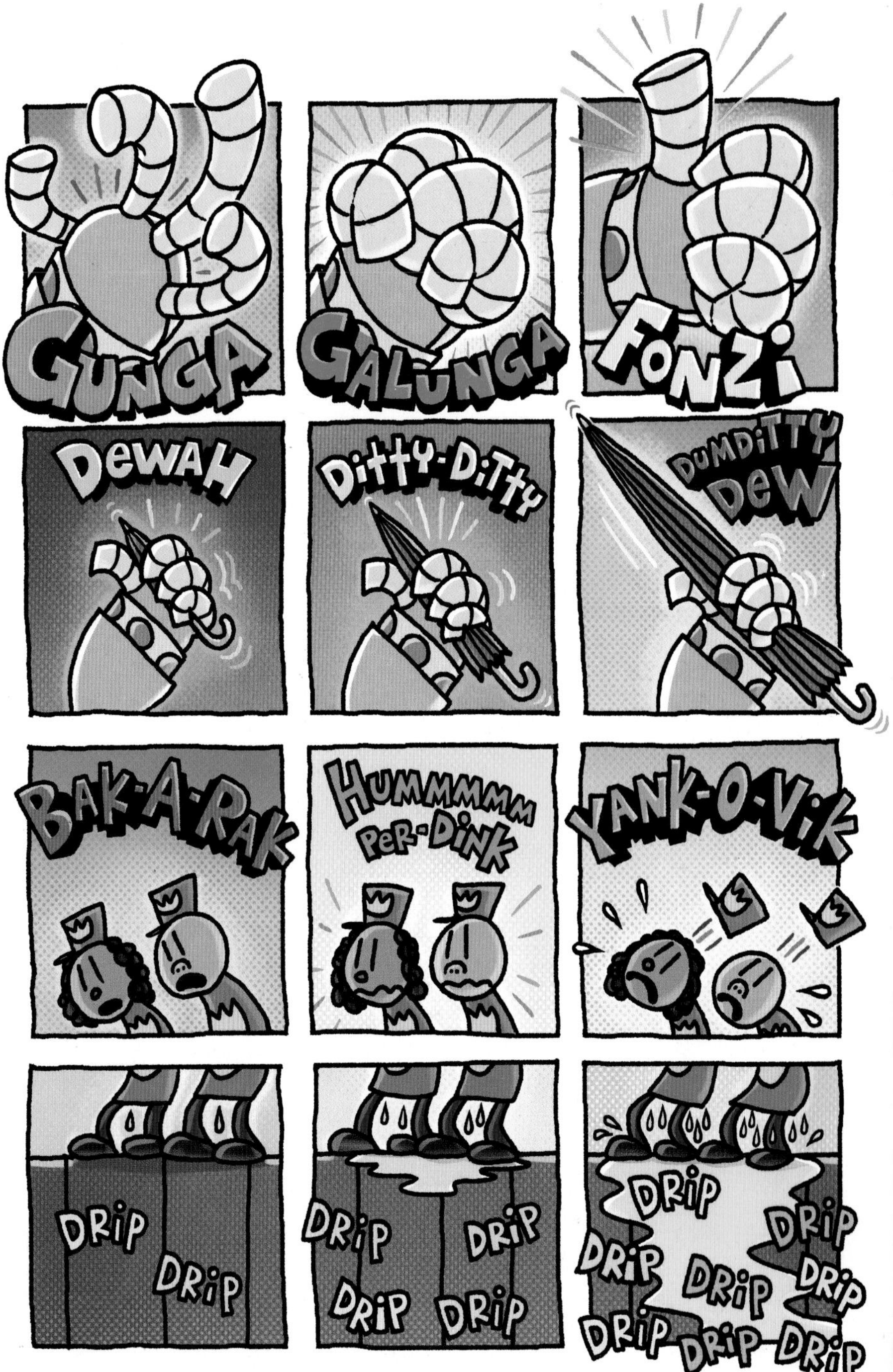
GUNGA
GALUNGA
FONZI
DEWAH
DITTY-DITTY
DUMDITTY DEW
BAK-A-RAK
HUMMMMM PER-DINK
YANK-O-VIK
DRIP
DRIP
DRIP
DRIP
DRIP
DRIP
DRIP
DRIP
DRIP
DRIP
DRIP
DRIP
DRIP
DRIP

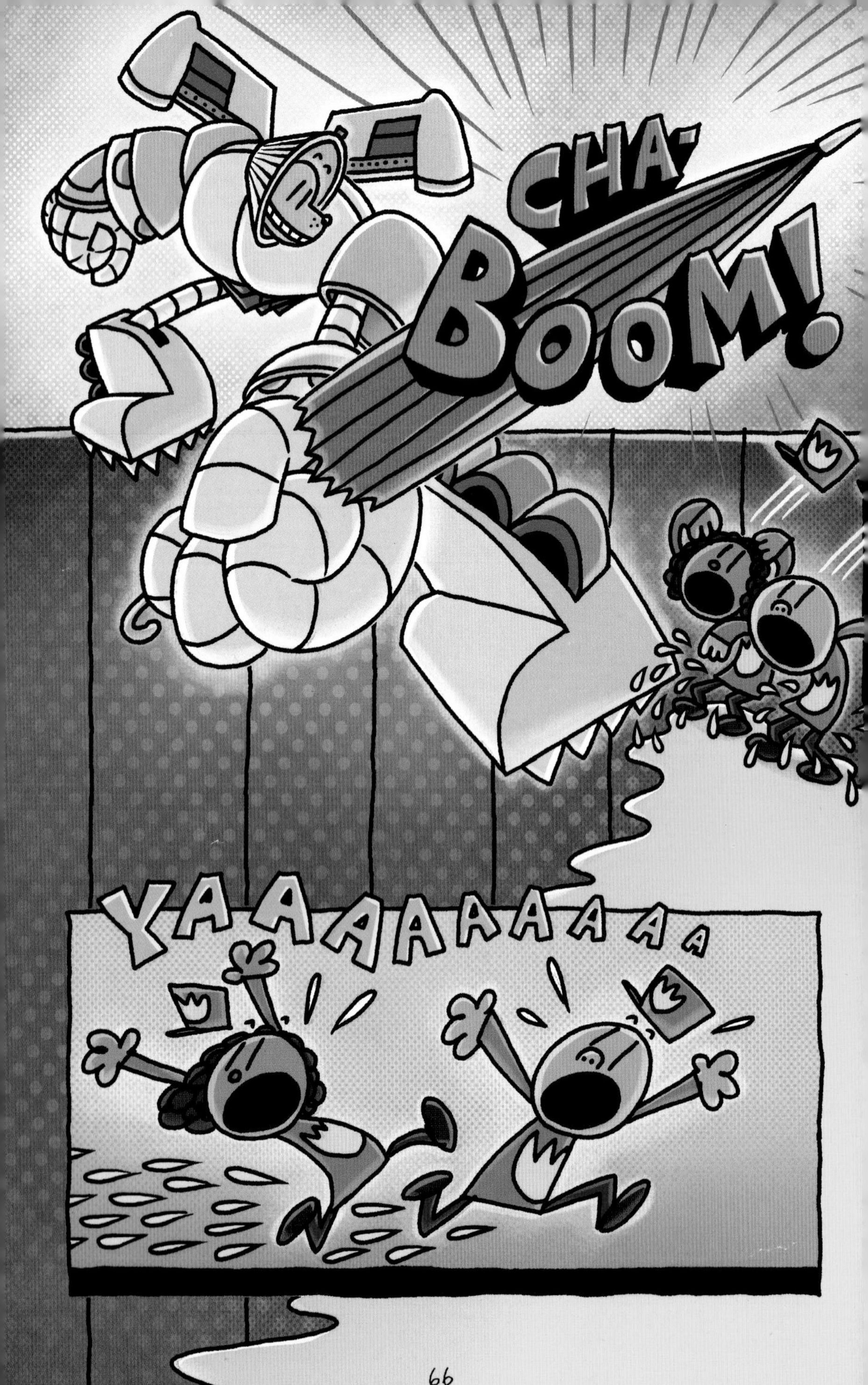
CHA-BOOM!
YAAAAAAAAAA

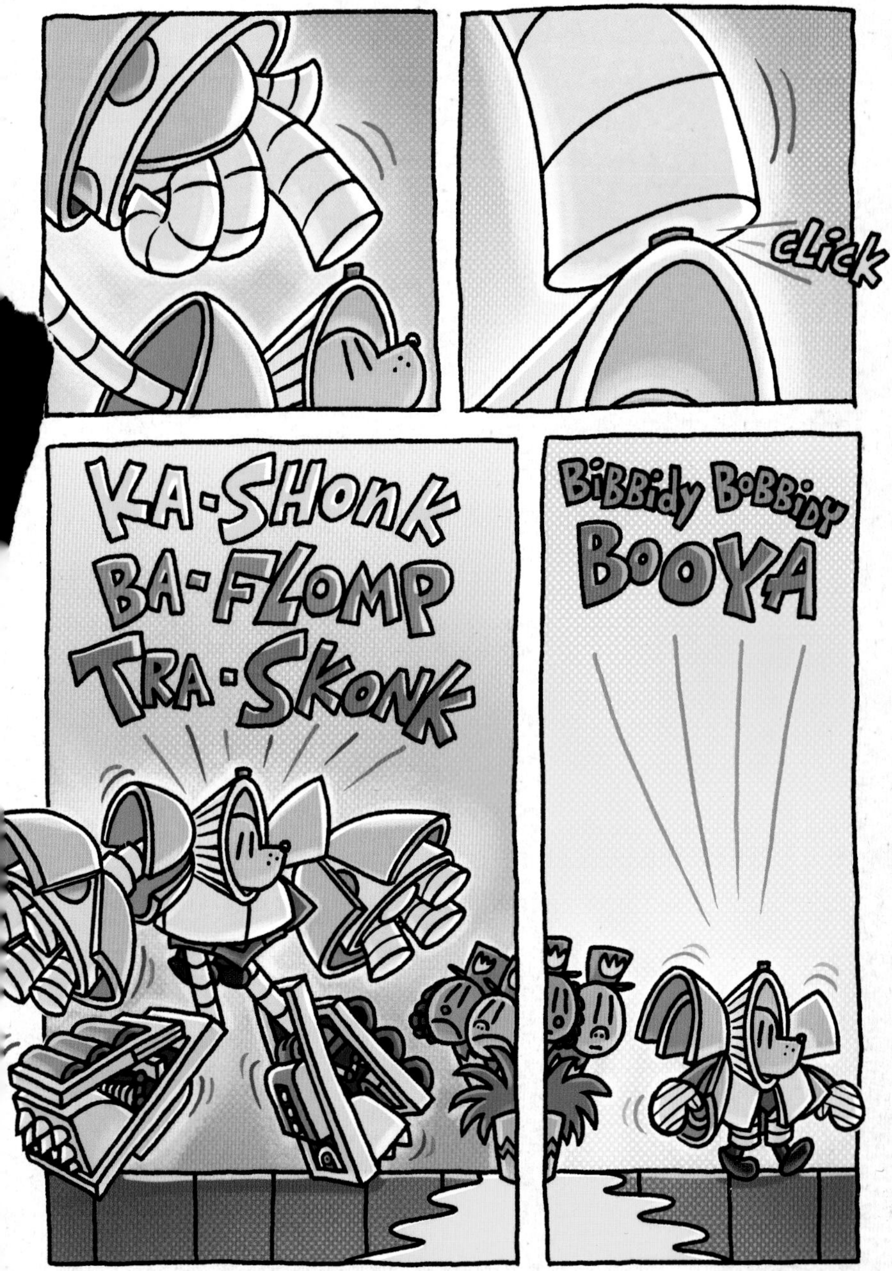
cLick
KA-SHONK
BA-FLOMP
TRA-SKONK
BiBBidy BoBBidy
BooYA

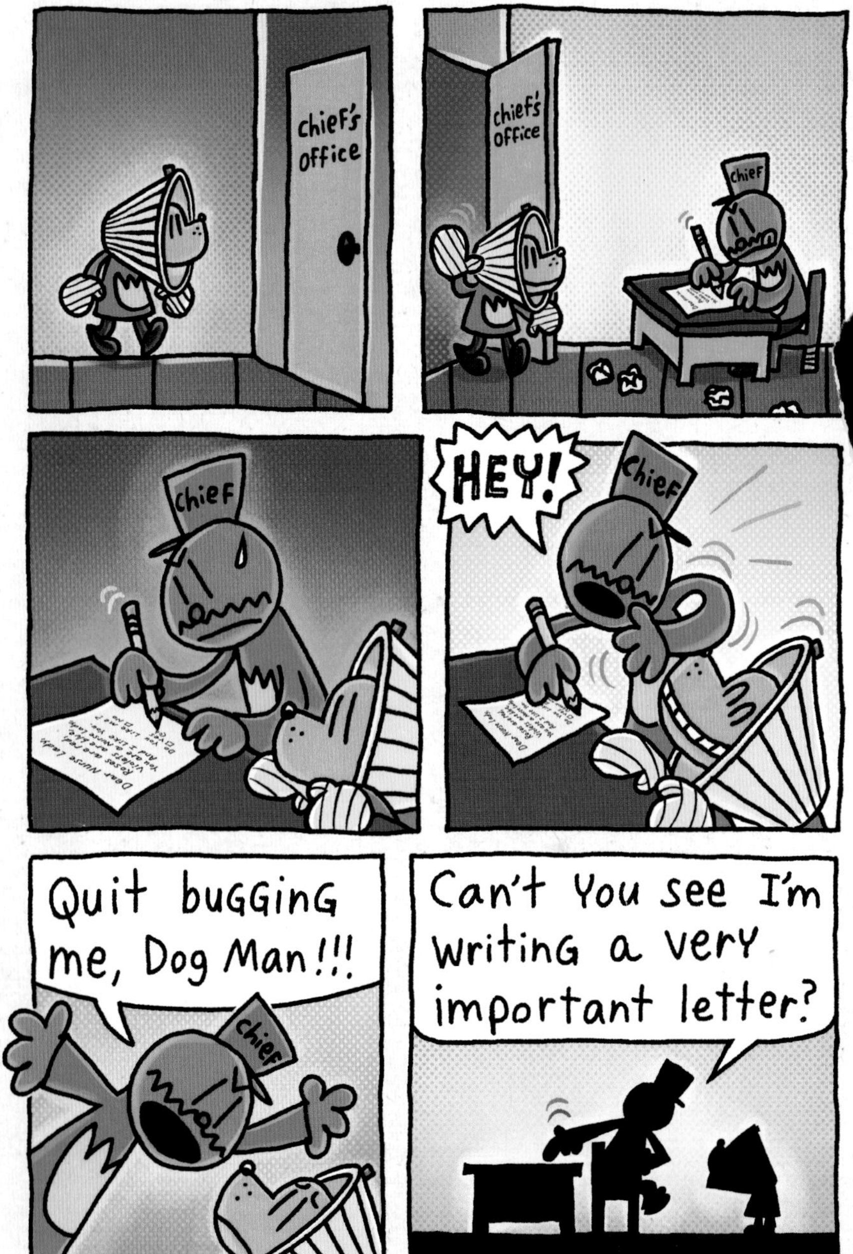
Chief's Office
Chief's Office
Chief
Chief
HEY!
Chief
Quit bugging me, Dog Man!!!
Chief
Can't you see I'm writing a very important letter?

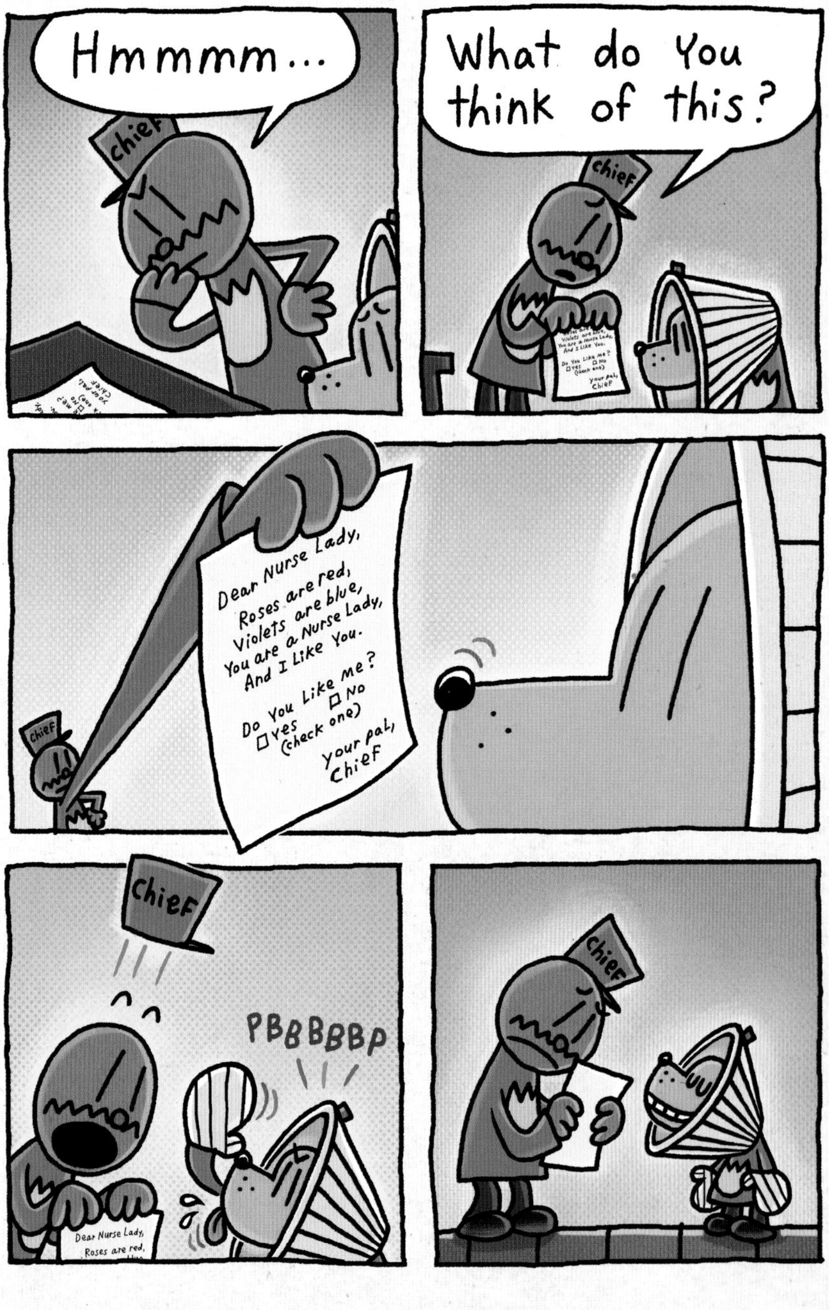
Hmmmm...
What do You think of this?
Dear Nurse Lady,
Roses are red,
Violets are blue,
You are a Nurse Lady,
And I Like You.
Do You Like me?
☐ Yes ☐ No
(check one)
your pal,
Chief
PBBBBBP

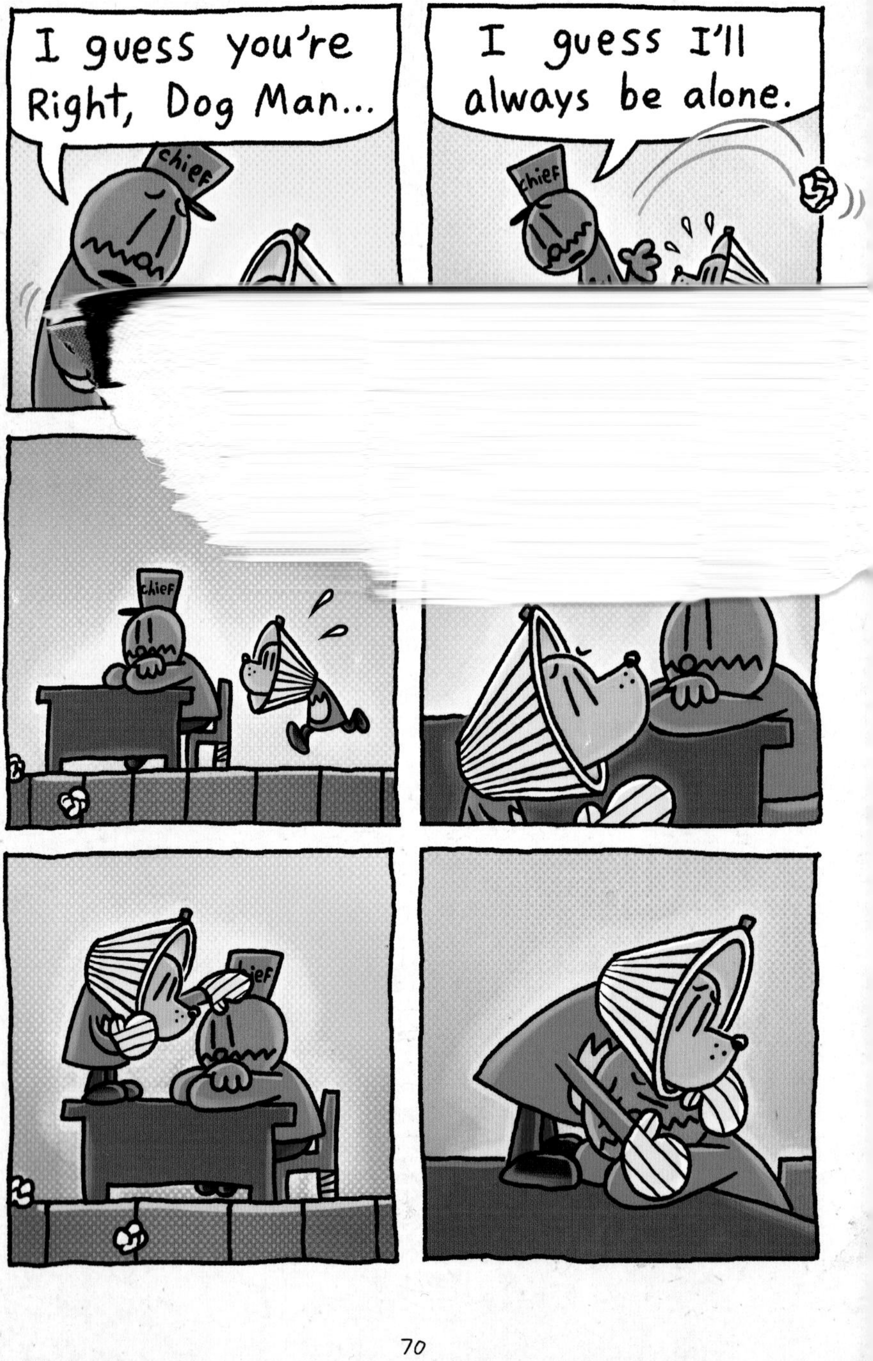
I guess you're Right, Dog Man...
I guess I'll always be alone.

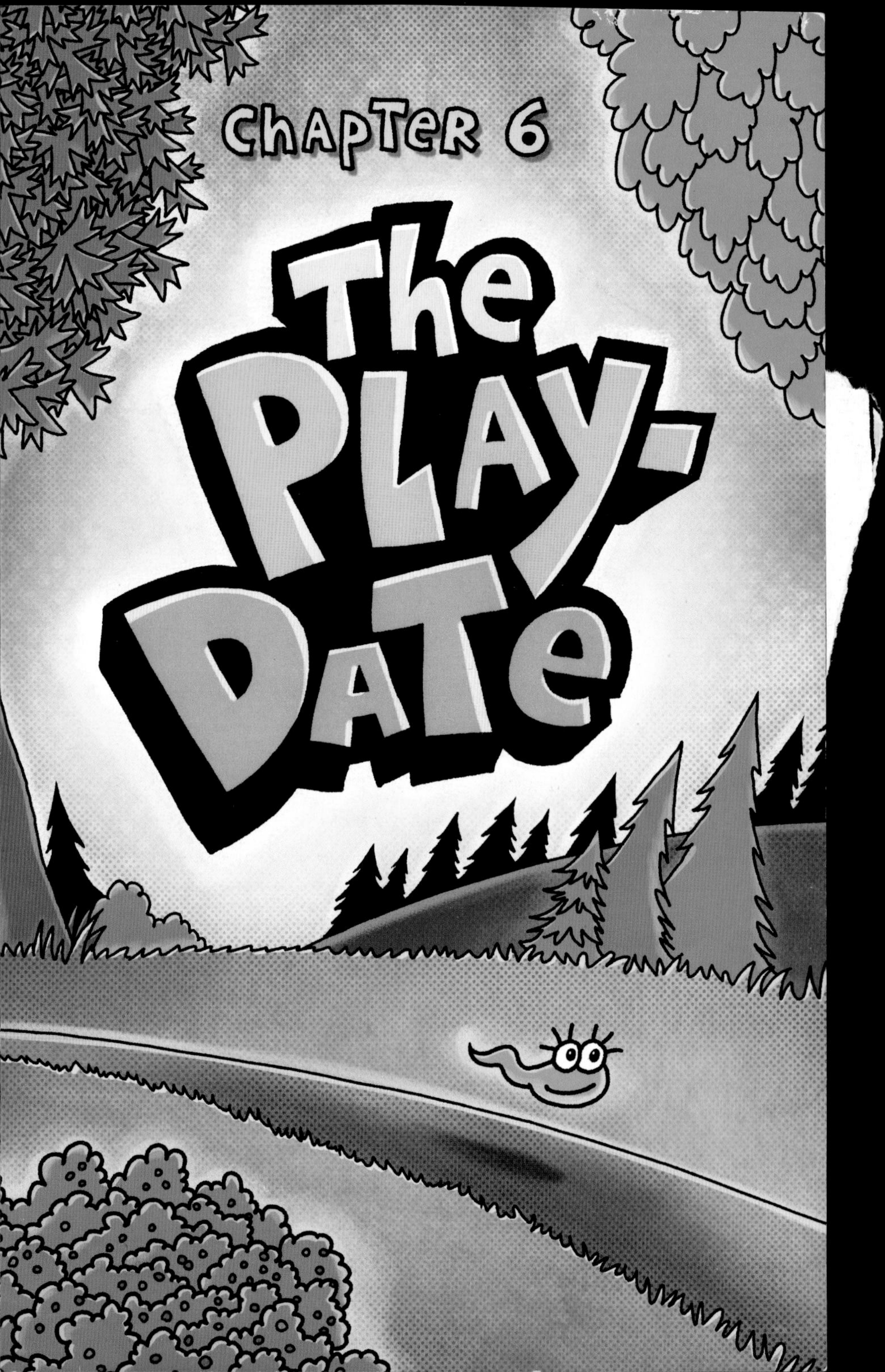
Chapter 6
The Play-Date

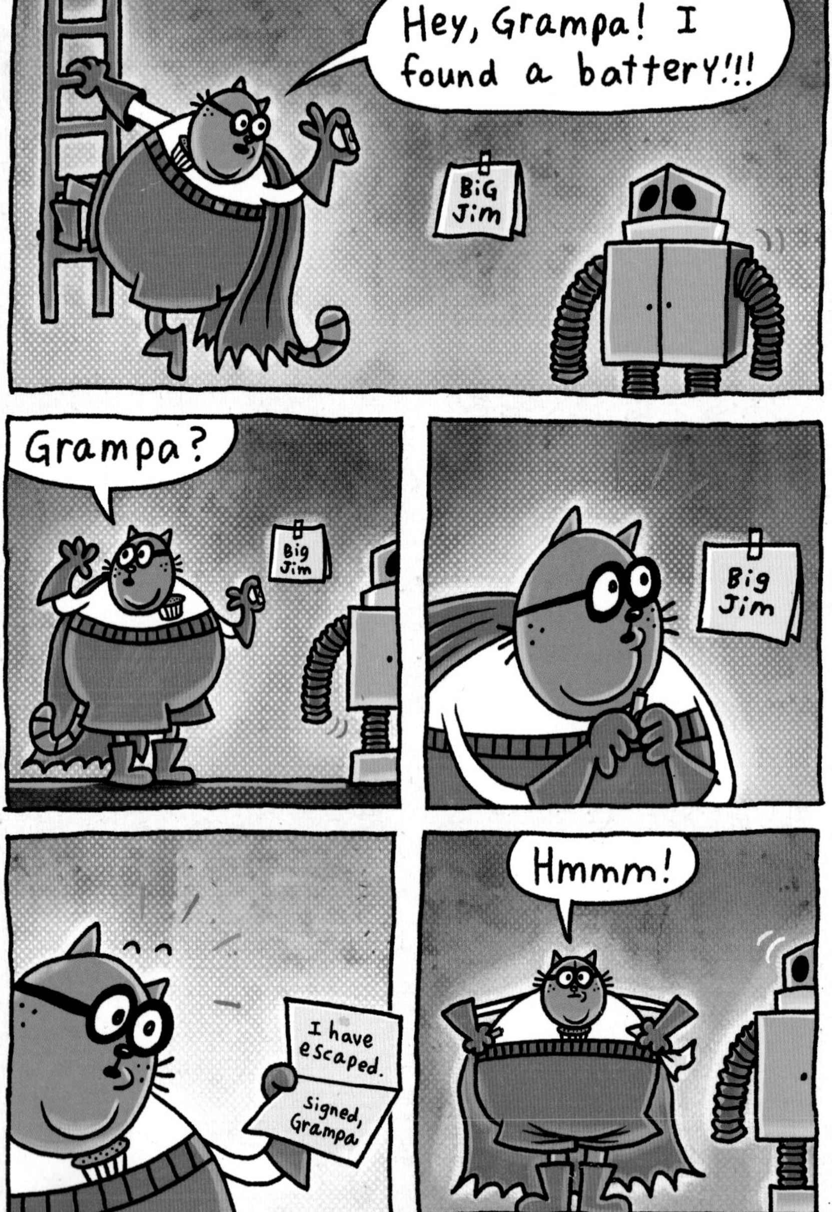
Hey, Grampa! I found a battery!!!
Big Jim
Grampa?
Big Jim
Big Jim
I have escaped.
Signed, Grampa
Hmmm!

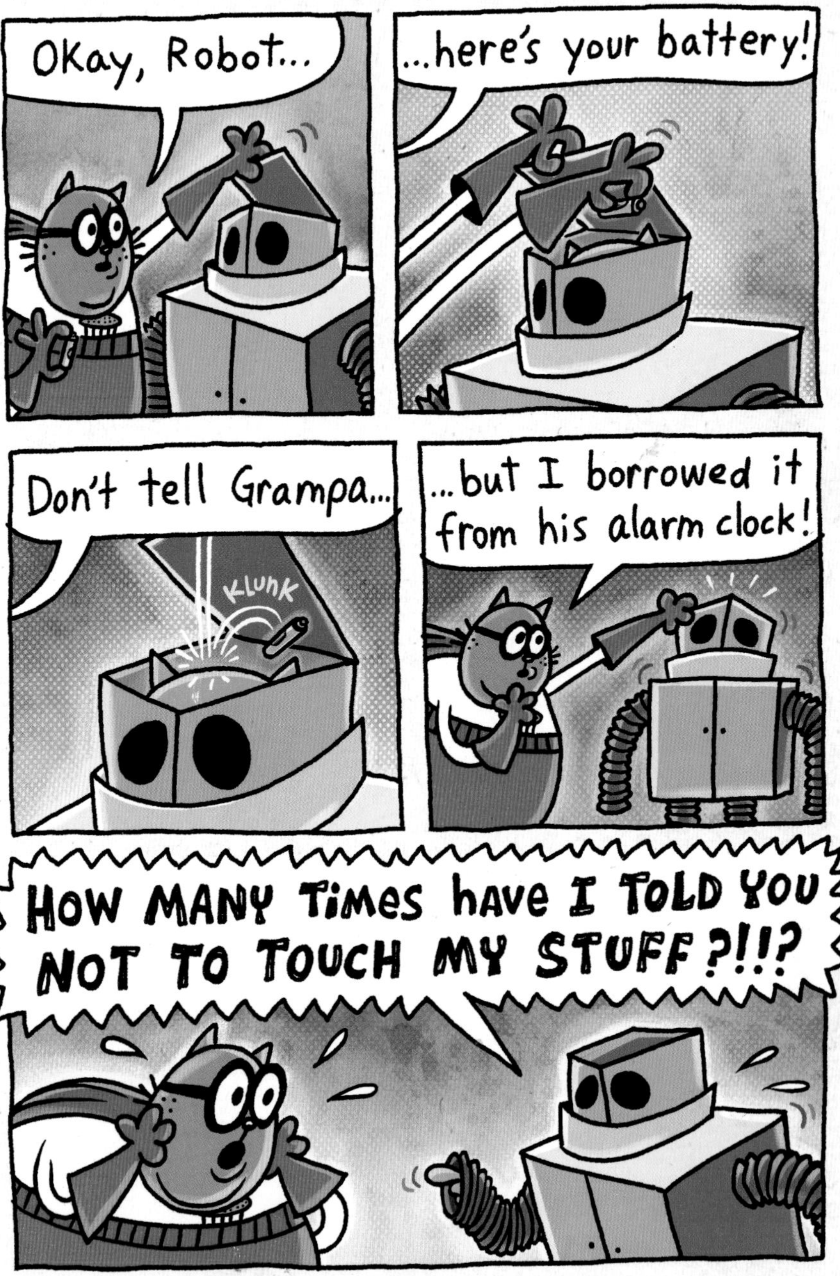
OKay, Robot...
...here's your battery!
Don't tell Grampa...
KLUNK
...but I borrowed it from his alarm clock!
HOW MANY TIMES have I TOLD YOU NOT TO TOUCH MY STUFF?!!?

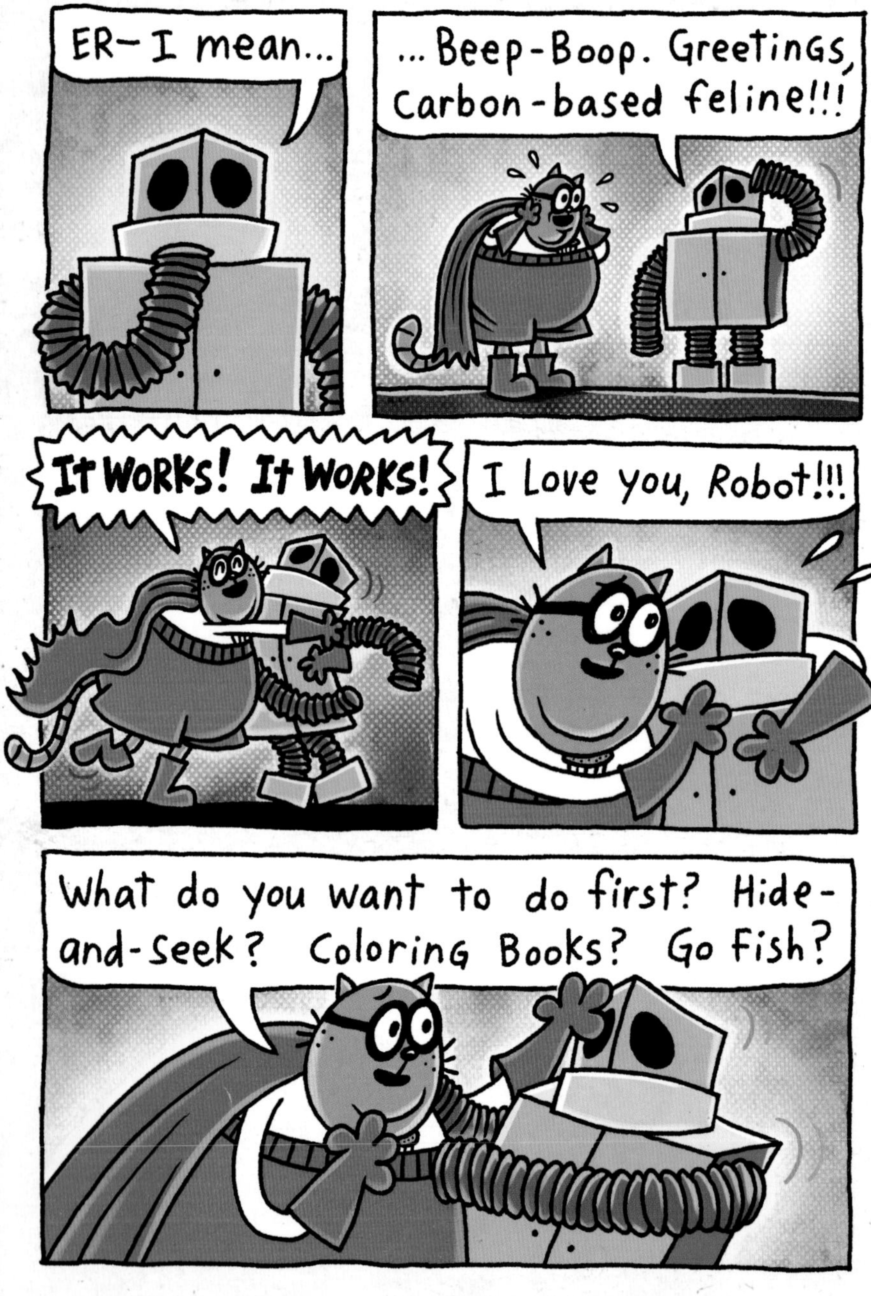
ER—I mean...
...Beep-Boop. Greetings, Carbon-based feline!!!
It WORKS! It WORKS!
I Love you, Robot!!!
What do you want to do first? Hide-and-seek? Coloring Books? Go Fish?

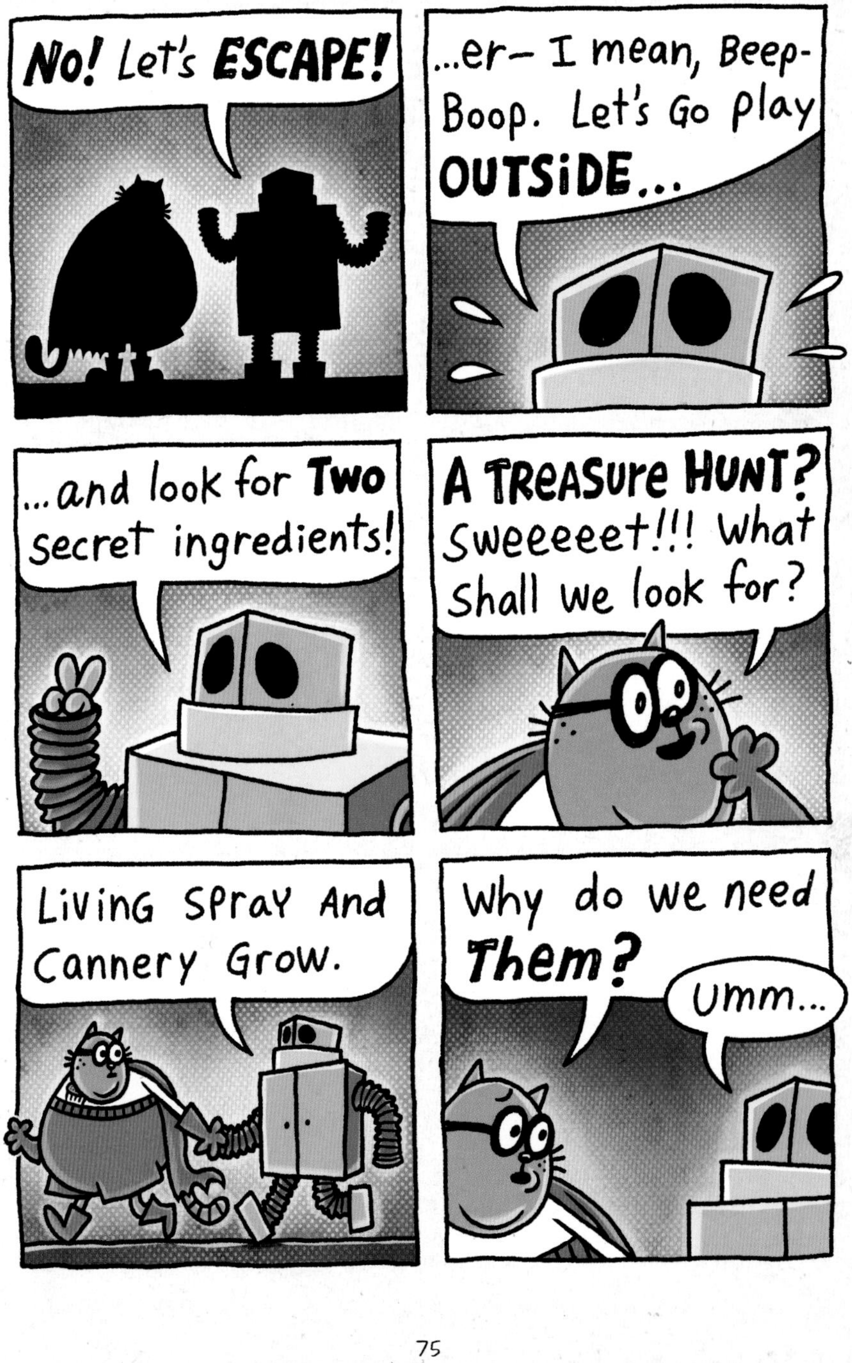
NO! Let's ESCAPE!
...er– I mean, Beep-Boop. Let's Go play OUTSIDE...
...and look for TWO secret ingredients!
A TREASURE HUNT? Sweeeeet!!! What Shall we look for?
LiViNG SPraY And Cannery Grow.
Why do we need Them?
Umm...

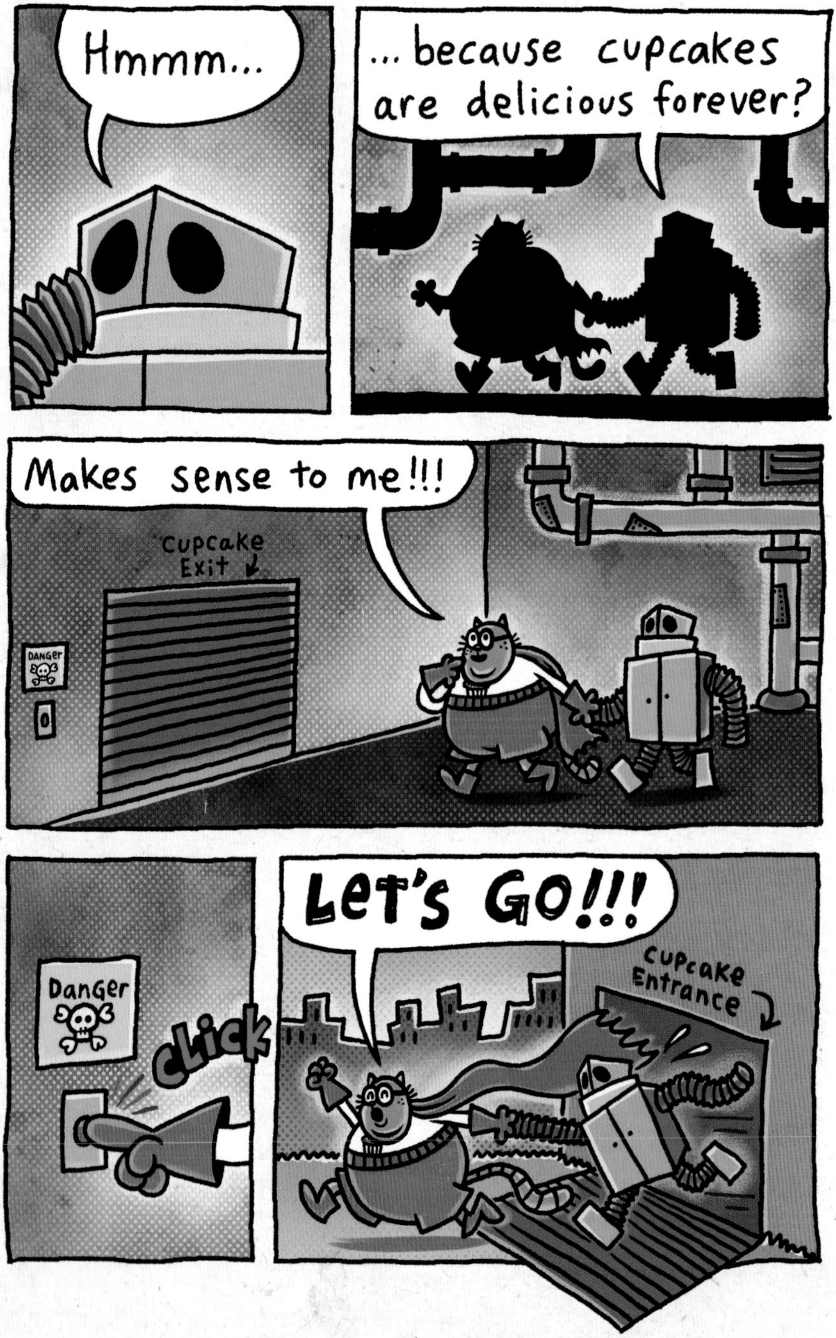
Hmmm...
...because cupcakes are delicious forever?
Makes sense to me!!!
Cupcake Exit
DANGER
Danger
CLICK
LET'S GO!!!
Cupcake Entrance

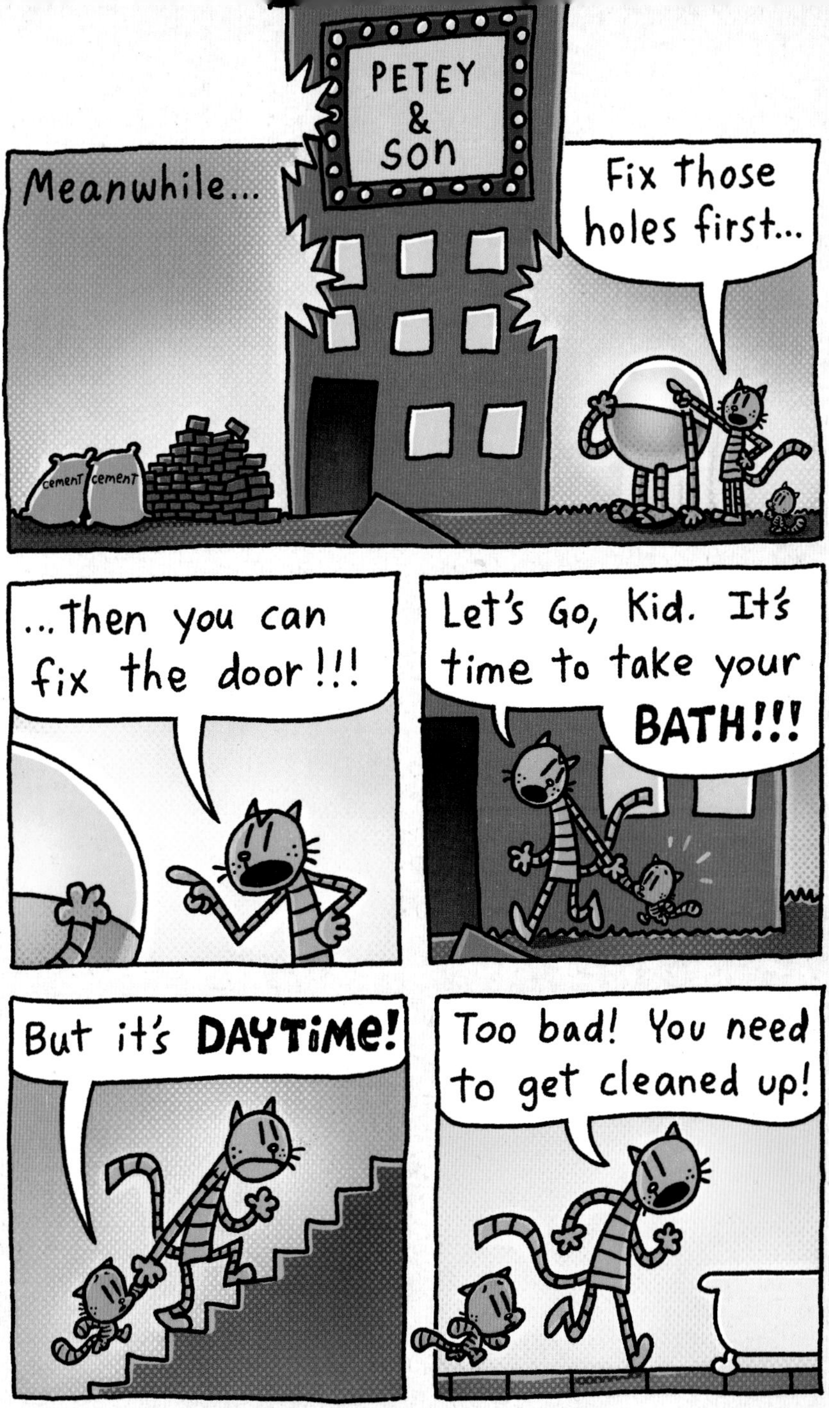
PETEY & SON
Meanwhile...
Fix those holes first...
cement
cement
...then you can fix the door!!!
Let's Go, Kid. It's time to take your BATH!!!
But it's DAYTIME!
Too bad! You need to get cleaned up!

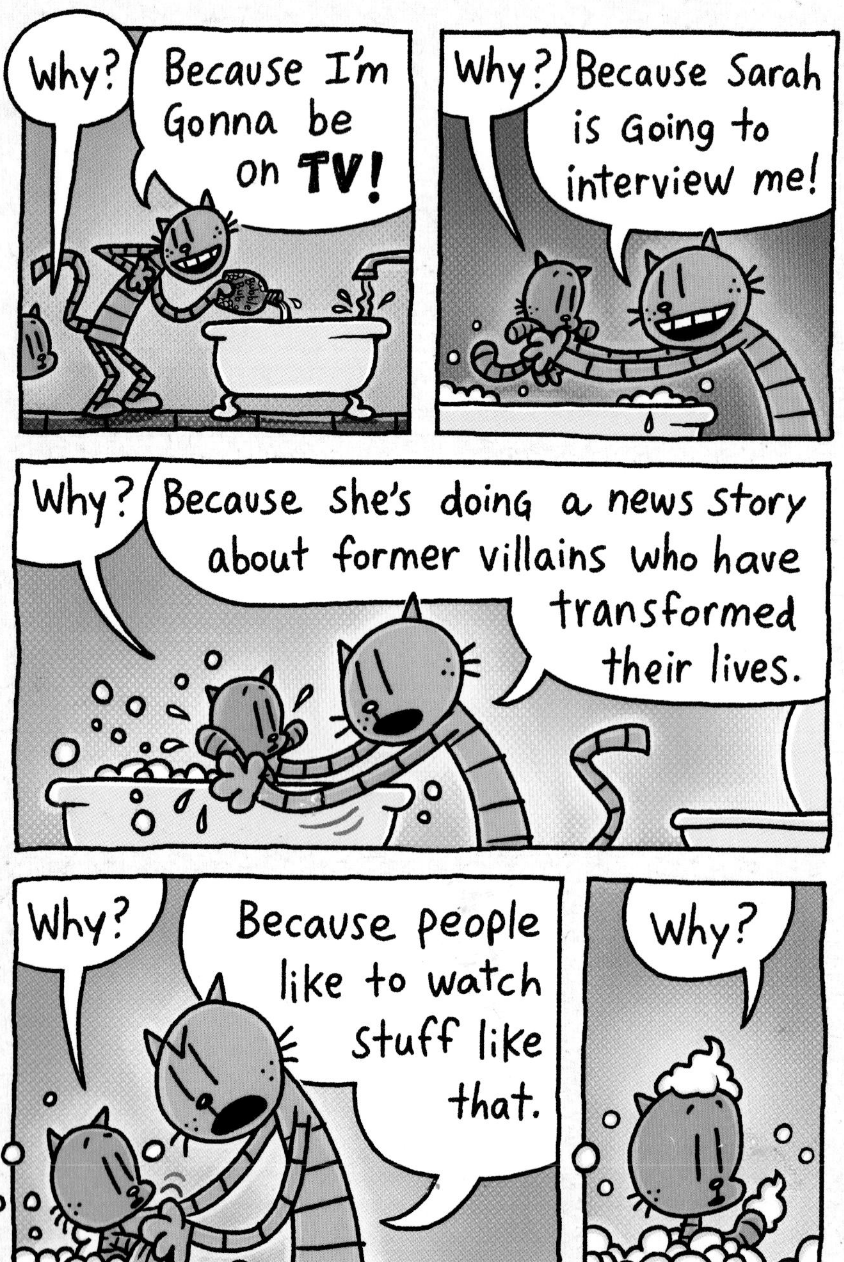

Why?
Because I'm Gonna be on TV!
Bubble Bub
Why?
Because Sarah is Going to interview me!
Why?
Because she's doing a news story about former villains who have transformed their lives.
Why?
Because people like to watch stuff like that.
Why?

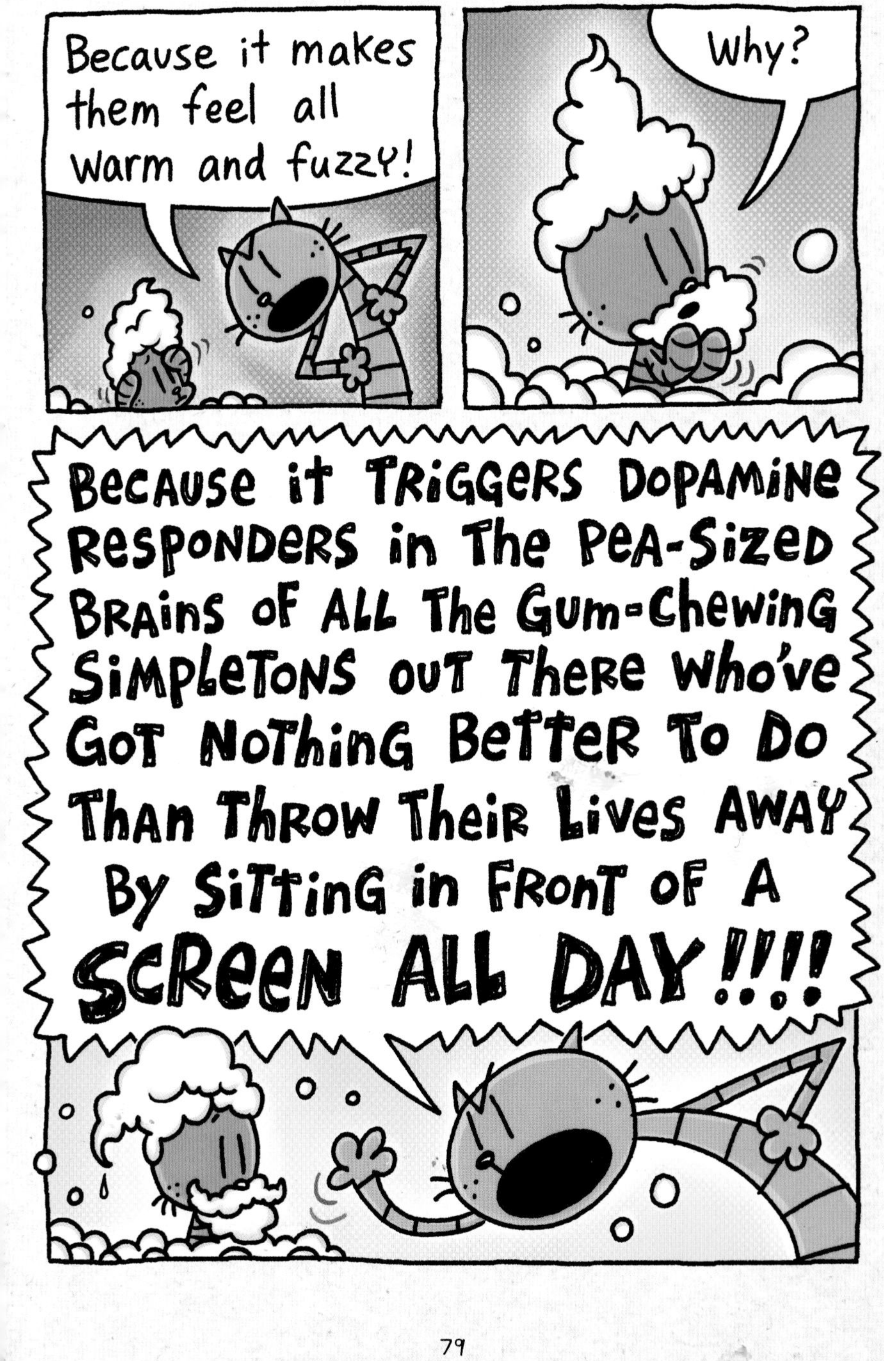
Because it makes them feel all warm and fuzzy!
Why?
BECAUSE iT TRIGGERS DOPAMiNE RESPONDERS iN THE PEA-SIZED BRAiNS OF ALL THE GUM-CHEWiNG SiMPLETONS OUT THERE WHO'VE GOT NOTHiNG BETTER TO DO THAN THROW THEiR LiVES AWAY BY SiTTiNG iN FRONT OF A SCREEN ALL DAY!!!!

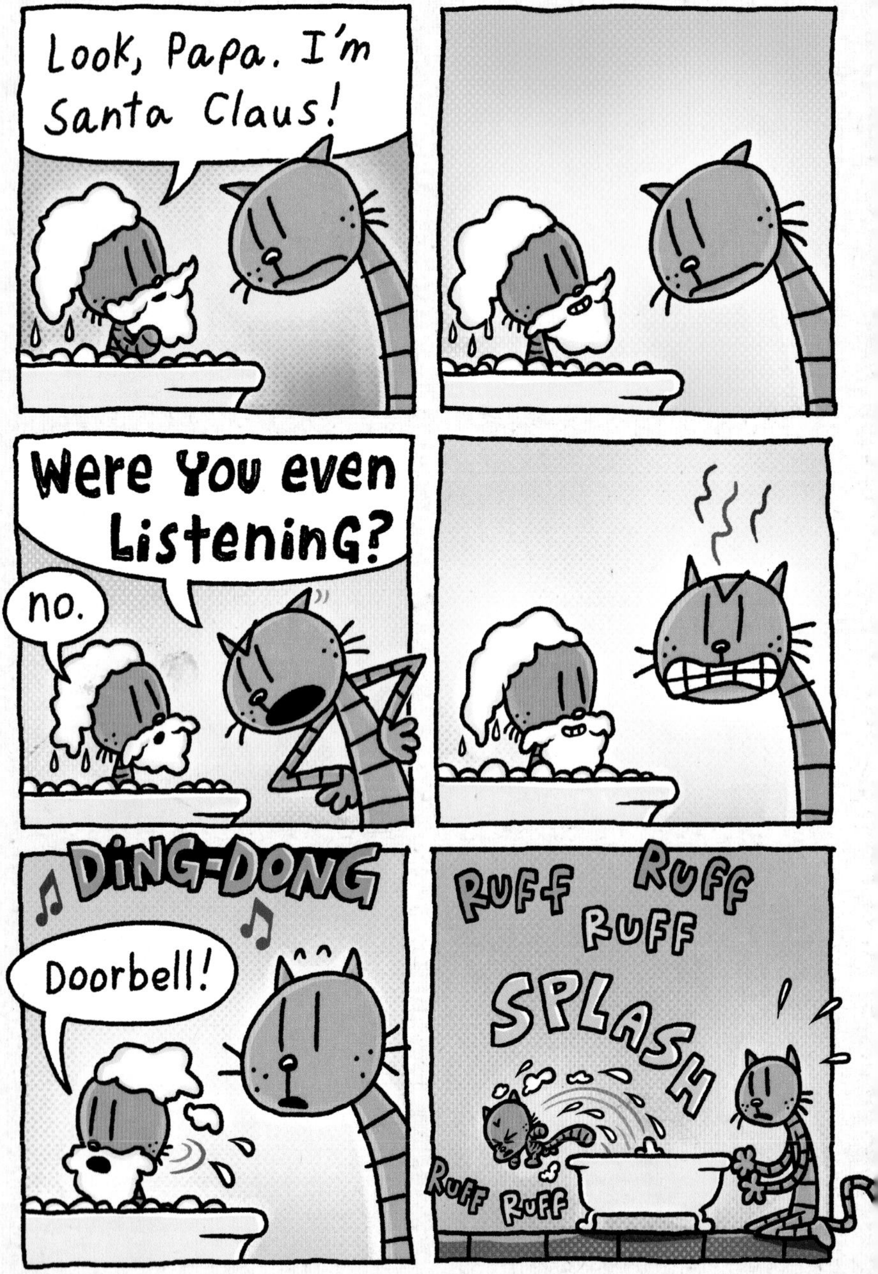
Look, Papa. I'm Santa Claus!
Were You even ListeninG?
no.
DiNG-DONG
Doorbell!
RUFF RUFF
RUFF
SPLASH
RUFF RUFF

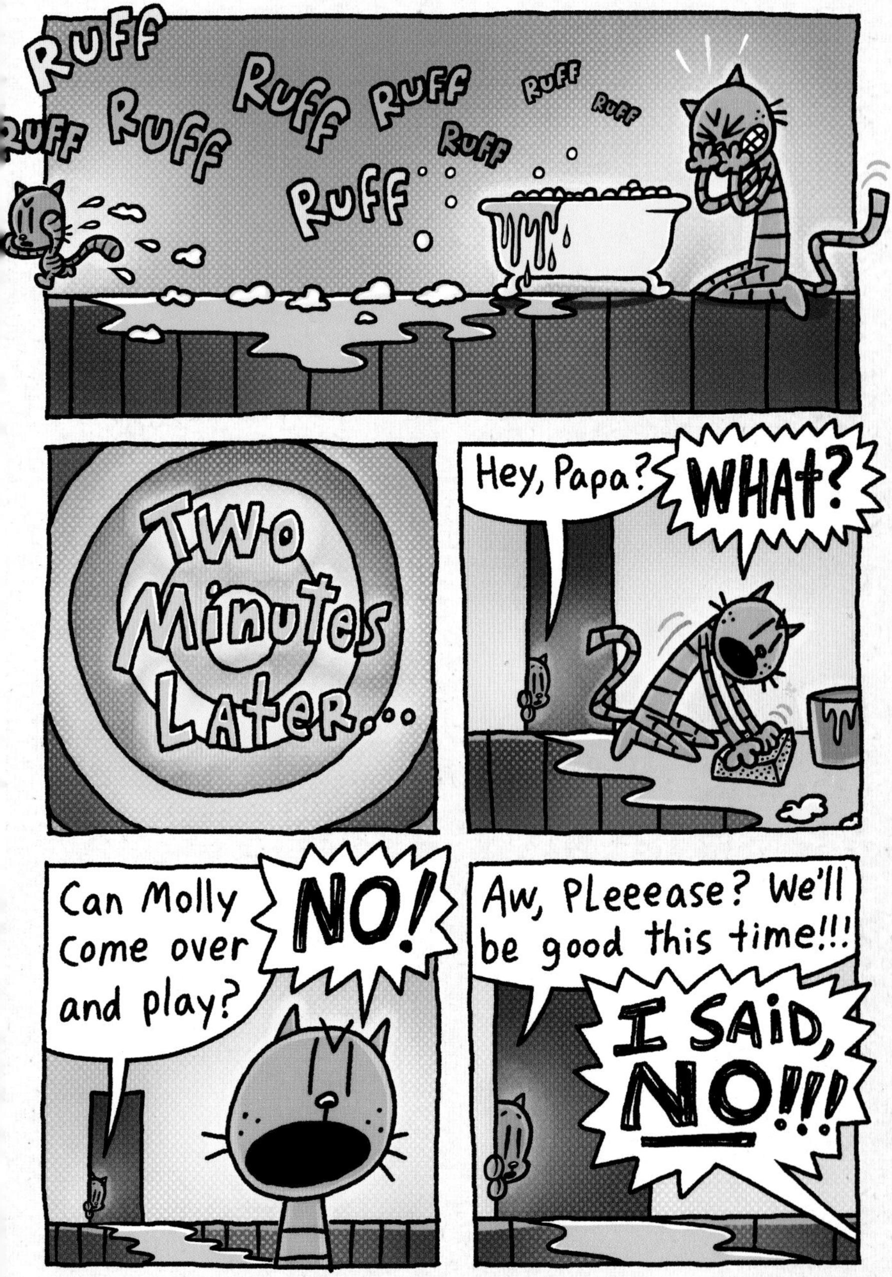
RUFF
RUFF RUFF
RUFF RUFF
RUFF
RUFF
RUFF
RUFF
RUFF
TWO Minutes LATER...
Hey, Papa?
WHAT?
Can Molly come over and play?
NO!
Aw, Pleeease? We'll be good this time!!!
I SAID, NO!!!

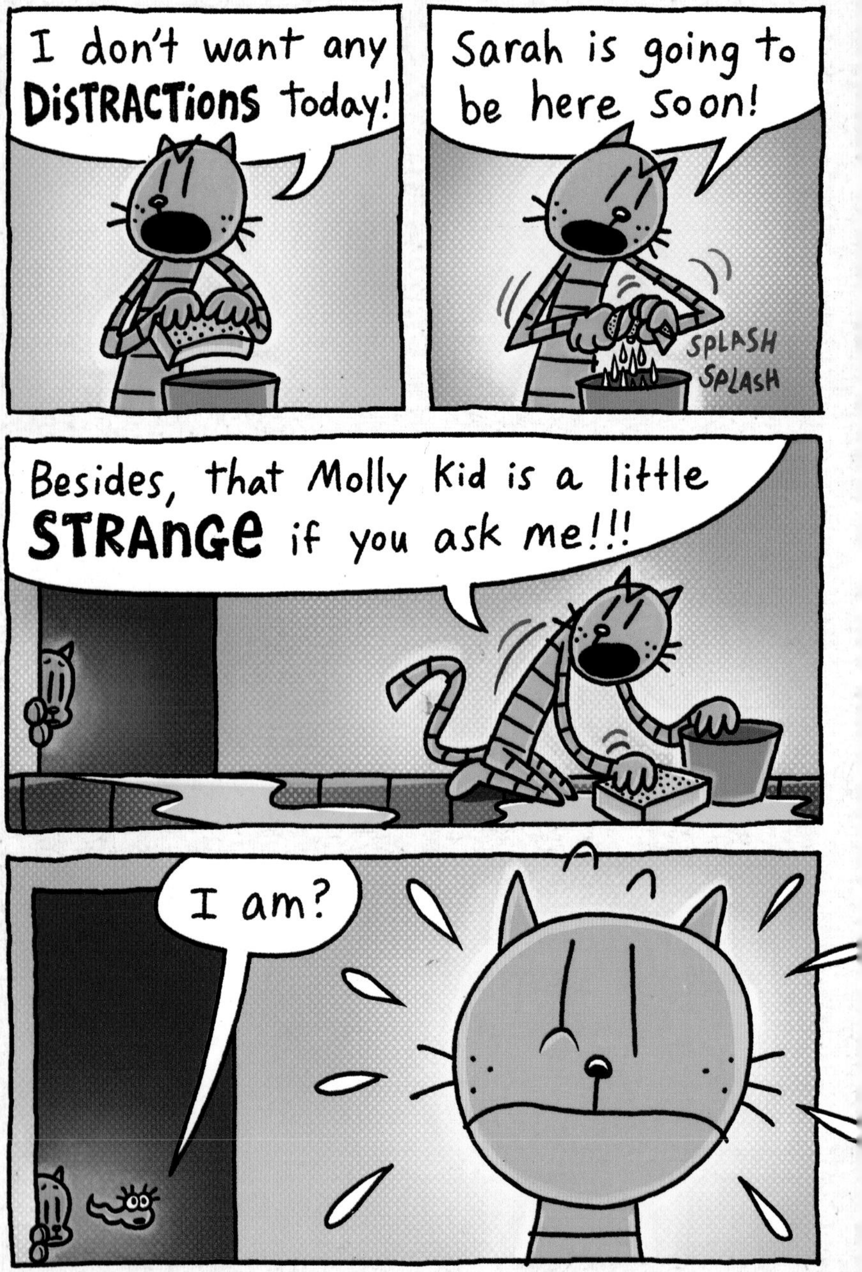
I don't want any DISTRACTIONS today!
Sarah is going to be here soon!
SPLASH SPLASH
Besides, that Molly kid is a little STRANGE if you ask me!!!
I am?

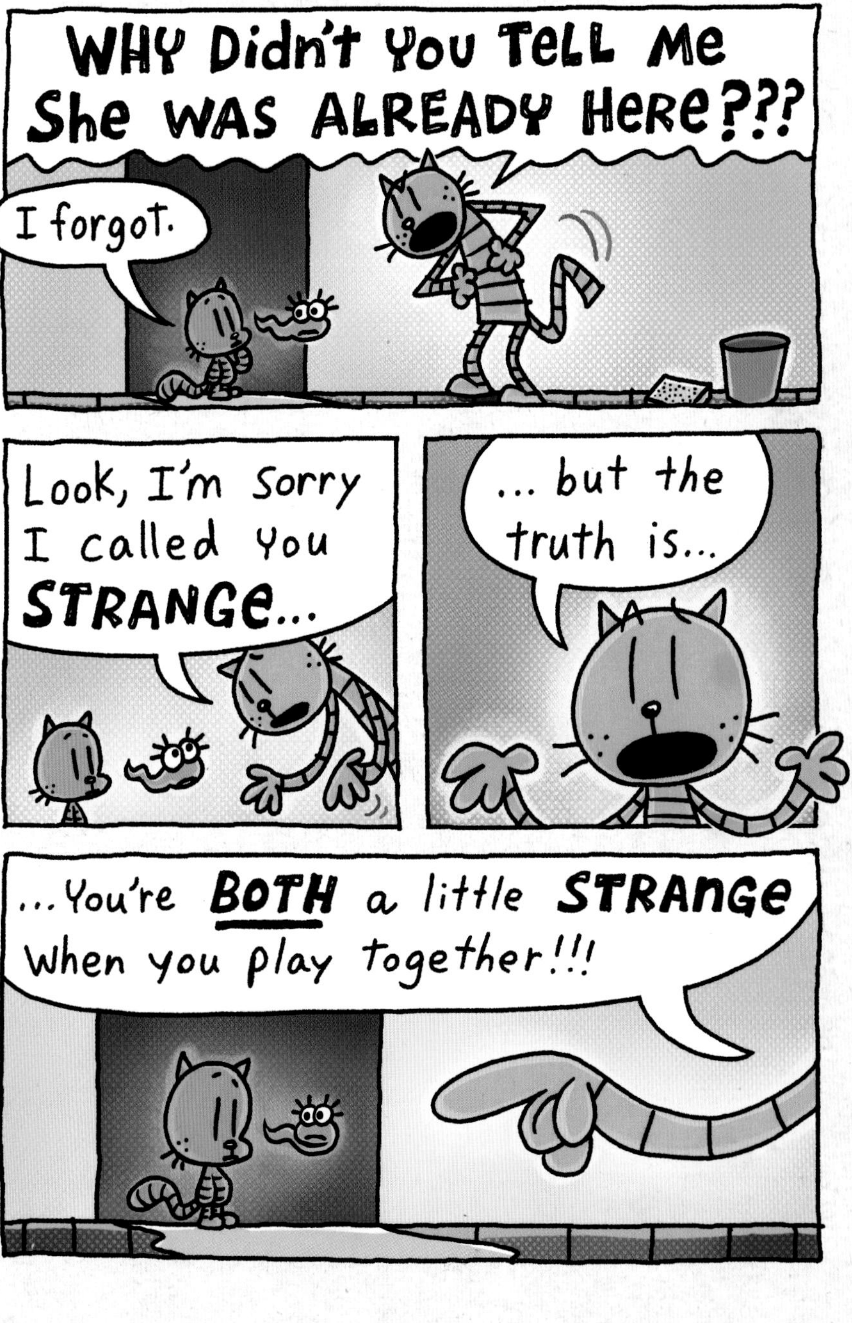
WHY Didn't You TELL Me She WAS ALREADY Here???
I forgot.
Look, I'm Sorry I called you STRANGE...
... but the truth is...
...You're BOTH a little STRANGE when you play together!!!

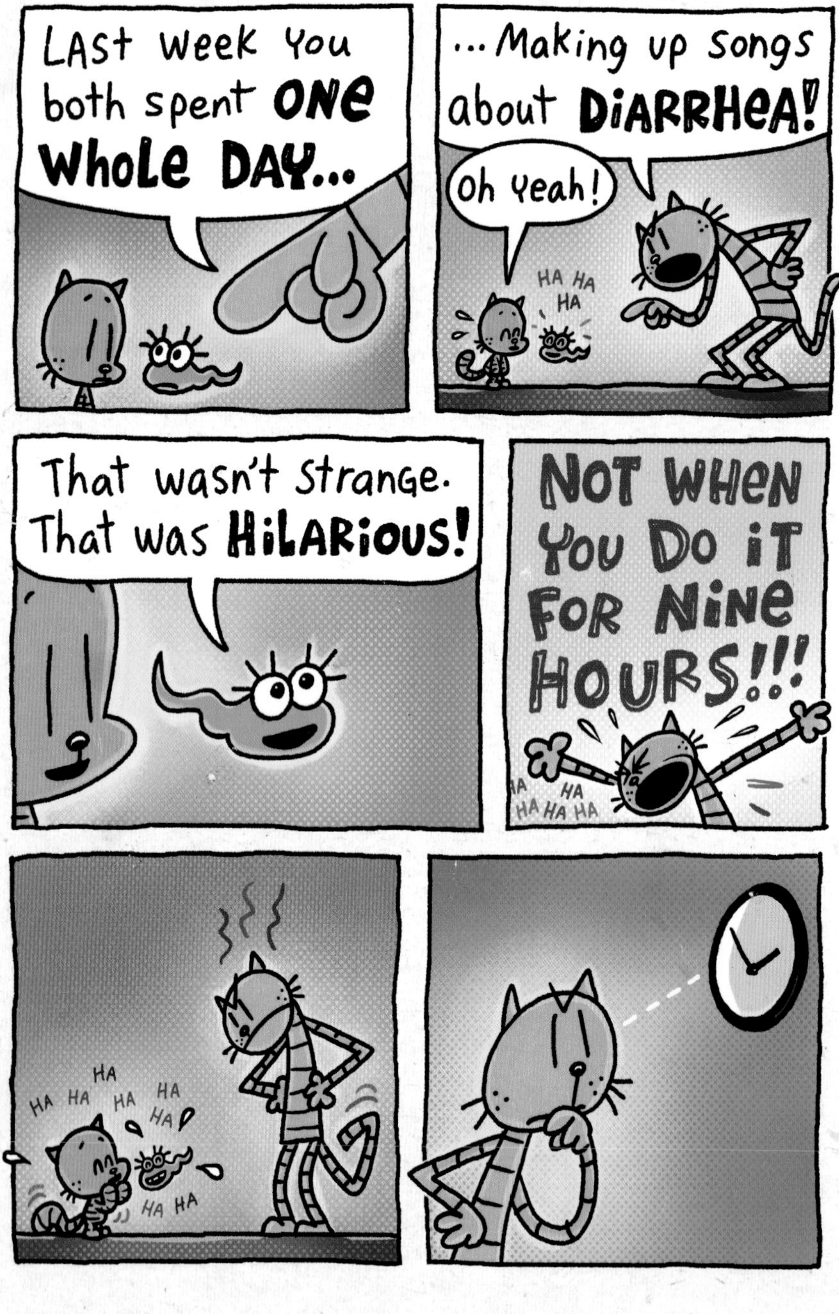
LAST week You both spent ONE WHOLE DAY...
...Making up songs about DIARRHEA!
Oh Yeah!
HA HA HA
That wasn't Strange. That was HILARIOUS!
NOT WHEN YOU DO IT FOR NINE HOURS!!!
HA HA HA HA HA
HA HA HA HA HA HA!
HA HA

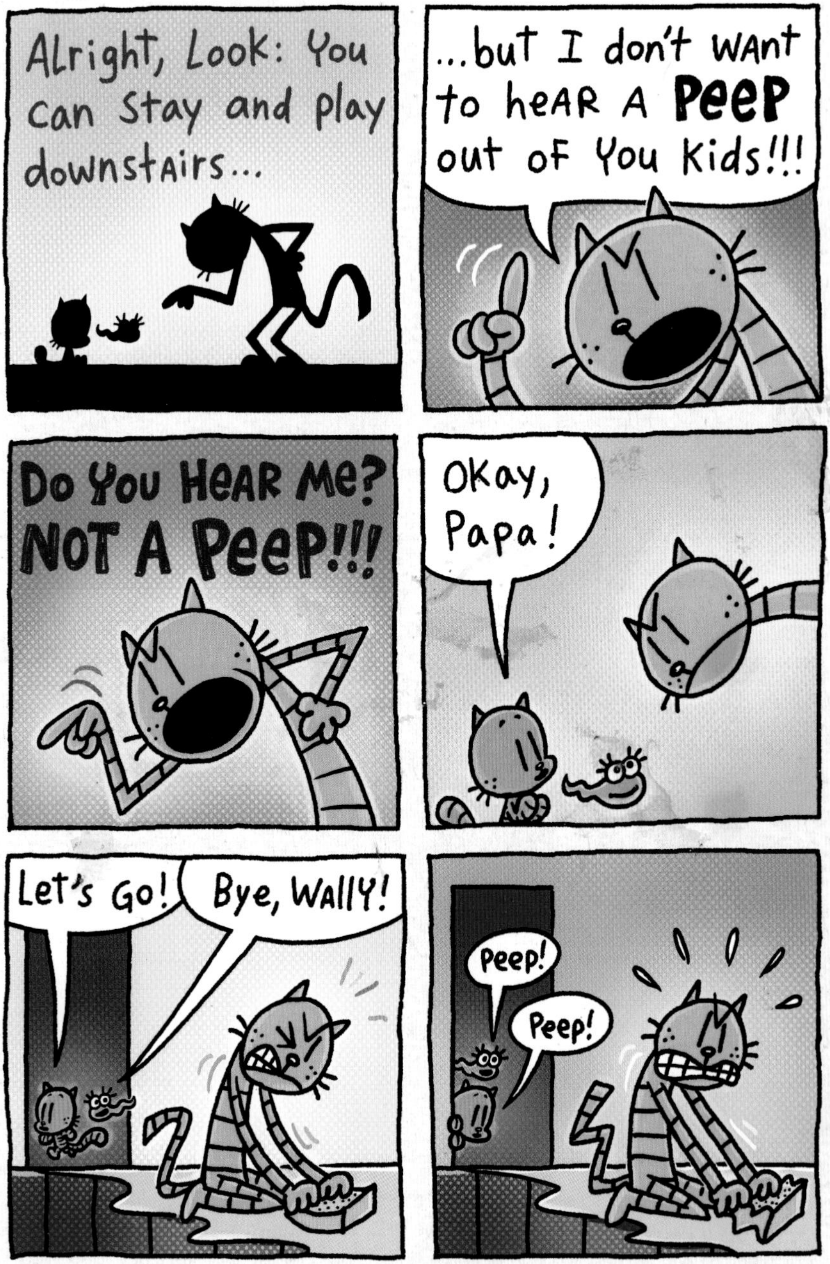
Alright, Look: You can Stay and play downstairs...
...but I don't WANT to hear A PEEP out of You kids!!!
Do You Hear Me? NOT A PeeP!!!
Okay, Papa!
Let's Go!
Bye, Wally!
Peep!
Peep!

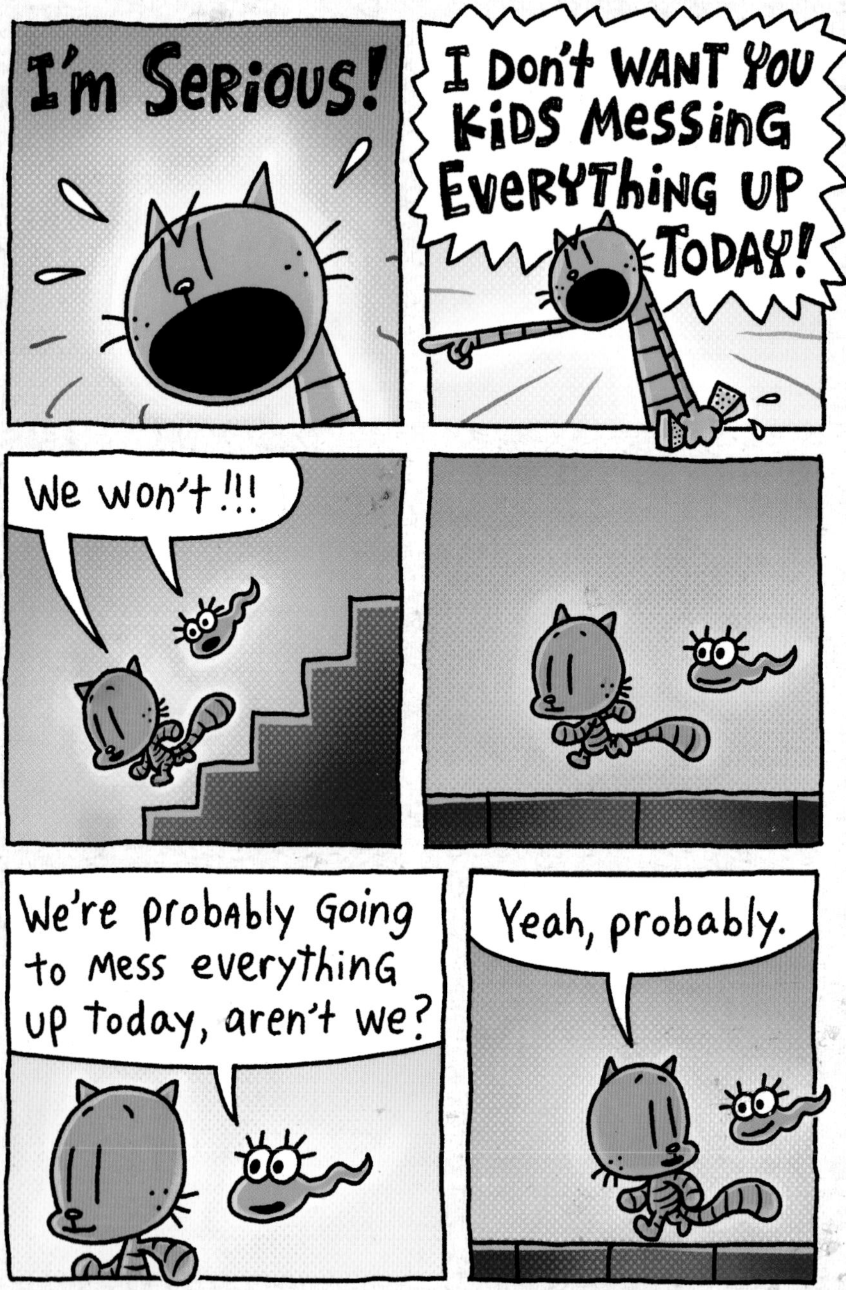
I'm SERIOUS!
I DON'T WANT YOU KIDS MESSING EVERYTHING UP TODAY!
We won't!!!
We're probably Going to Mess everything up today, aren't we?
Yeah, probably.

CHAPTER 7

A Buncha Stuff That Happened Next

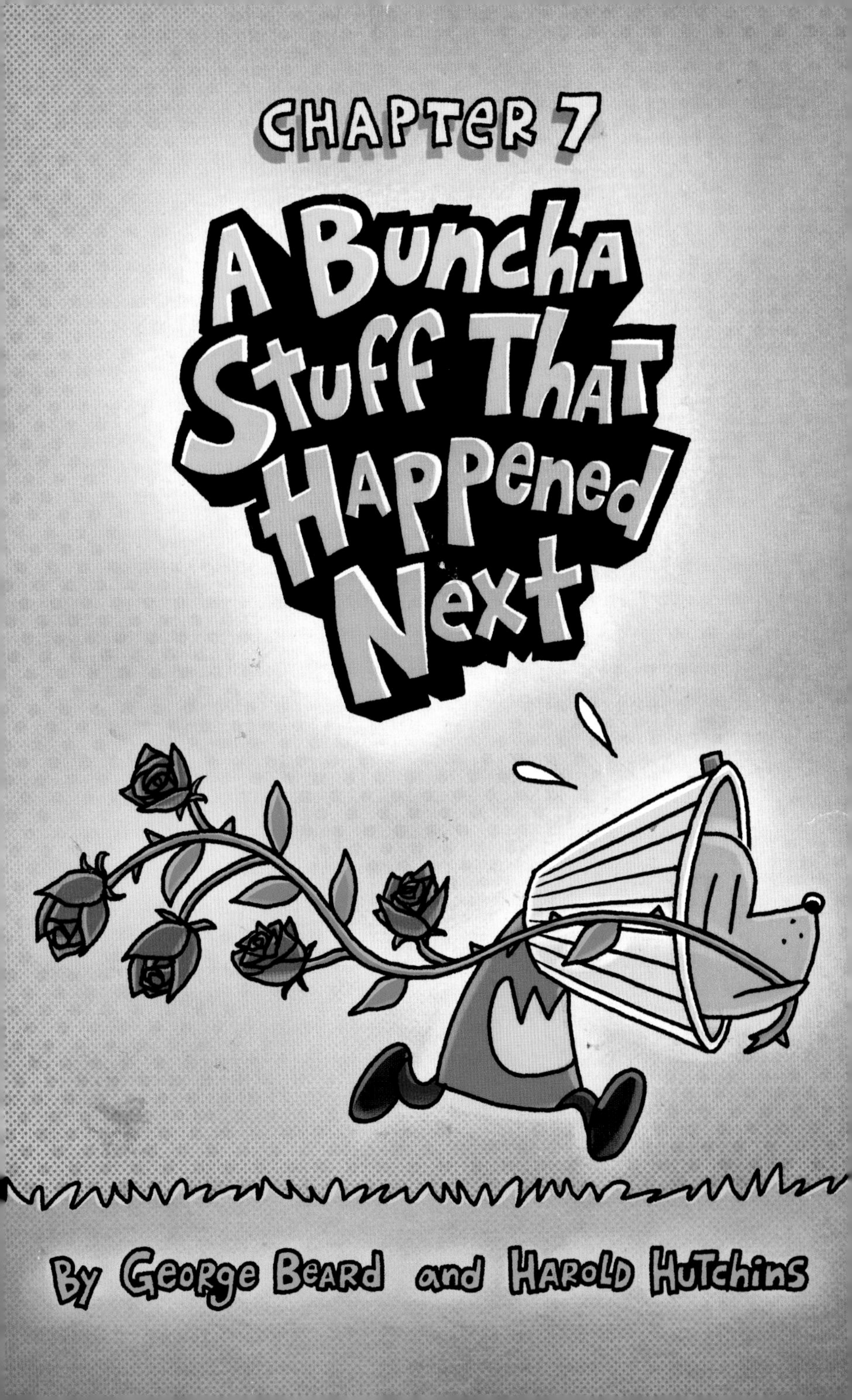

By George Beard and Harold Hutchins

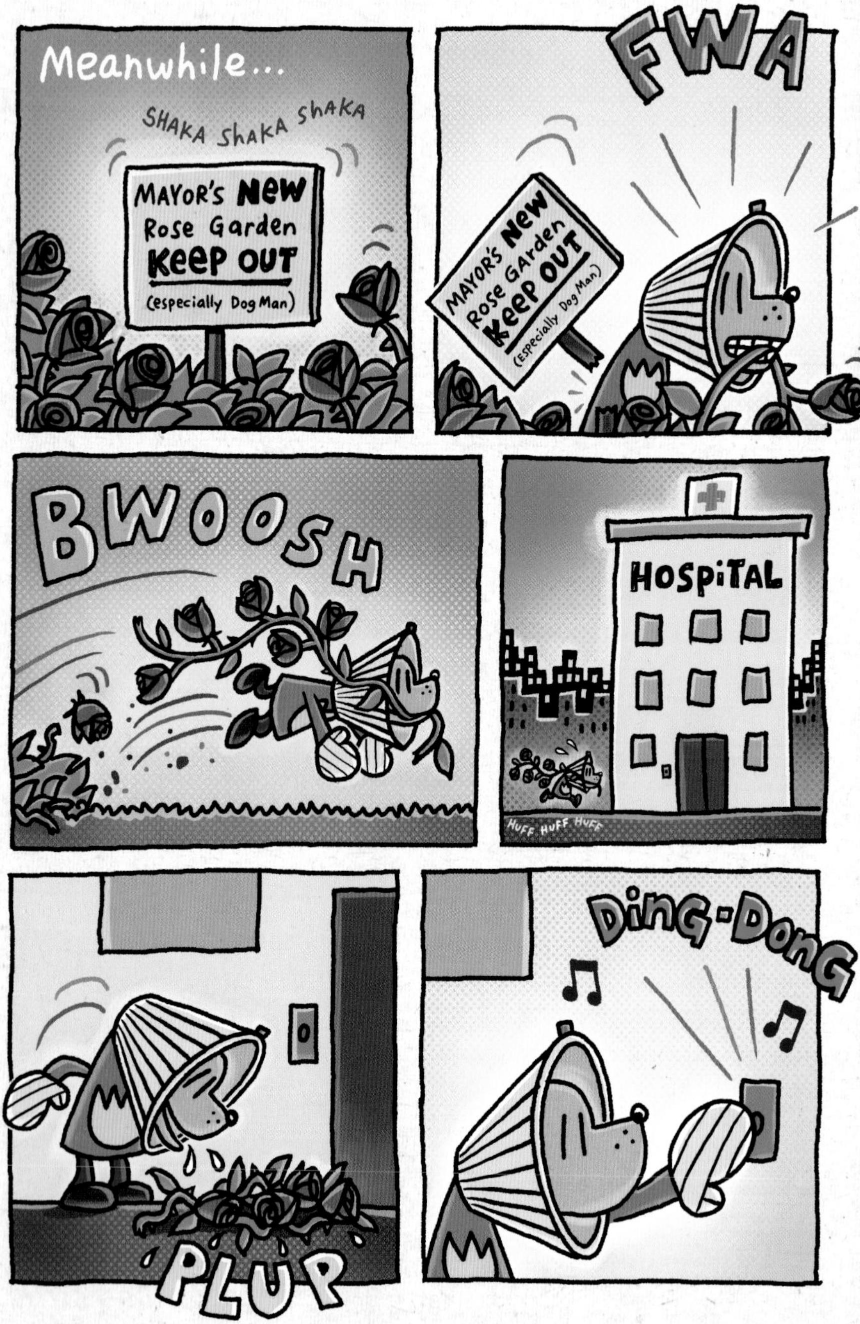
Meanwhile...
SHAKA ShaKA ShaKA
MAYOR'S NEW Rose Garden KEEP OUT (especially Dog Man)
FWA
MAYOR'S NEW Rose Garden KEEP OUT (especially Dog Man)
BWOOSH
HOSPITAL
HUFF HUFF HUFF
PLUP
DING-DONG

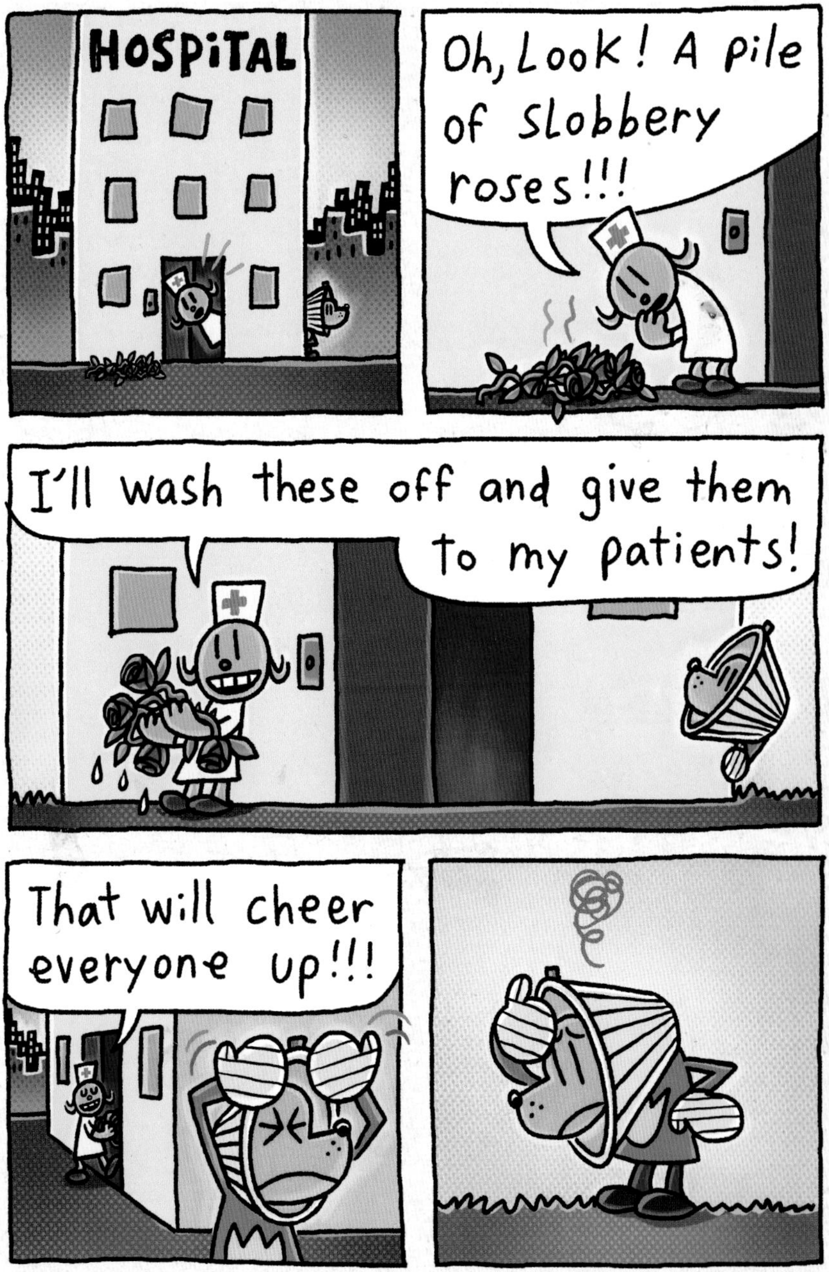
HOSPITAL
Oh, Look! A pile of Slobbery roses!!!
I'll wash these off and give them to my patients!
That will cheer everyone up!!!

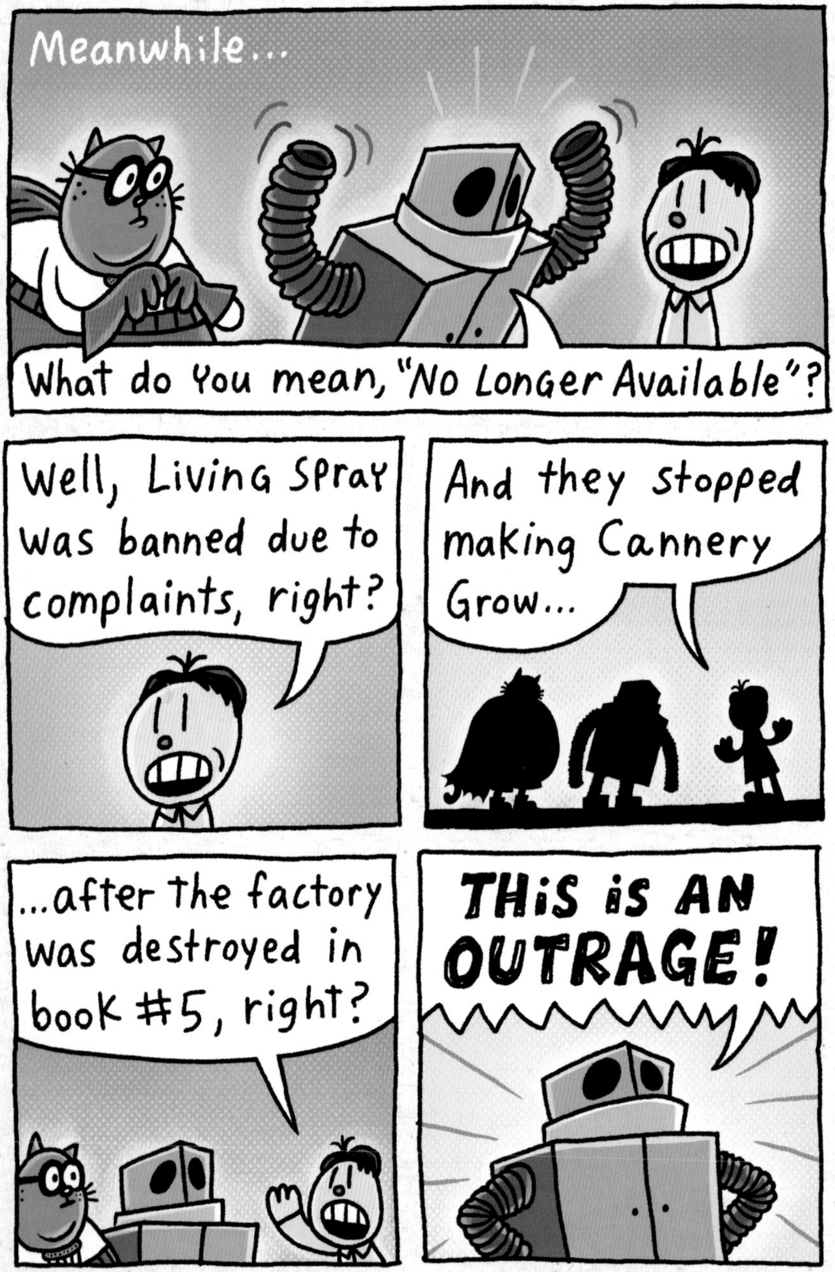
Meanwhile...
What do you mean, "No Longer Available"?
Well, Living Spray was banned due to complaints, right?
And they stopped making Cannery Grow...
...after the factory was destroyed in book #5, right?
THiS iS AN OUTRAGE!

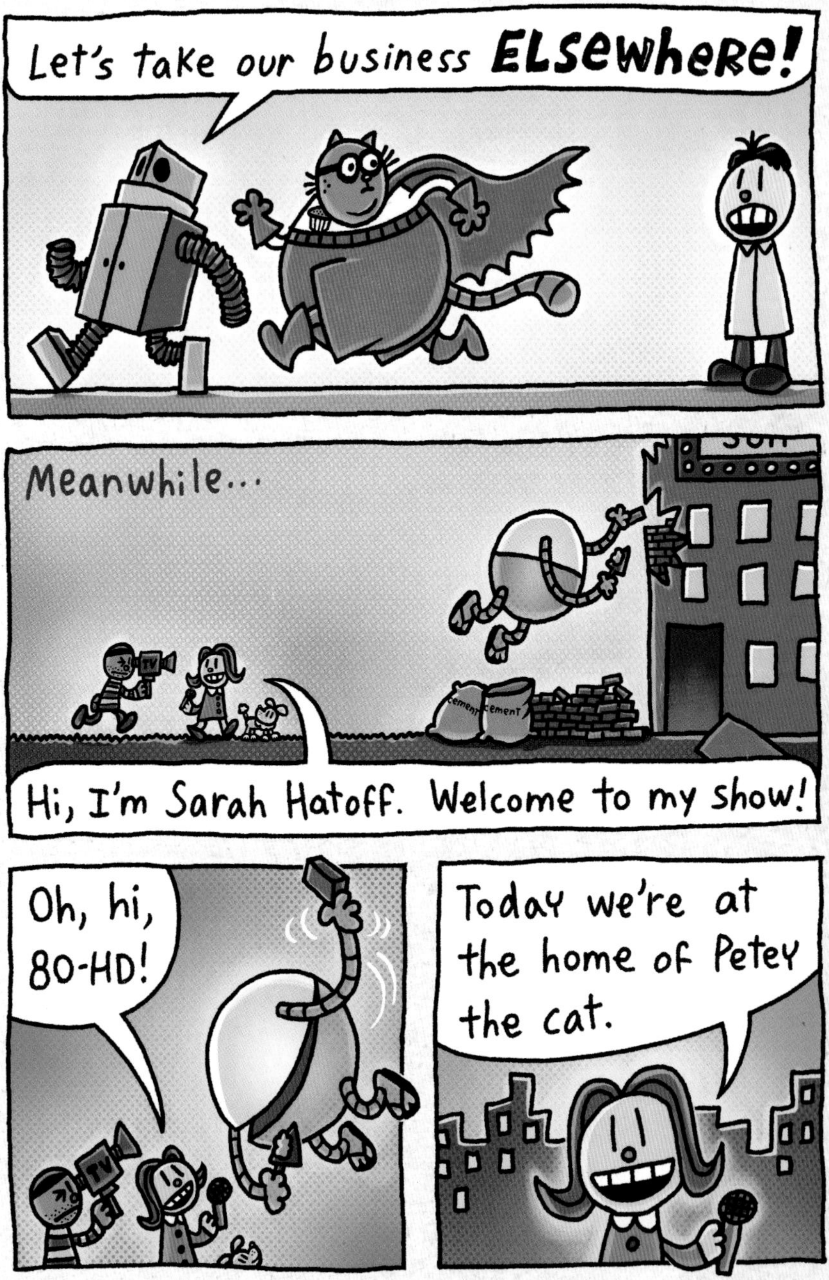
Let's take our business ELSEWHERE!
Meanwhile...
Hi, I'm Sarah Hatoff. Welcome to my show!
Oh, hi, 80-HD!
TV
Today we're at the home of Petey the cat.

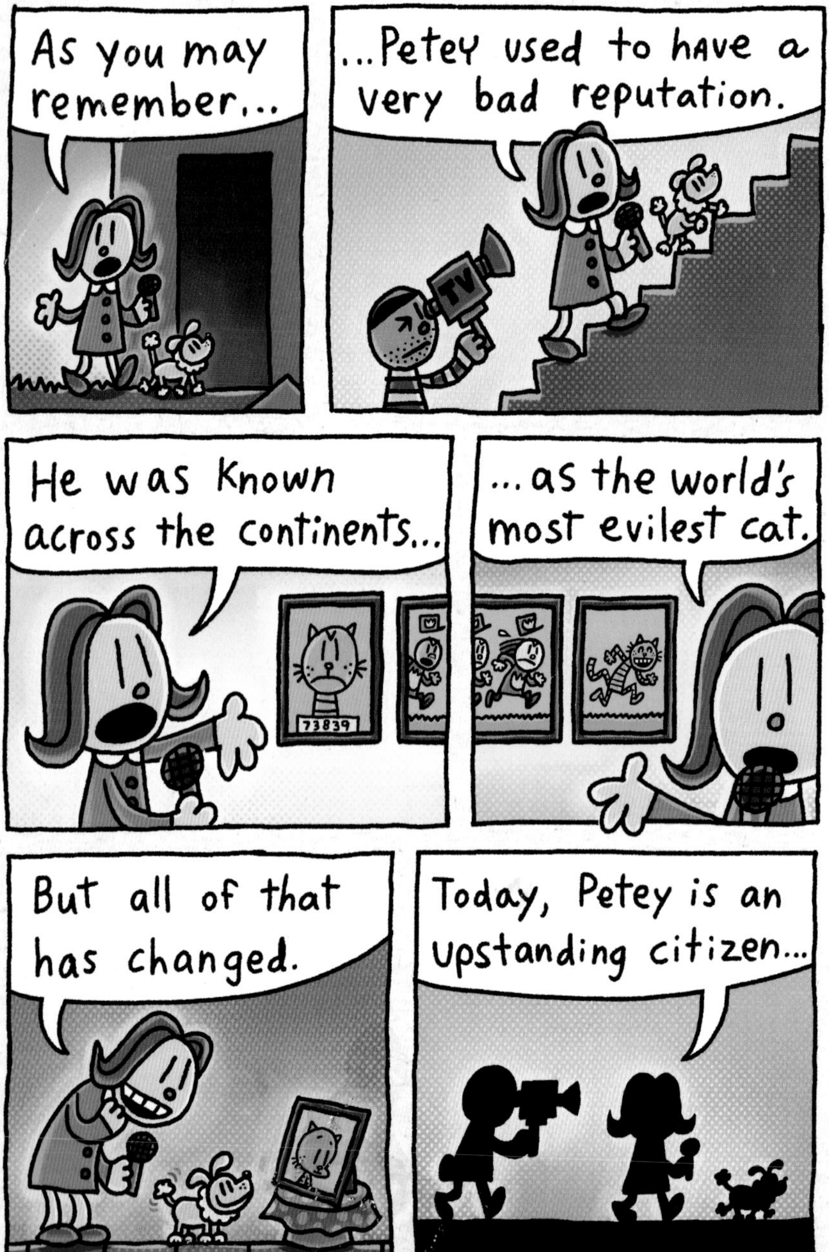
As you may remember...
...Petey used to have a very bad reputation.
TV
He was known across the continents...
73839
...as the world's most evilest cat.
But all of that has changed.
Today, Petey is an upstanding citizen...

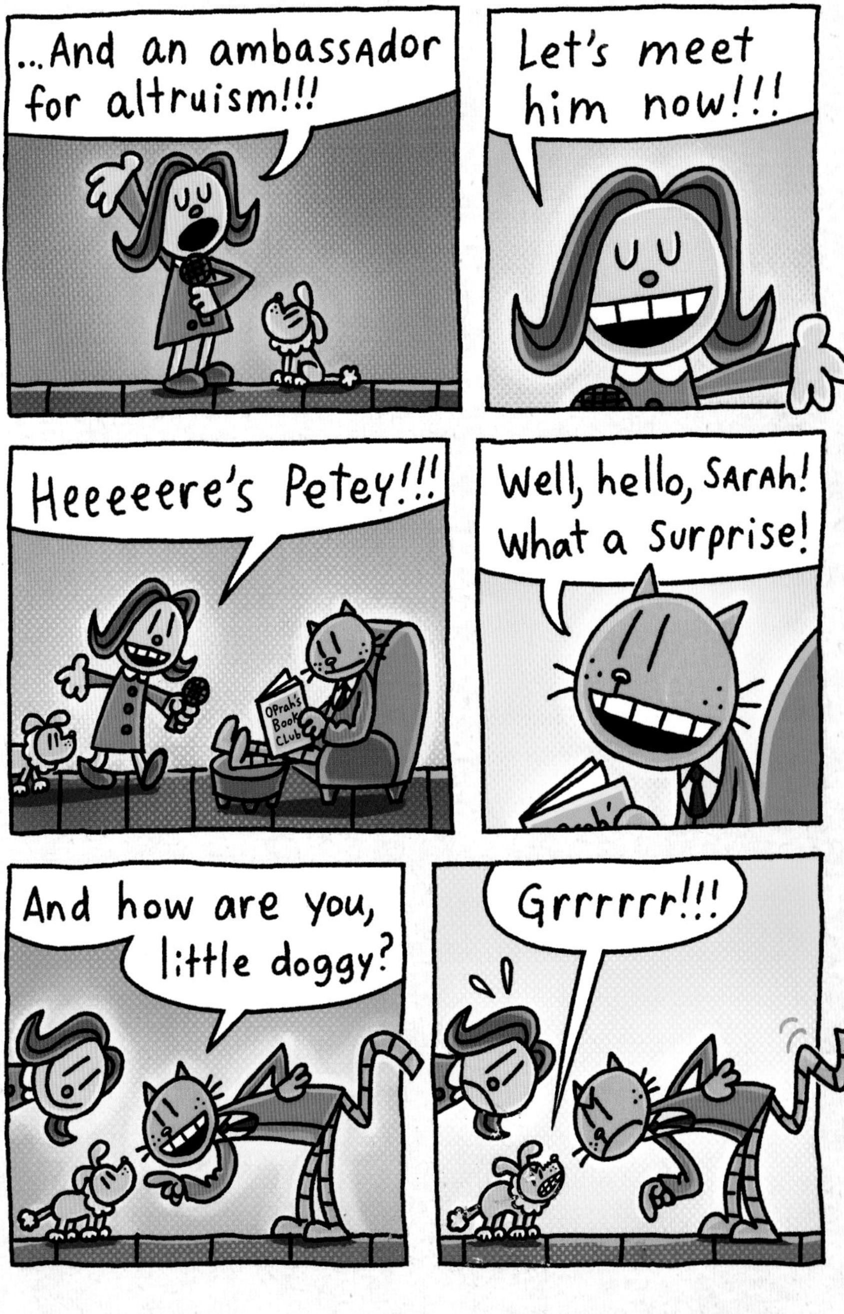
...And an ambassador for altruism!!!
Let's meet him now!!!
Heeeeere's Petey!!!
Oprah's Book Club
Well, hello, Sarah! What a surprise!
And how are you, little doggy?
Grrrrrr!!!

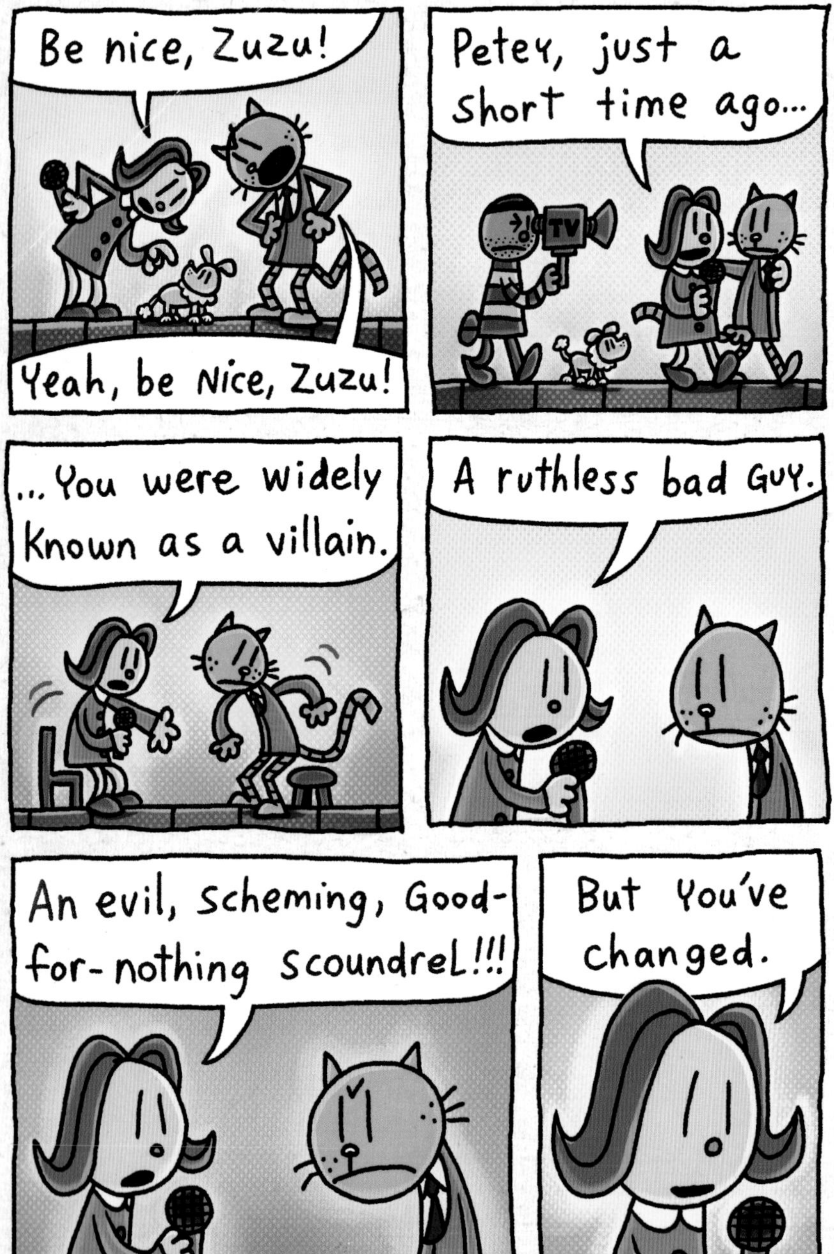
Be nice, Zuzu!
Yeah, be Nice, Zuzu!
TV
Petey, just a short time ago...
...You were widely Known as a villain.
A ruthless bad GUY.
An evil, scheming, Good-for-nothing scoundreL!!!
But You've changed.

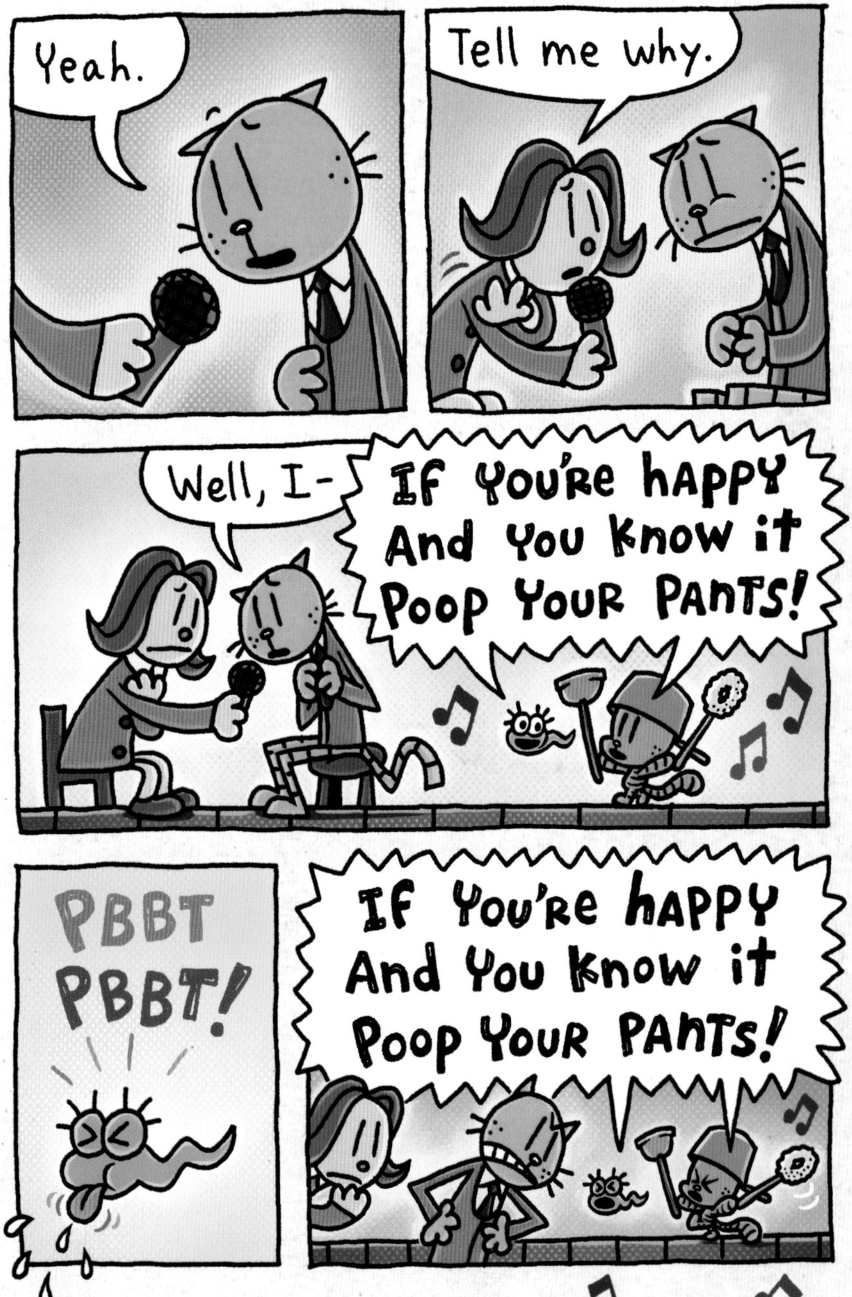
Yeah.
Tell me why.
Well, I-
If You're happy And You Know it Poop Your PANTS!
PBBT PBBT!
If You're happy And You Know it Poop Your PANTS!

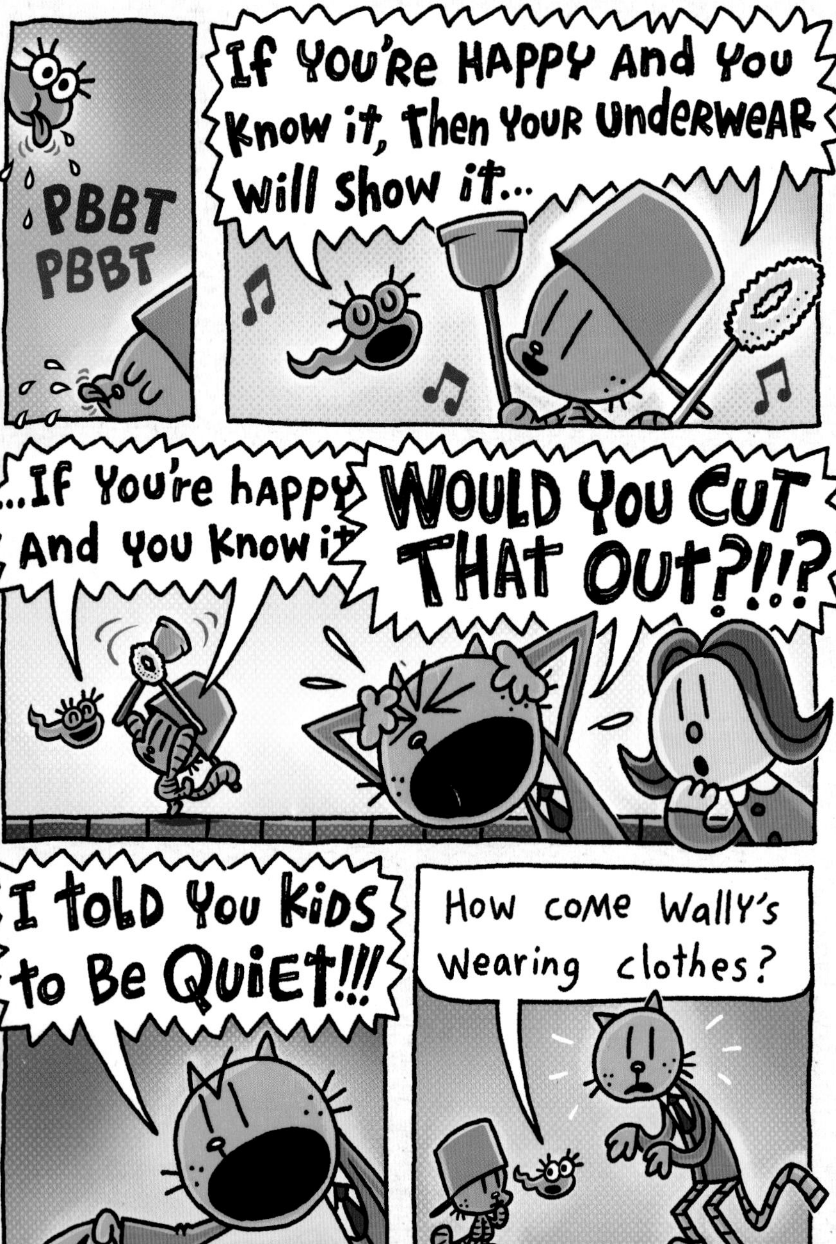
PBBT
PBBT
If YOU'RE HAPPY And YOU Know it, Then YOUR UndERWEAR will Show it...
...If You're happy And you know it
WOULD YOU CUT THAT OUT?!!?
I TOLD YOU KIDS to Be QUIET!!!
How come Wally's wearing clothes?

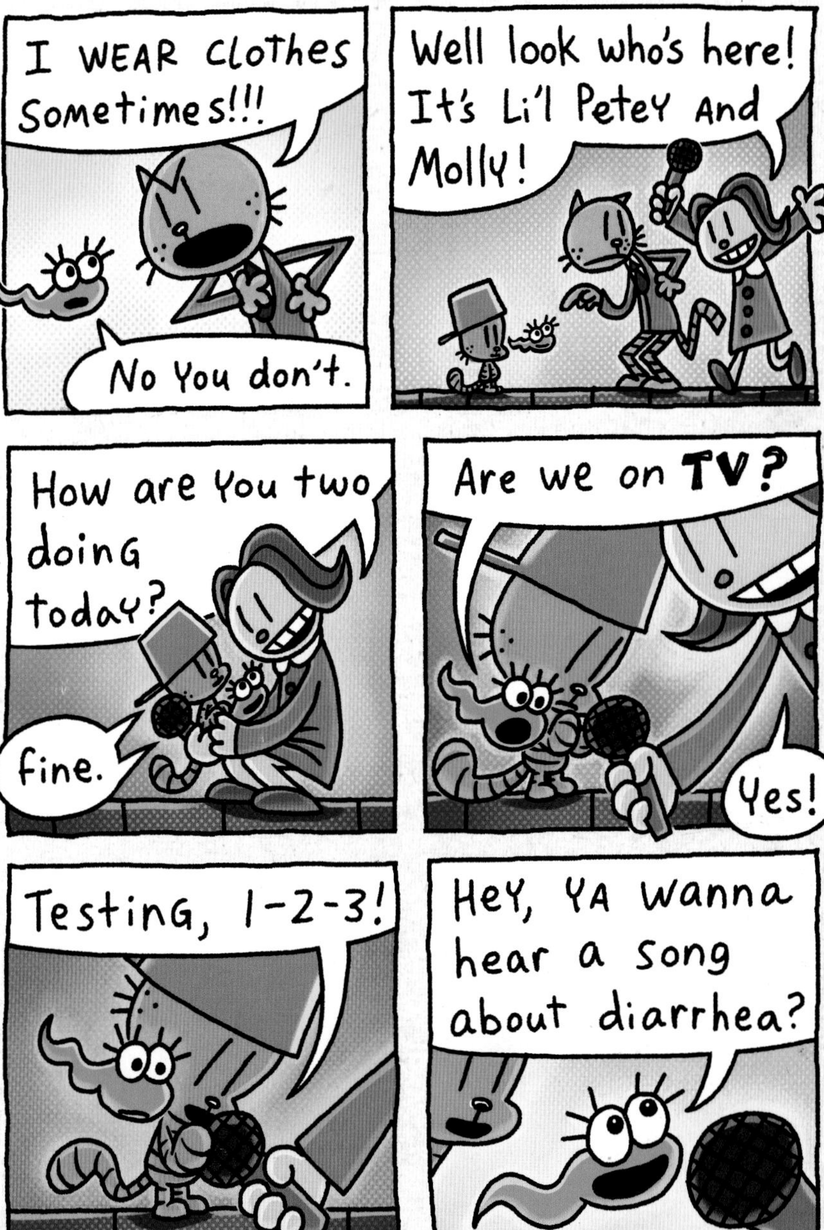
I WEAR CLothes Sometimes!!!
No You don't.
Well look who's here! It's Li'l Petey And Molly!
How are You two doing today?
fine.
Are we on TV?
Yes!
Testing, 1-2-3!
Hey, YA wanna hear a song about diarrhea?

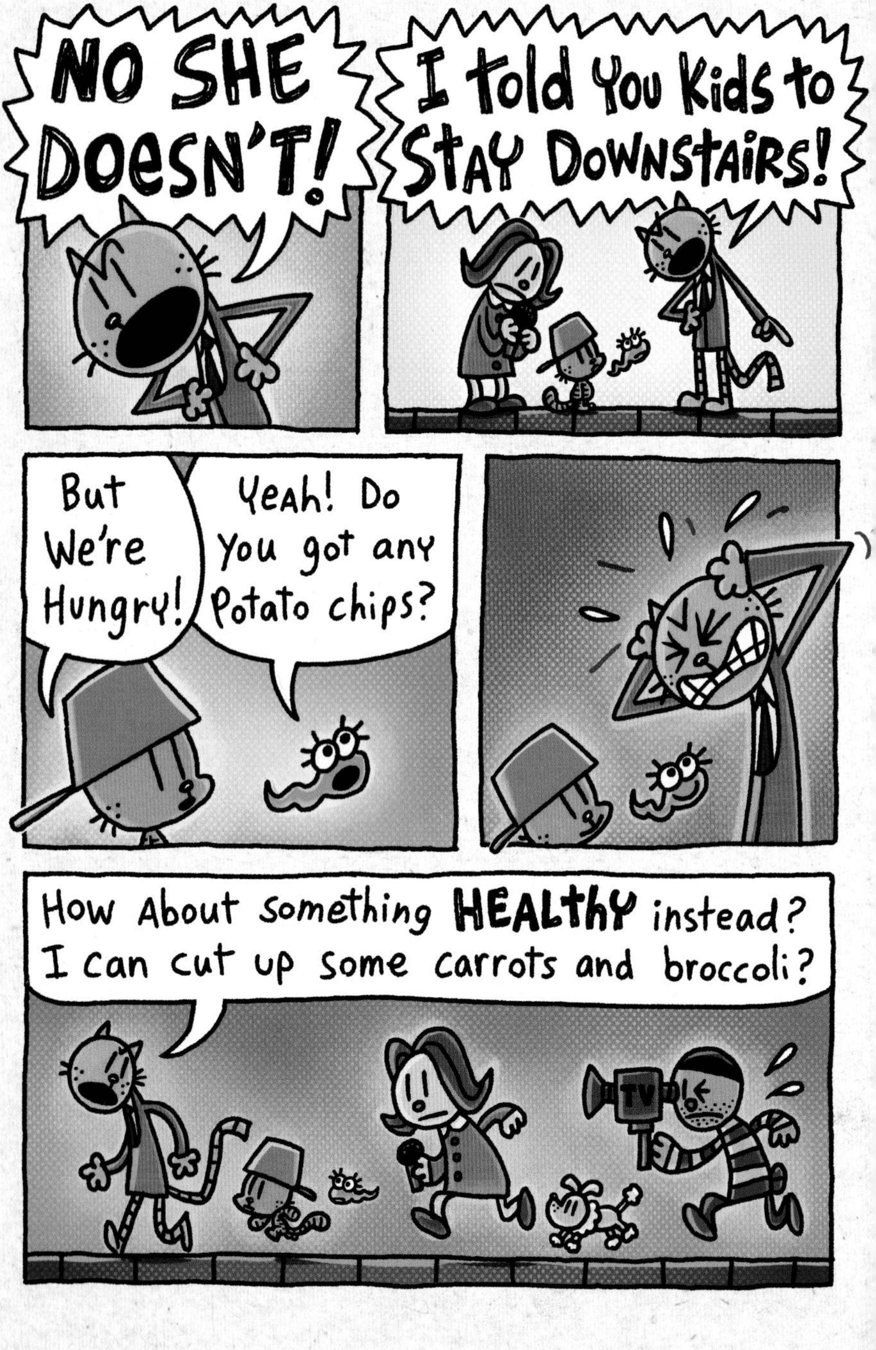
NO SHE DOESN'T!
I told You Kids to STAY DOWNSTAIRS!
But We're Hungry!
Yeah! Do You got any Potato chips?
How About something HEALTHY instead? I can cut up some carrots and broccoli?
TV

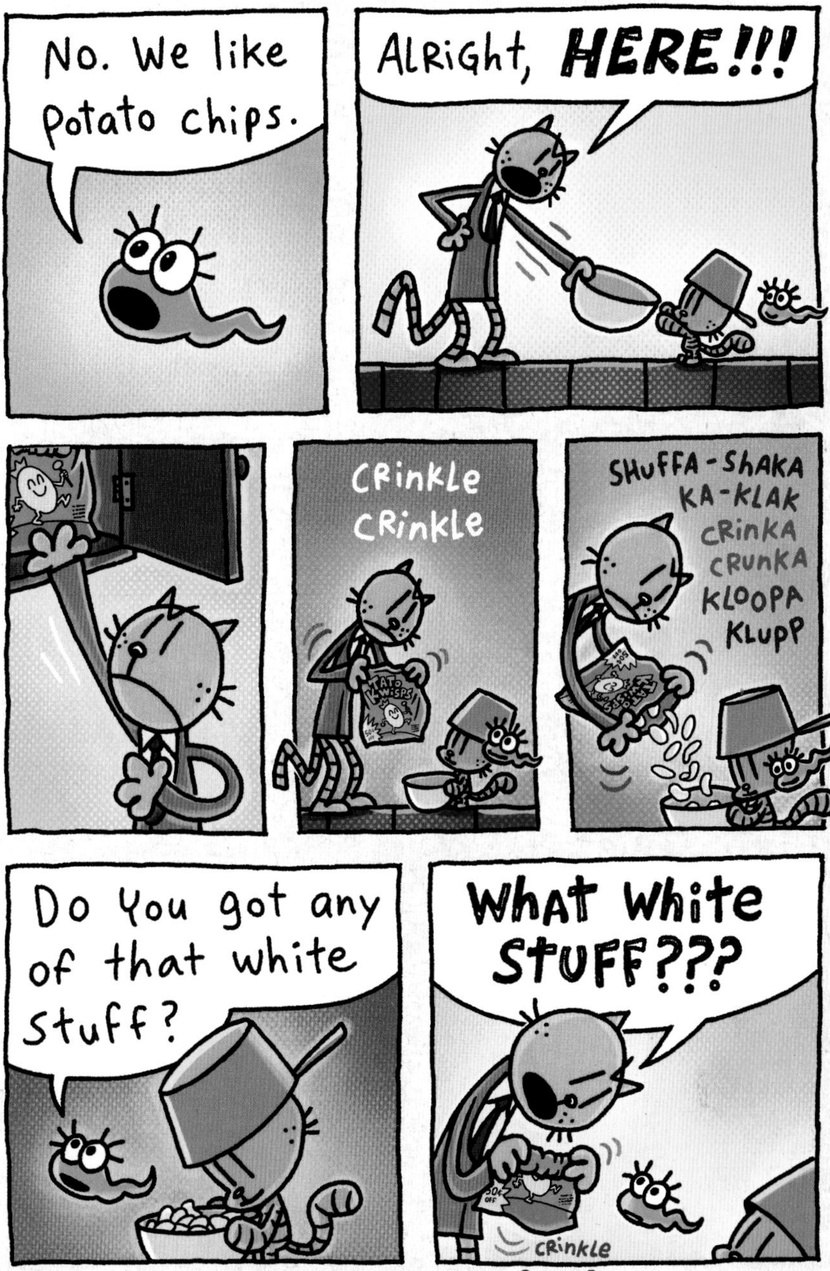
No. We like potato chips.
ALRIGHT, HERE!!!
CRINKLE CRINKLE
SHUFFA-SHAKA KA-KLAK CRINKA CRUNKA KLOOPA KLUPP
Do you got any of that white stuff?
What White STUFF???
CRINKLE
CRINKLE

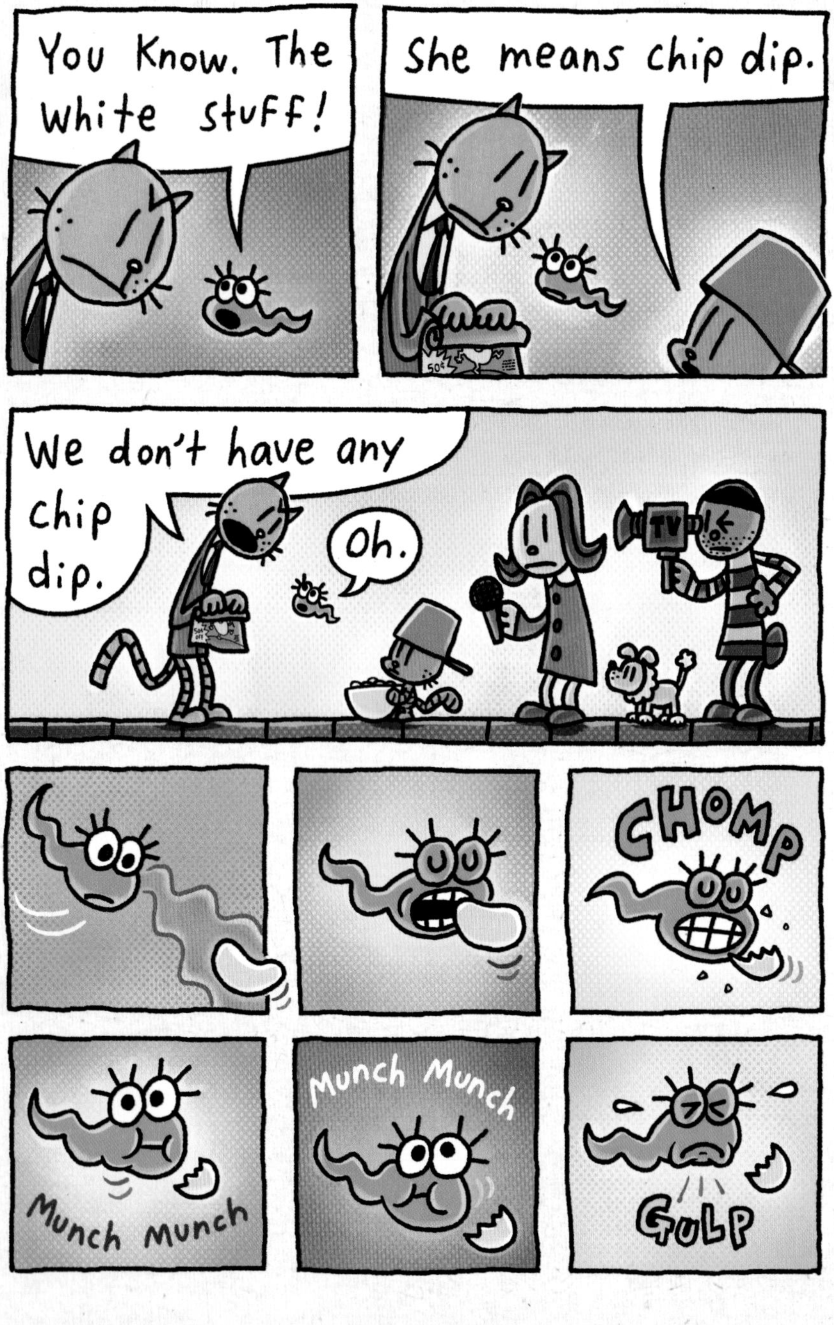
You Know. The white stuff!
She means chip dip.
We don't have any chip dip.
Oh.
CHOMP
Munch Munch
Munch Munch
GULP

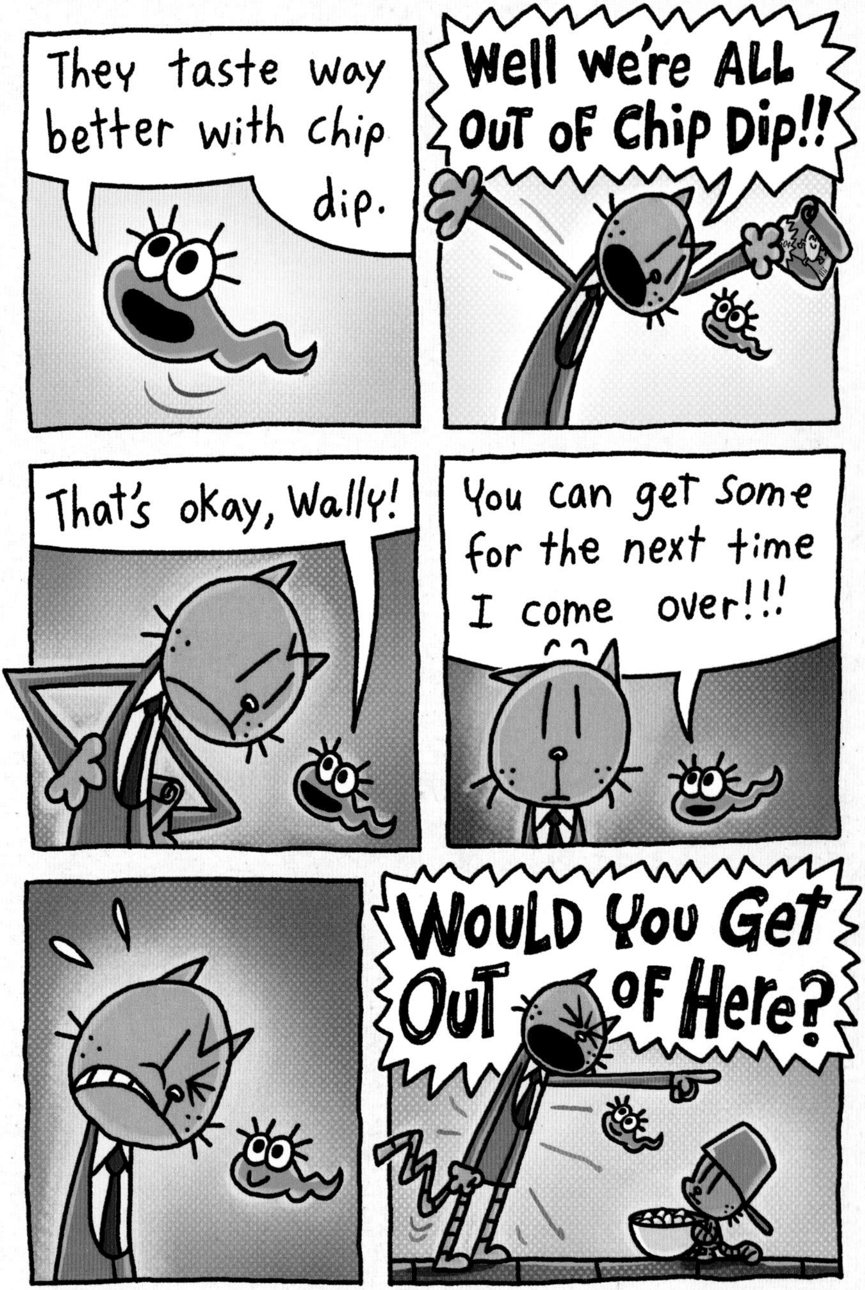
They taste way better with chip dip.
Well we're ALL OUT OF Chip Dip!!
That's okay, Wally!
You can get some for the next time I come over!!!
WOULD YOU GET OUT OF Here?

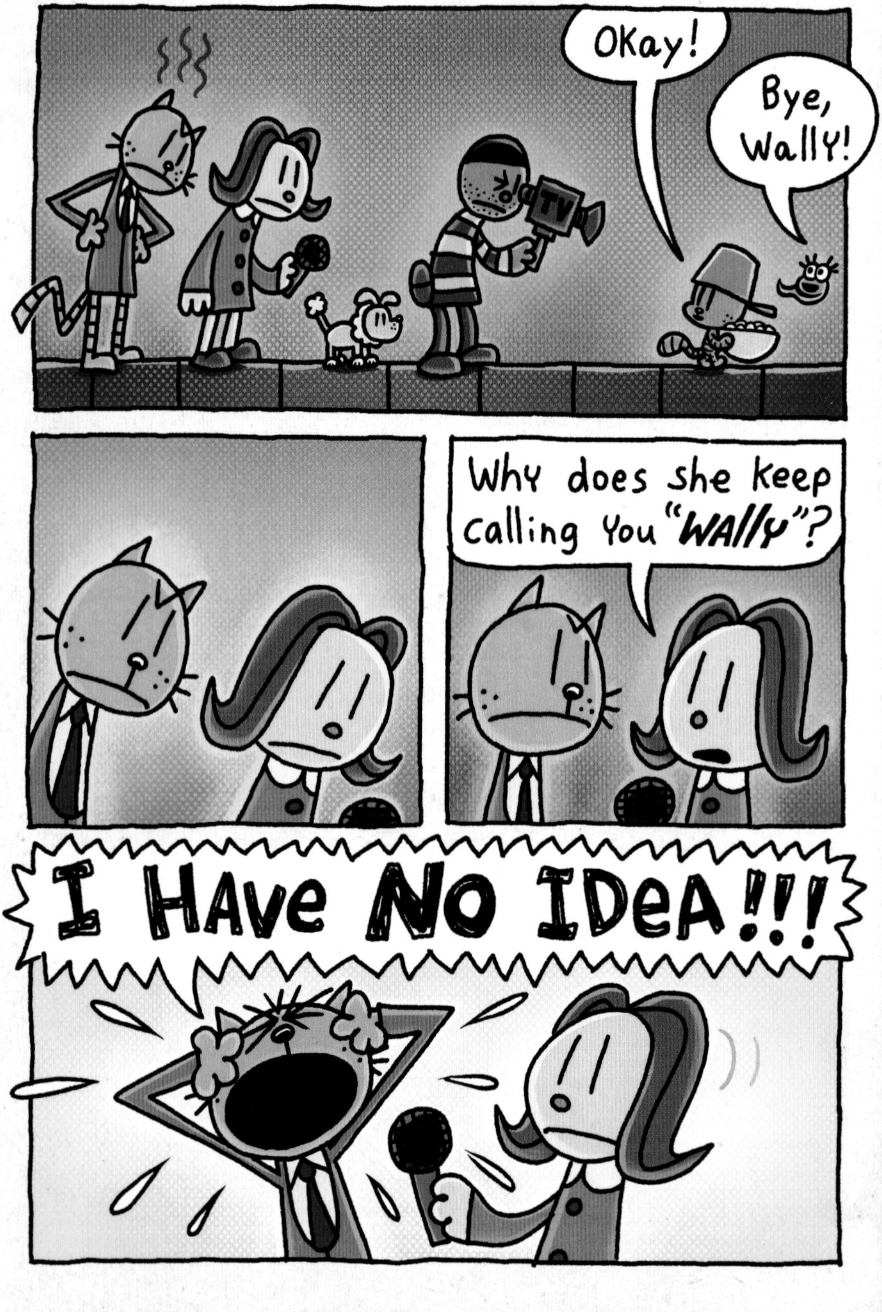
OKay!
Bye, Wally!
Why does she keep calling You "WALLY"?
I HAVE NO IDEA!!!

CHAPTER #8

BECOMING PETEY

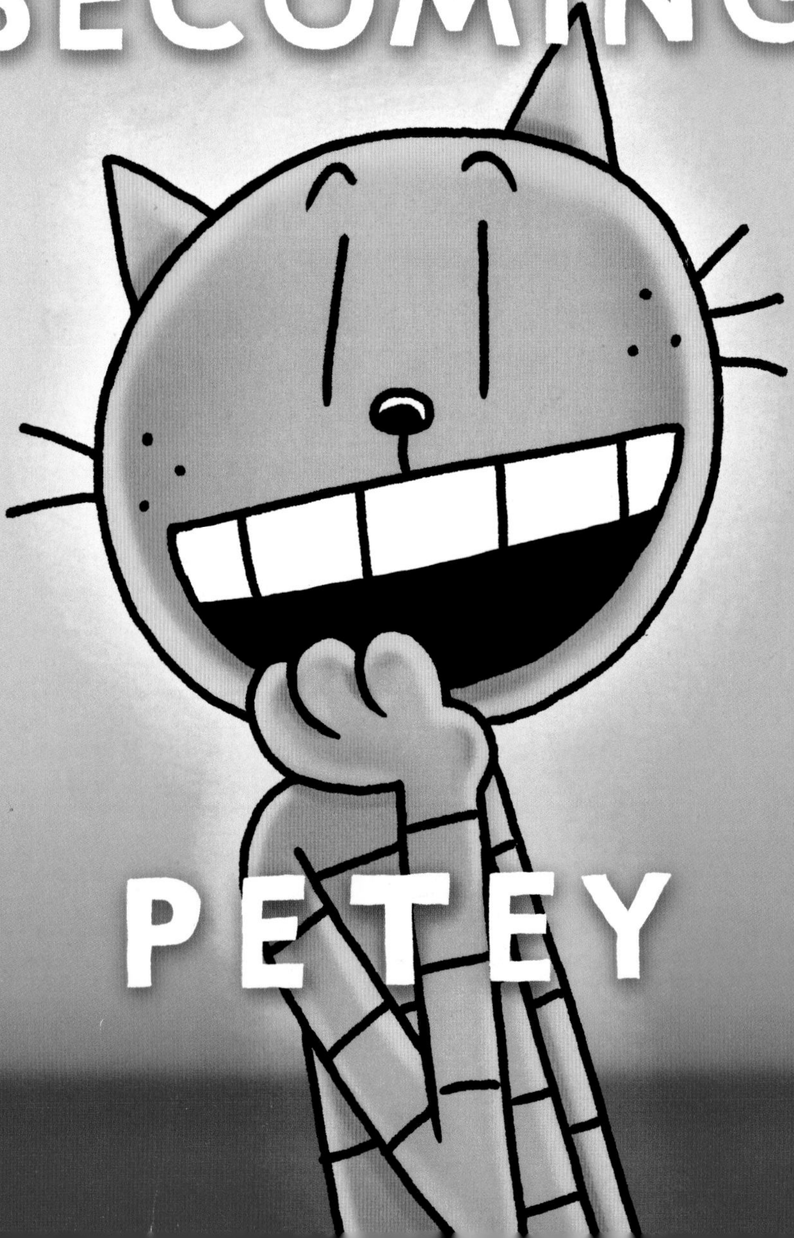

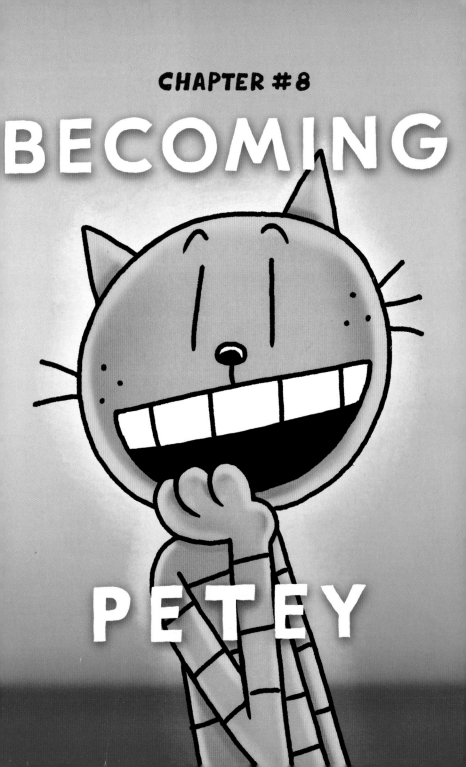

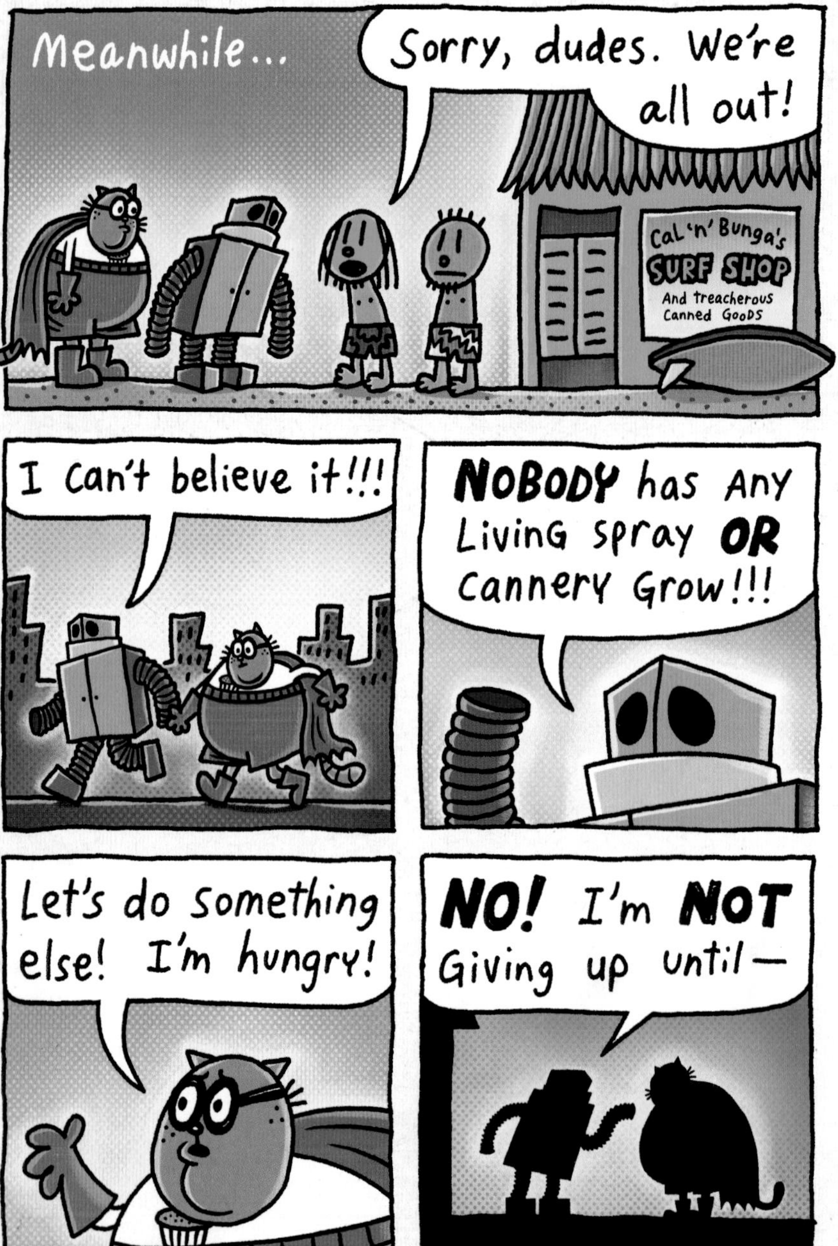
Meanwhile...
Sorry, dudes. We're all out!
Cal 'n' Bunga's
SURF SHOP
And treacherous Canned GooDS
I can't believe it!!!
NOBODY has Any Living spray OR cannery Grow!!!
Let's do something else! I'm hungry!
NO! I'm NOT Giving up until—

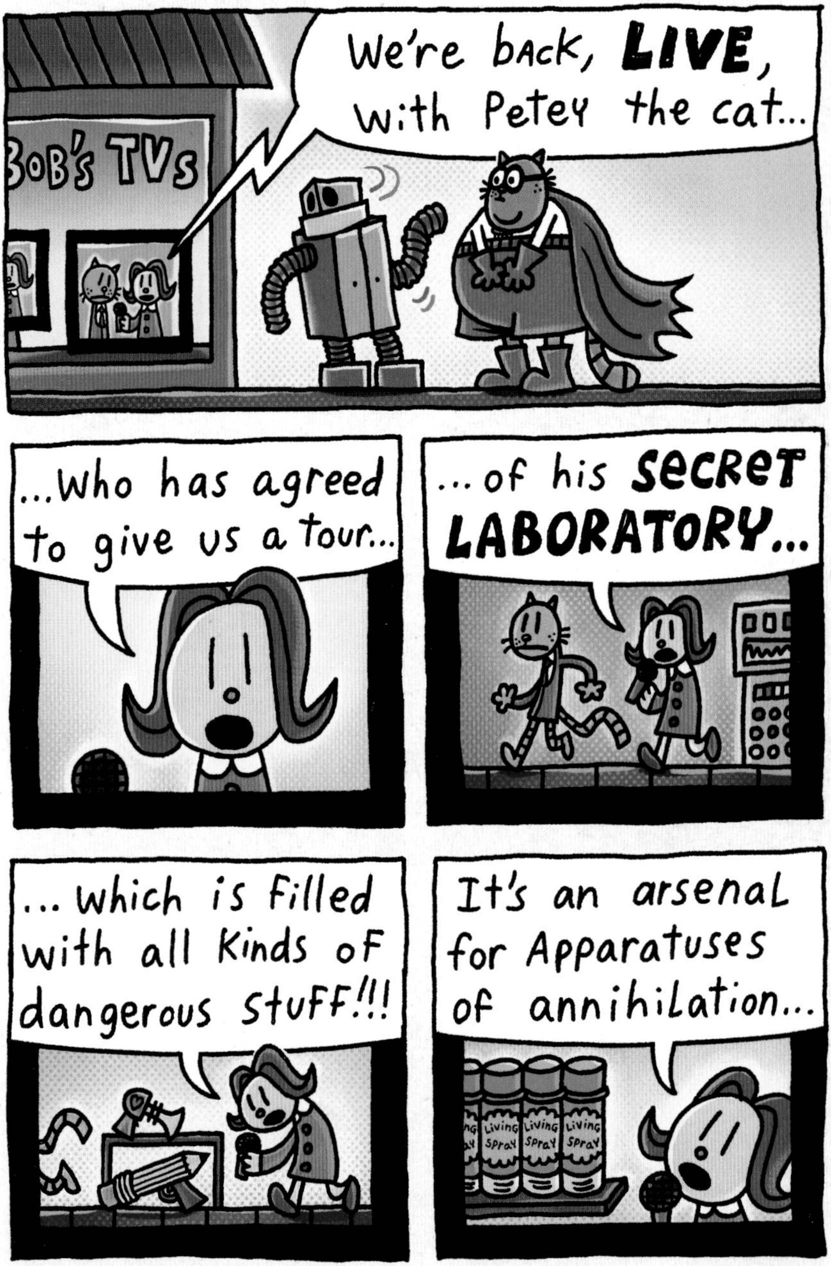
BOB'S TVs
We're back, LIVE, with Petey the cat...
...Who has agreed to give us a tour...
...of his SECRET LABORATORY...
...which is Filled with all Kinds of dangerous stuff!!!
It's an arsenal for Apparatuses of annihilation...
Living Spray
Living Spray
Living Spray

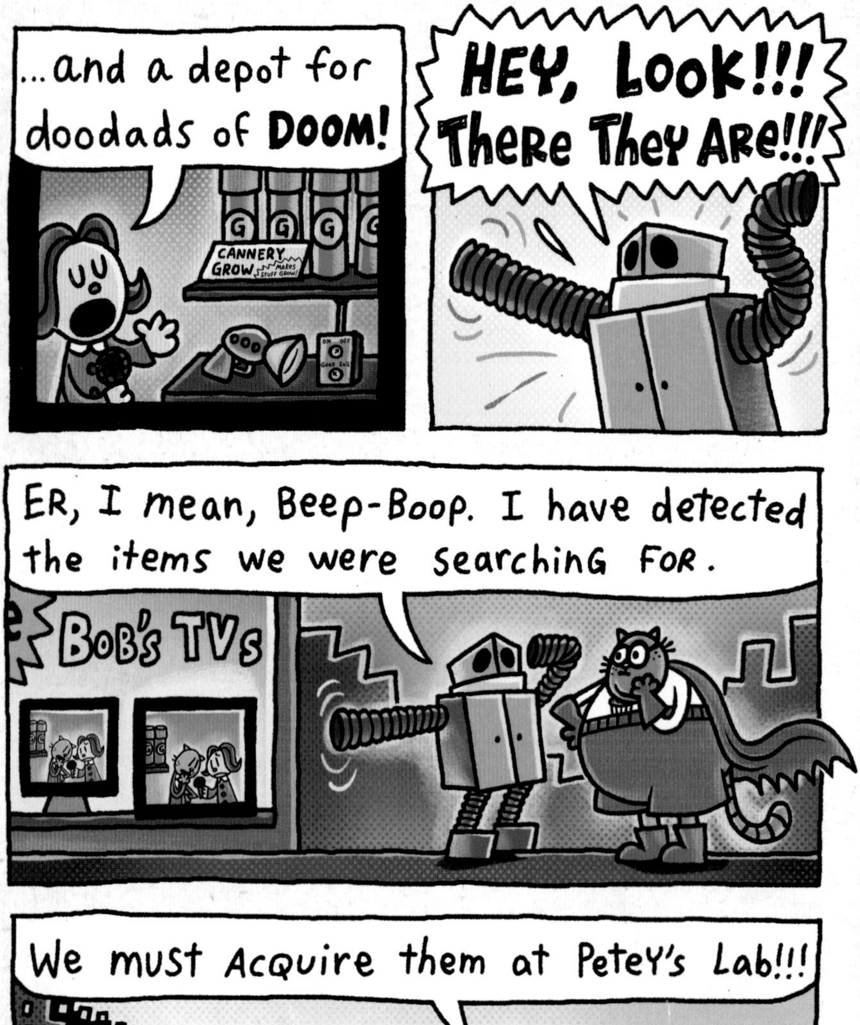
...and a depot for doodads of DOOM!
CANNERY GROW
HEY, LOOK!!! There They Are!!!
ER, I mean, Beep-Boop. I have detected the items we were searching FOR.
BOB'S TVs
We must Acquire them at Petey's Lab!!!

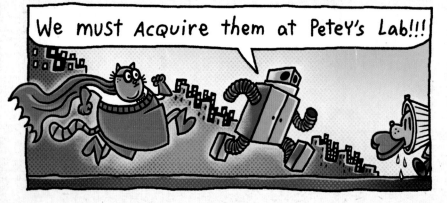

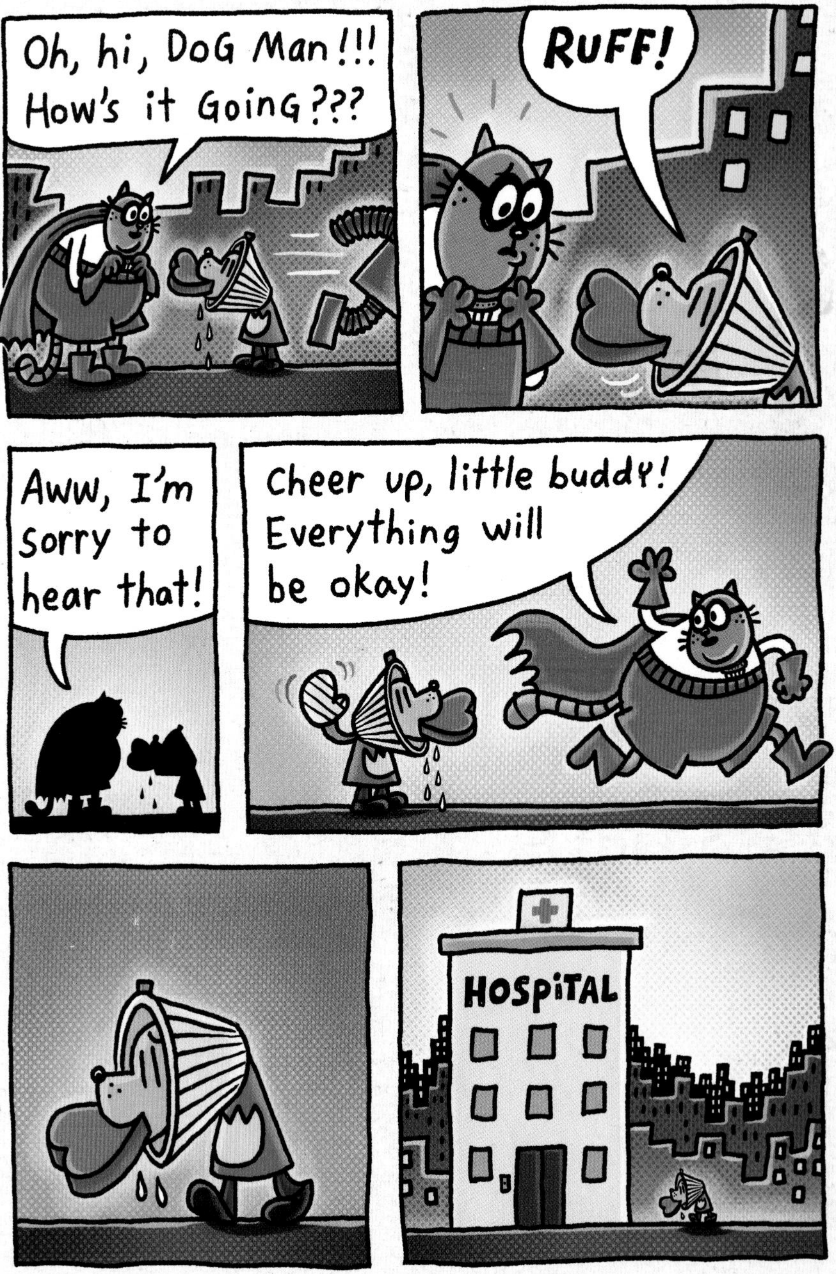
Oh, hi, DoG Man!!! How's it GoinG???
RUFF!
Aww, I'm sorry to hear that!
Cheer up, little buddy! Everything will be okay!
HOSPITAL

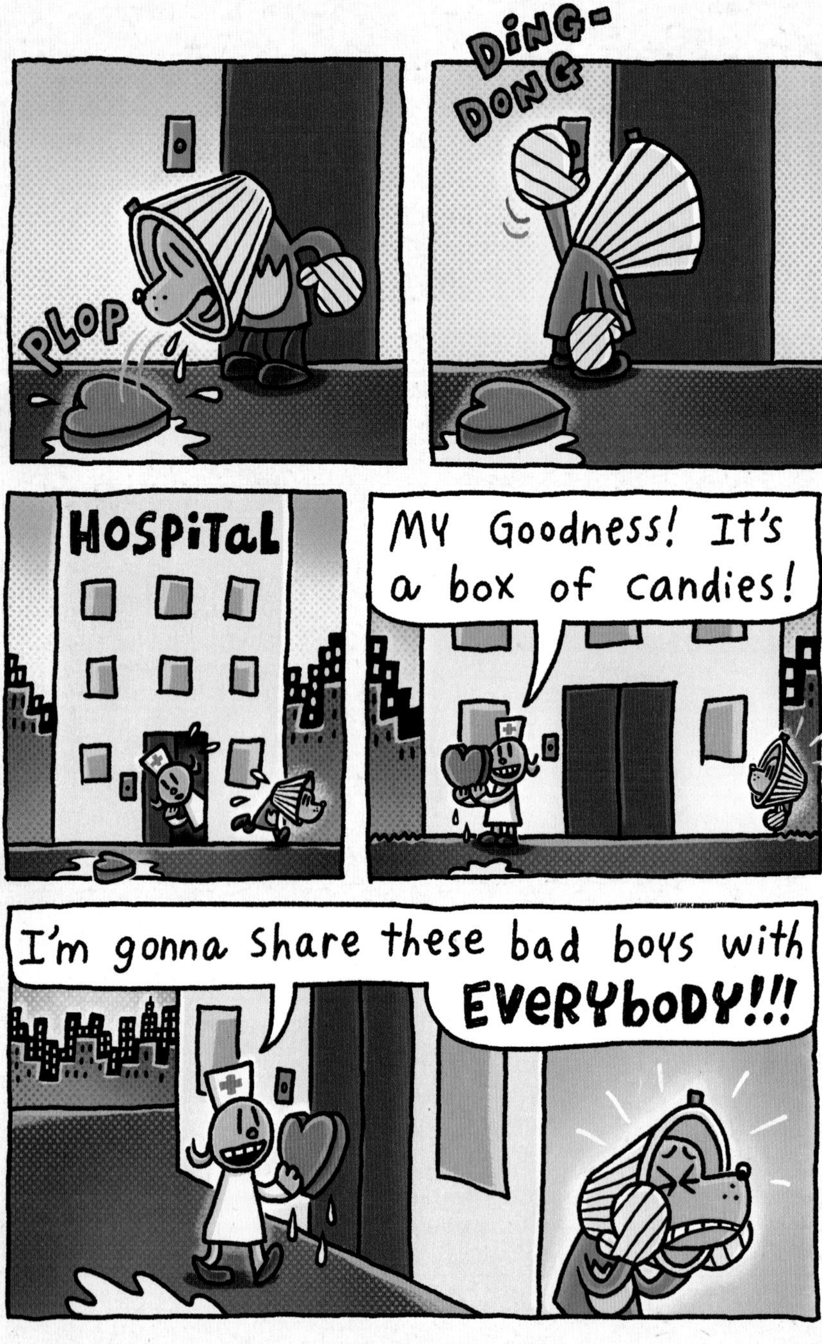
PLOP
DING-DONG
HOSPITAL
MY Goodness! It's a box of candies!
I'm gonna share these bad boys with EVERYBODY!!!

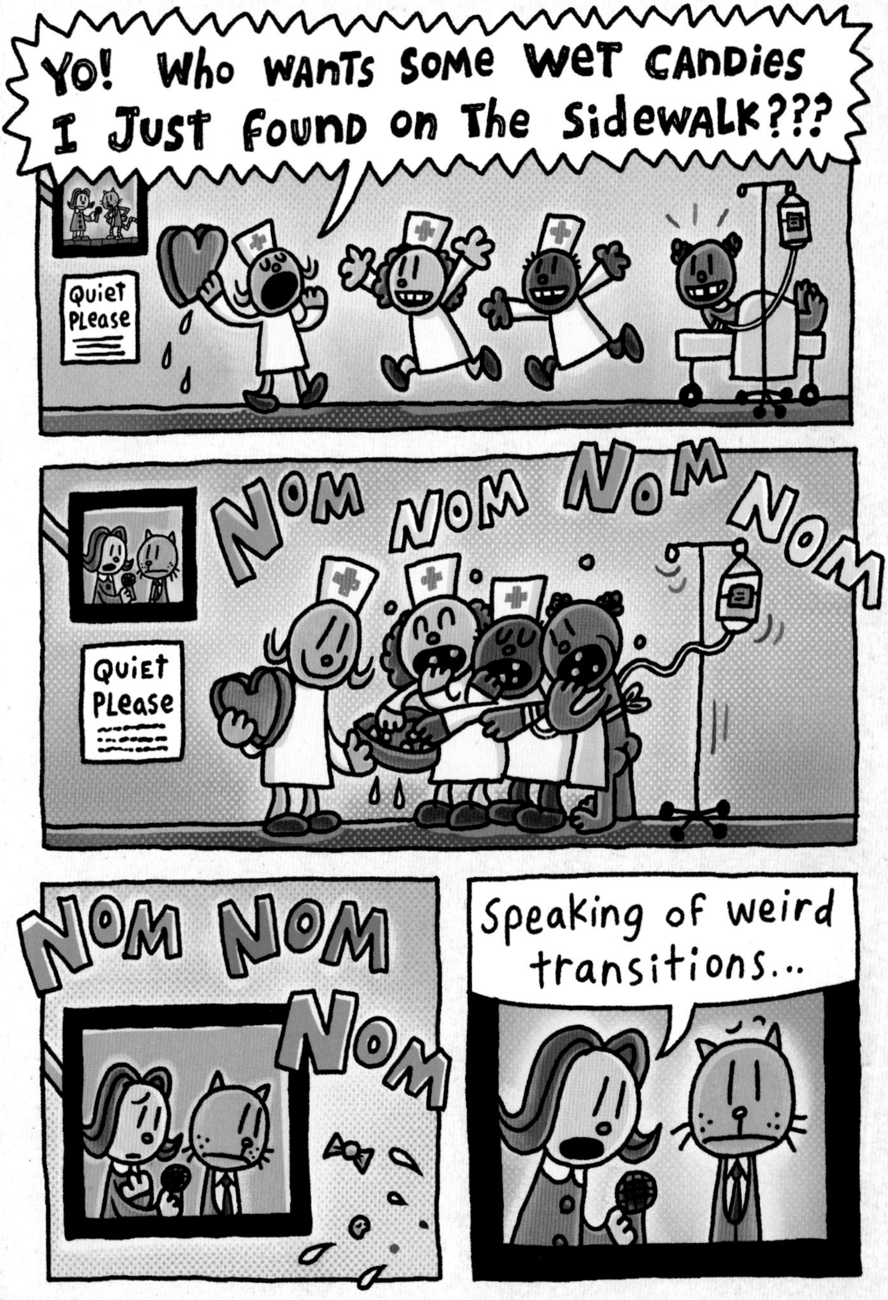
YO! Who WANTS SOME WET CANDIES I JUST FOUND ON The SideWALK???
Quiet Please
NOM NOM NOM NOM
Quiet Please
NOM NOM NOM
Speaking of weird transitions...

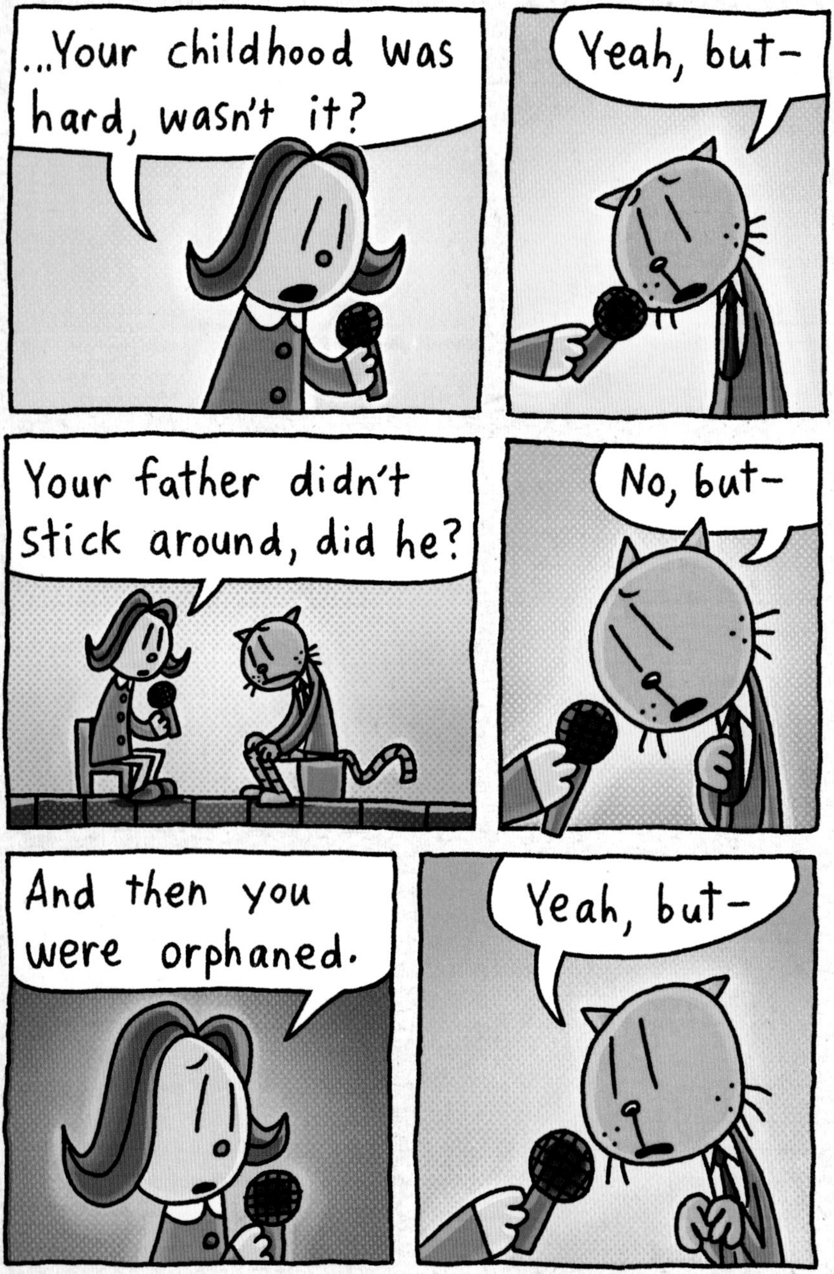
...Your childhood was hard, wasn't it?
Yeah, but-
Your father didn't stick around, did he?
No, but-
And then you were orphaned.
Yeah, but-

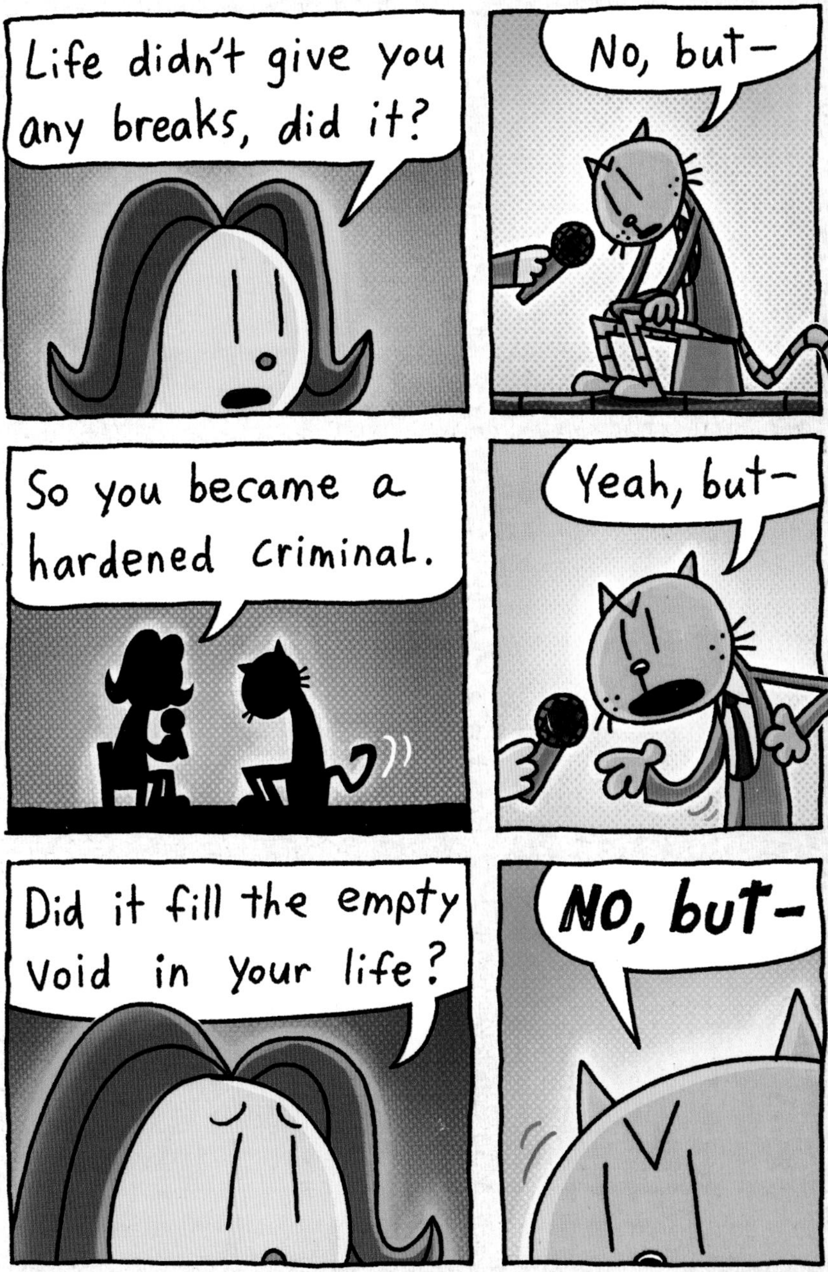
Life didn't give you any breaks, did it?
No, but—
So you became a hardened criminal.
Yeah, but—
Did it fill the empty void in your life?
NO, but—

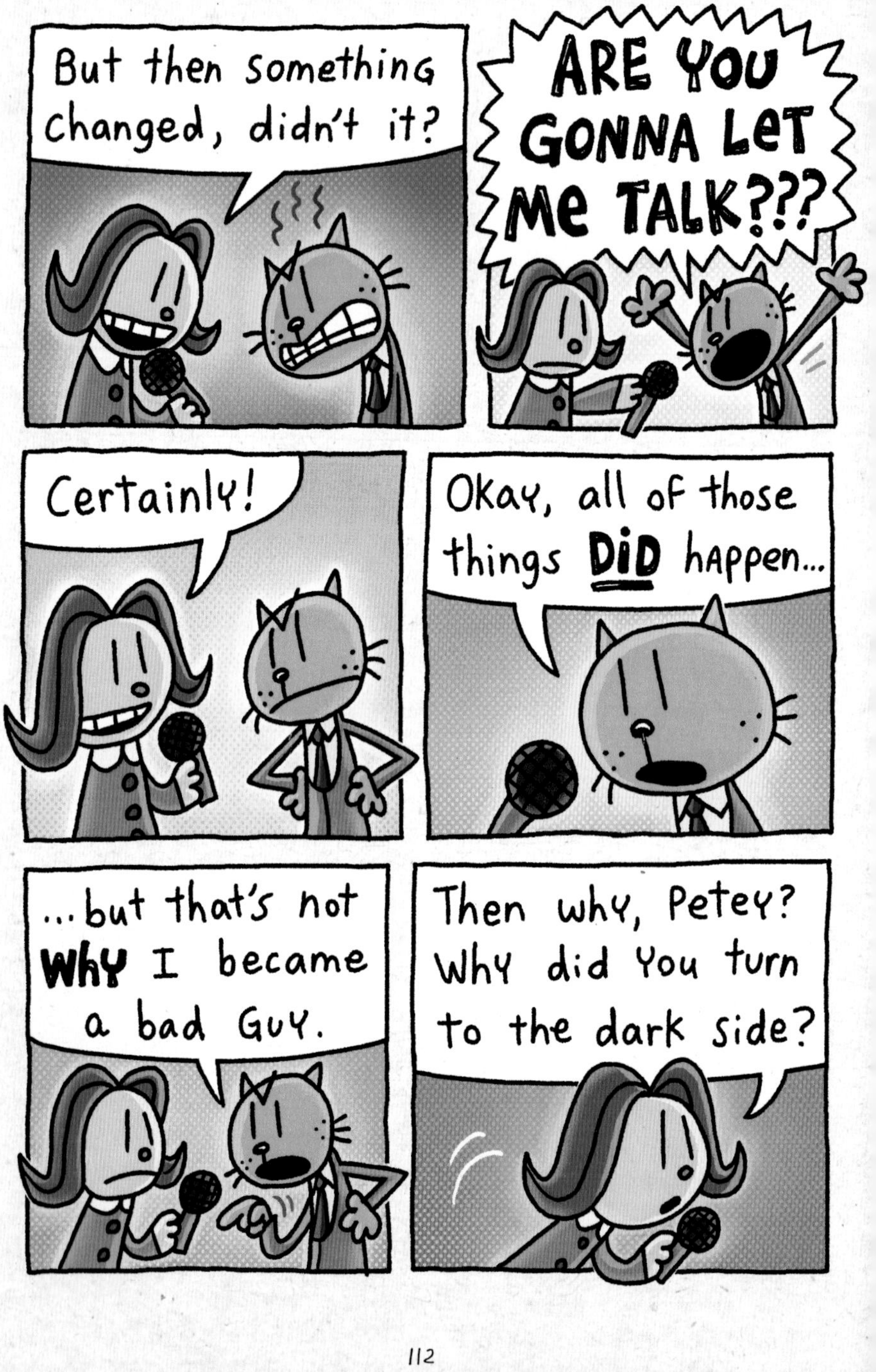
But then something changed, didn't it?
ARE YOU GONNA LET ME TALK???
Certainly!
Okay, all of those things DID happen...
...but that's not WHY I became a bad Guy.
Then why, Petey? Why did You turn to the dark side?

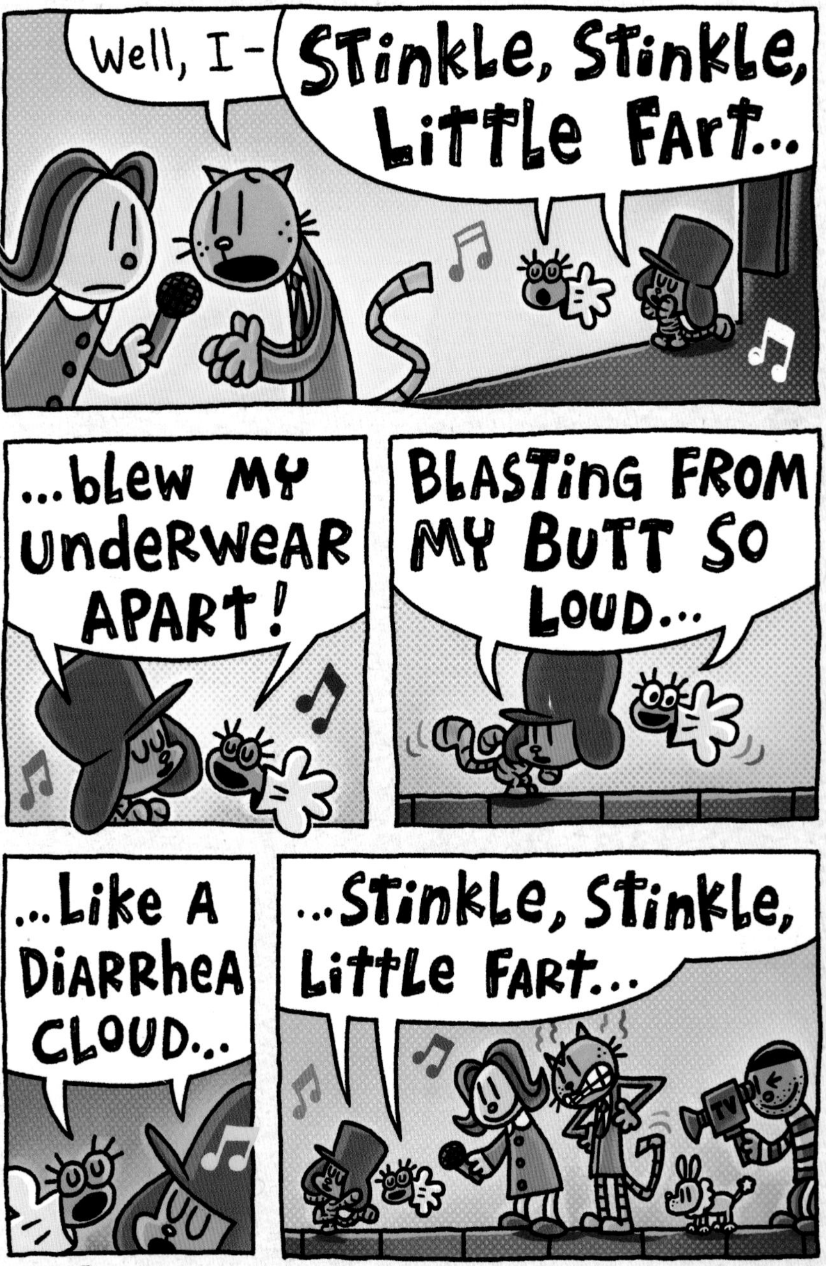
Well, I–
Stinkle, Stinkle, Little Fart...
...blew my underwear apart!
Blasting from my butt so loud...
...like a diarrhea cloud...
...Stinkle, Stinkle, Little Fart...
TV

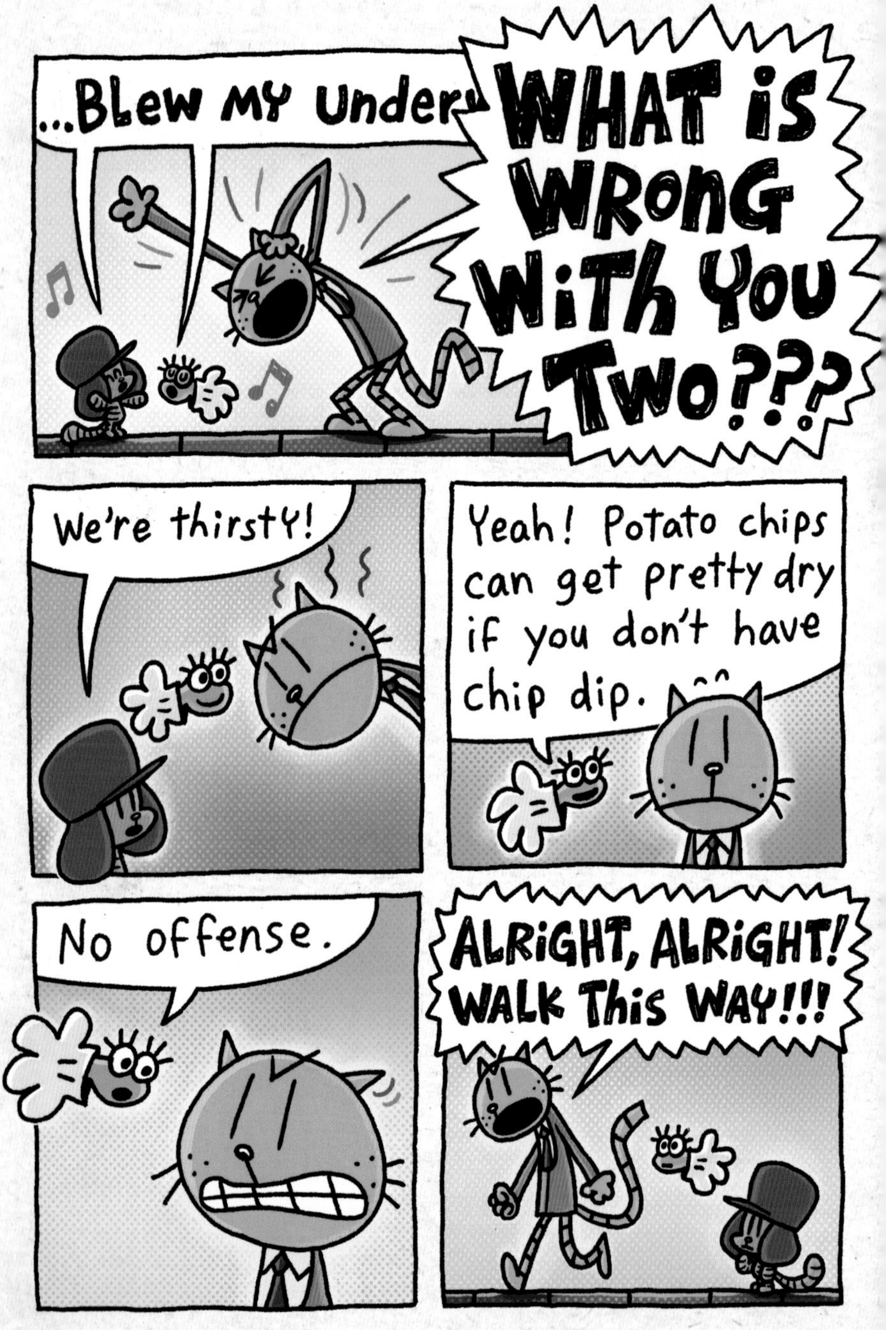
...Blew my Under
WHAT is WRONG WiTh You Two???
We're thirsty!
Yeah! Potato chips can get pretty dry if you don't have chip dip.
No offense.
ALRiGHT, ALRiGHT! WALK This WAY!!!

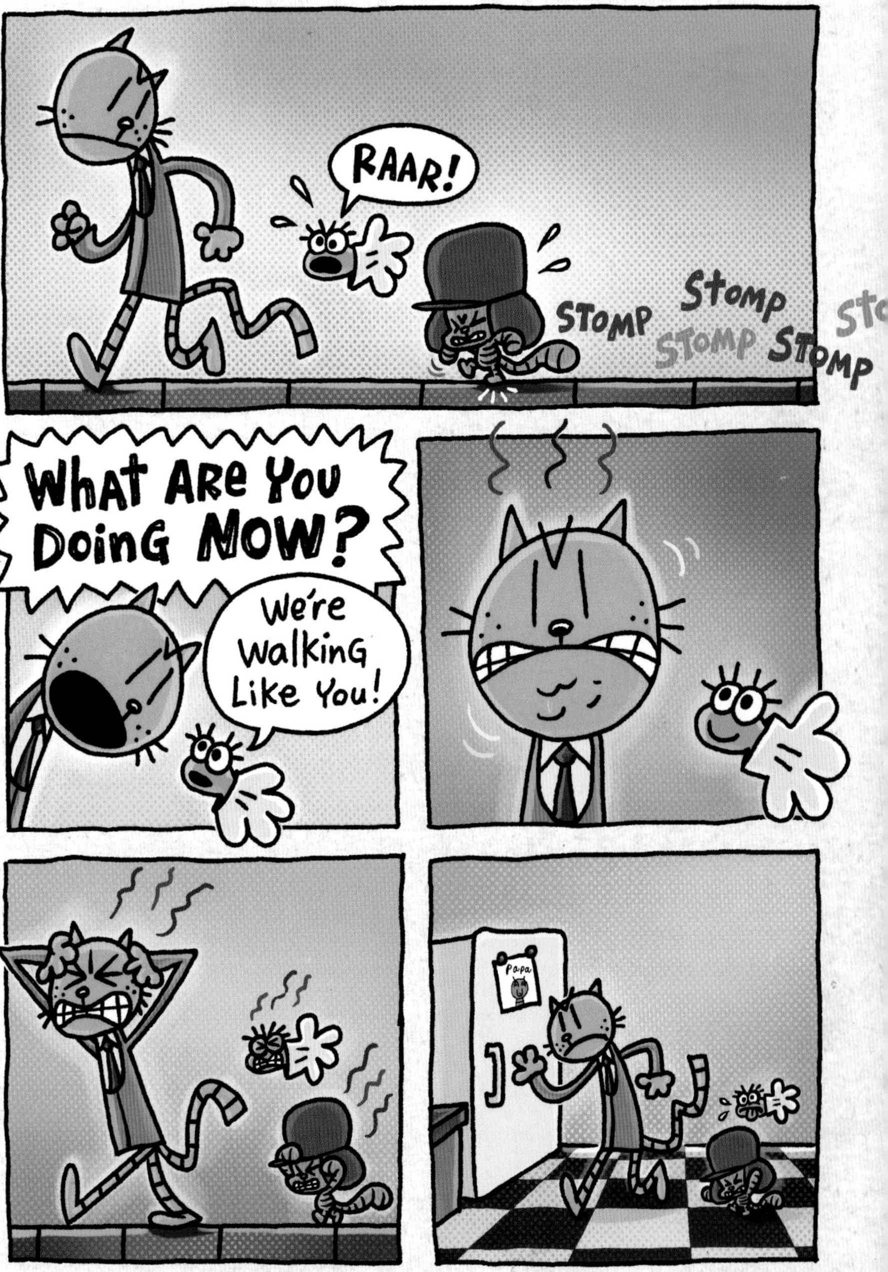
RAAR!
STOMP
STOMP
STOMP STOMP
STOMP
What Are You Doing NOW?
We're Walking Like You!
Papa

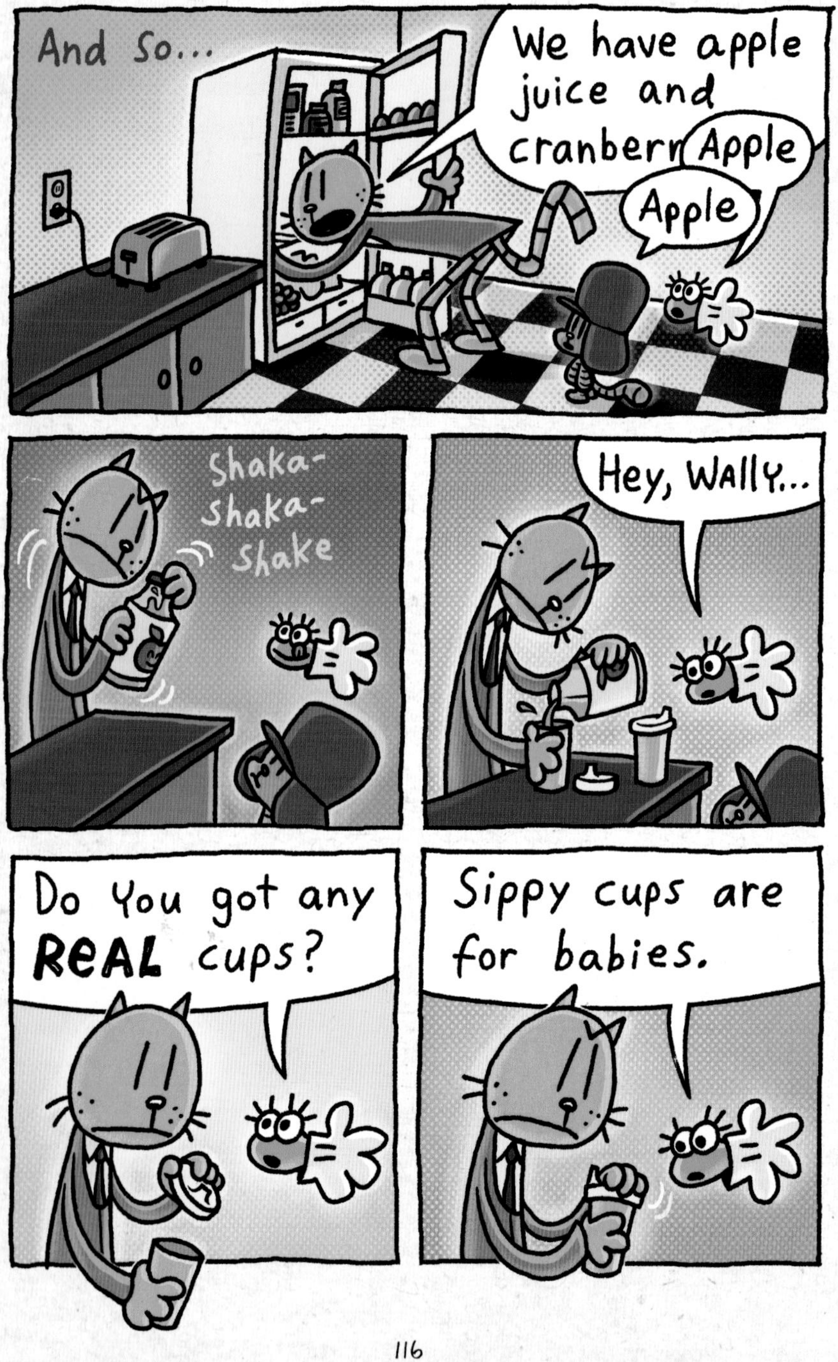
And So...
We have apple juice and cranberr
Apple
Apple
Shaka-shaka-shake
Hey, WALLY...
Do You got any REAL cups?
Sippy cups are for babies.

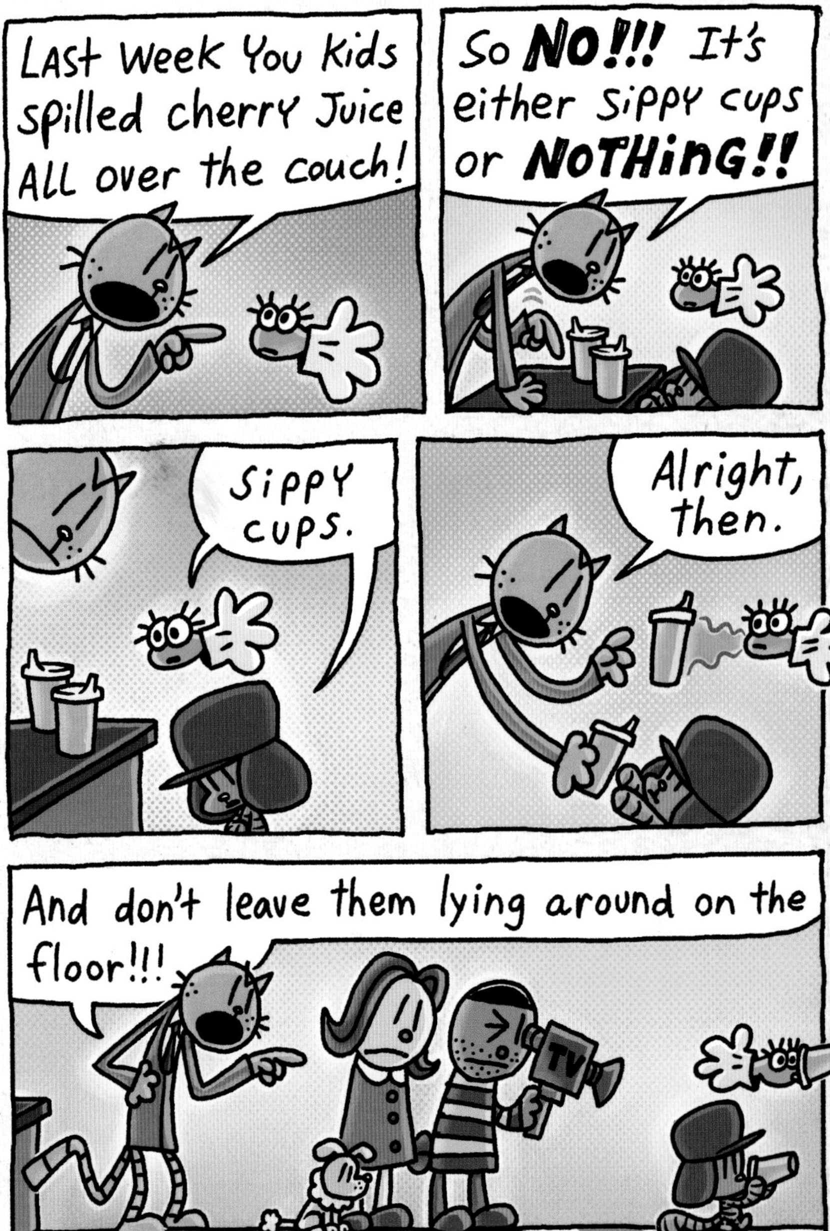
LAST WEEK YOU KIDS spilled cherry Juice ALL over the couch!
So NO!!! It's either Sippy cups or NOTHING!!
Sippy cups.
Alright, then.
And don't leave them lying around on the floor!!!
TV

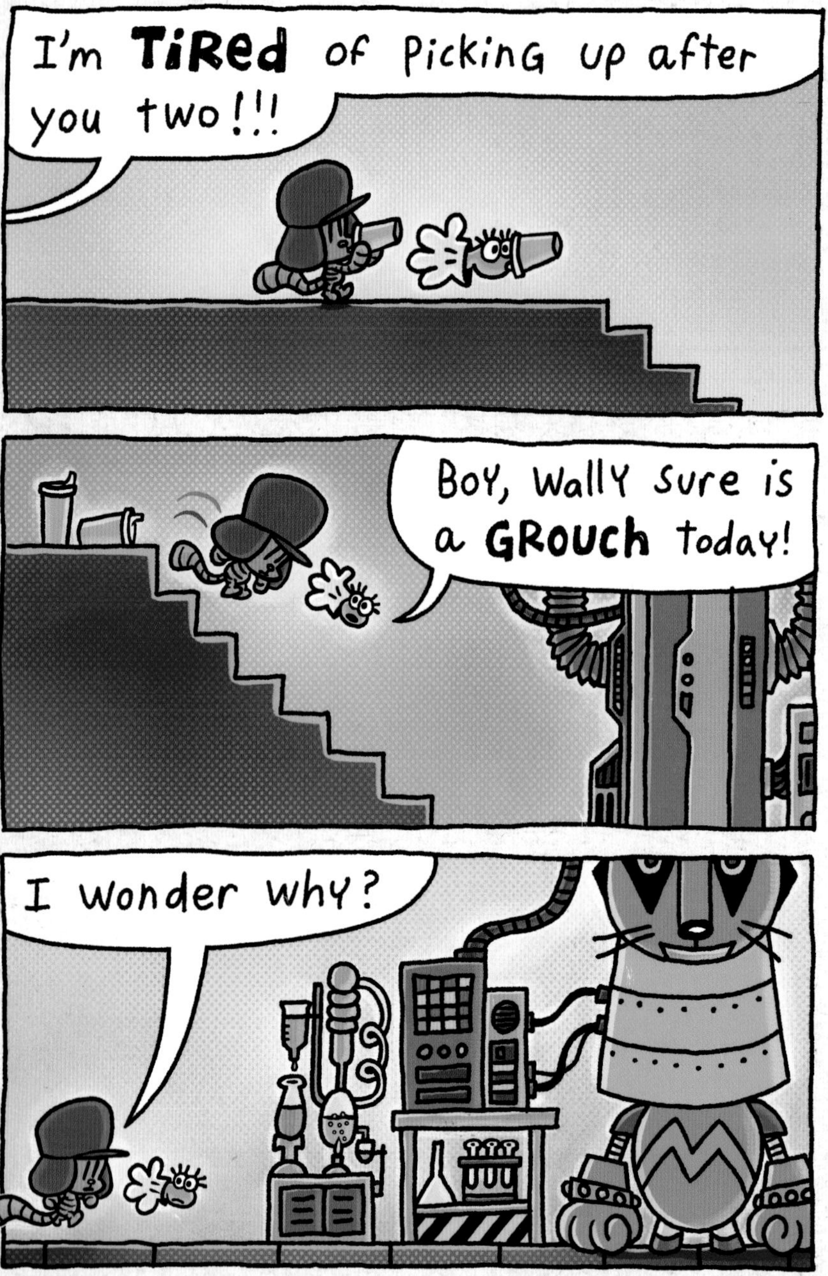
I'm TIRED of picking up after you two!!!
Boy, Wally sure is a GROUCH today!
I wonder why?

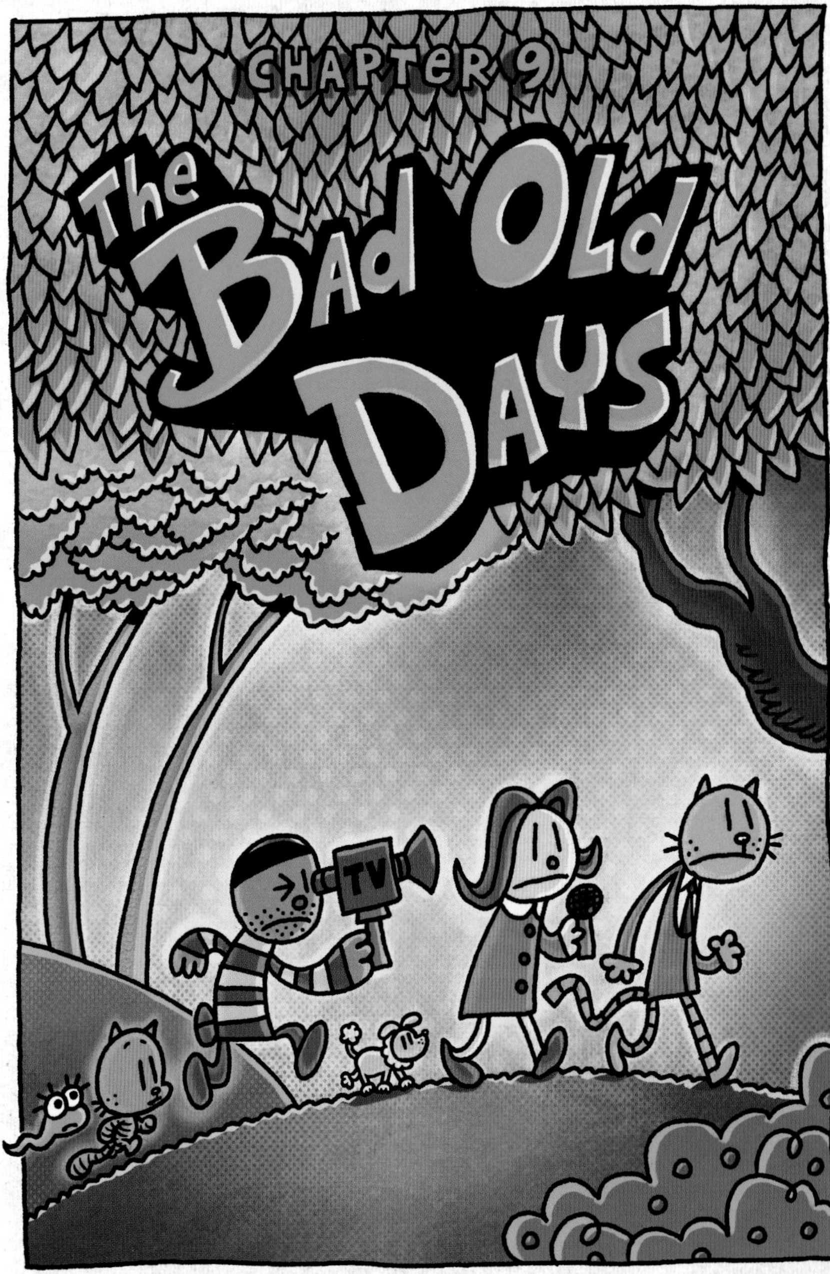
CHAPTER 9
The Bad Old Days
TV

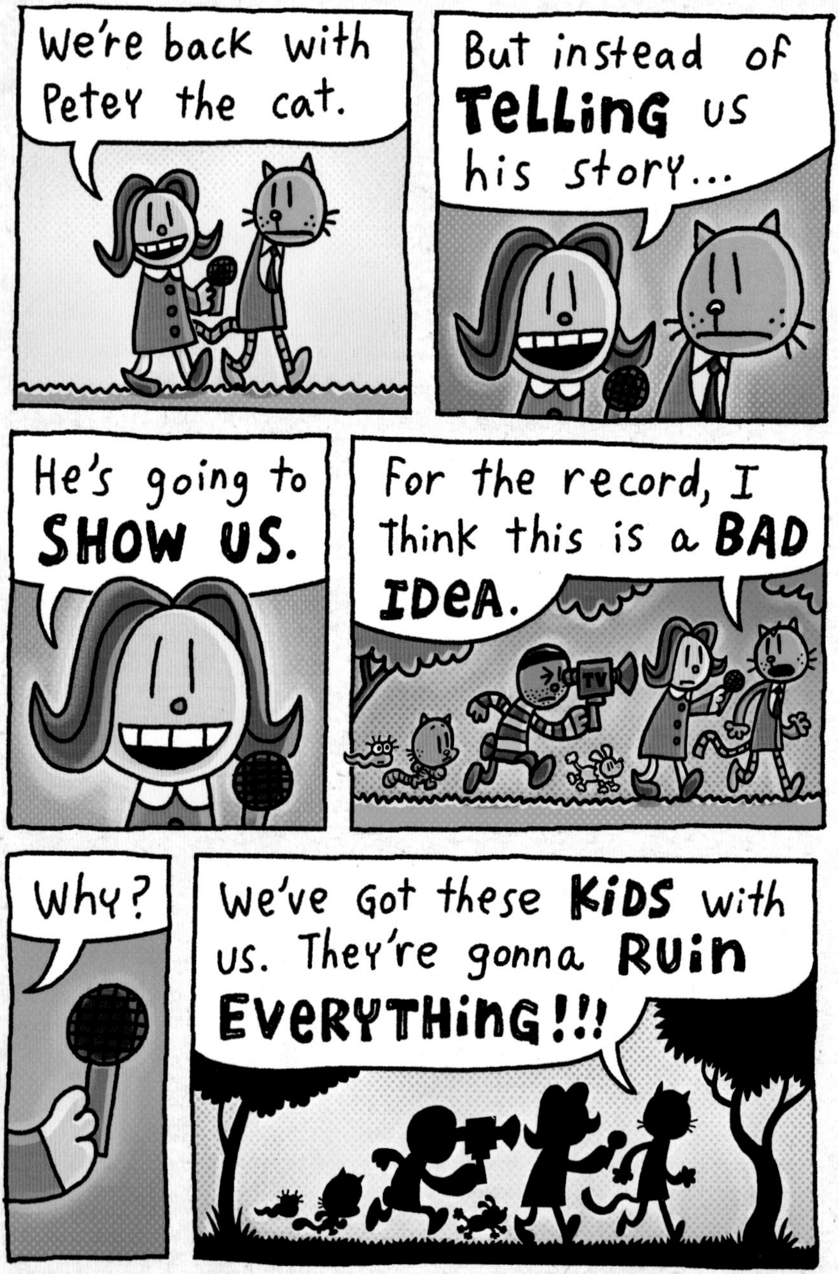
We're back with Petey the cat.
But instead of TELLING us his story...
He's going to SHOW US.
For the record, I think this is a BAD IDEA.
TV
Why?
We've Got these KIDS with us. They're gonna RUIN EVERYTHING!!!

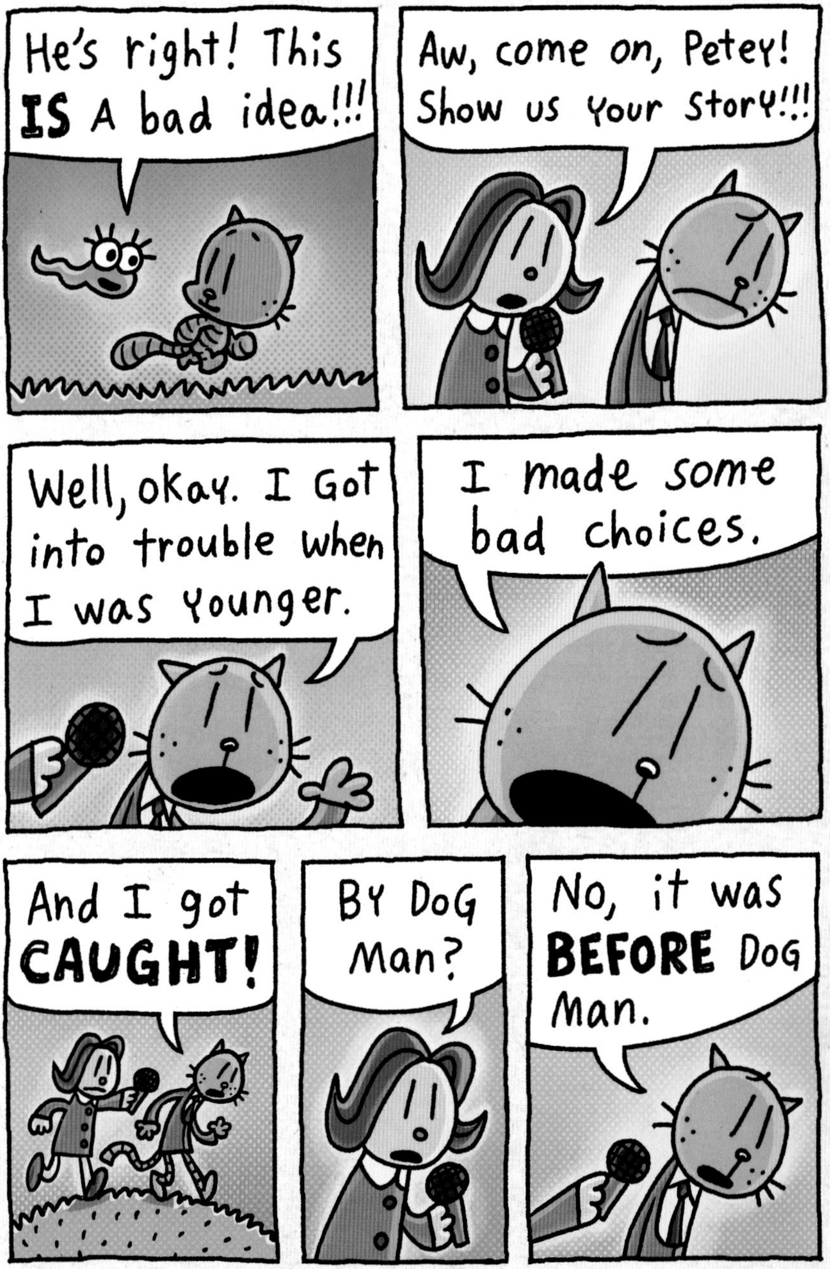
He's right! This IS A bad idea!!!
Aw, come on, Petey! Show us your story!!!
Well, okay. I got into trouble when I was younger.
I made some bad choices.
And I got CAUGHT!
By Dog Man?
No, it was BEFORE Dog Man.

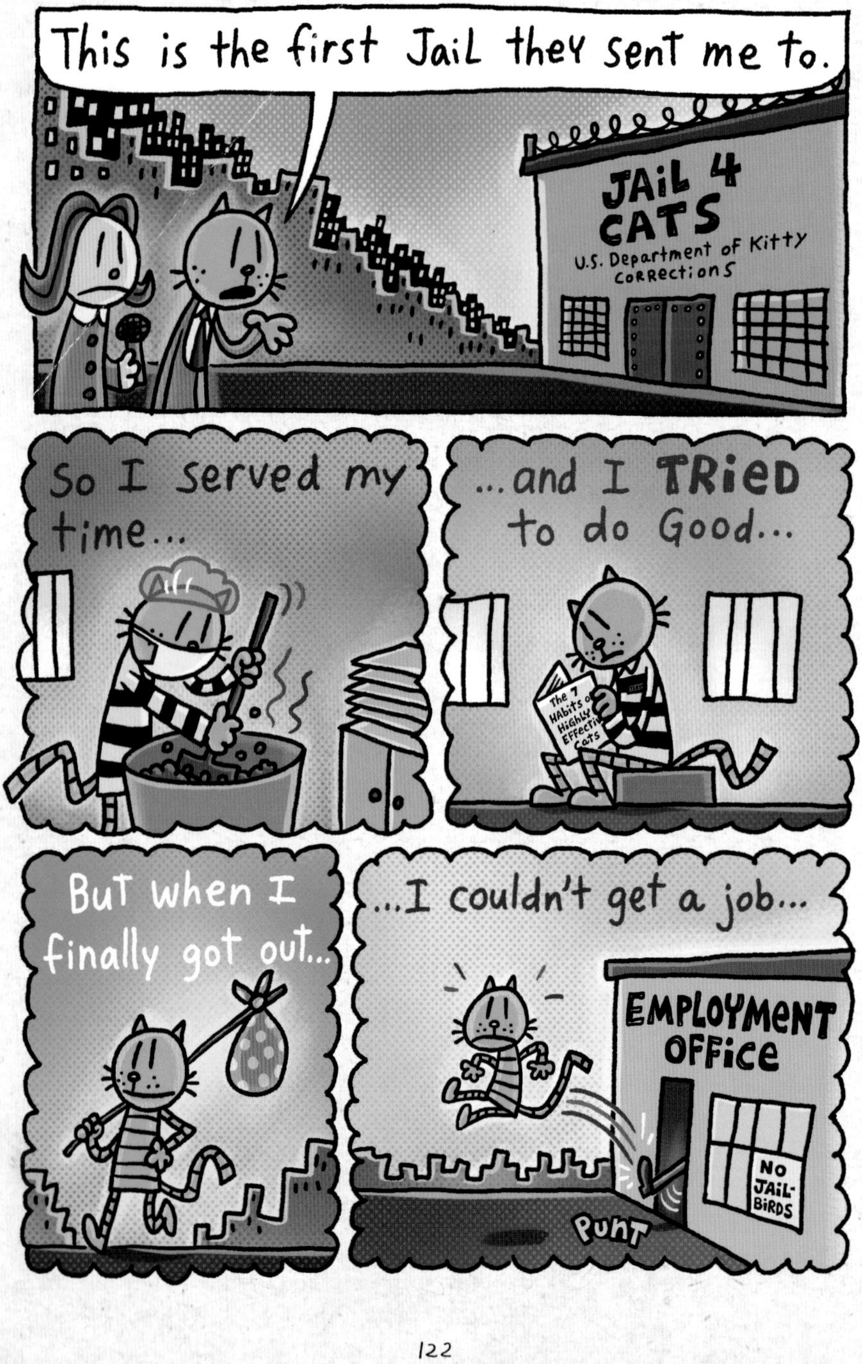
This is the first Jail they sent me to.
JAIL 4 CATS
U.S. Department of Kitty Corrections
So I served my time...
...and I TRIED to do Good...
The 7 Habits of Highly Effective Cats
But when I finally got out...
...I couldn't get a job...
EMPLOYMENT OFFICE
NO JAIL-BIRDS
PUNT

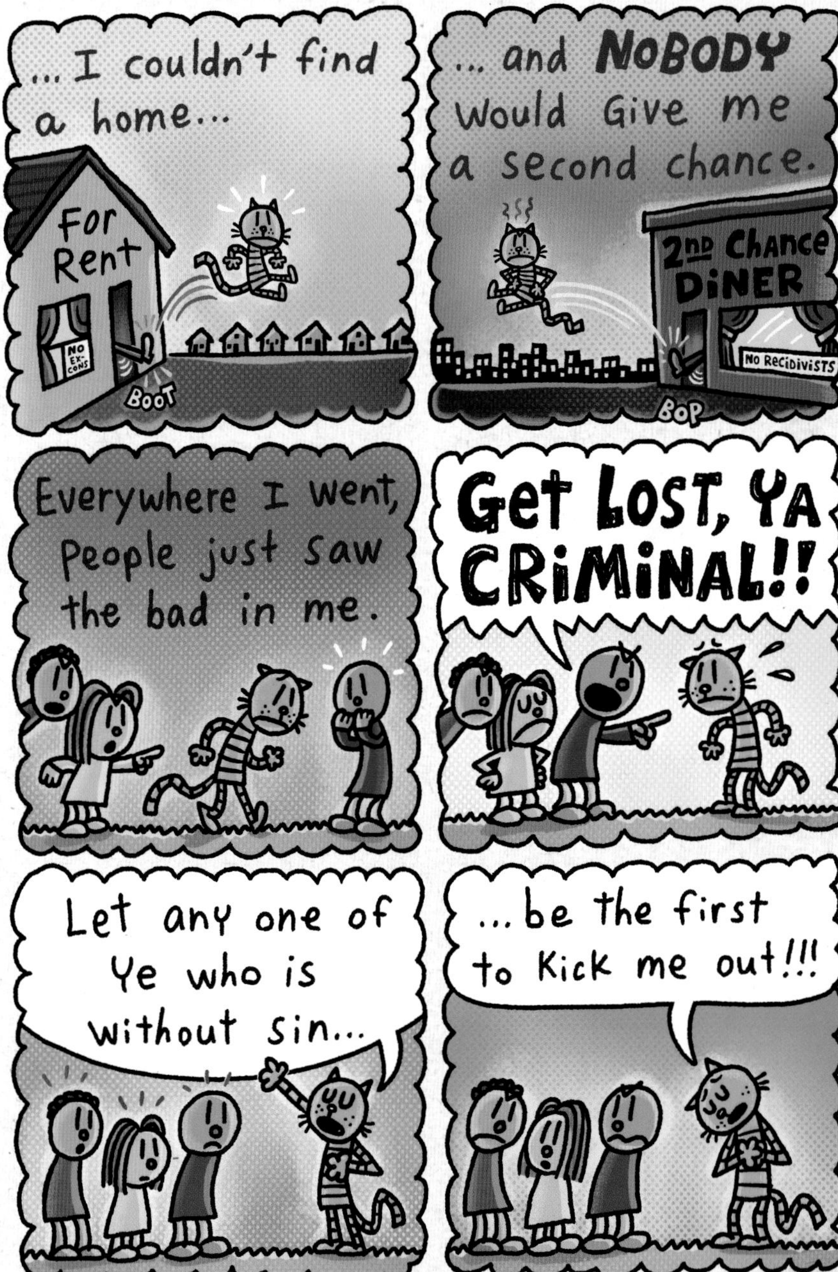
...I couldn't find a home...
For Rent
NO EX-CONS
BOOT
...and NOBODY Would Give me a second chance.
2ND Chance DINER
NO RECIDIVISTS
BOP
Everywhere I went, People just saw the bad in me.
Get LOST, YA CRIMINAL!!
Let any one of ye who is without sin...
...be the first to Kick me out!!!

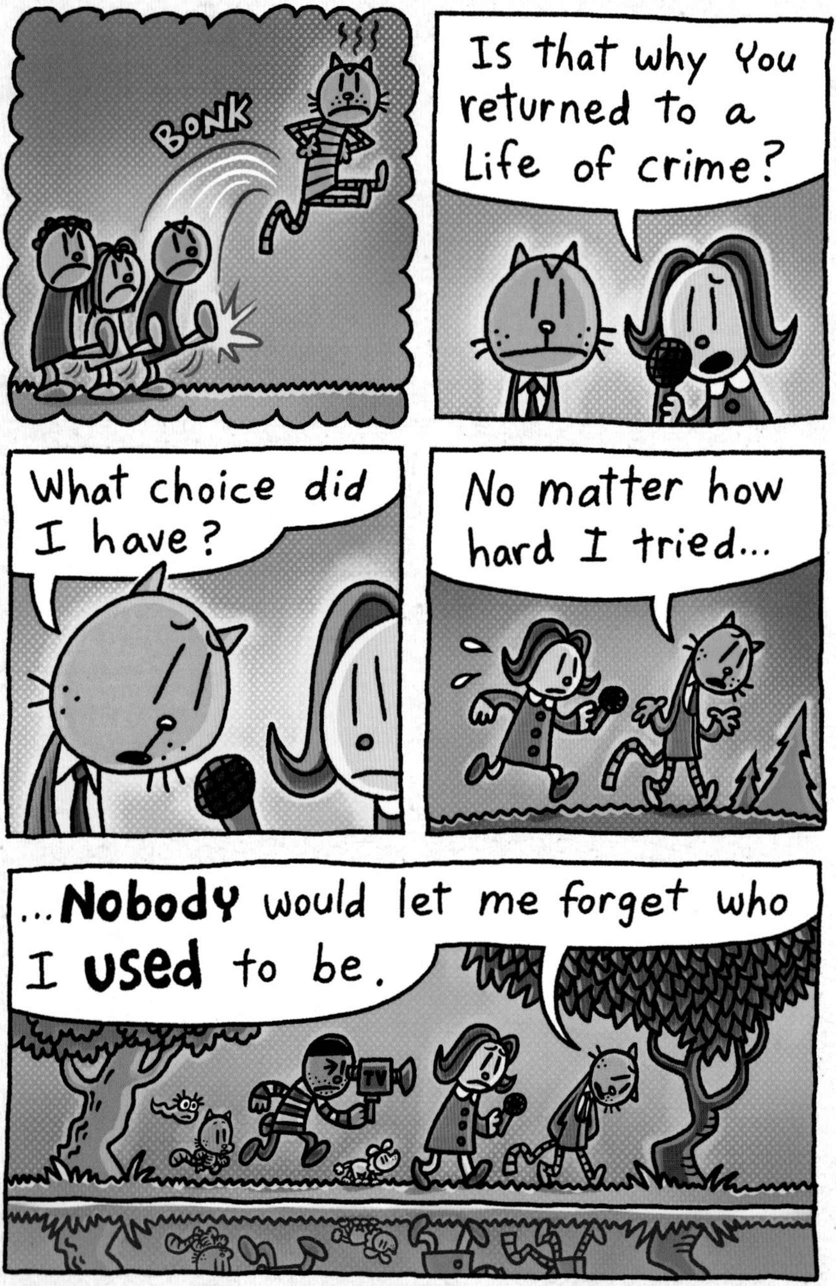
BONK
Is that why you returned to a life of crime?
What choice did I have?
No matter how hard I tried...
...Nobody would let me forget who I used to be.
TV

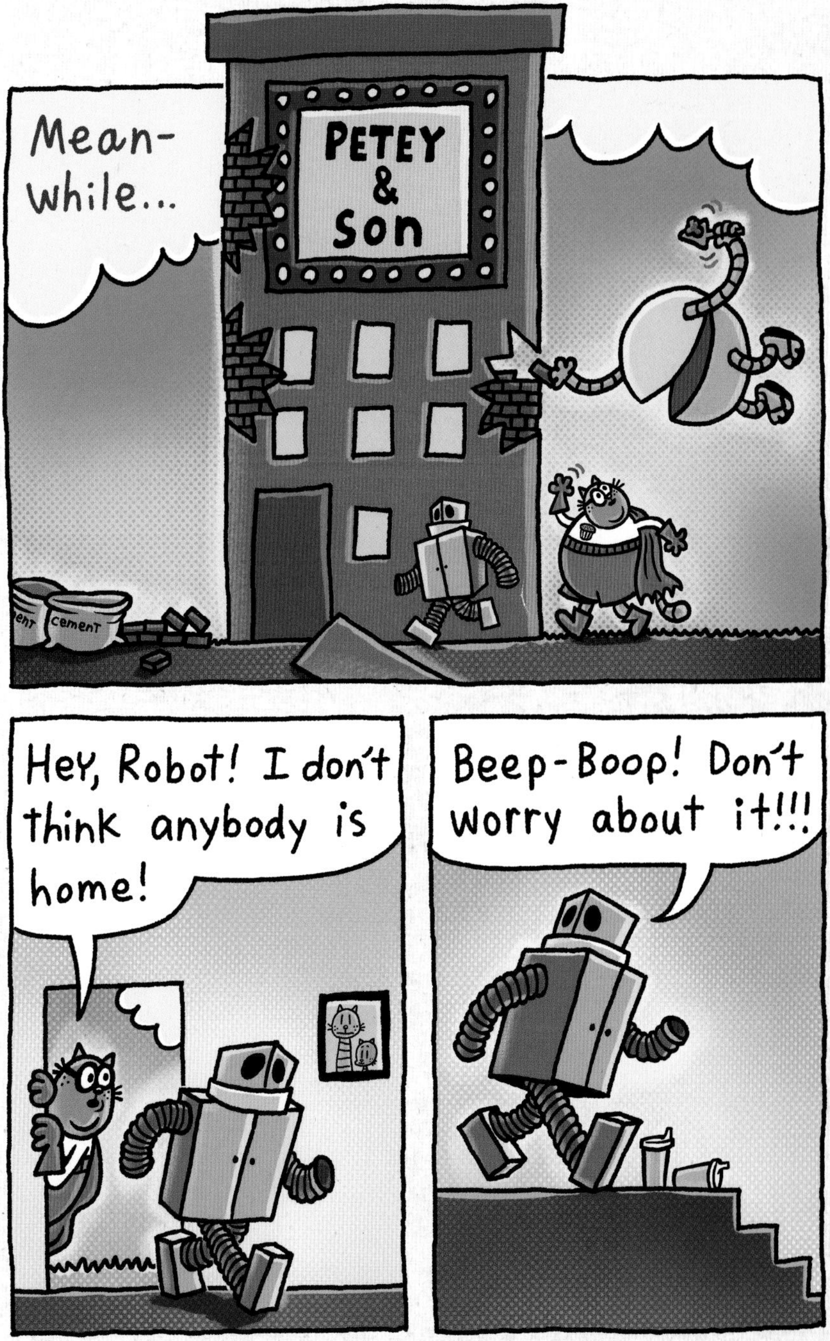
Mean-while...
PETEY & SON
CEMENT
CEMENT
Hey, Robot! I don't think anybody is home!
Beep-Boop! Don't worry about it!!!

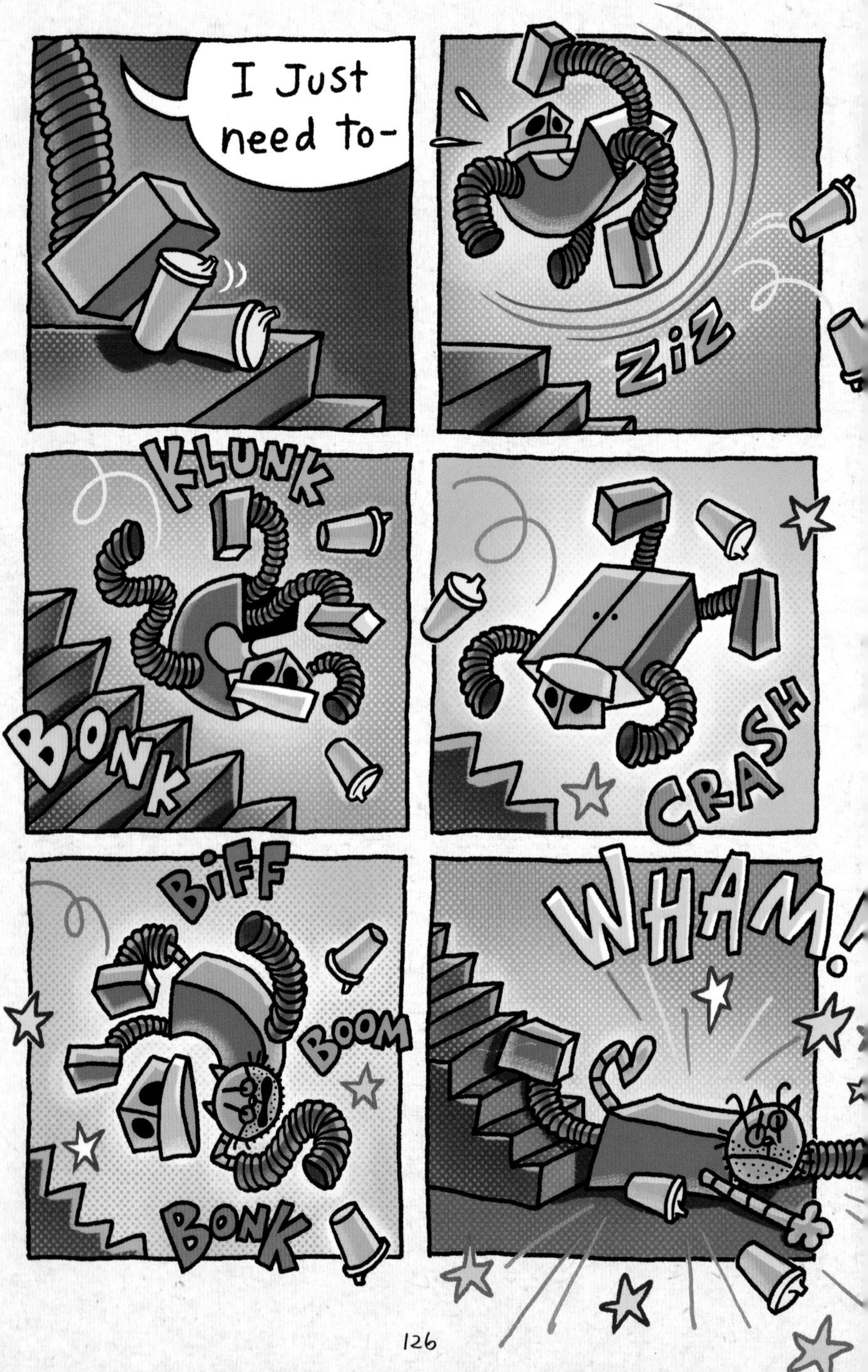
I Just need to-
ZiZ
KLUNK
BONK
CRASH
BiFF
BOOM
BONK
WHAM!

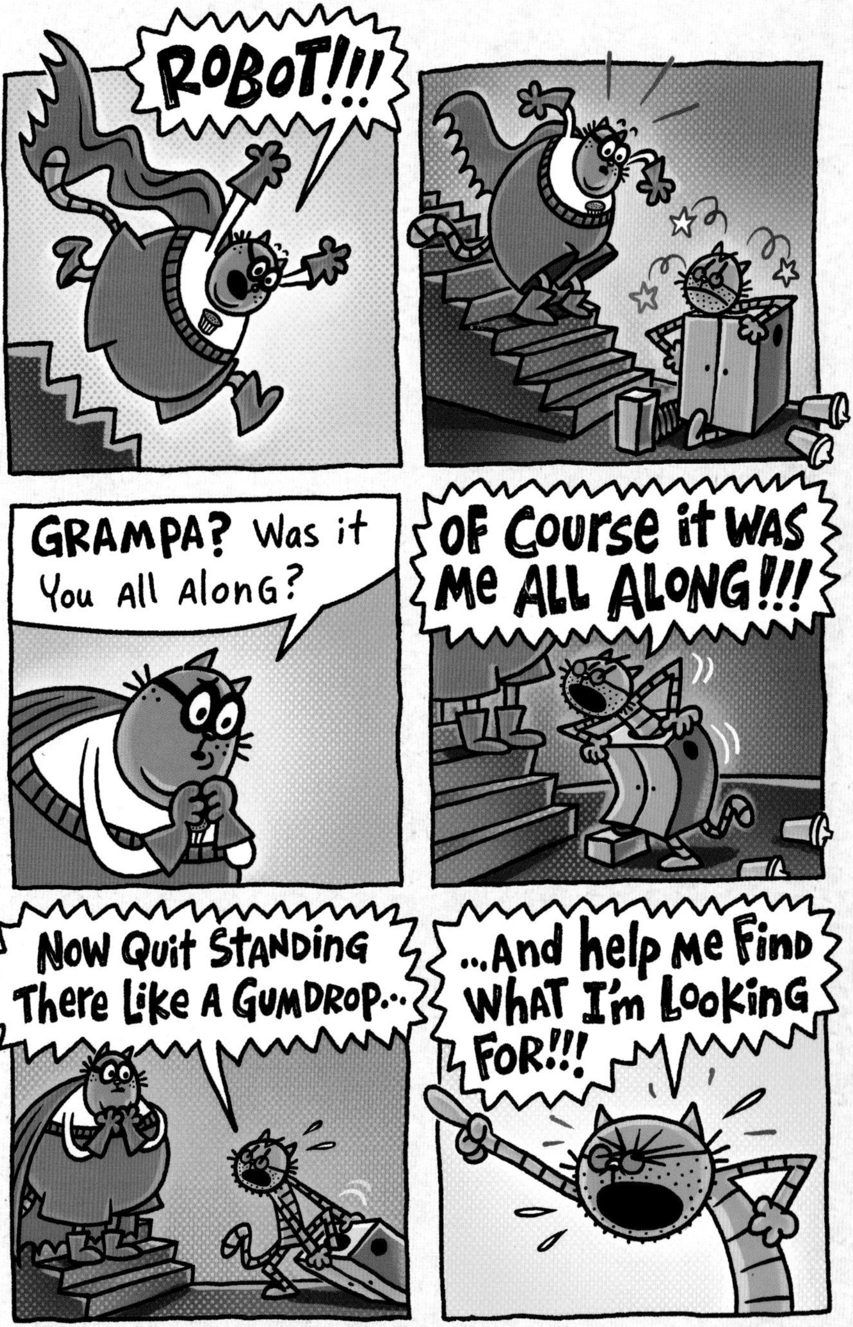
ROBOT!!!
GRAMPA? Was it You All AlonG?
OF Course it WAS Me ALL ALONG!!!
Now Quit STANDING There Like A GUMDROP...
...And help Me Find WHAT I'm Looking FOR!!!

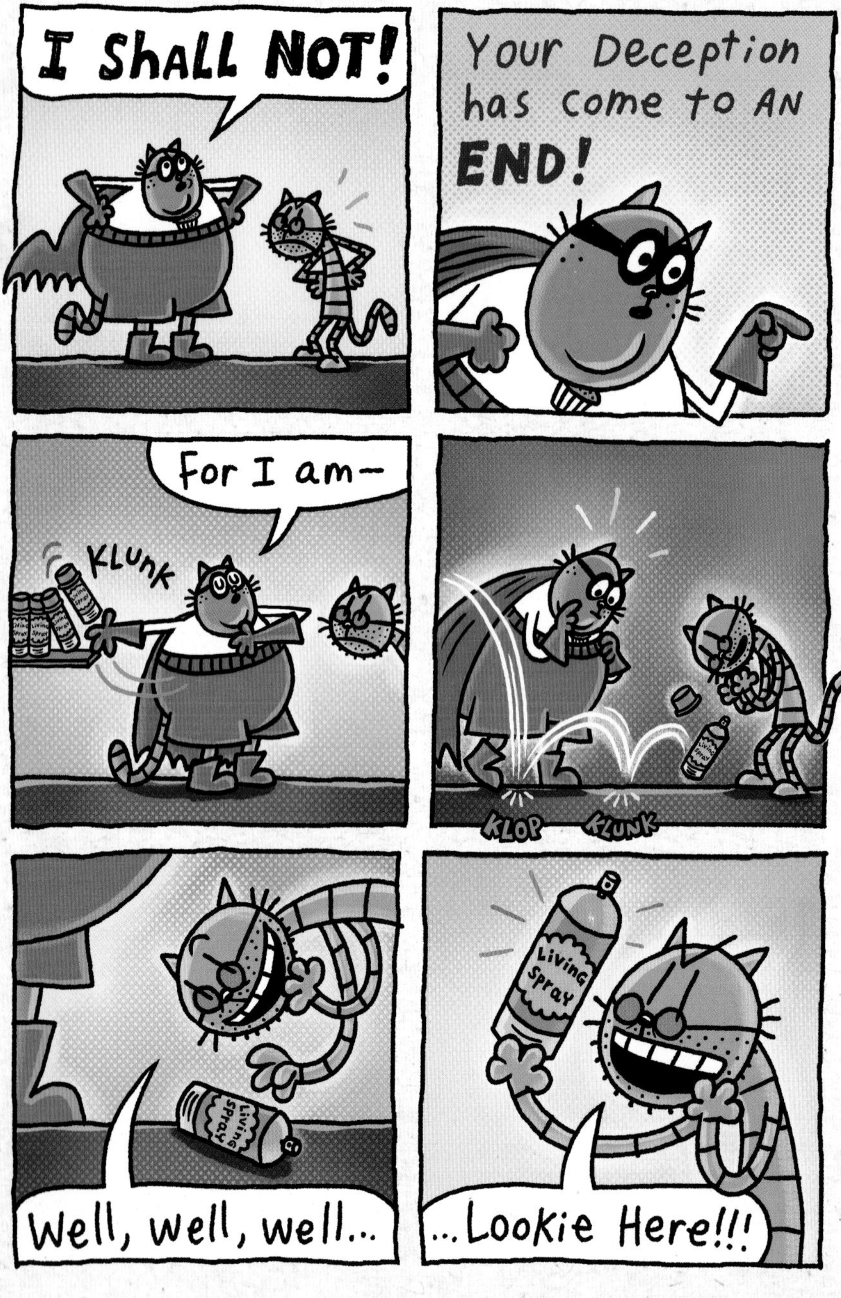
I ShALL NOT!
Your Deception has come to AN END!
For I am—
KLUNK
KLOP
KLUNK
Well, well, well...
...Lookie Here!!!

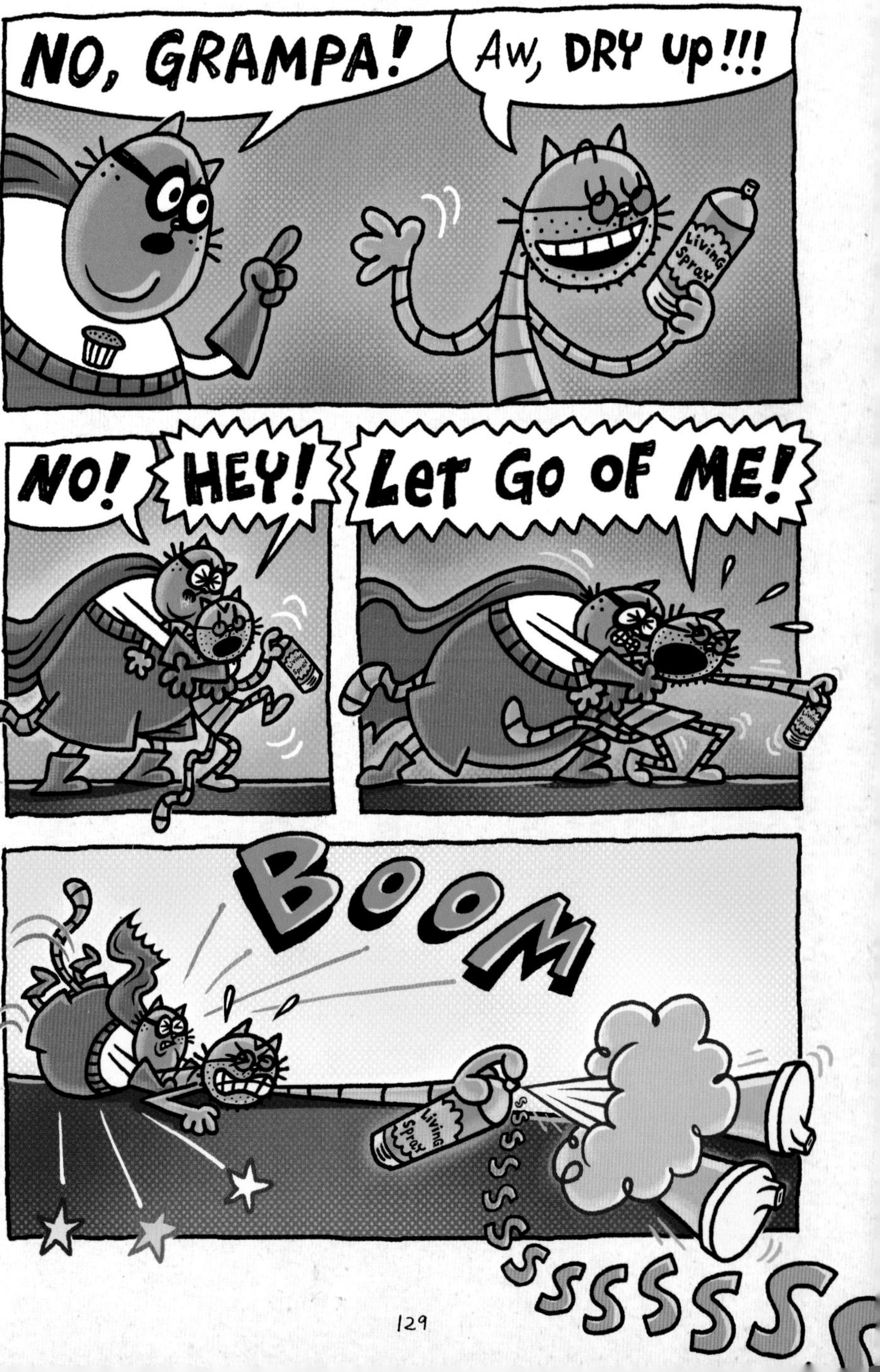
NO, GRAMPA!
Aw, DRY up!!!
Living Spray
NO!
HEY!
Let Go OF ME!
BOOM
Living Spray

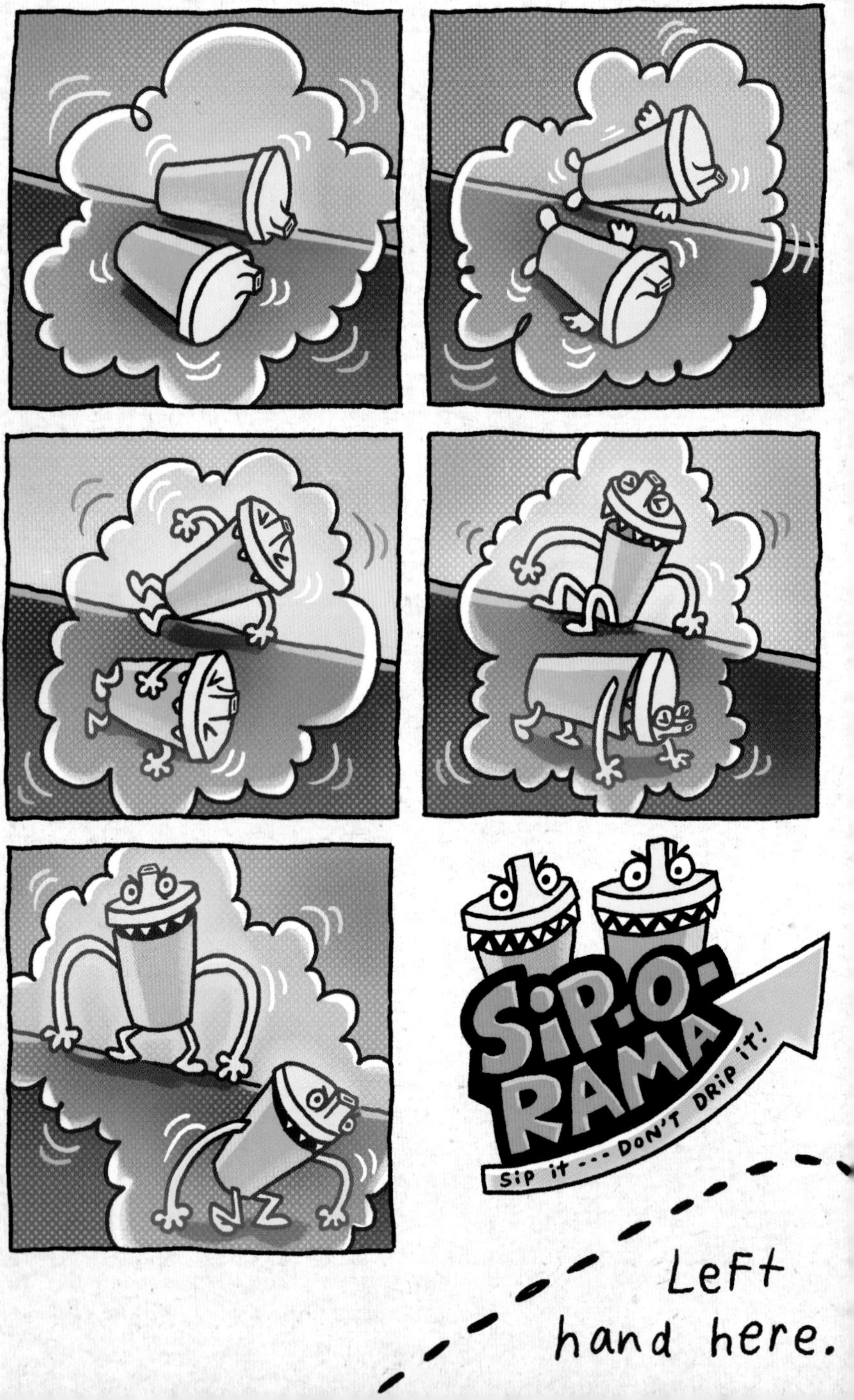
SIP-O-RAMA
Sip it --- DON'T DRIP it!
Left hand here.

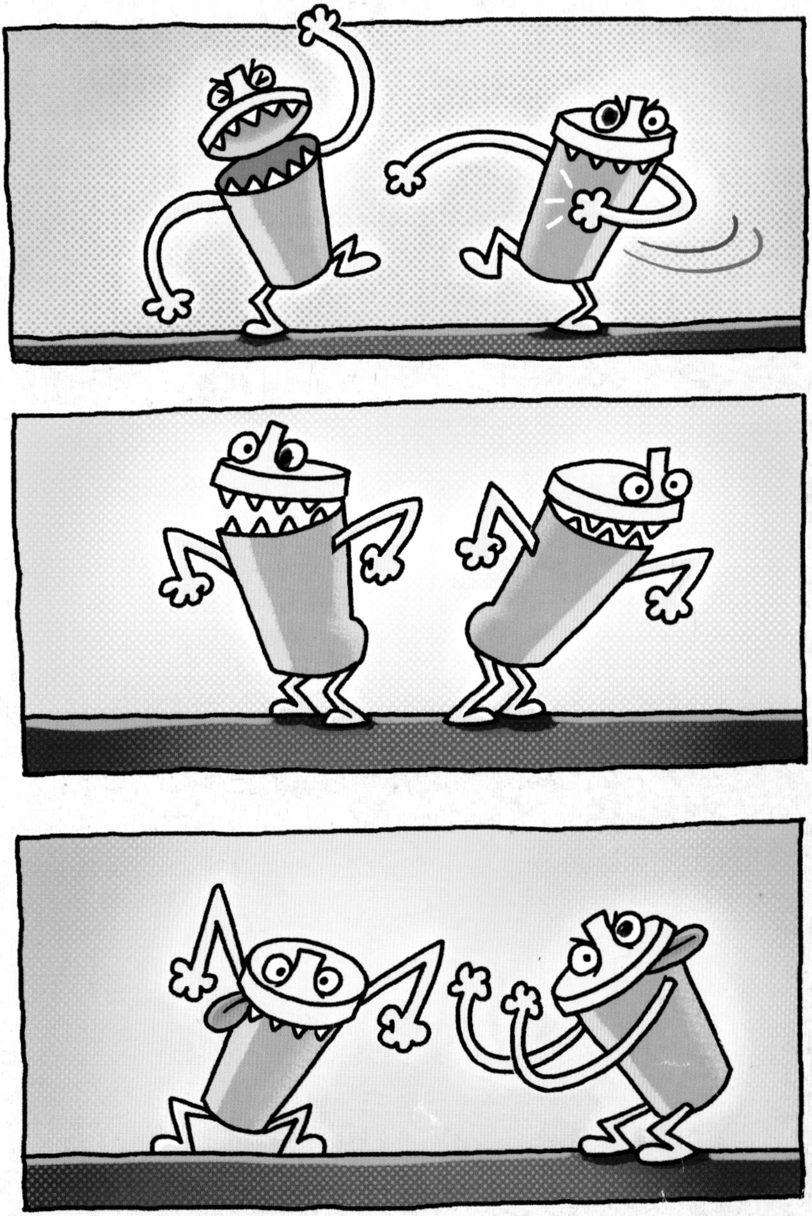

Right
Thumb
here.

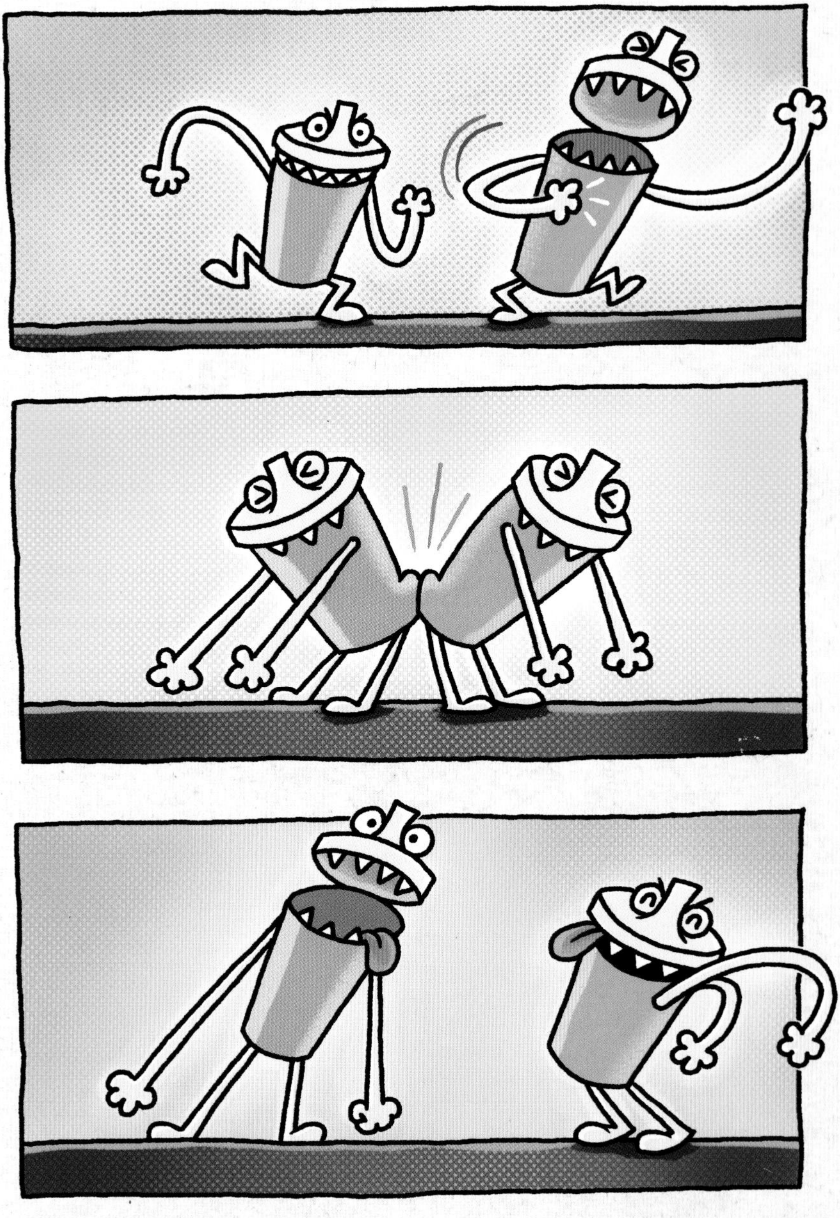

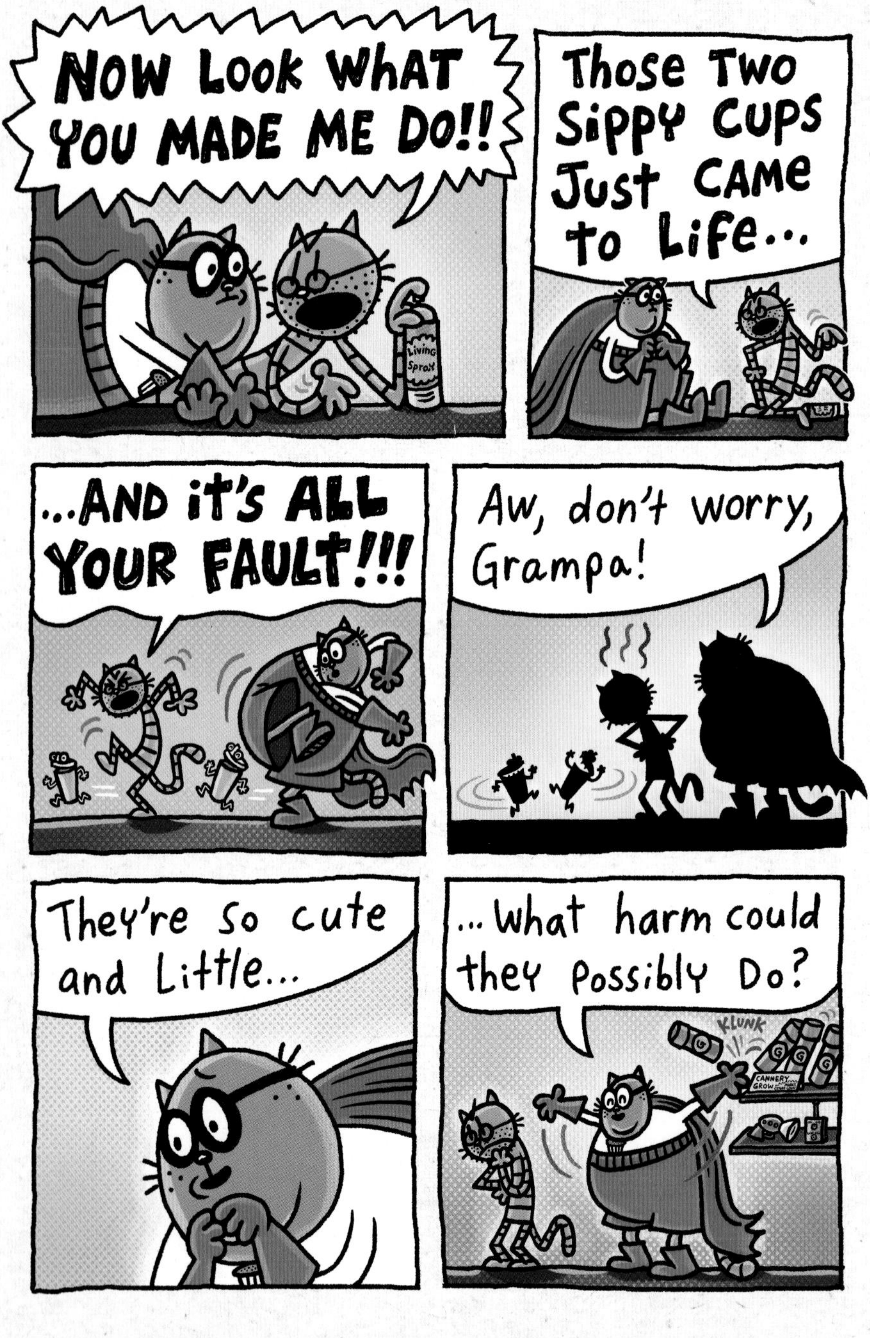
NOW LOOK WHAT YOU MADE ME DO!!
Living Spray
Those Two Sippy Cups Just CAME to Life...
...AND it's ALL YOUR FAULT!!!
Aw, don't worry, Grampa!
They're so cute and Little...
...What harm could they Possibly Do?
KLUNK
CANNERY GROW

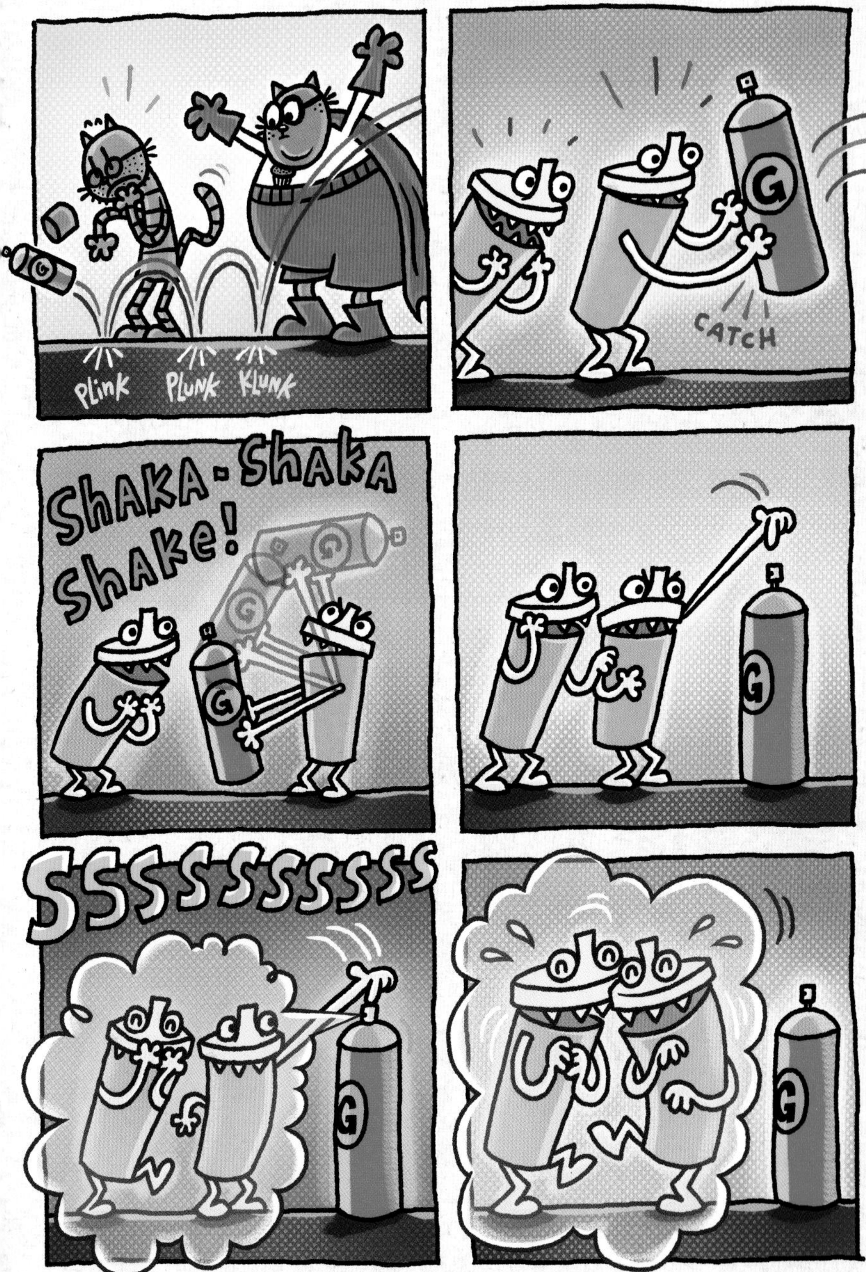
PLINK
PLUNK
KLUNK
CATCH
SHAKA-SHAKA
SHAKE!
SSSSSSSSSS

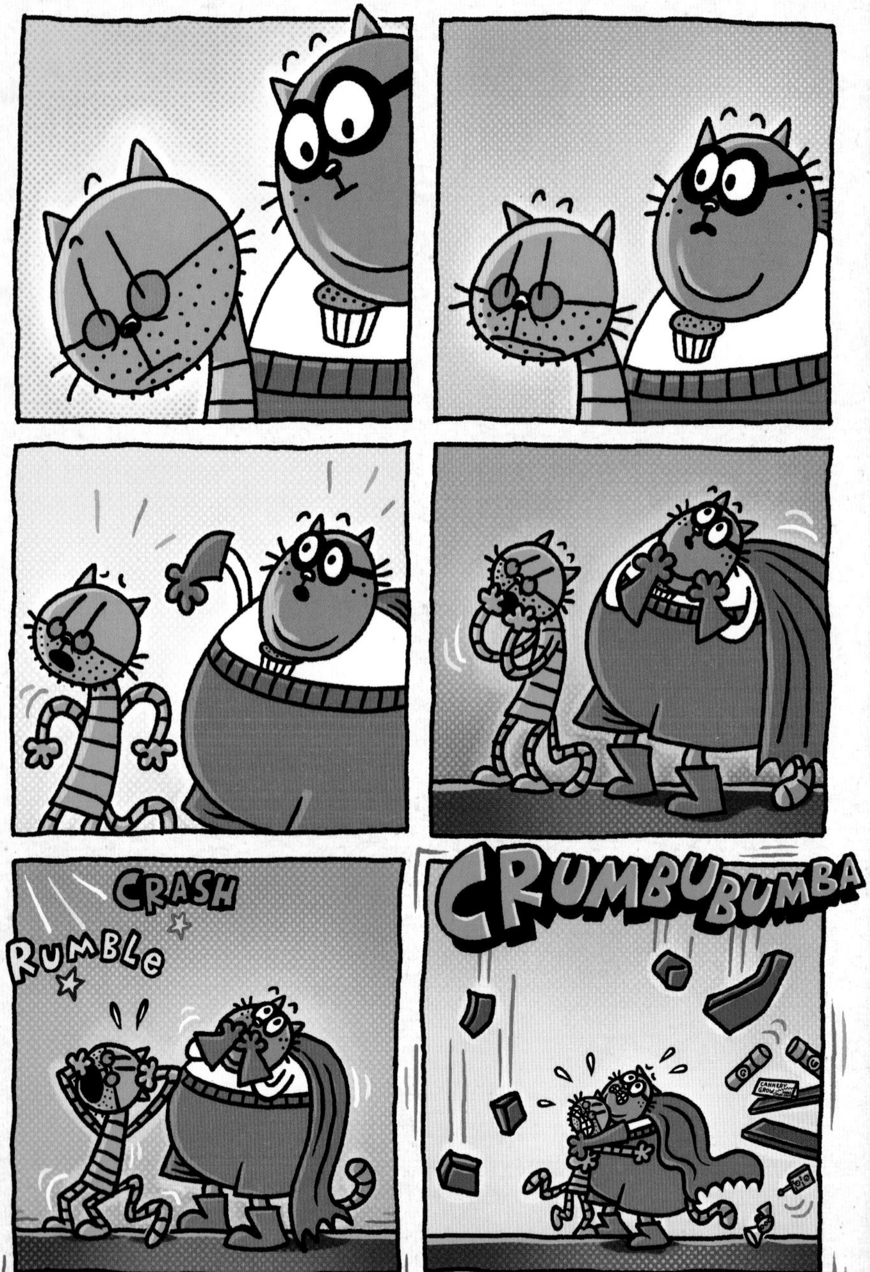
CRASH
RUMBLE
CRUMBUBUMBA

CHAPTER 10

NIGHT OF THE LIVING SIPPY CUPS

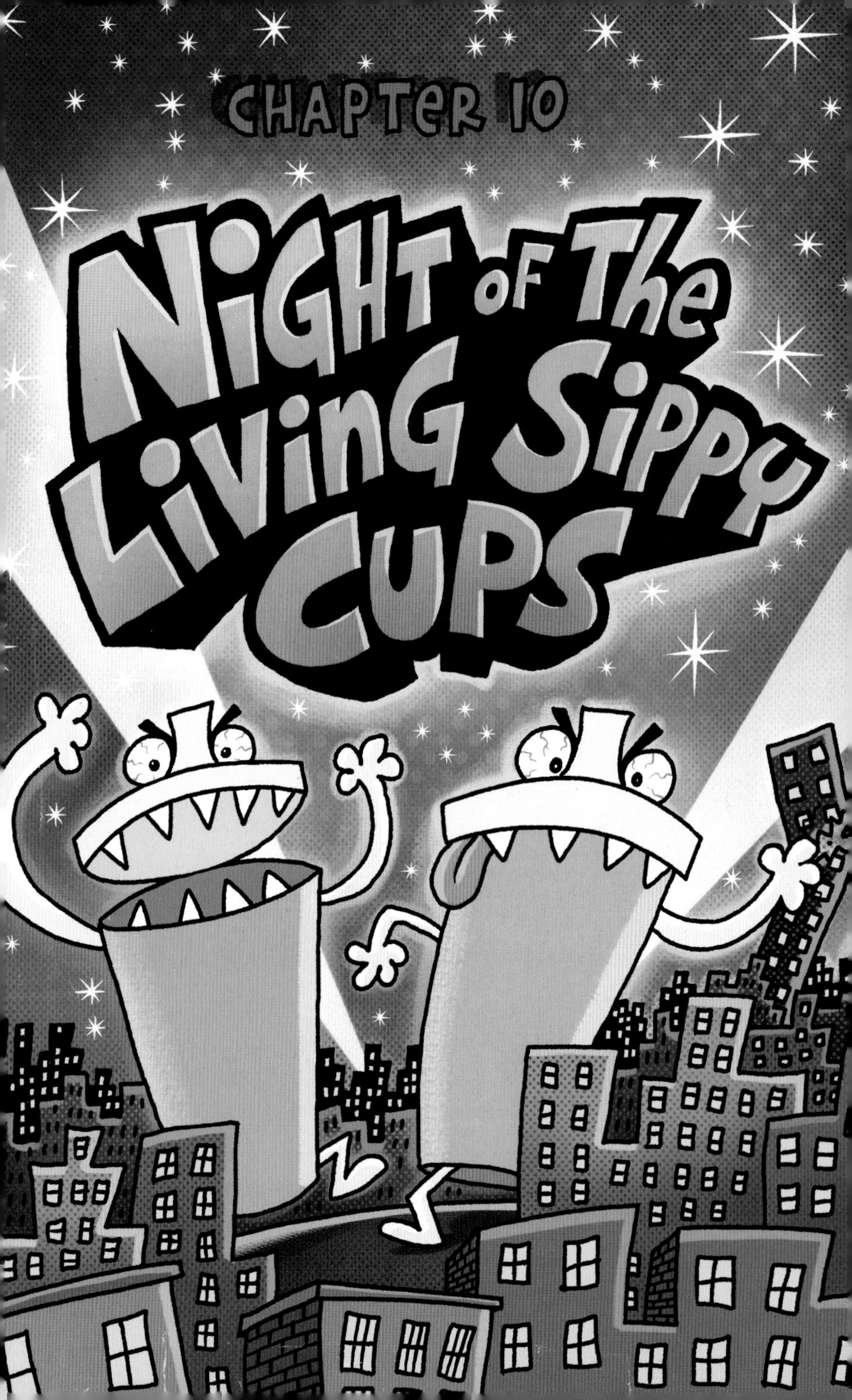

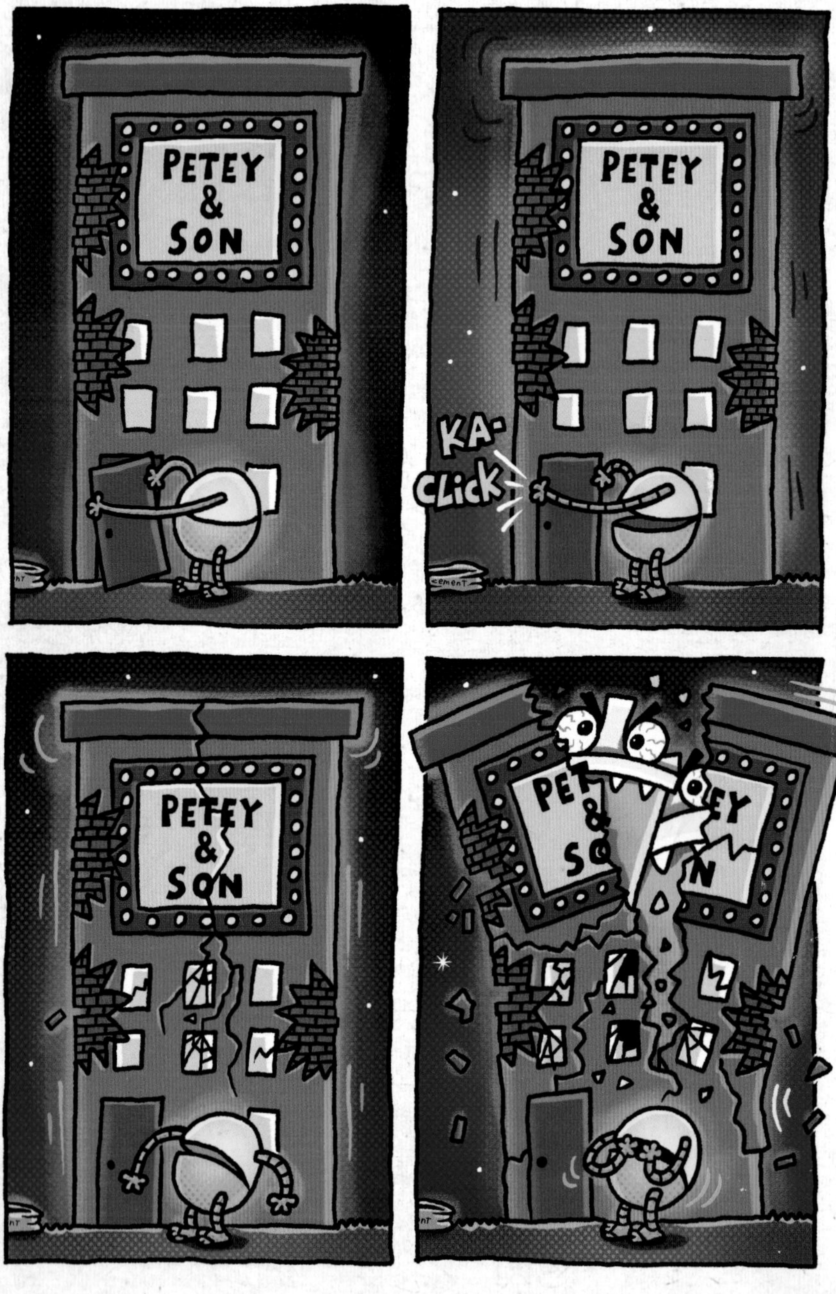
PETEY & SON
PETEY & SON
KA-CLICK
cement
PETEY & SON

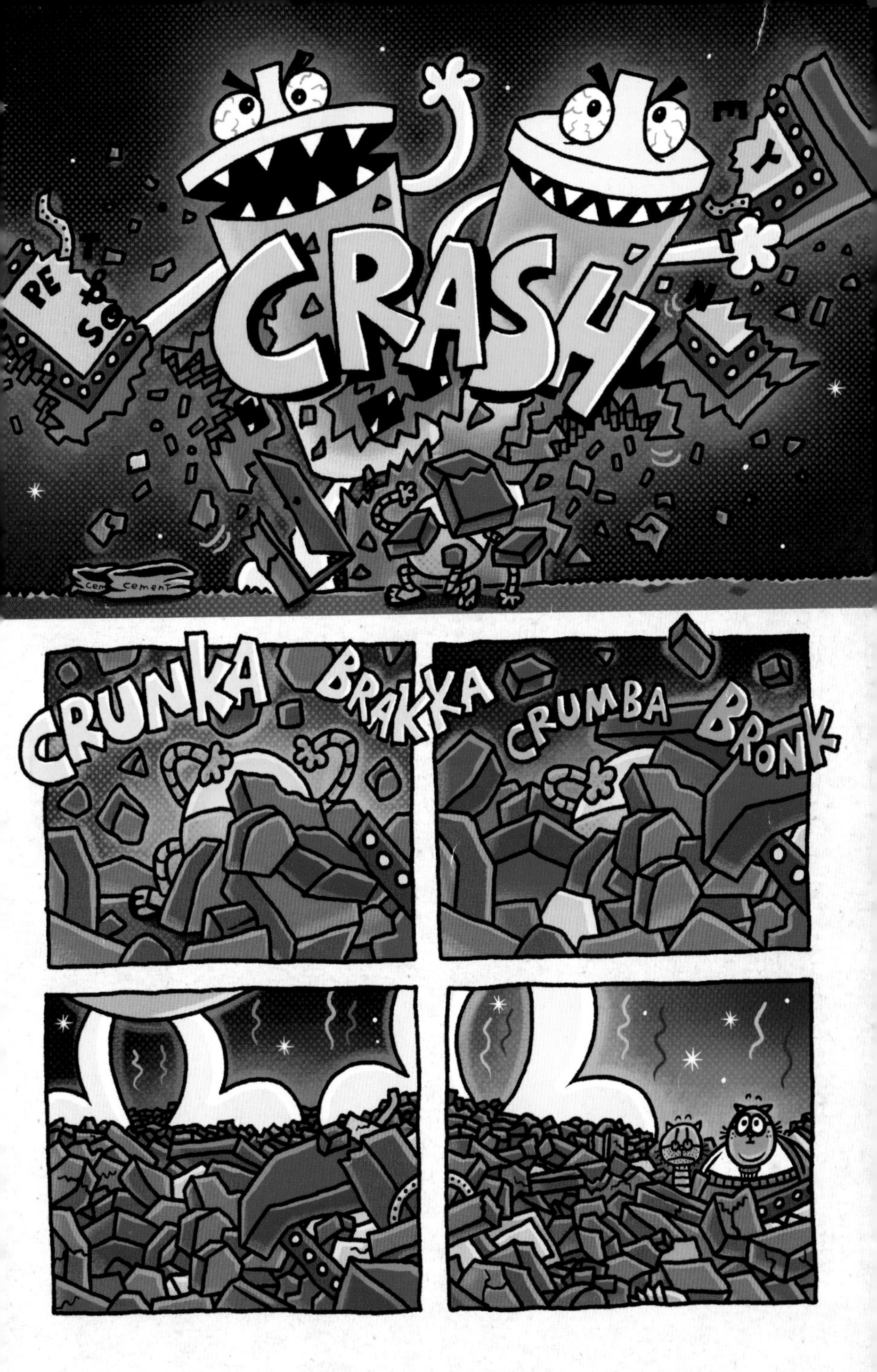
CRASH
CRUNKA
BRAKKA
CRUMBA
BRONK

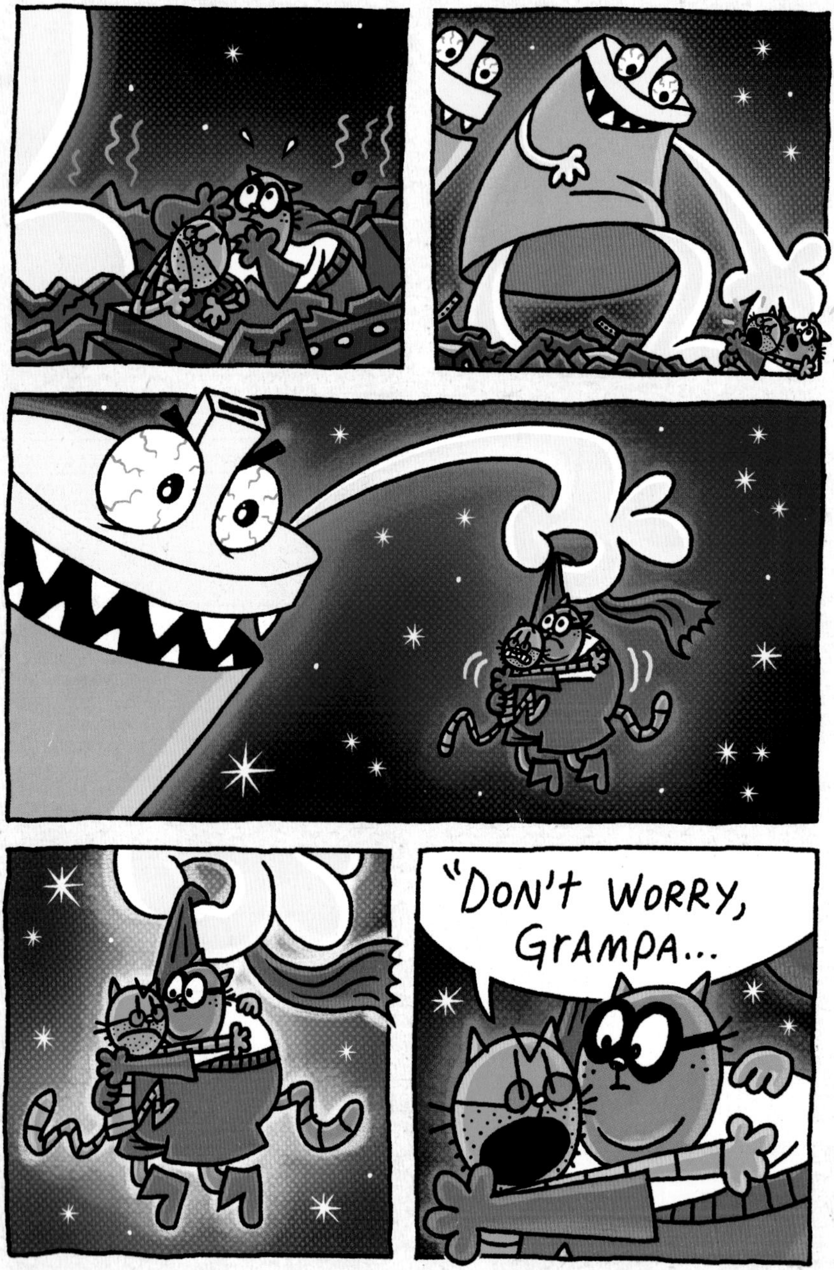
"DON'T WORRY, GrAMPA...

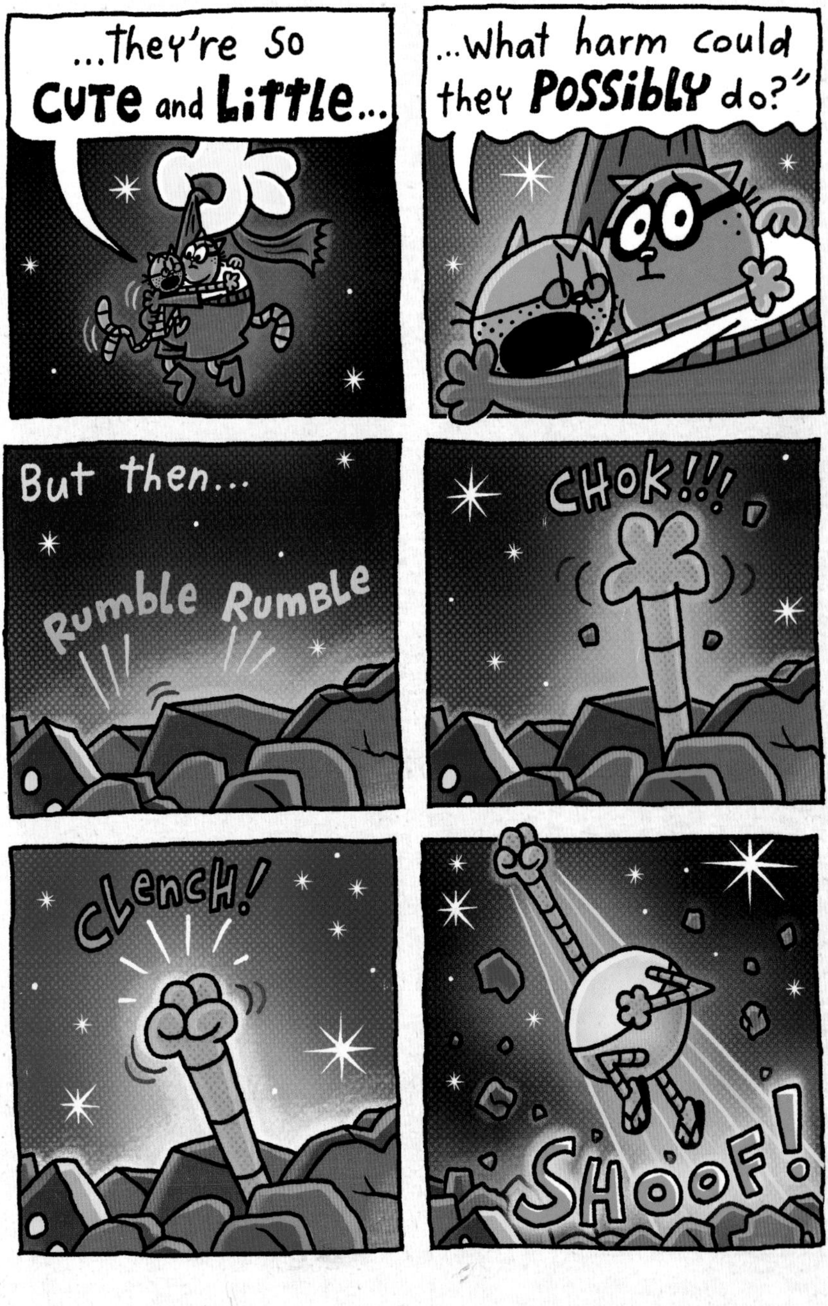
...they're so CUTE and LITTLE...
...What harm could they POSSIBLY do?"
But then...
Rumble Rumble
CHOK!!!
CLENCH!
SHOOF!

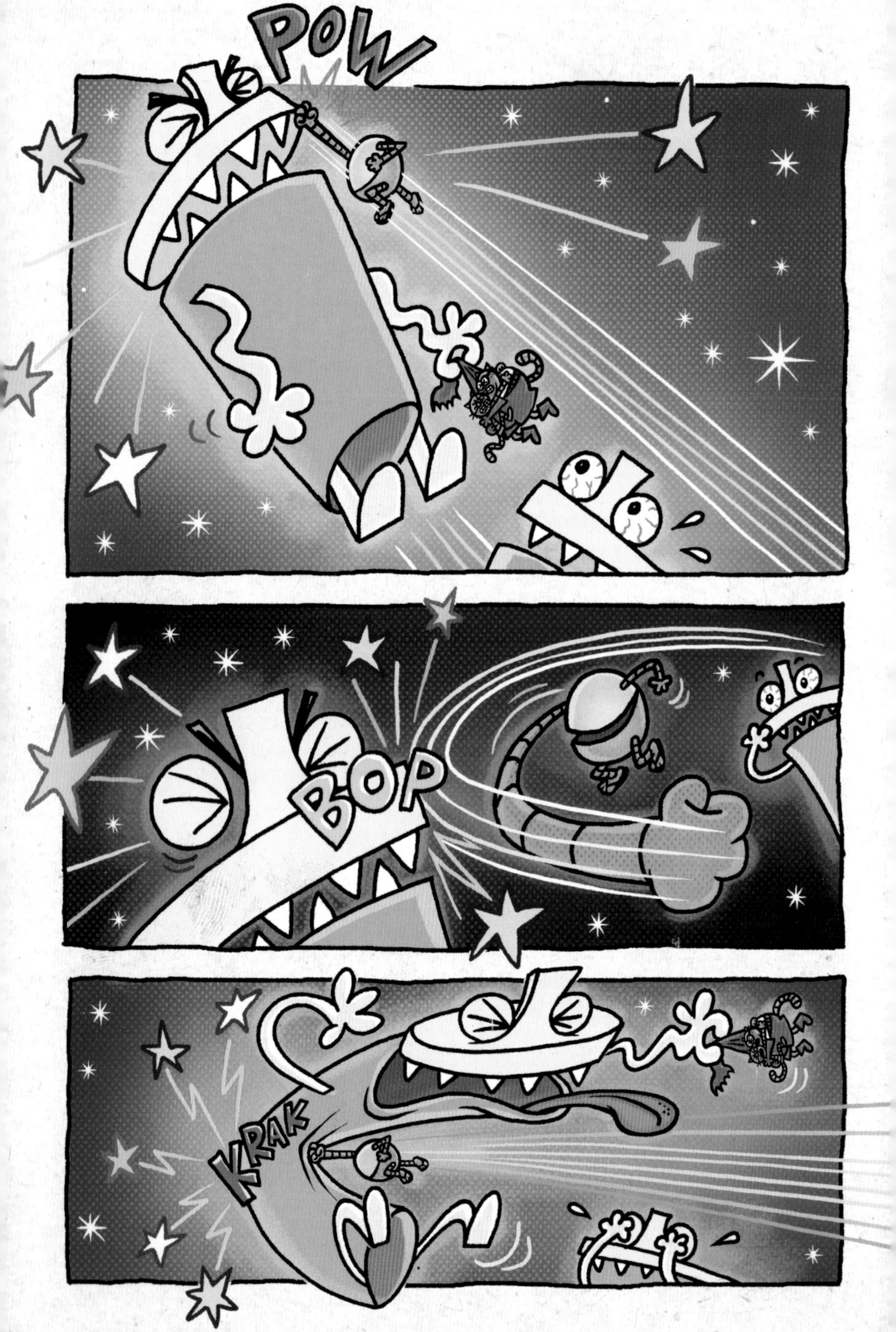
POW
BOP
KRAK

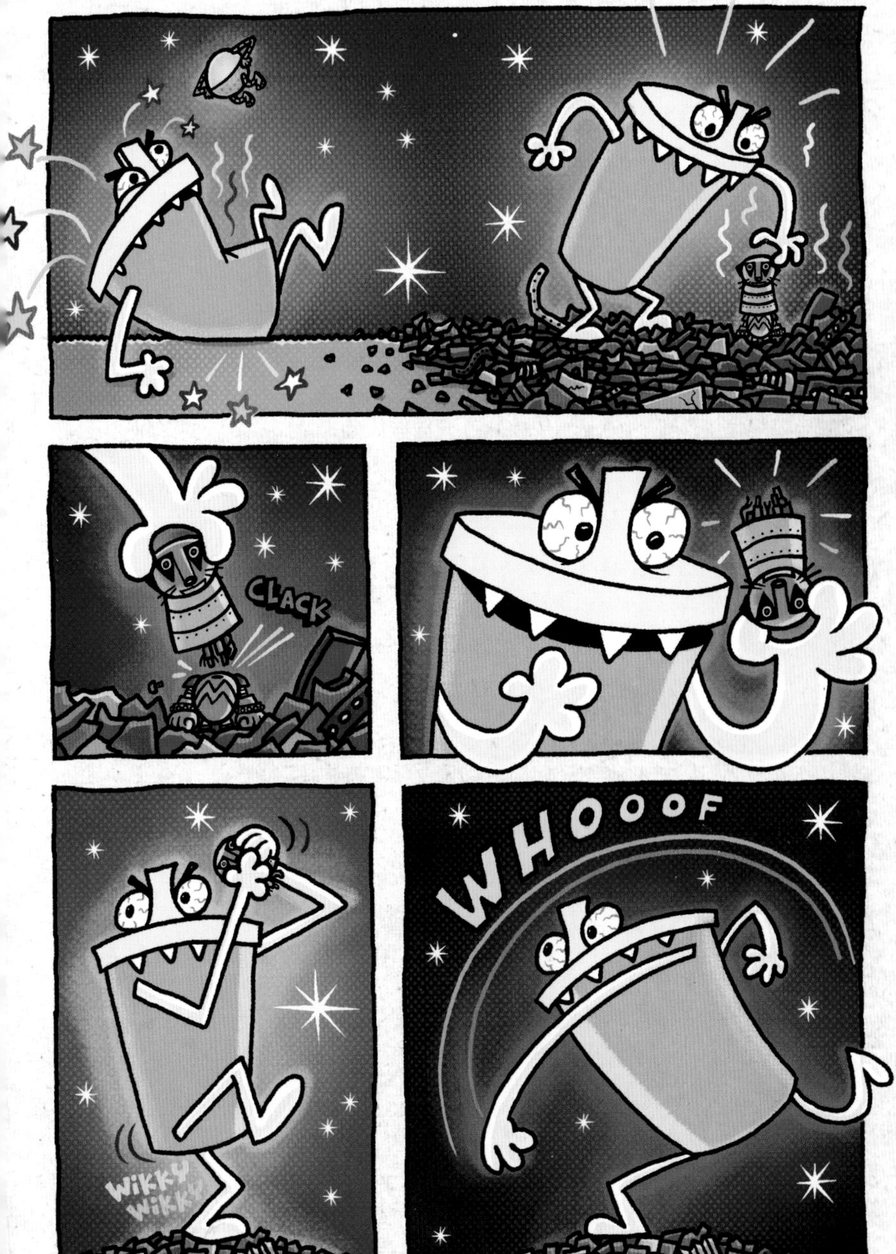

CLACK
WHOOOF
WIKKY WIKKY

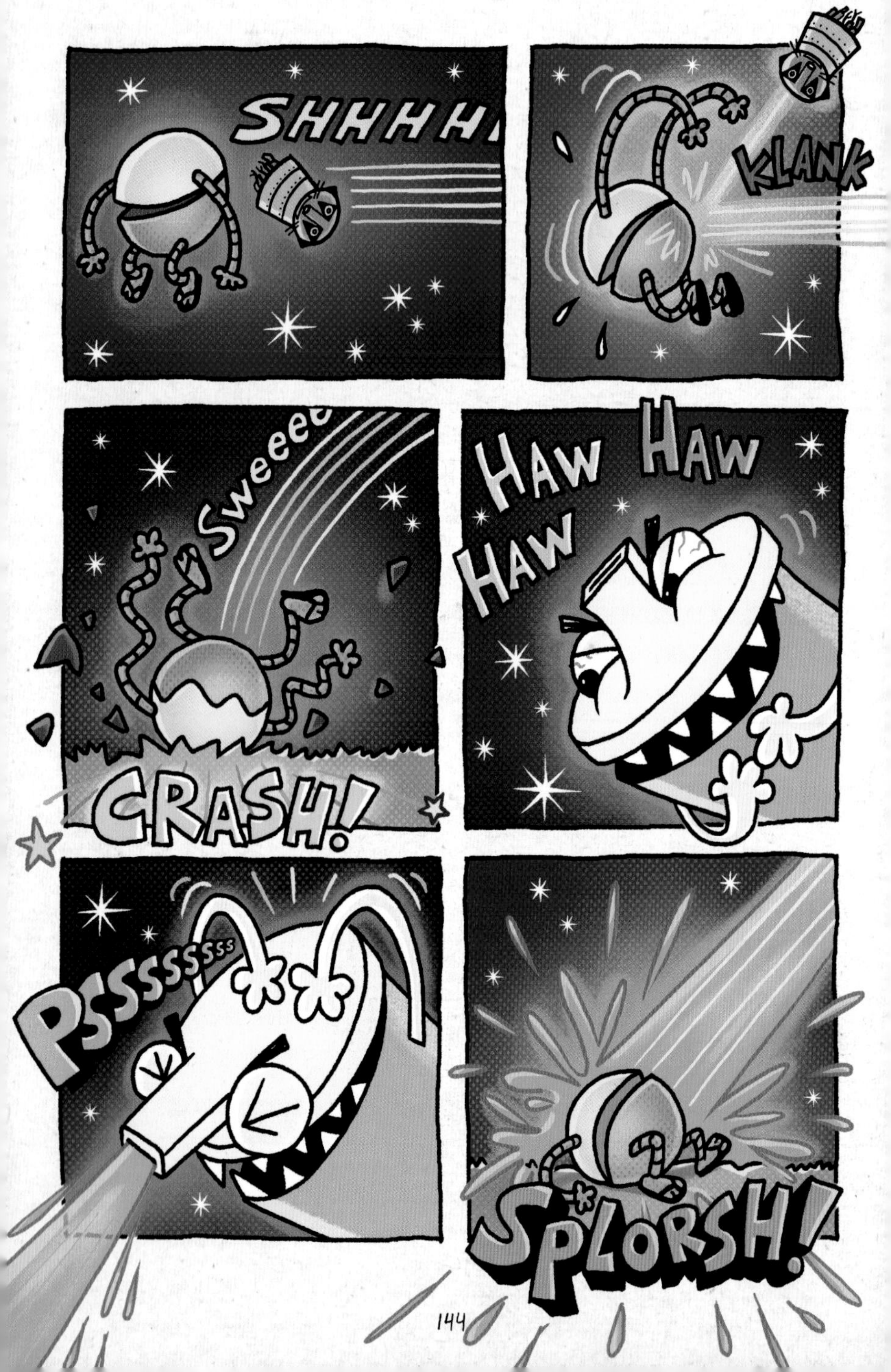
SHHHHH
KLANK
Sweeee
CRASH!
HAW HAW
HAW HAW
PSSSSSSSS
SPLORSH!

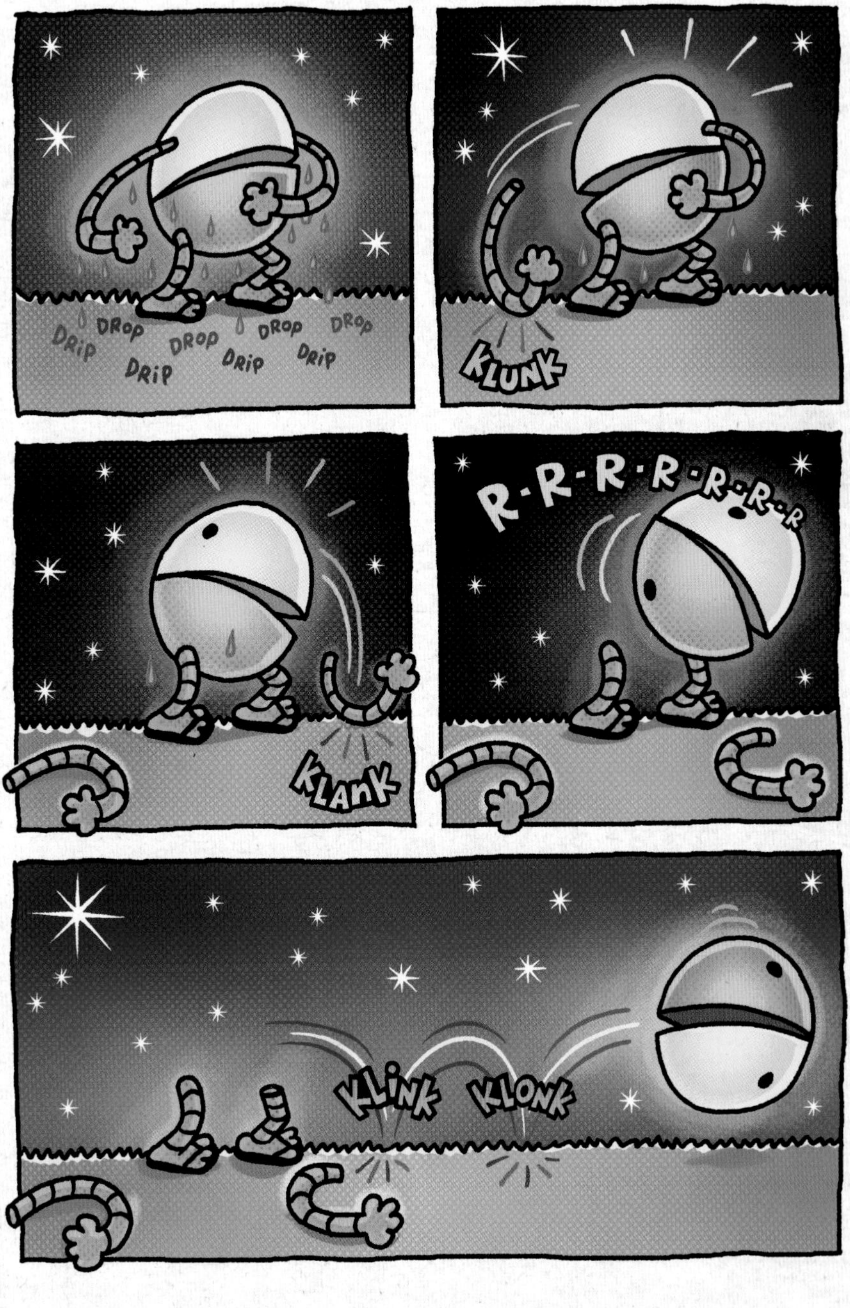
DRIP DROP DRIP DROP DRIP DROP DRIP DROP
KLUNK
KLANK
R-R-R-R-R-R-R
KLINK KLONK

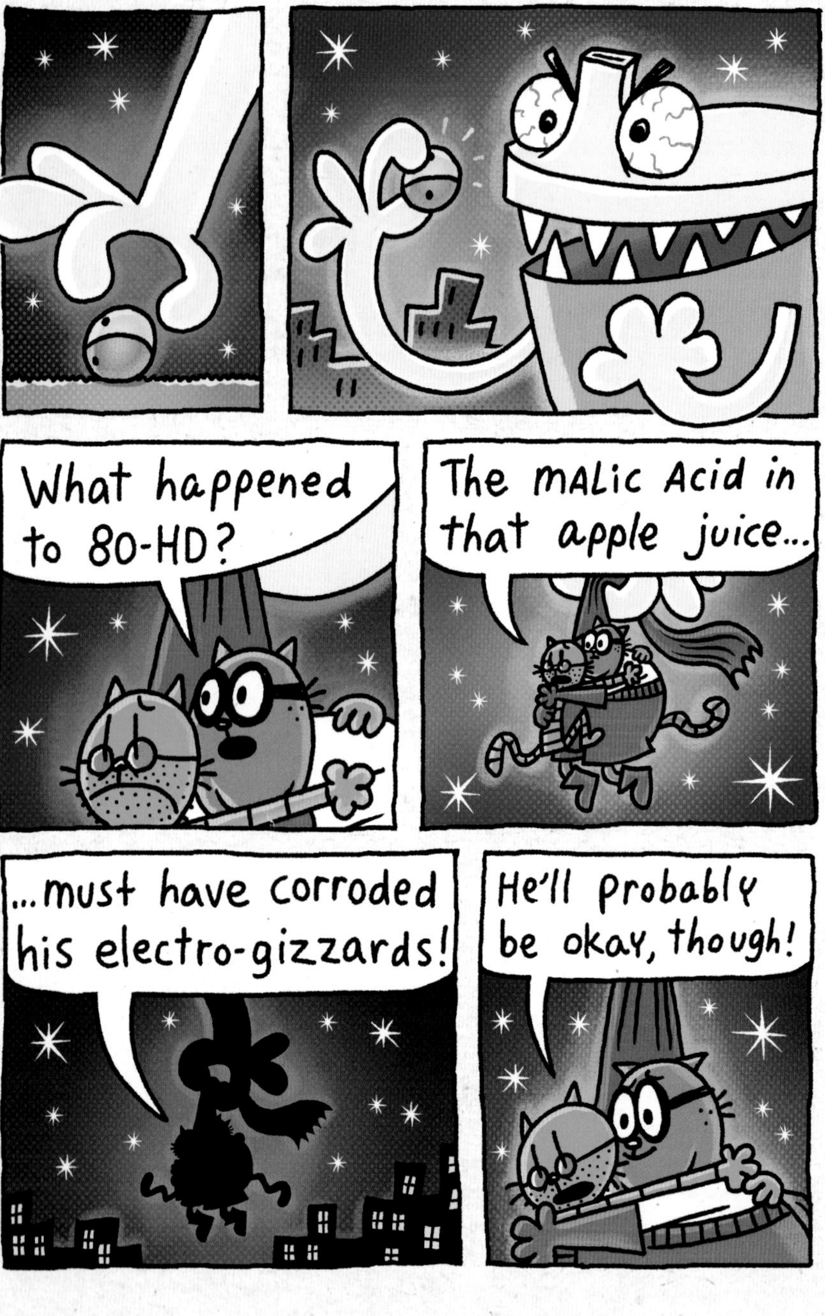
What happened to 80-HD?
The MALIC Acid in that apple juice...
...must have corroded his electro-gizzards!
He'll probably be okay, though!

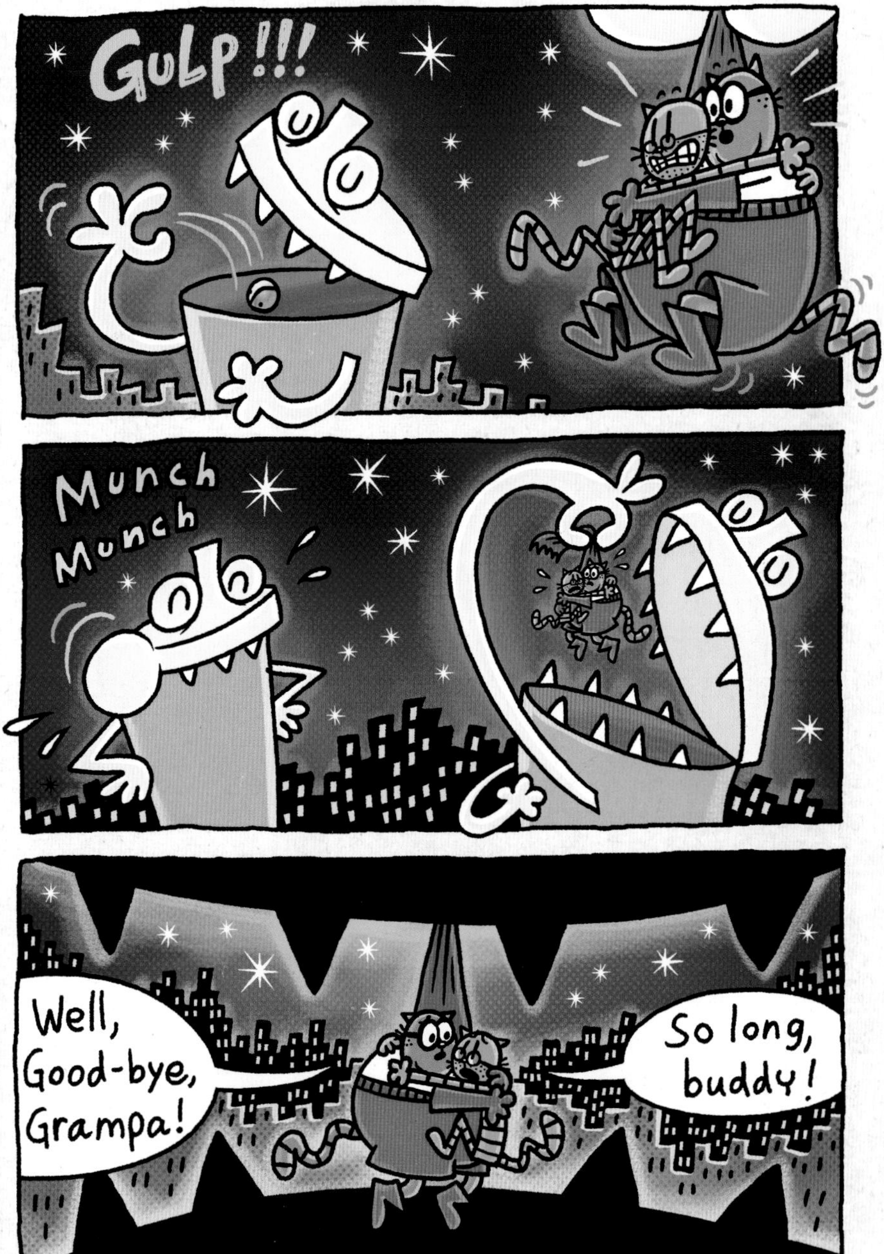
GULP!!!
Munch
Munch
Well, Good-bye, Grampa!
So long, buddy!

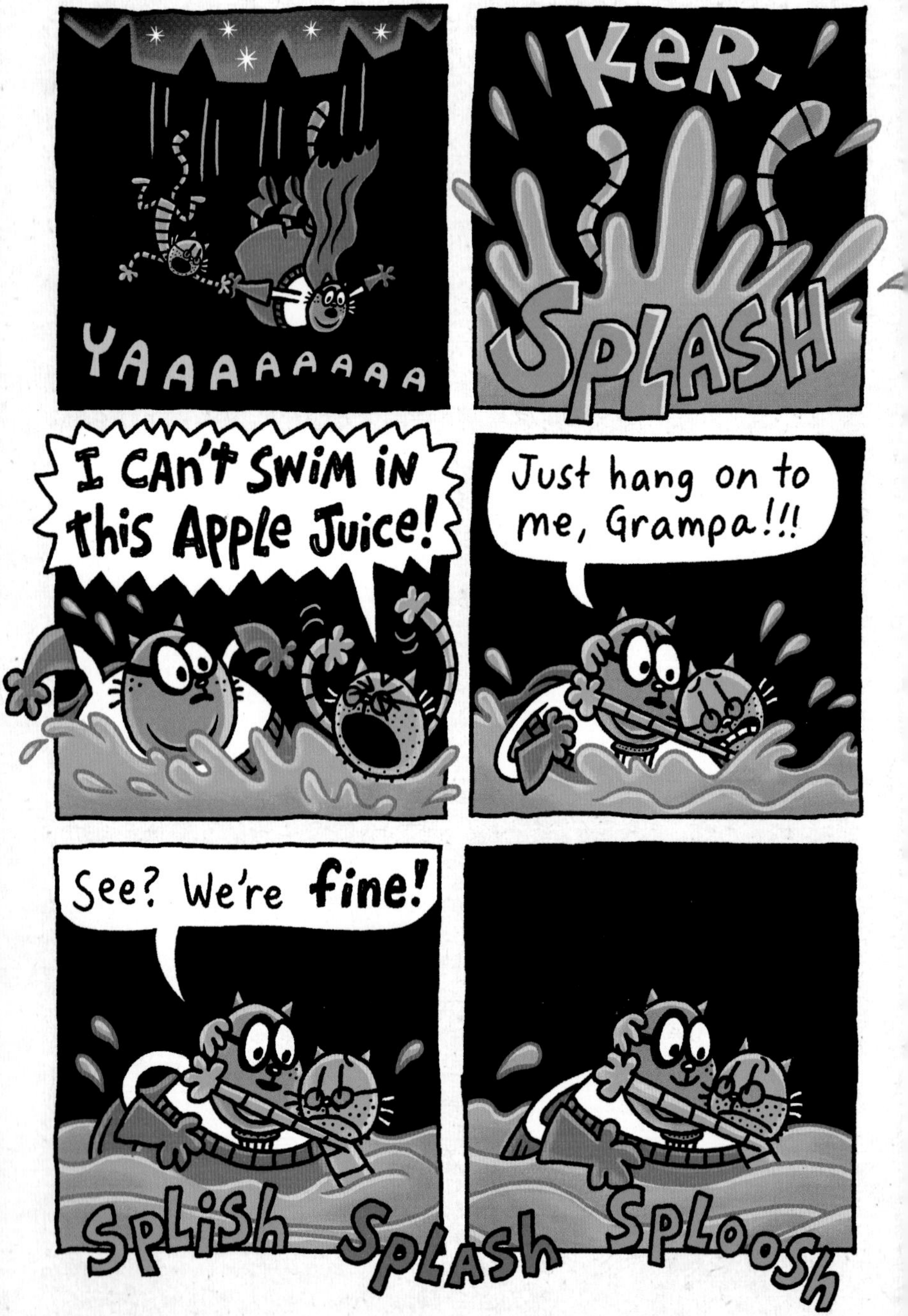
YAAAAAAAA
KER-SPLASH
I CAN'T SWIM IN this APPLE Juice!
Just hang on to me, Grampa!!!
See? We're fine!
SPLiSh SPLASh SPLoosh

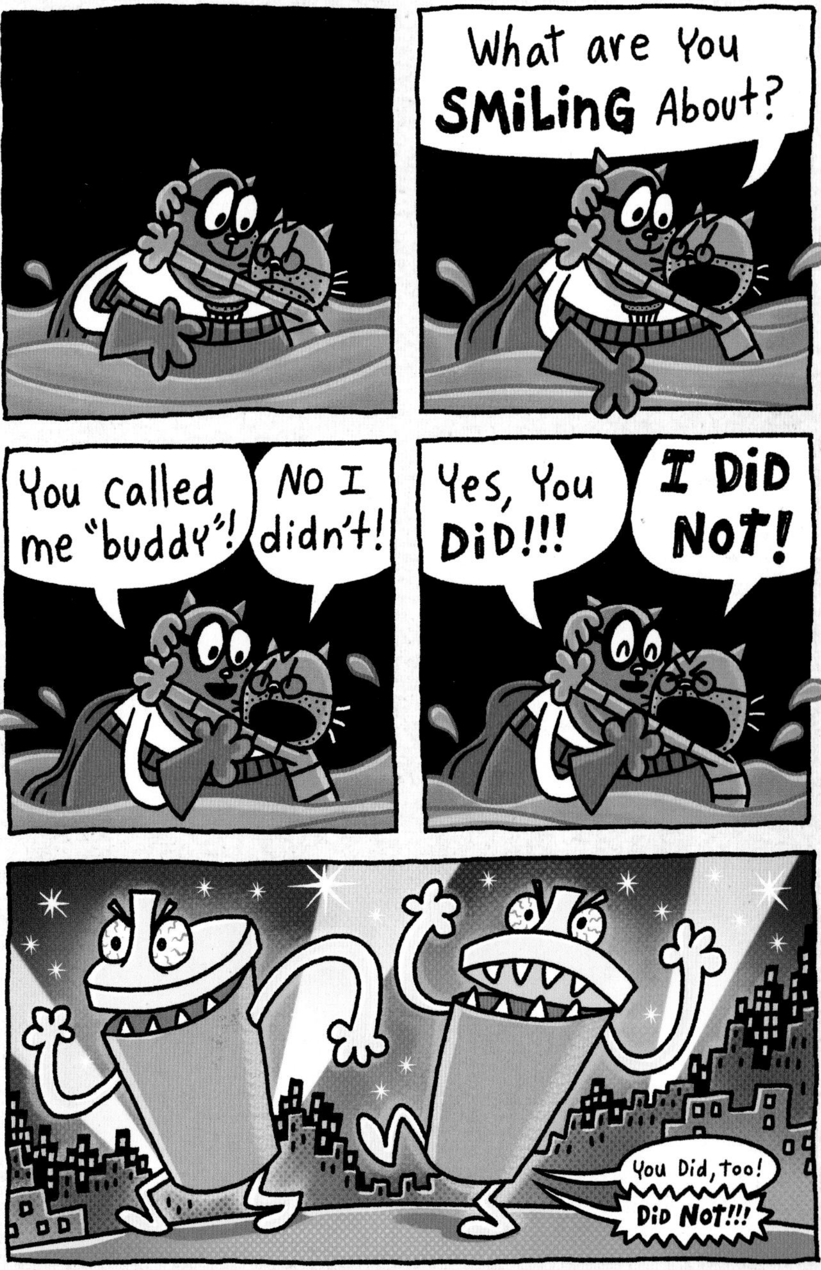
What are You SMILING About?
You called me "buddy"!
NO I didn't!
Yes, You DID!!!
I DID NOT!
You Did, too!
DID NOT!!!

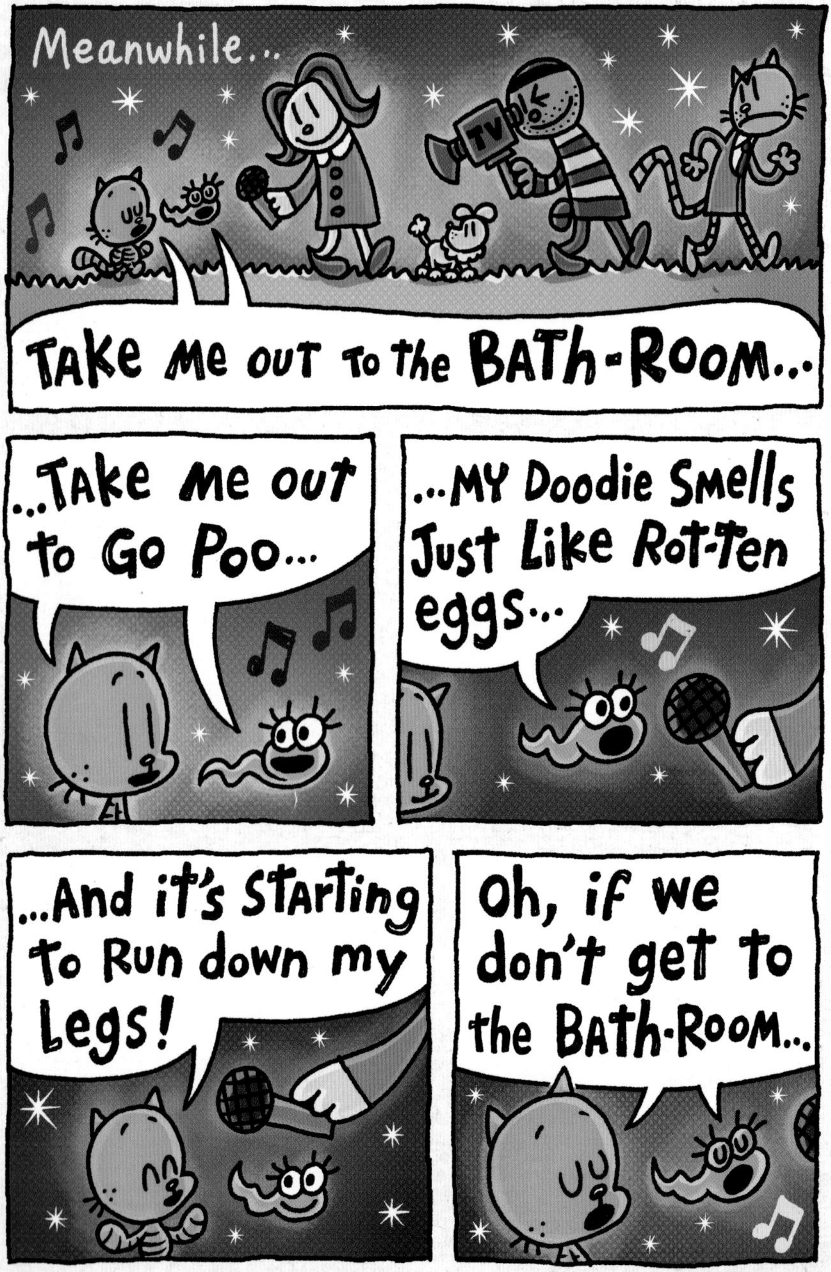

Meanwhile...
TAKE ME OUT TO THE BATH-ROOM...
...TAKE ME OUT TO GO POO...
...MY DOODIE SMELLS JUST LIKE ROT-TEN EGGS...
...AND IT'S STARTING TO RUN DOWN MY LEGS!
OH, IF WE DON'T GET TO THE BATH-ROOM...

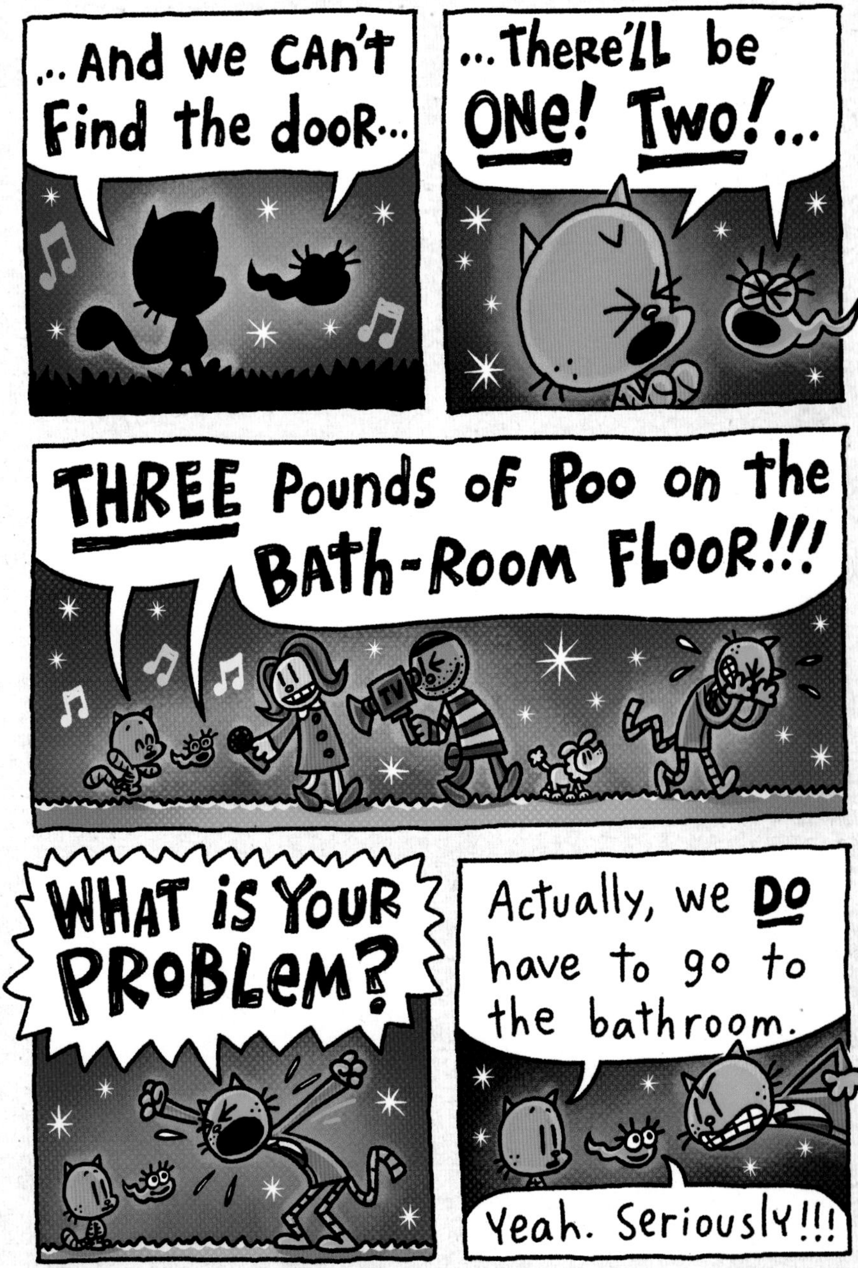
...And we CAN'T Find the door...
...There'll be ONE! TWO!...
THREE Pounds of Poo on the BATH-ROOM FLOOR!!!
WHAT IS YOUR PROBLEM?
Actually, we DO have to go to the bathroom.
Yeah. Seriously!!!

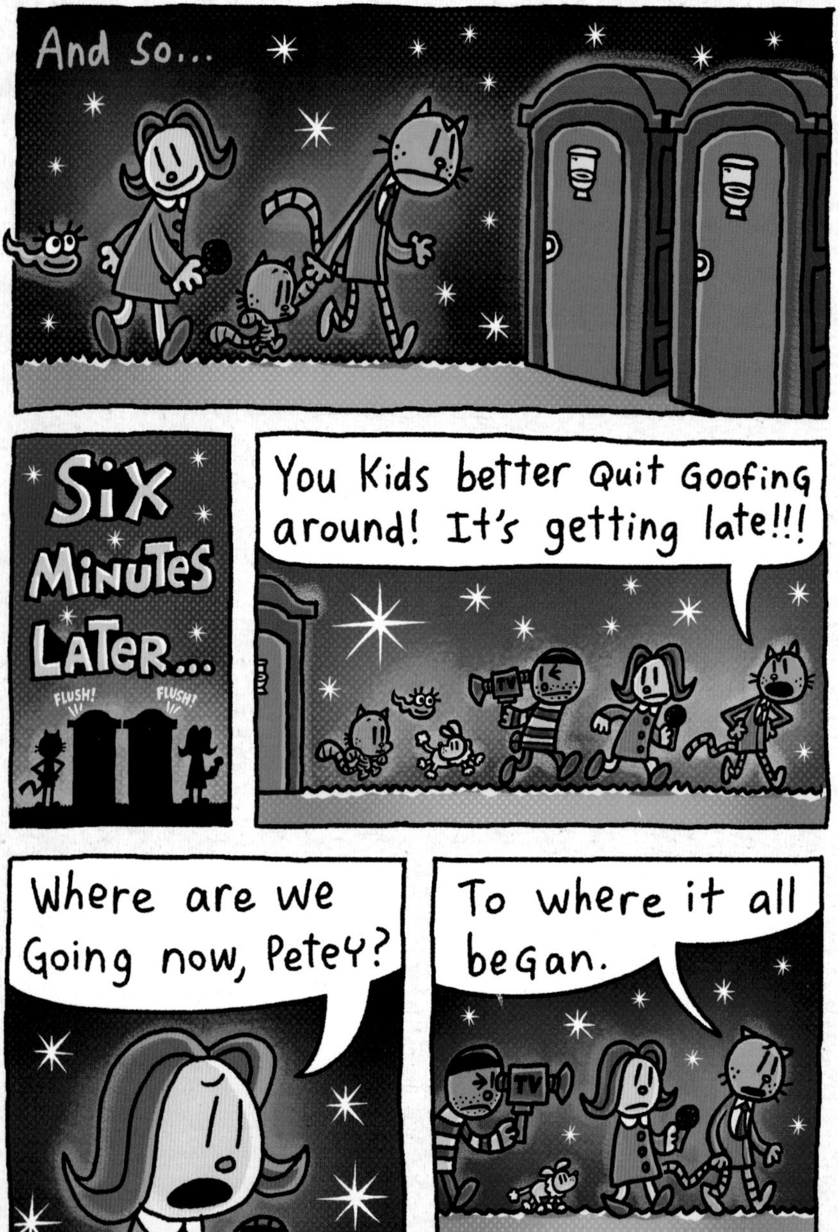
And so...
Six Minutes Later...
FLUSH!
FLUSH!
You Kids better Quit Goofing around! It's getting late!!!
TV
Where are we Going now, Petey?
To where it all beGan.
TV

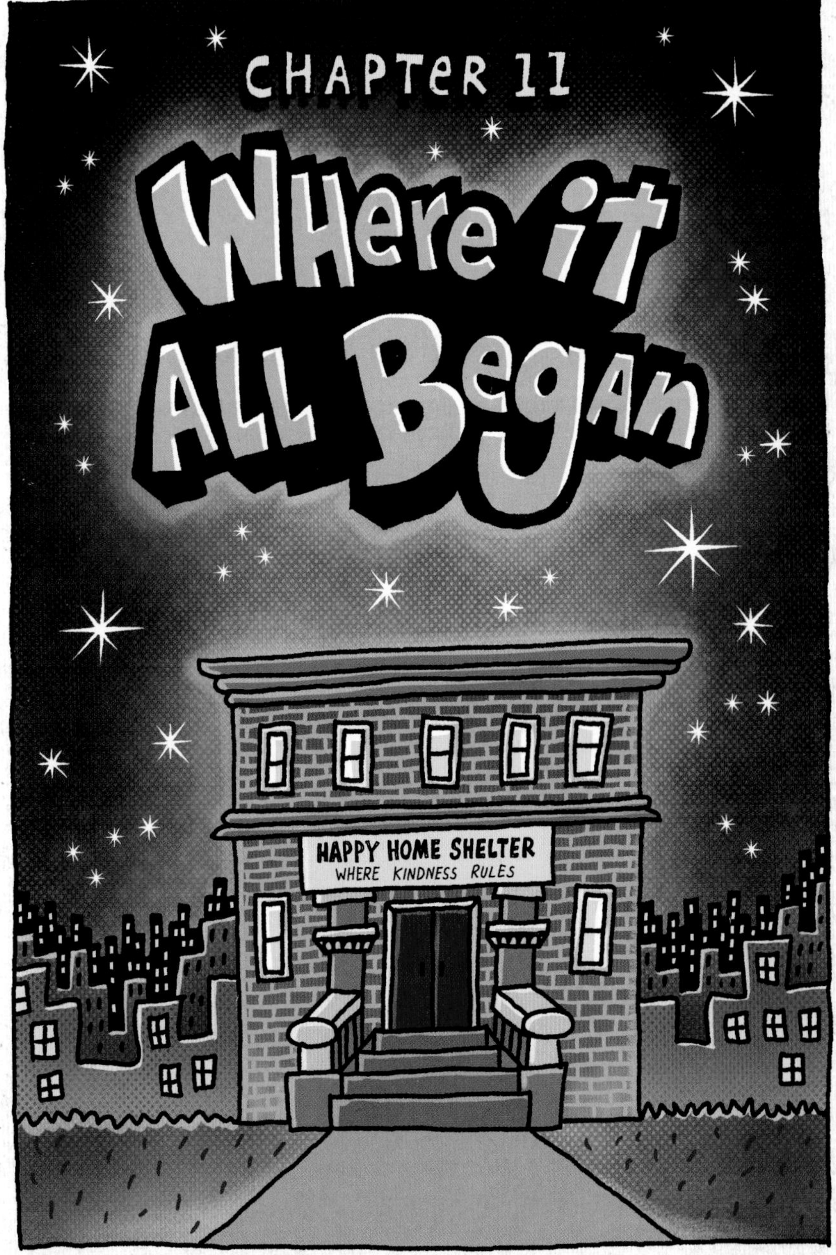
CHAPTER 11
Where it All Began
HAPPY HOME SHELTER
WHERE KINDNESS RULES

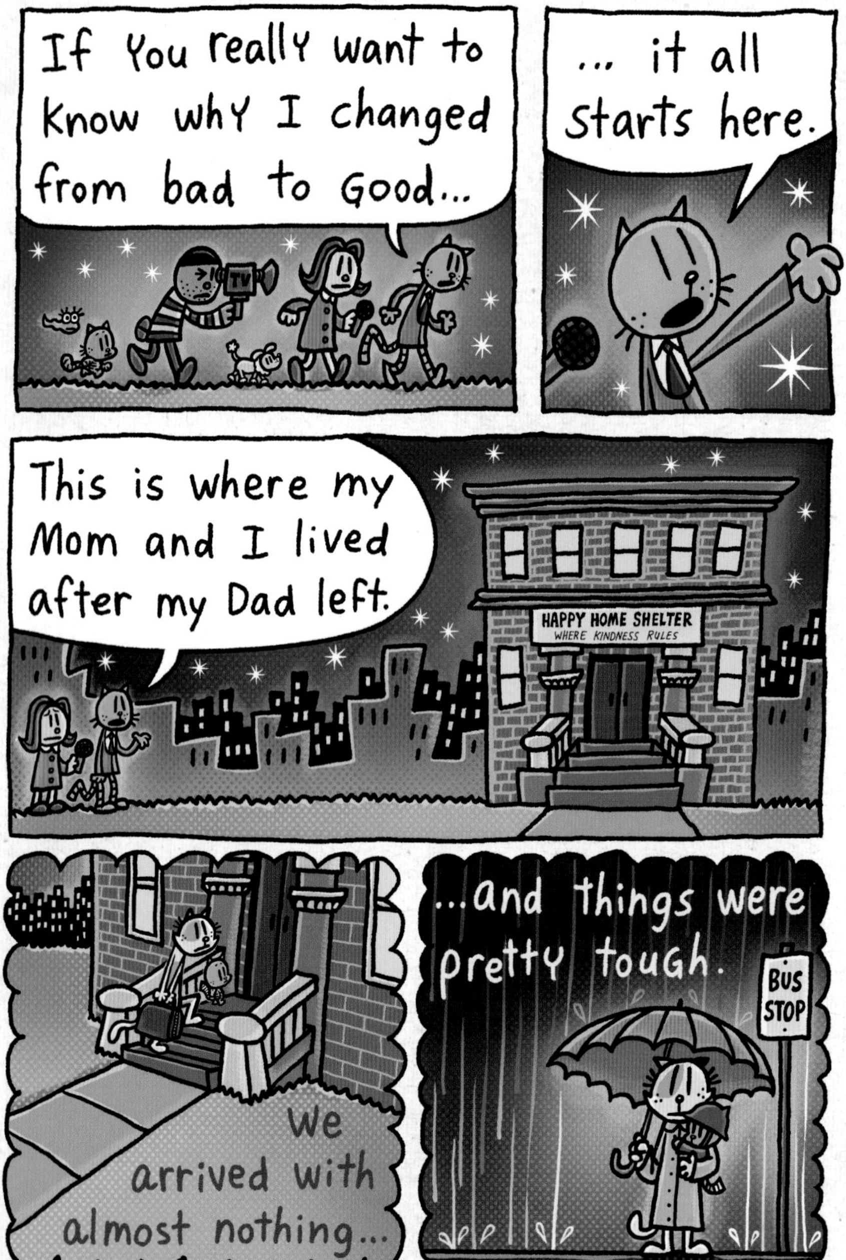
If You really want to Know why I changed from bad to Good...
TV
... it all starts here.
This is where my Mom and I lived after my Dad left.
HAPPY HOME SHELTER
WHERE KINDNESS RULES
We arrived with almost nothing...
...and things were pretty tough.
BUS STOP

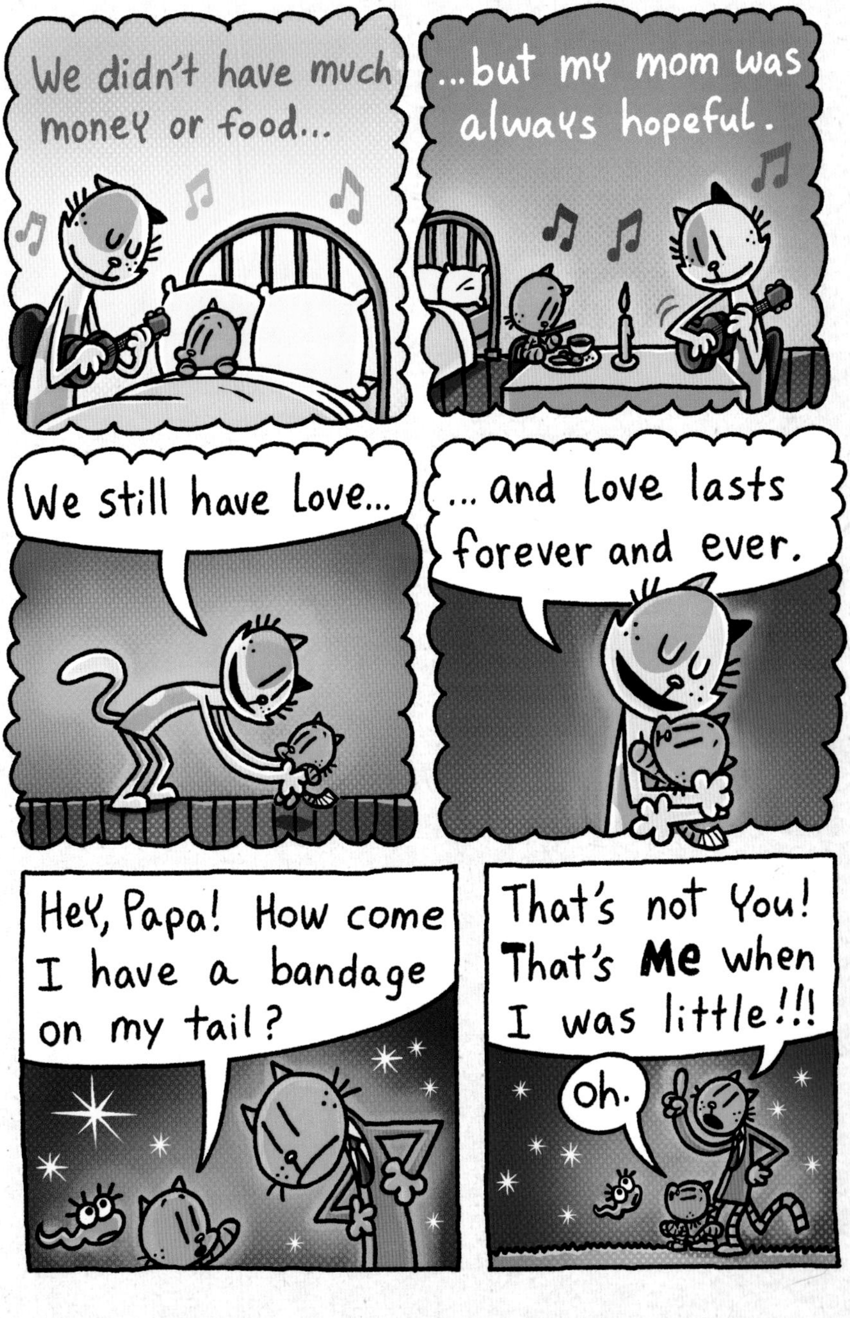
We didn't have much money or food...
...but my mom was always hopeful.
We still have love...
...and love lasts forever and ever.
Hey, Papa! How come I have a bandage on my tail?
That's not You! That's **Me** when I was little!!!
Oh.

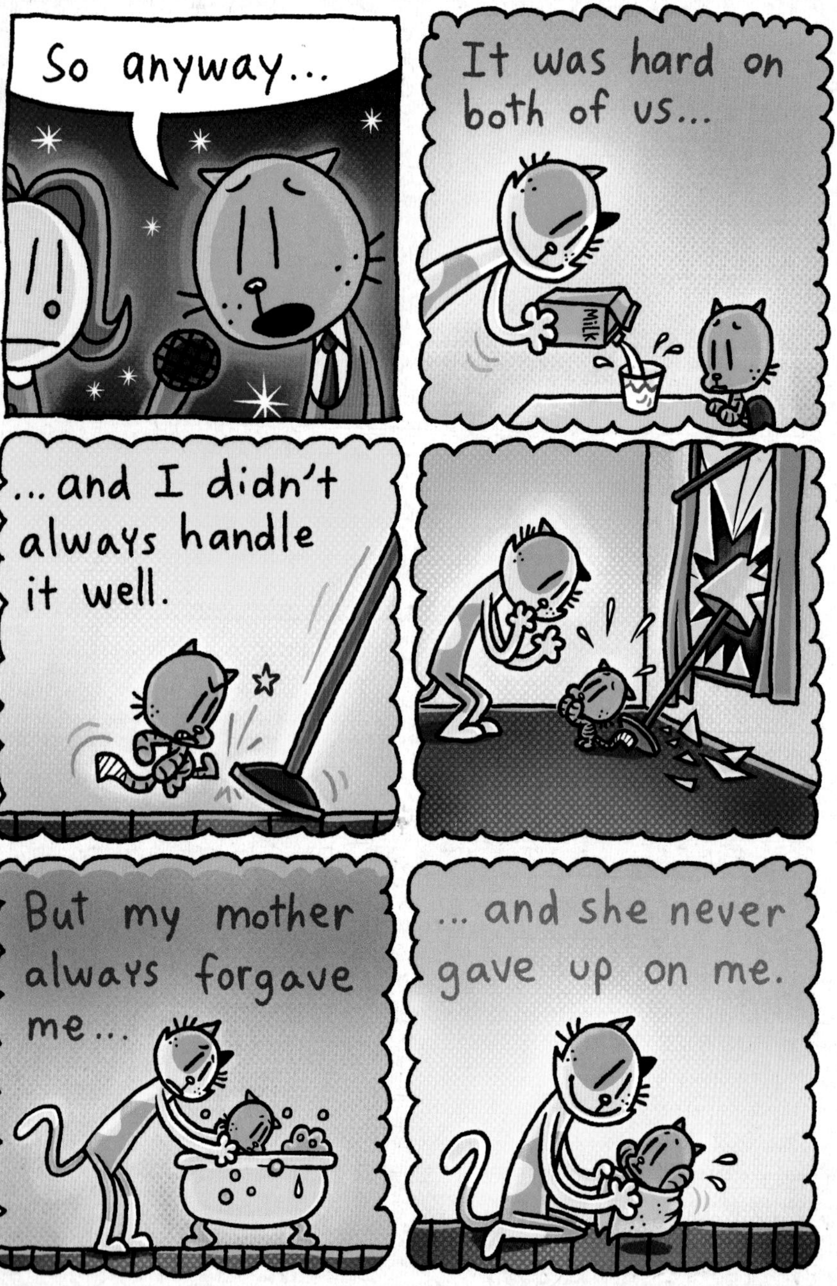
So anyway...
It was hard on both of us...
MILK
...and I didn't always handle it well.
But my mother always forgave me...
...and she never gave up on me.

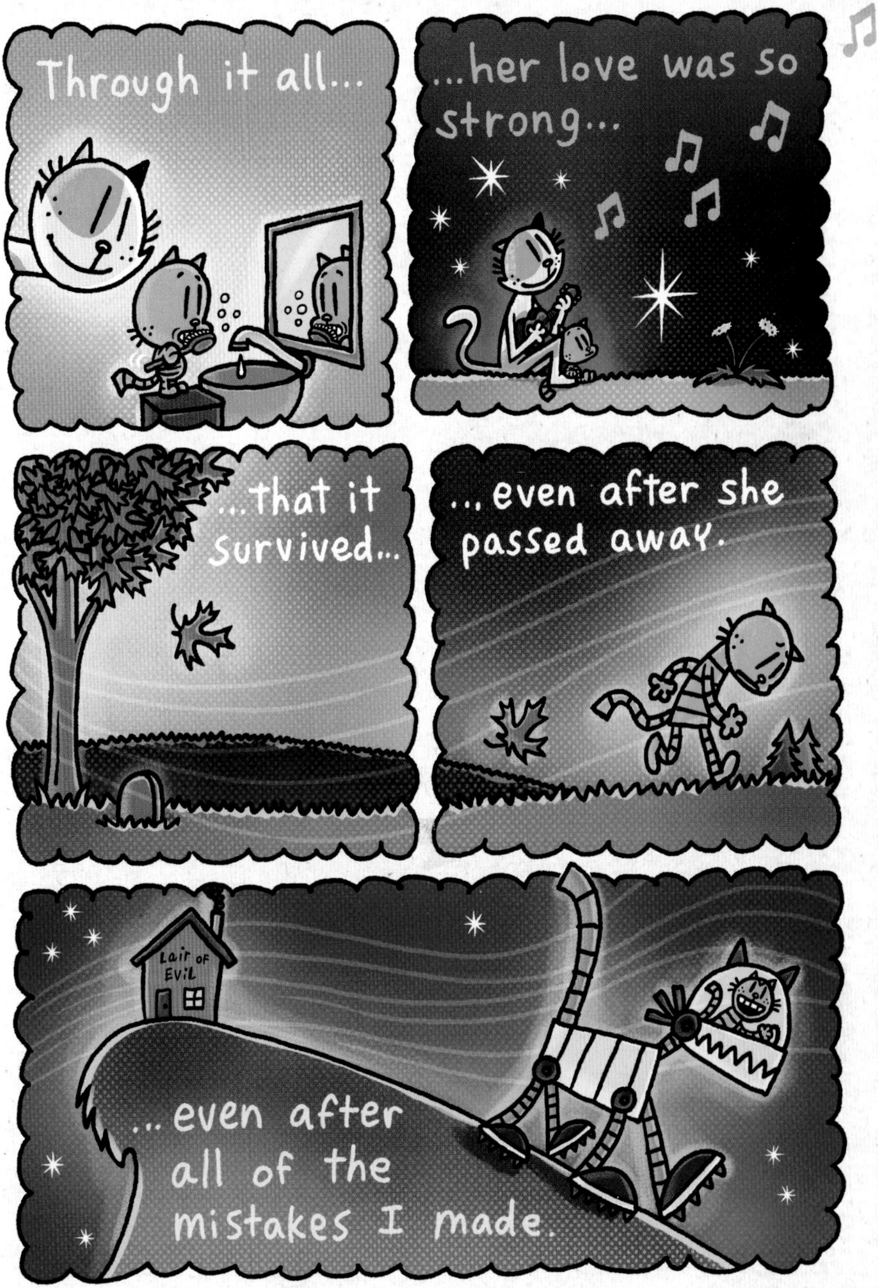
Through it all...
...her love was so strong...
...that it survived...
...even after she passed away.
Lair of Evil
...even after all of the mistakes I made.

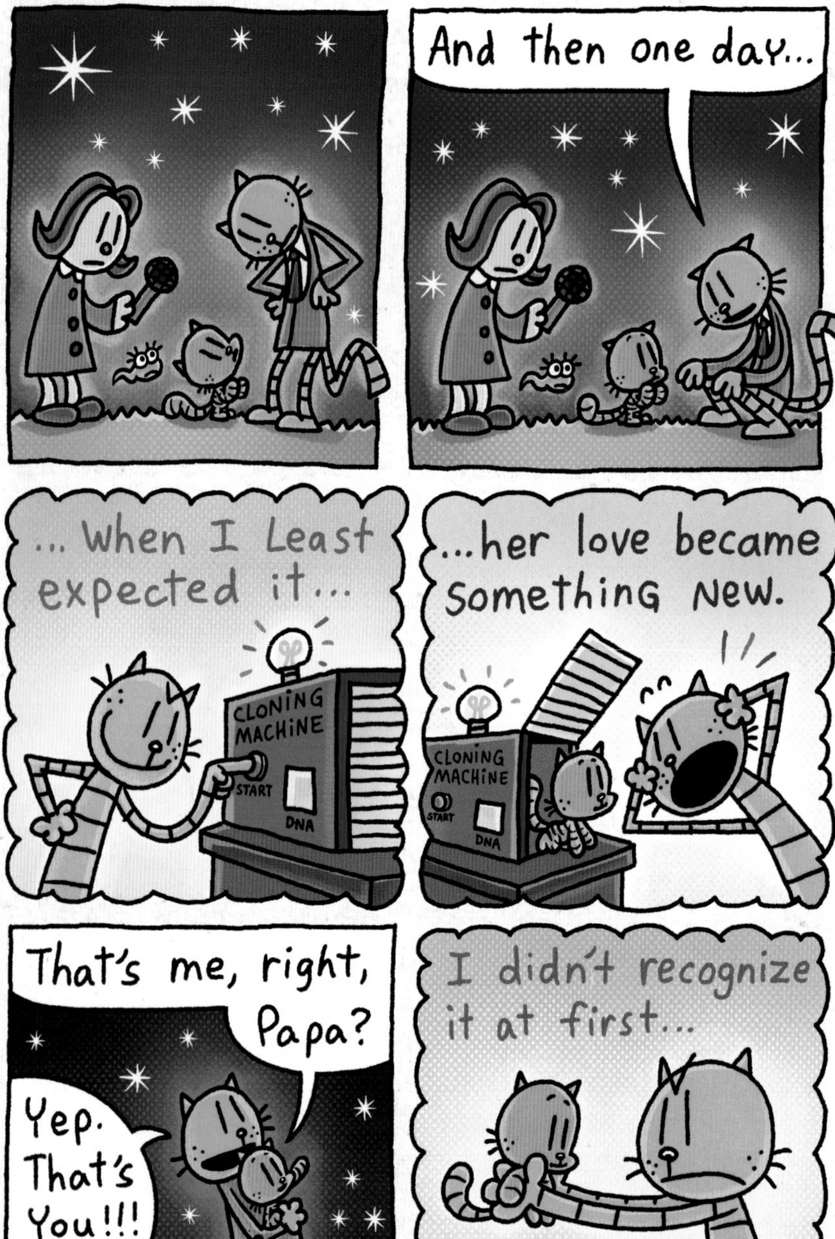
And then one day...
... When I Least expected it...
CLONING MACHINE
START
DNA
...her love became Something New.
CLONING MACHINE
START
DNA
That's me, right, Papa?
Yep. That's You!!!
I didn't recognize it at first...

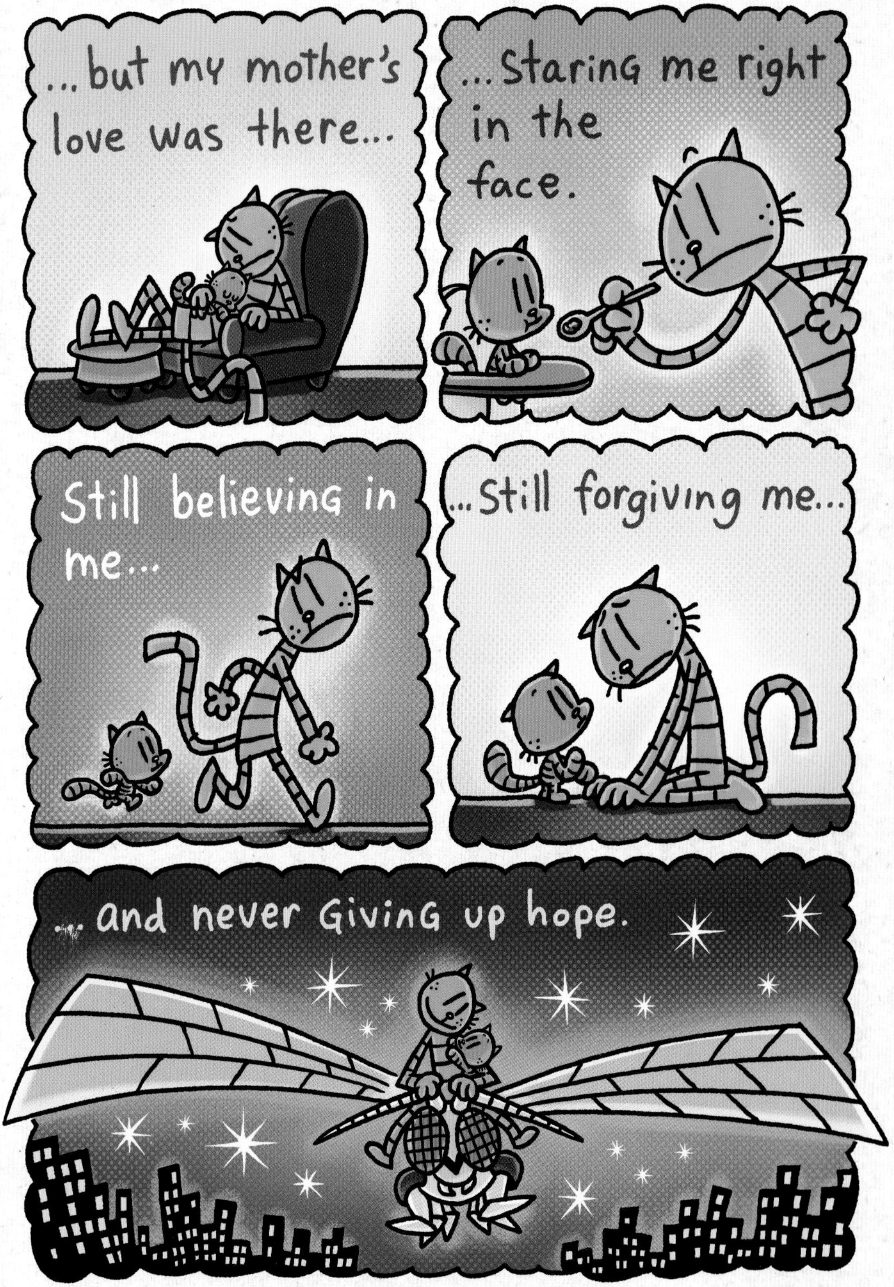
...but my mother's love was there...
...Staring me right in the face.
Still believing in me...
...Still forgiving me...
...and never giving up hope.

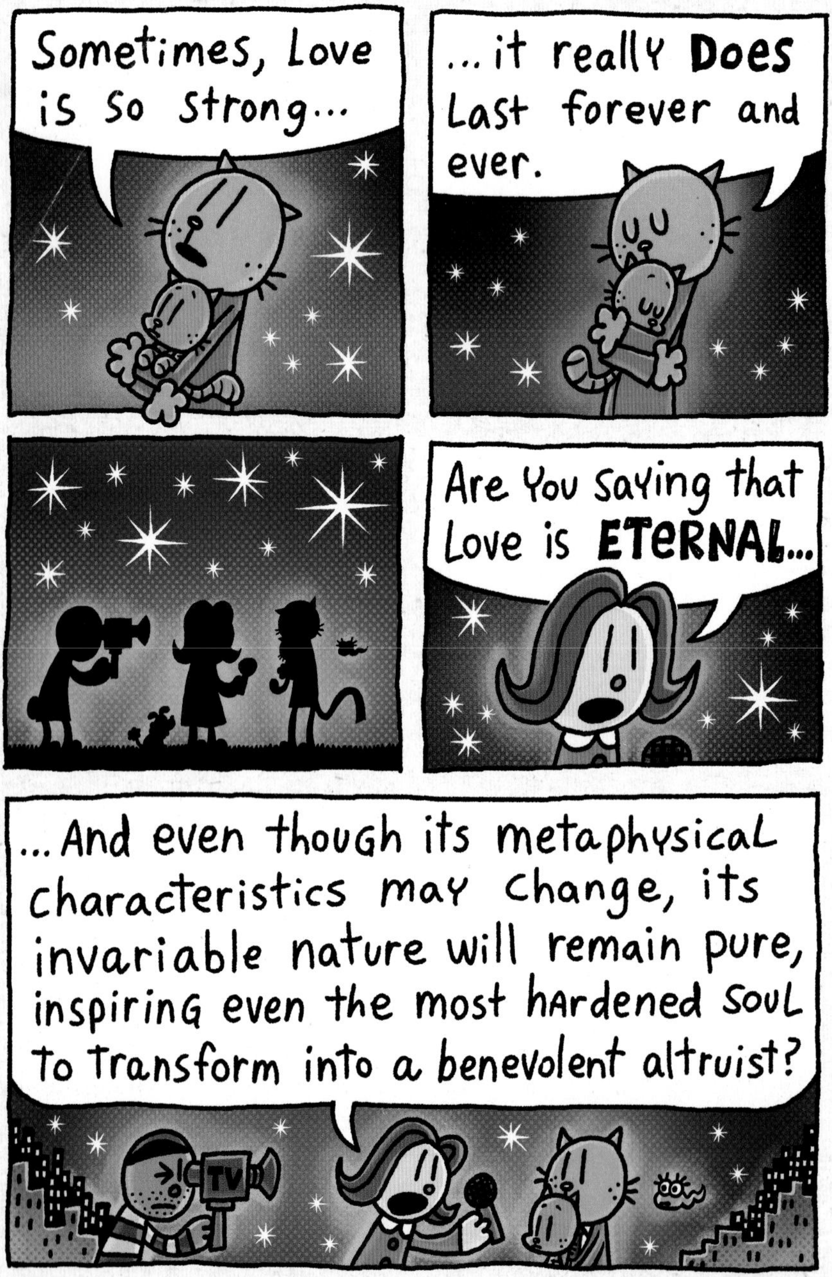
Sometimes, Love is So strong...
...it really DOES Last forever and ever.
Are You saying that Love is ETERNAL...
...And even though its metaphysical characteristics may change, its invariable nature will remain pure, inspiring even the most hardened soul to transform into a benevolent altruist?
TV

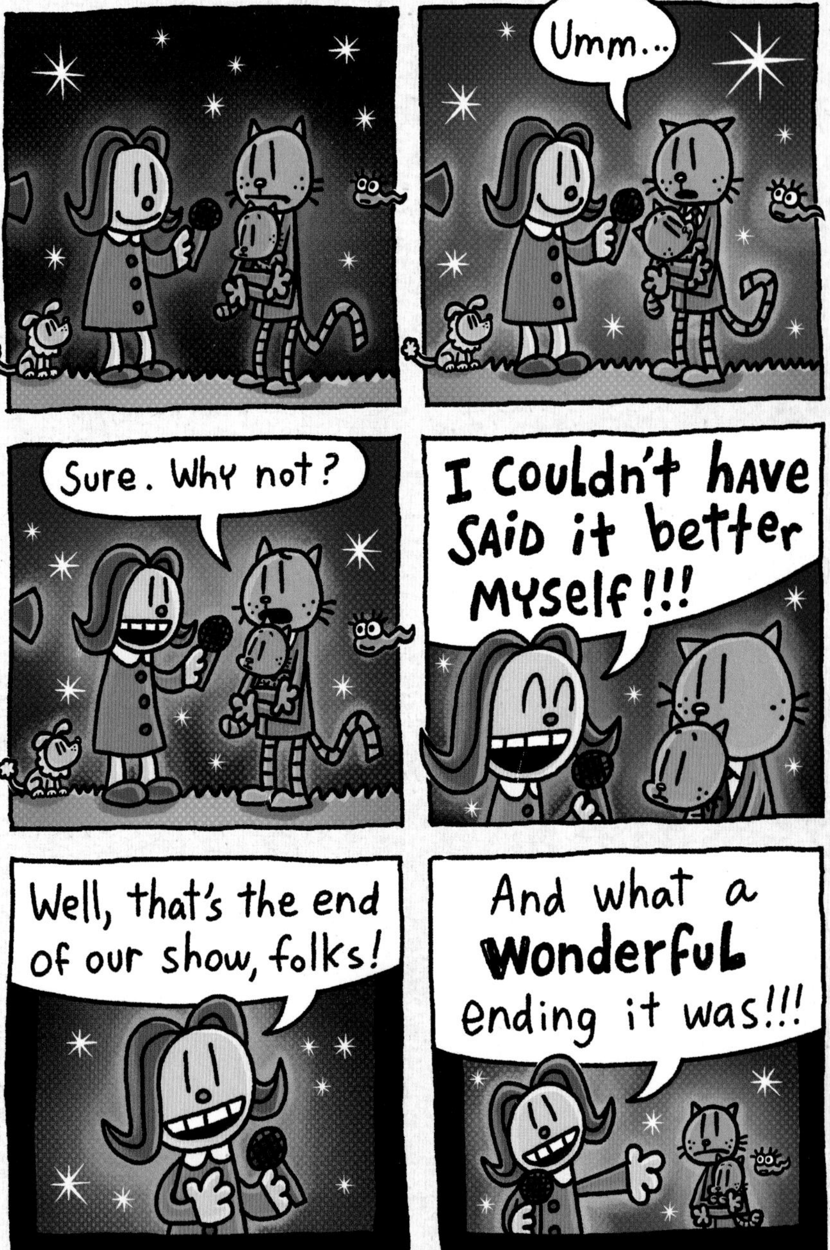
Umm...
Sure. Why not?
I couldn't have SAID it better MYSELF!!!
Well, that's the end of our show, folks!
And what a wonderful ending it was!!!

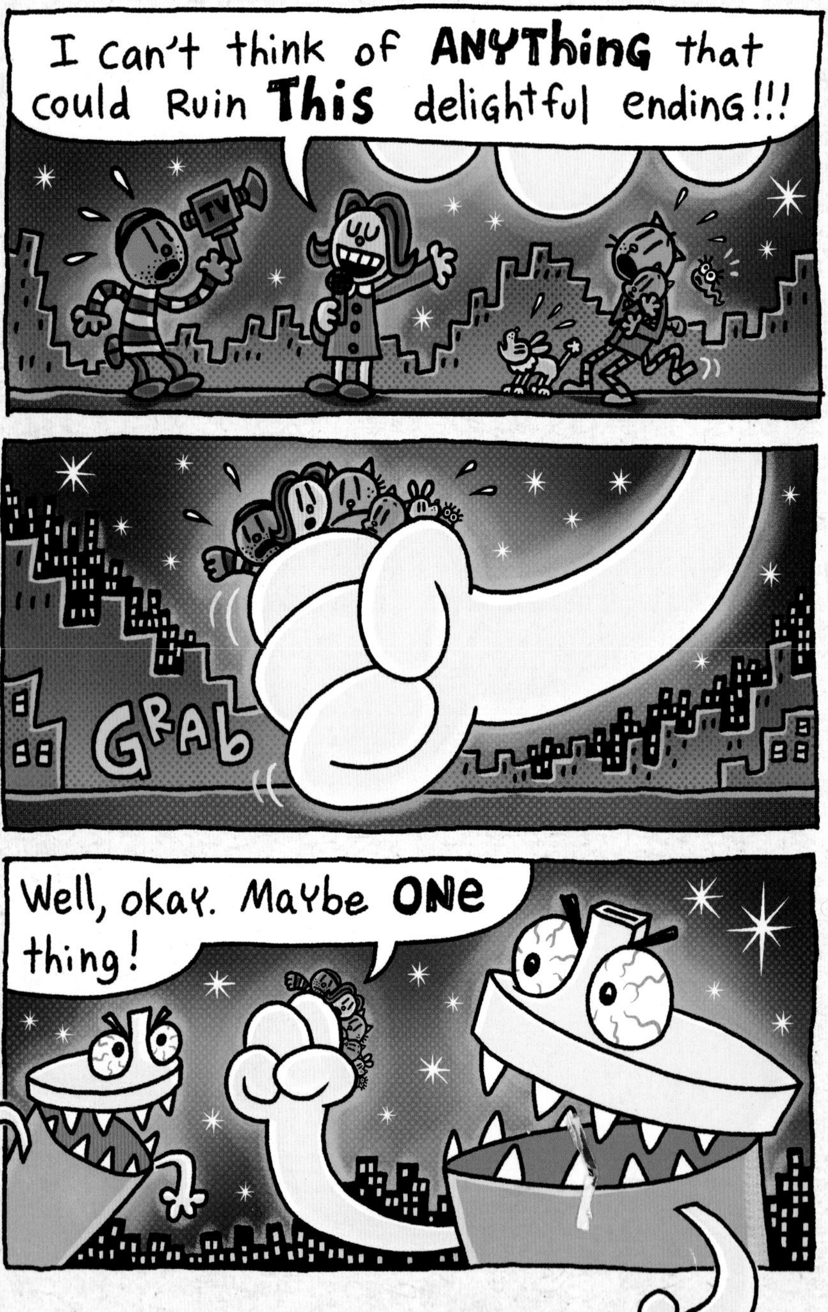
I can't think of ANYThing that could Ruin This delightful ending!!!
TV
GRAb
Well, okay. Maybe ONE thing!

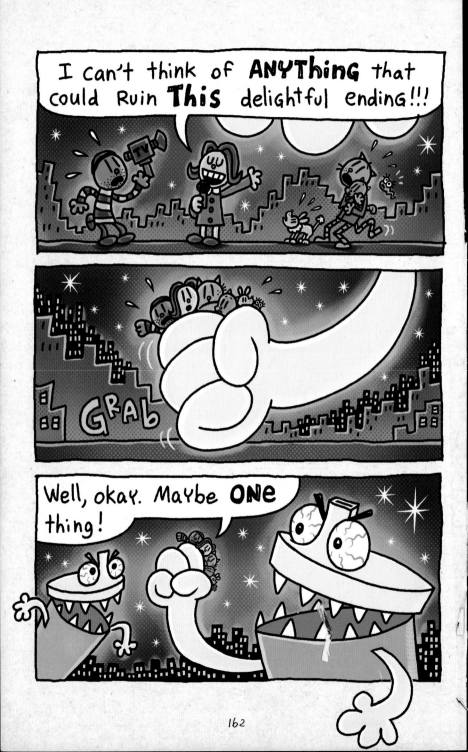

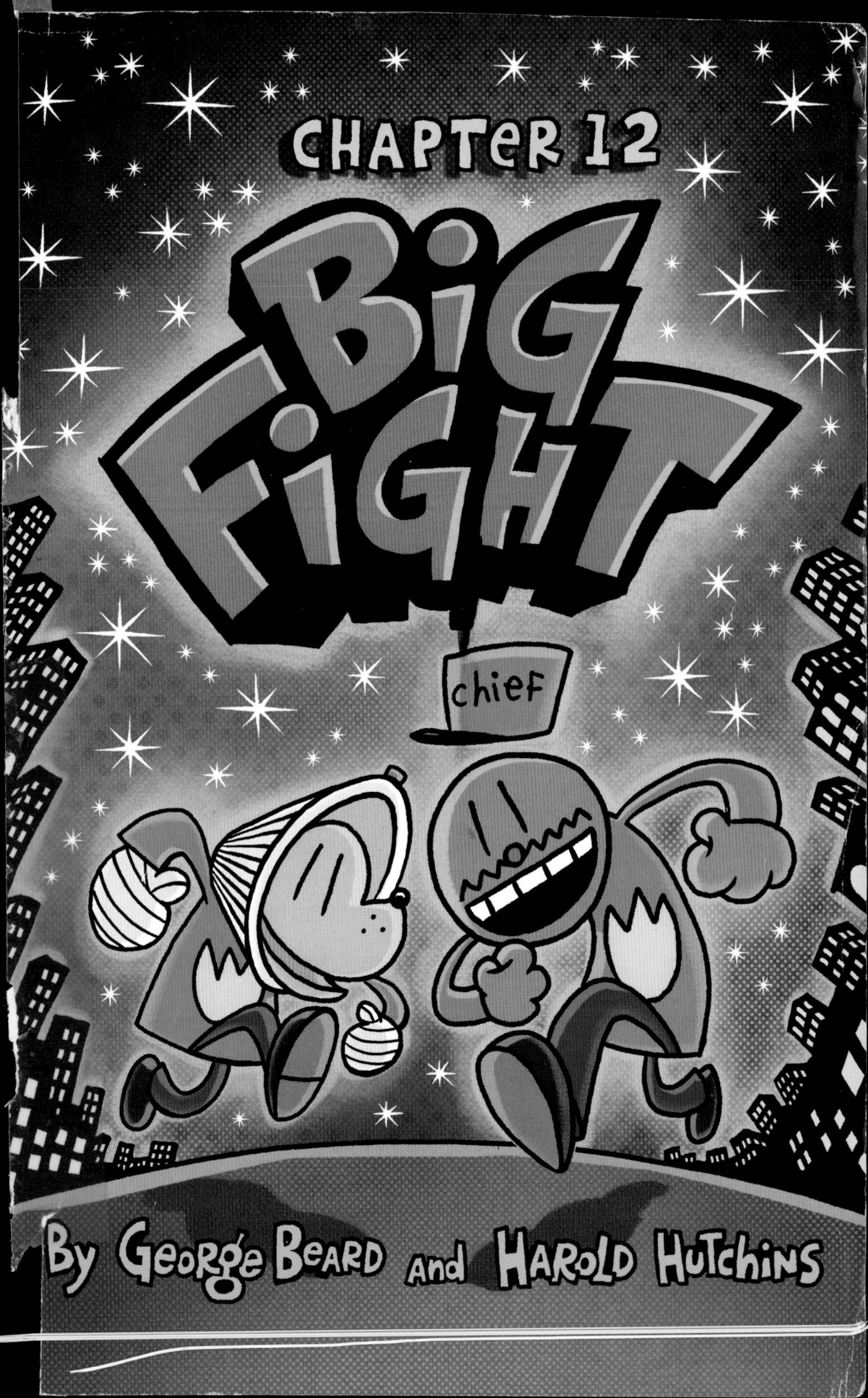
CHAPTER 12
BIG FIGHT
chief
By George Beard and Harold Hutchins

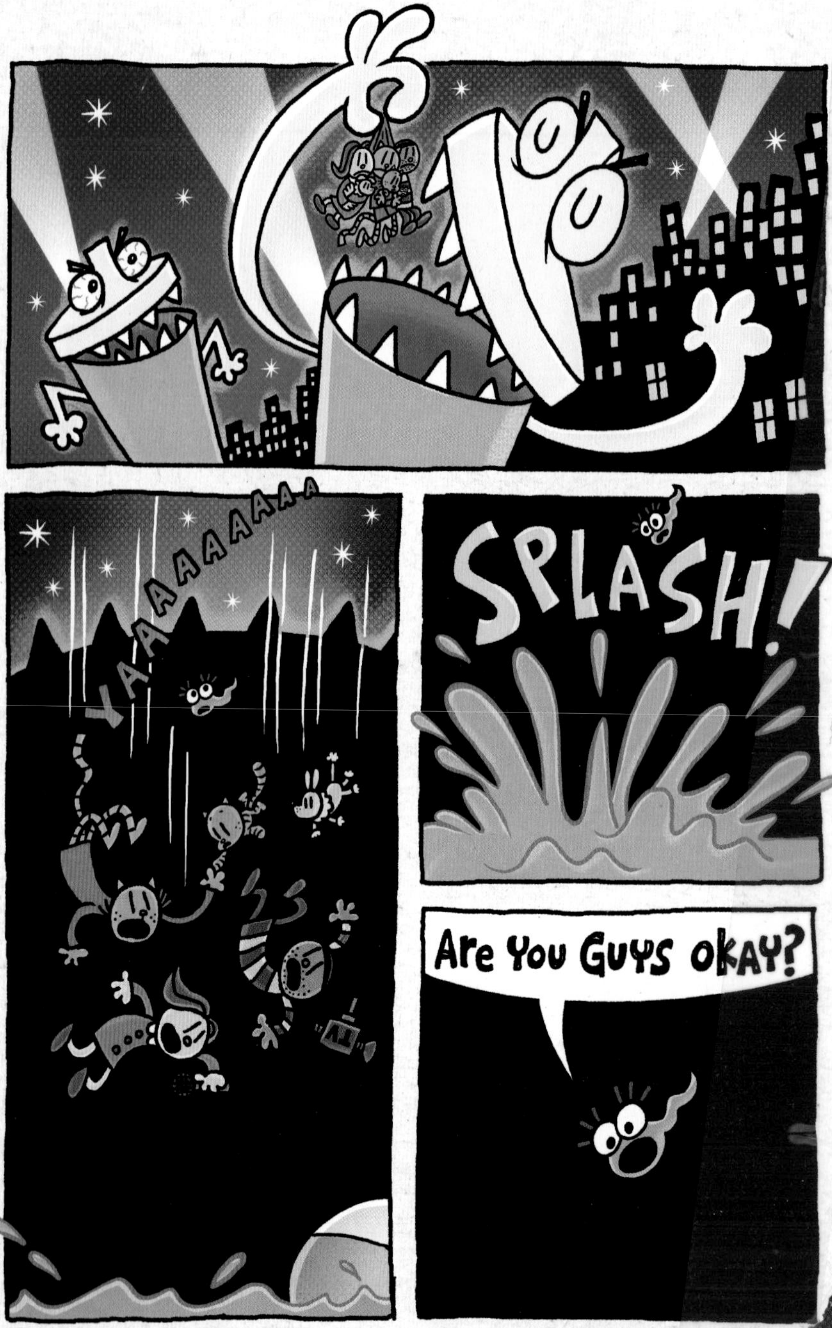
YAAAAAAAAAAA
SPLASH!
Are You Guys okay?

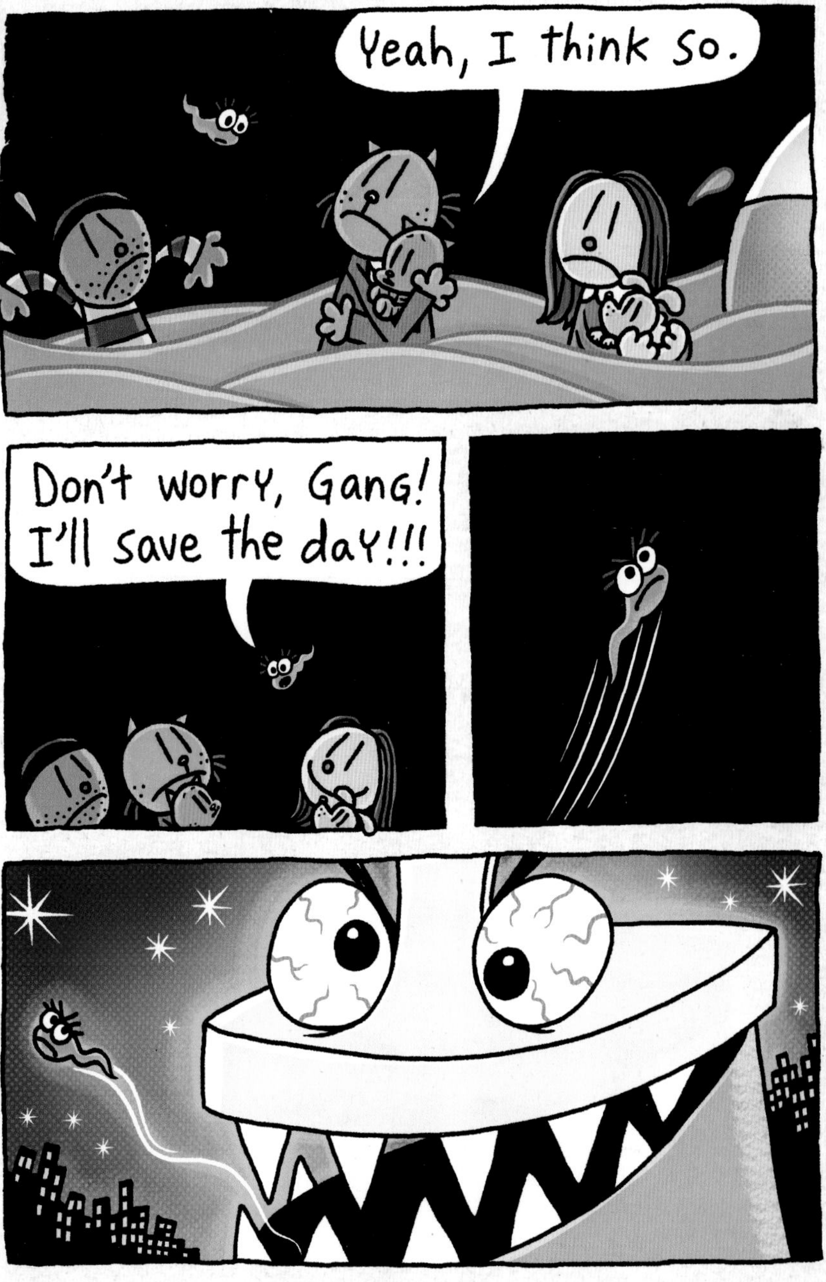
Yeah, I think so.
Don't worry, Gang! I'll save the day!!!

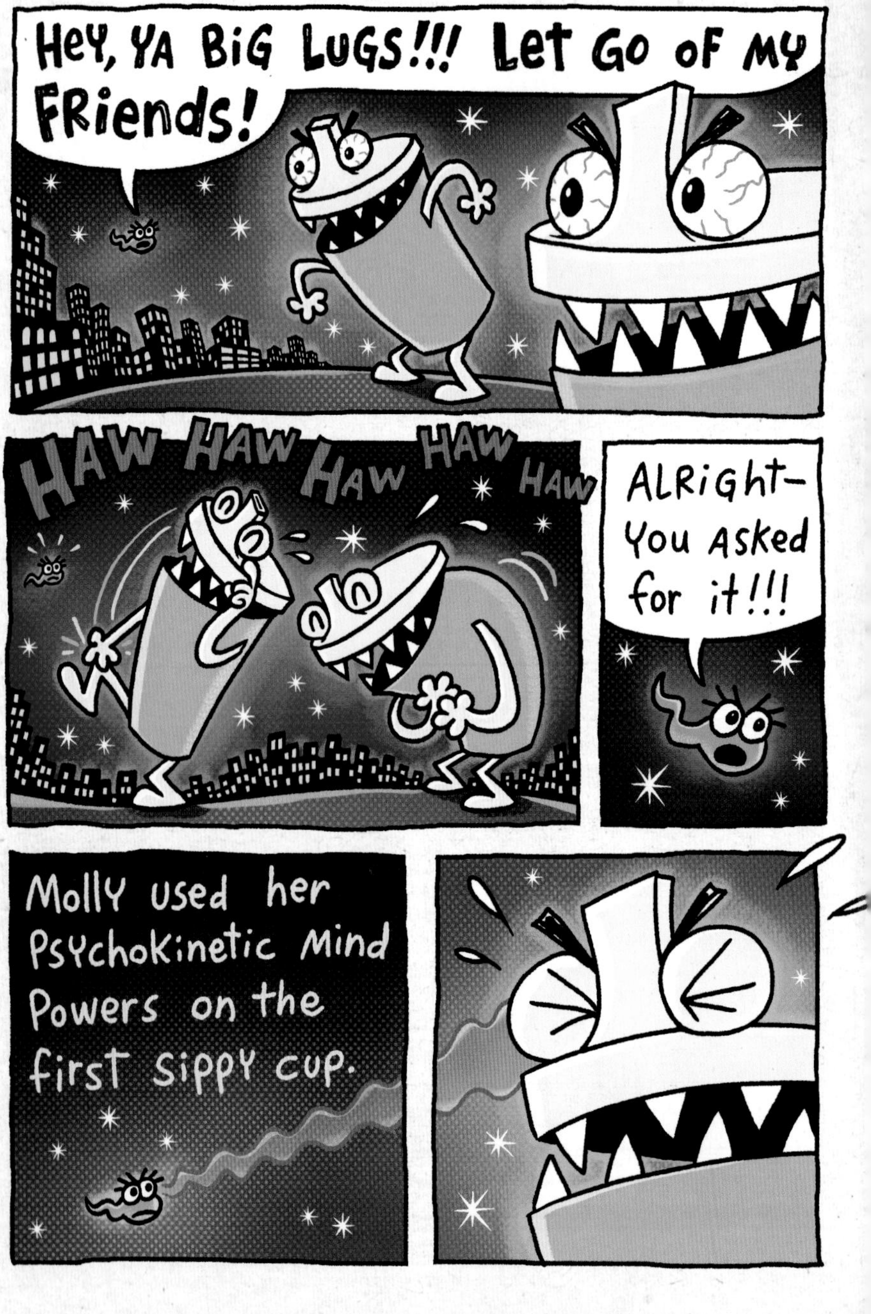
HEY, YA BIG LUGS!!! LET GO OF MY FRIENDS!
HAW HAW HAW HAW HAW
ALRIGHT– YOU ASKED FOR IT!!!
Molly used her Psychokinetic Mind Powers on the first sippy cup.

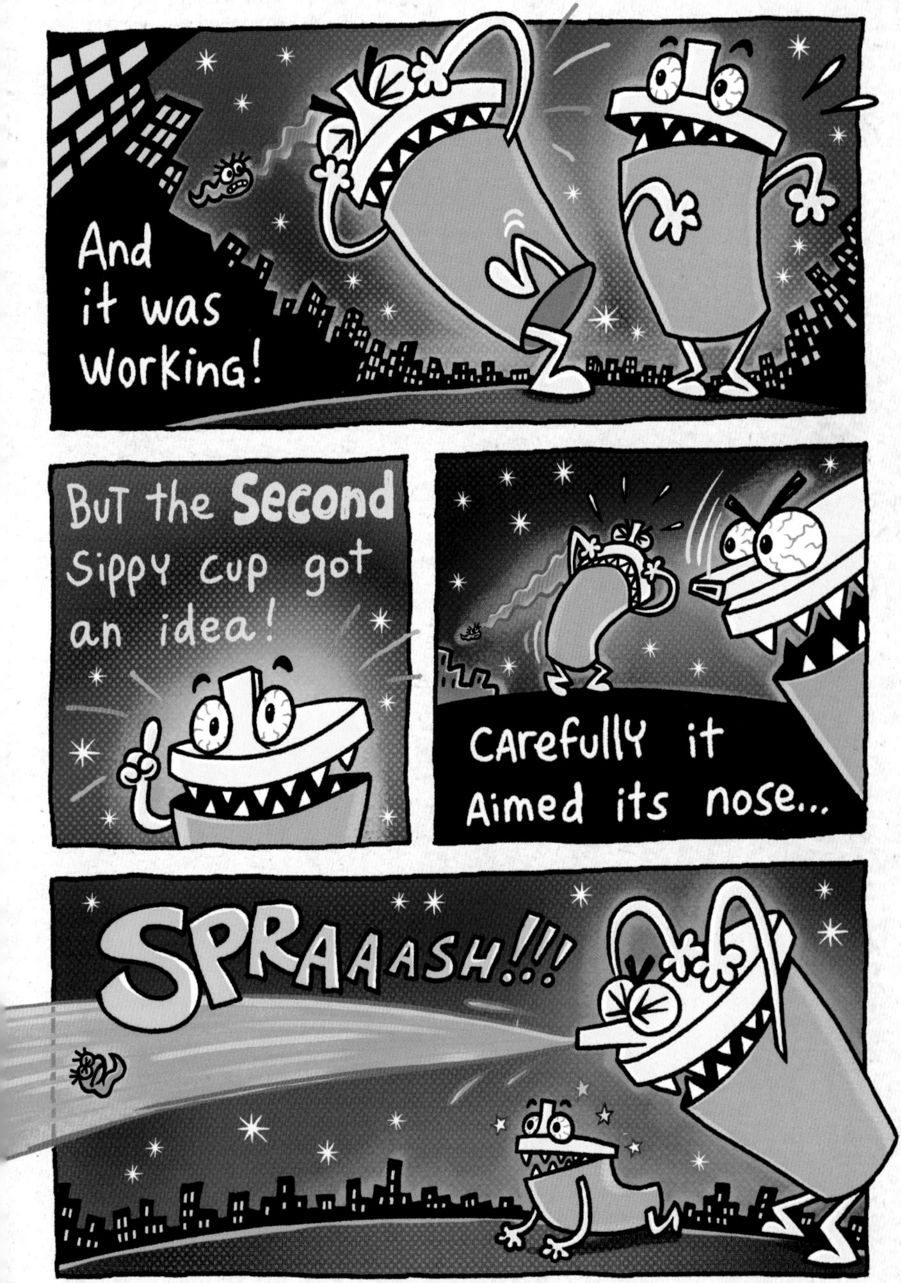
And it was working!
But the second sippy cup got an idea!
Carefully it aimed its nose...
SPRAAASH!!!

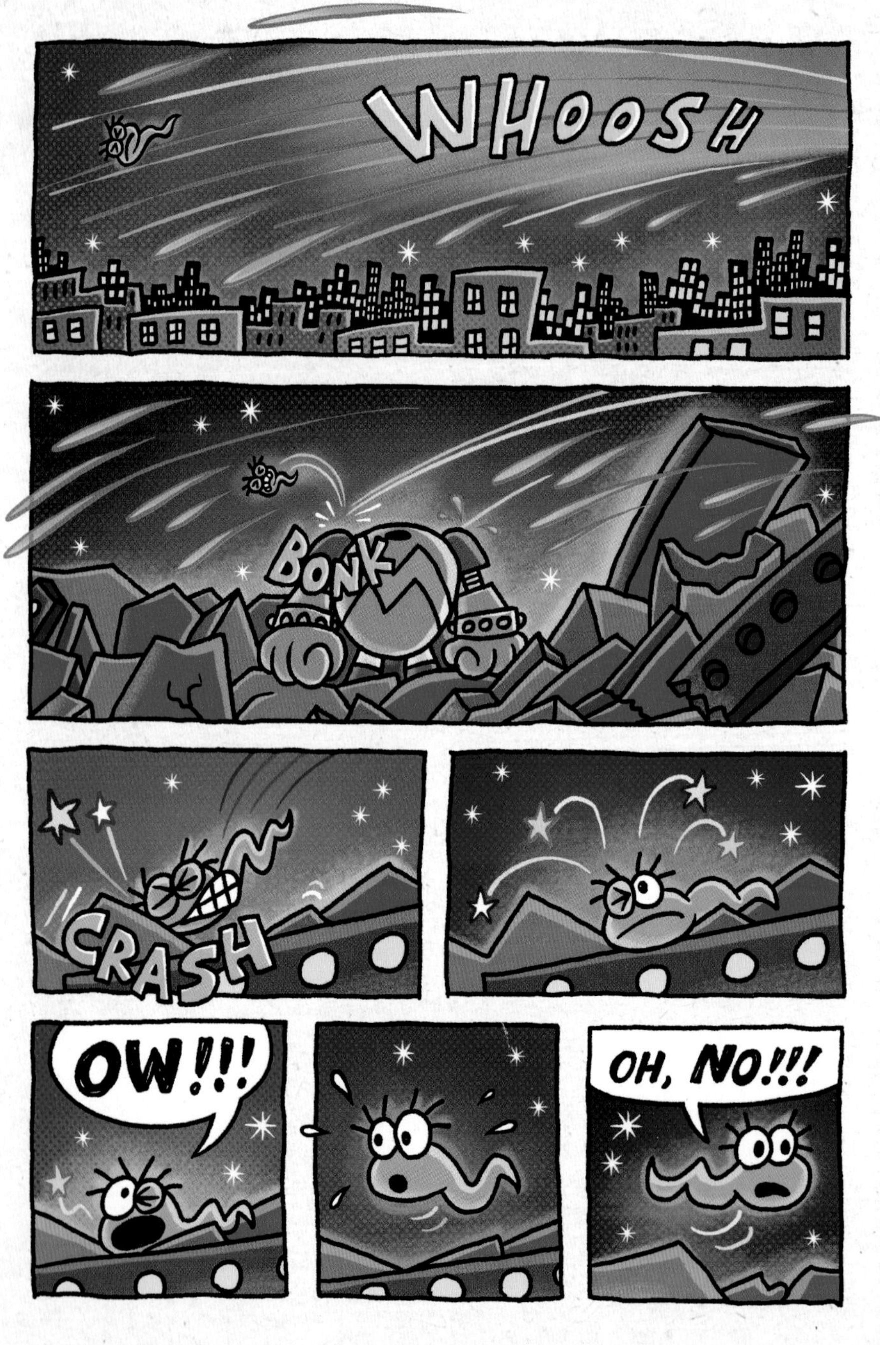
WHOOSH
BONK
CRASH
OW!!!
OH, NO!!!

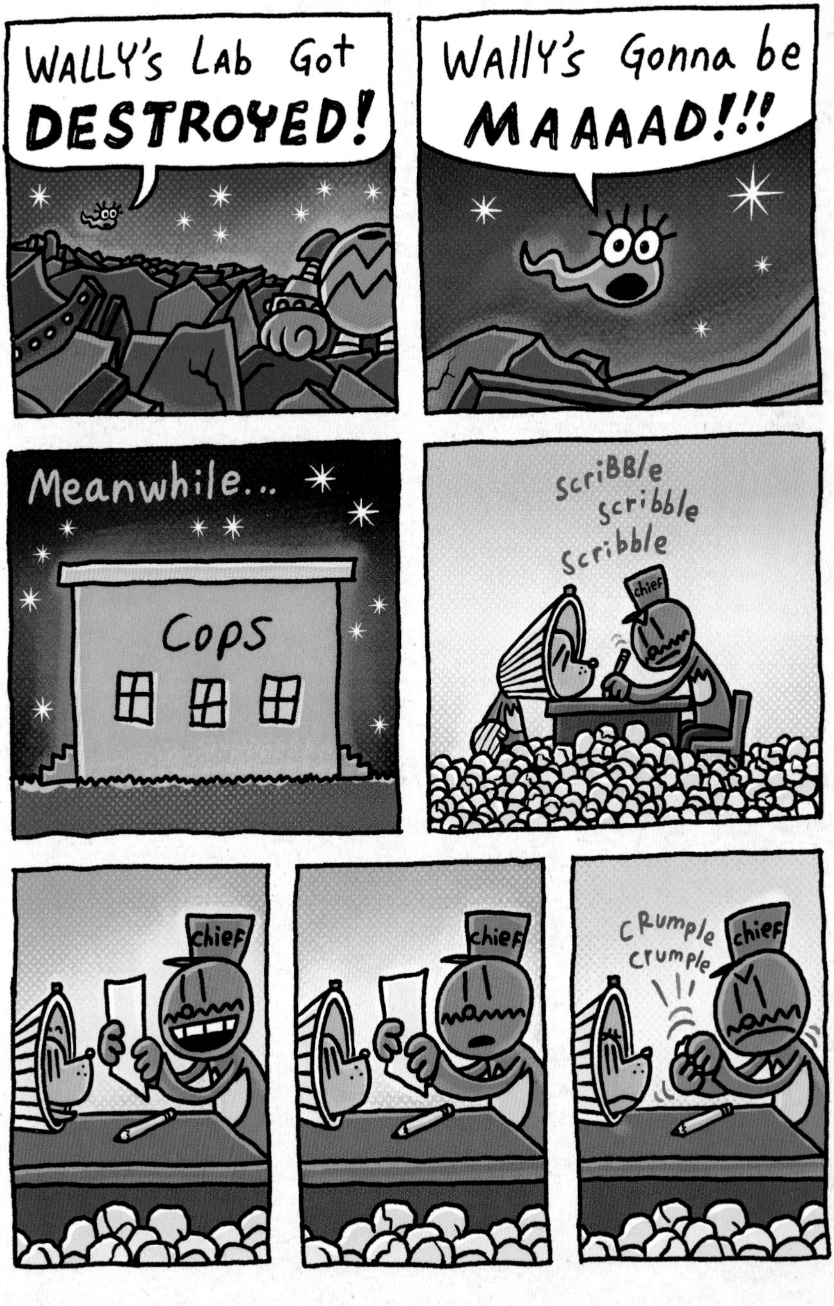
WALLY's Lab Got DESTROYED!
WALLY's Gonna be MAAAAD!!!
Meanwhile...
Cops
chief
Scribble scribble scribble
chief
chief
chief
CRumple crumple

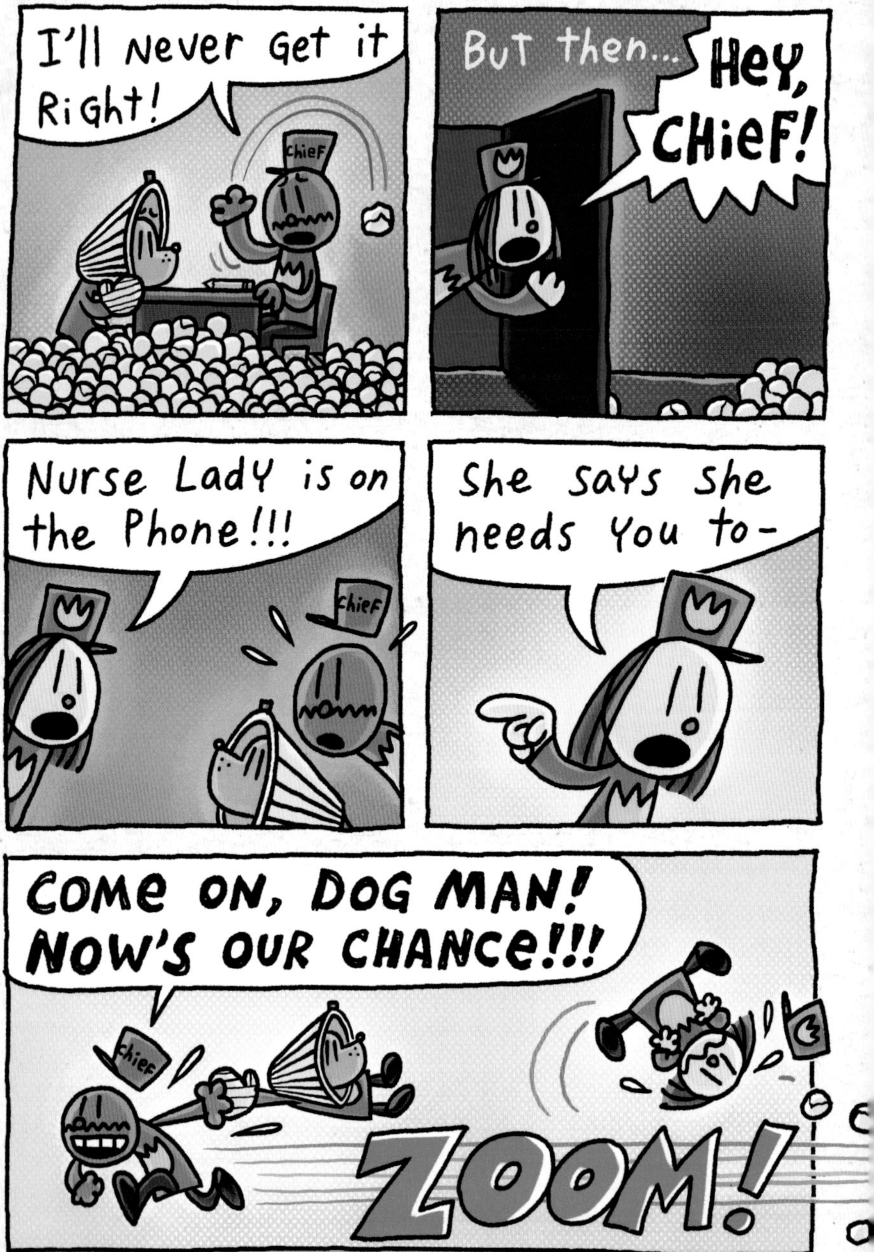
I'll Never Get it Right!
But then...
Hey, Chief!
Chief
Nurse Lady is on the Phone!!!
Chief
She says she needs You to-
COME ON, DOG MAN! NOW'S OUR CHANCE!!!
Chief
ZOOM!

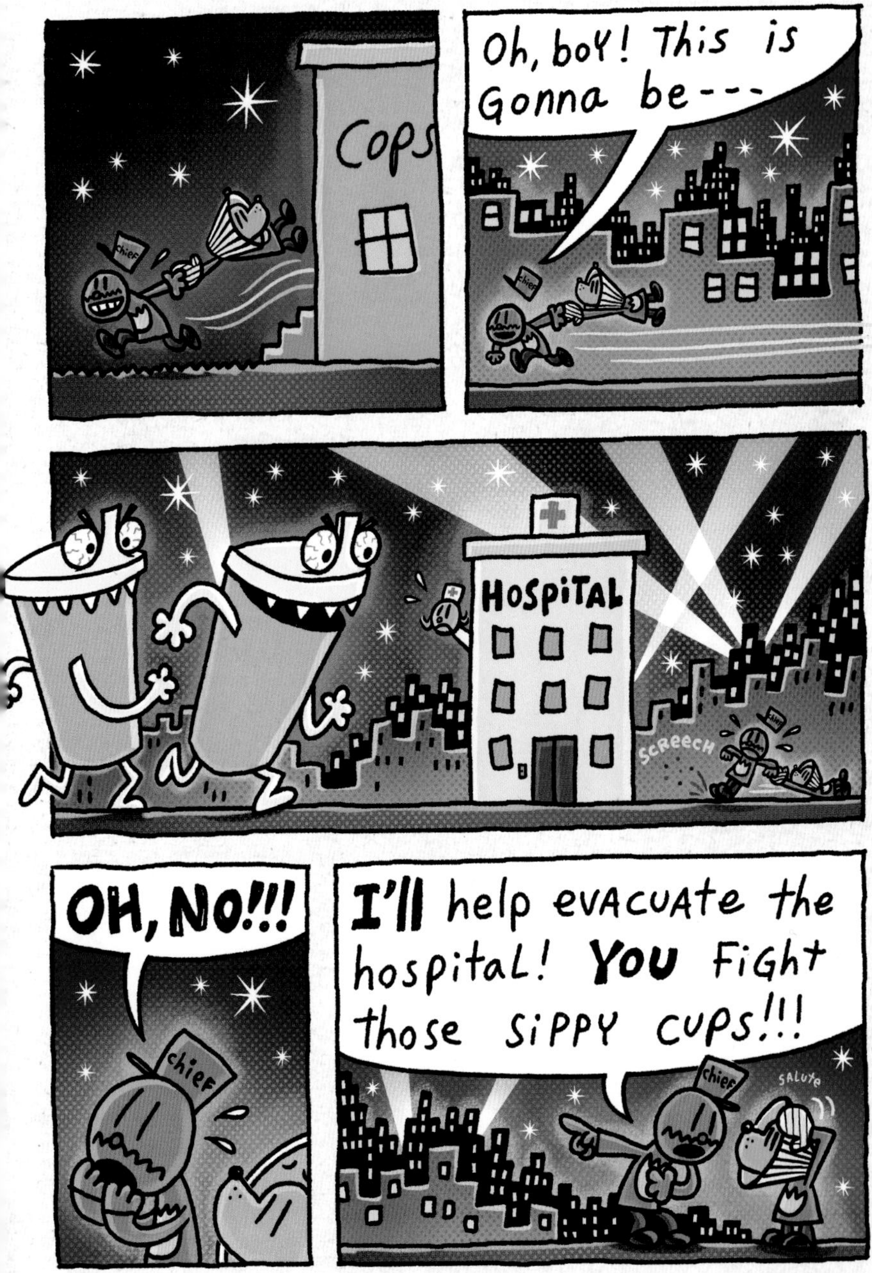
Cops
Oh, boy! This is Gonna be---
HOSPITAL
SCREECH
OH, NO!!!
I'll help evacuate the hospital! YOU Fight those sippy cups!!!
SALUTE

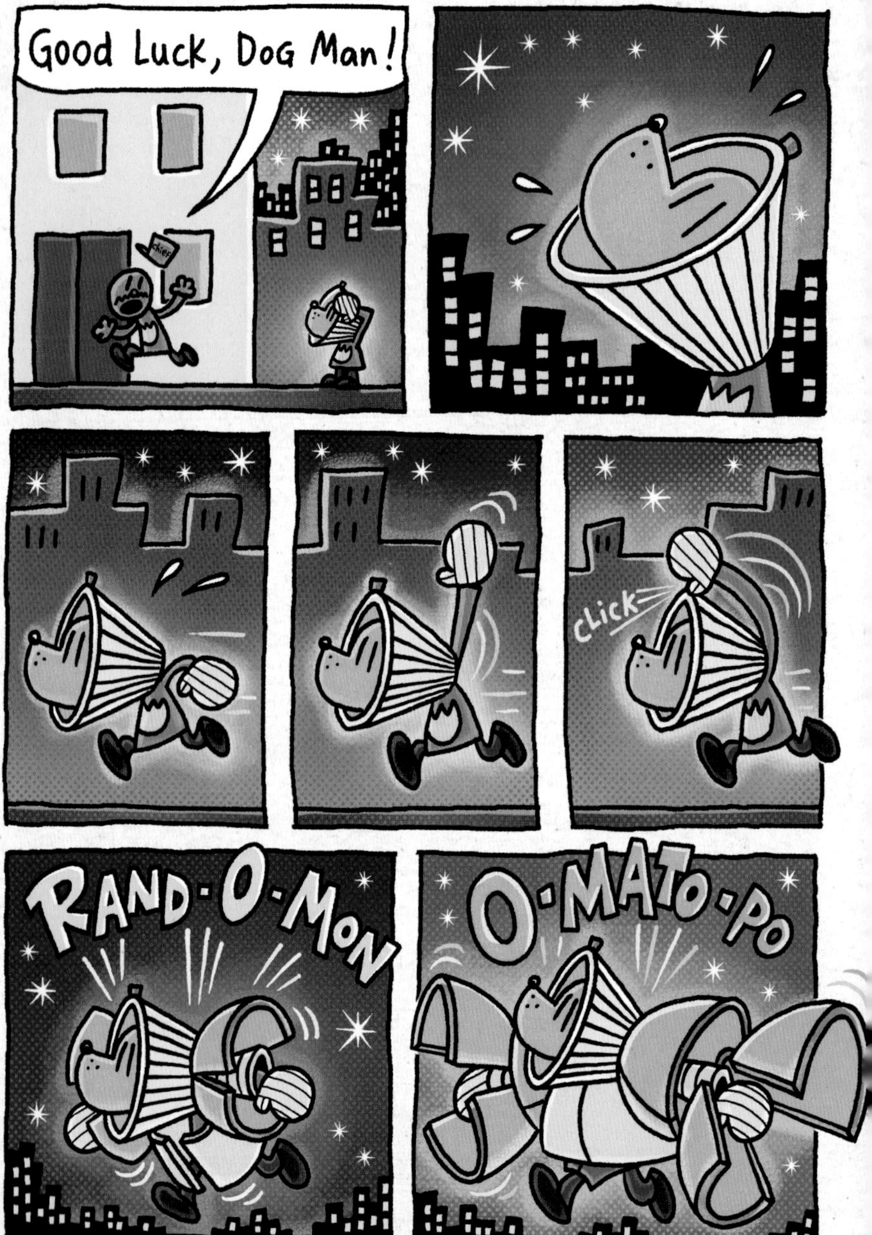
Good Luck, Dog Man!
CHIEF
CLICK
RAND-O-MON
O-MATO-PO

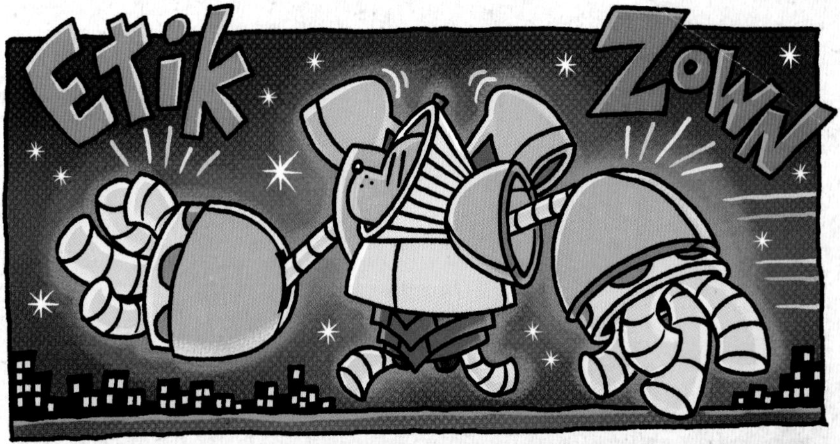
Etik
Zown

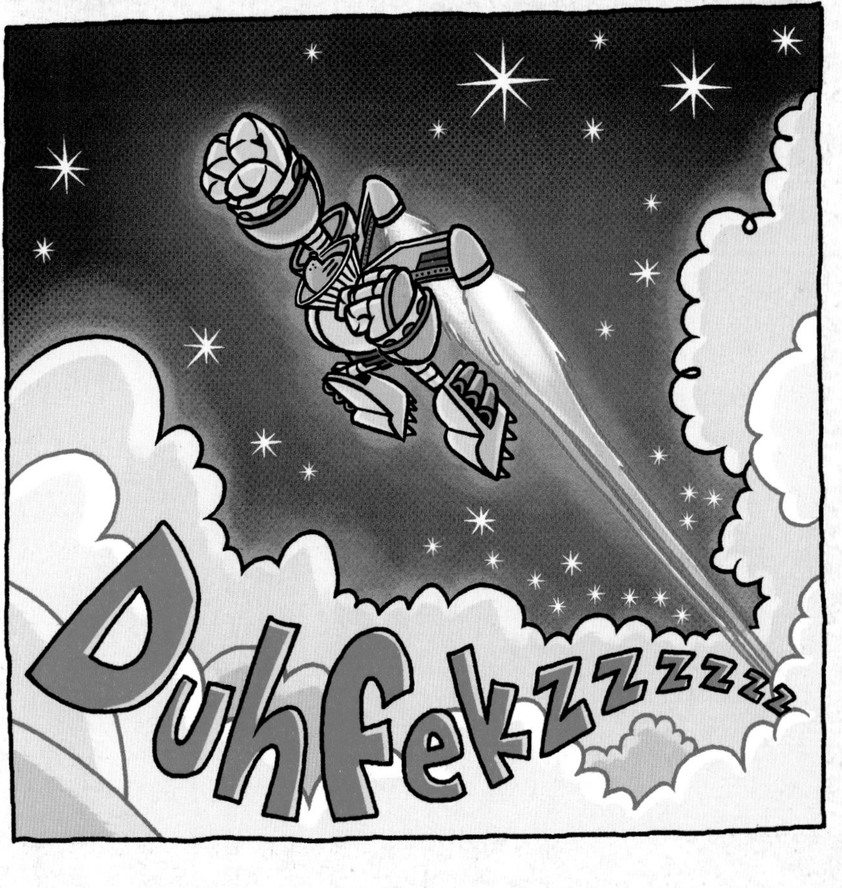
Duhfekzzzzzz

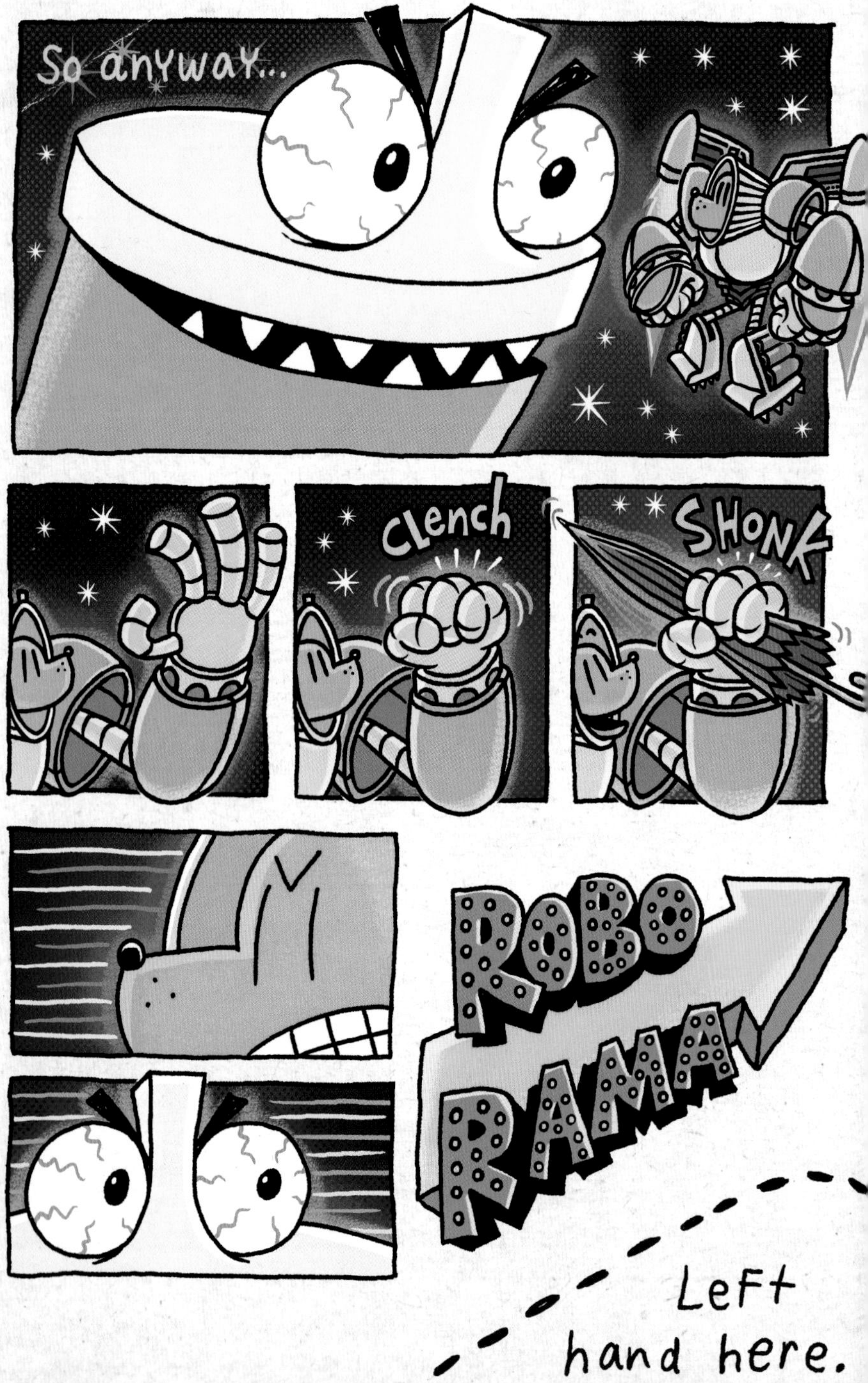
So anyway...
CLENCH
SHONK
ROBO RAMA
Left hand here.

175

Right
Thumb
here.

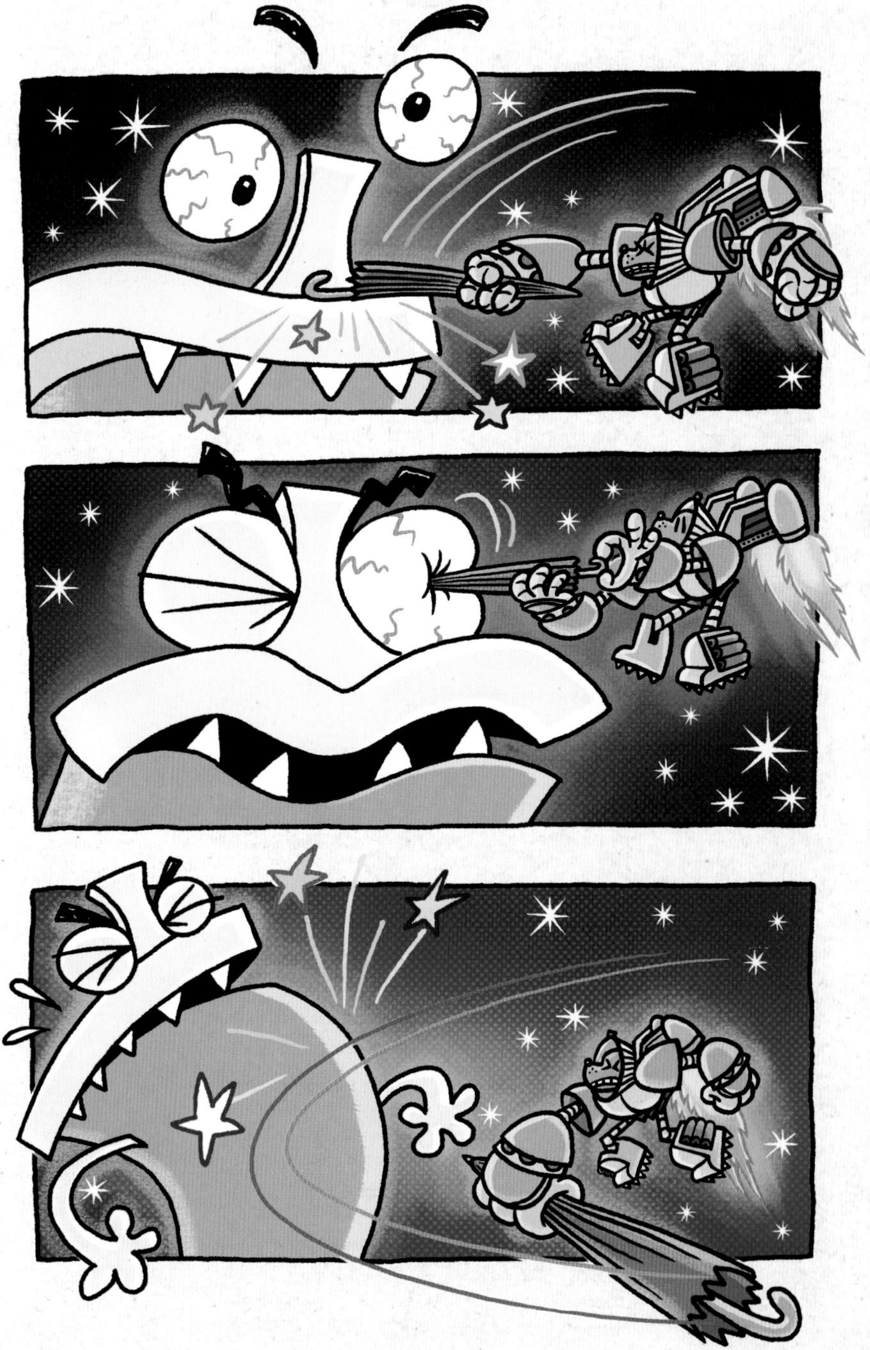

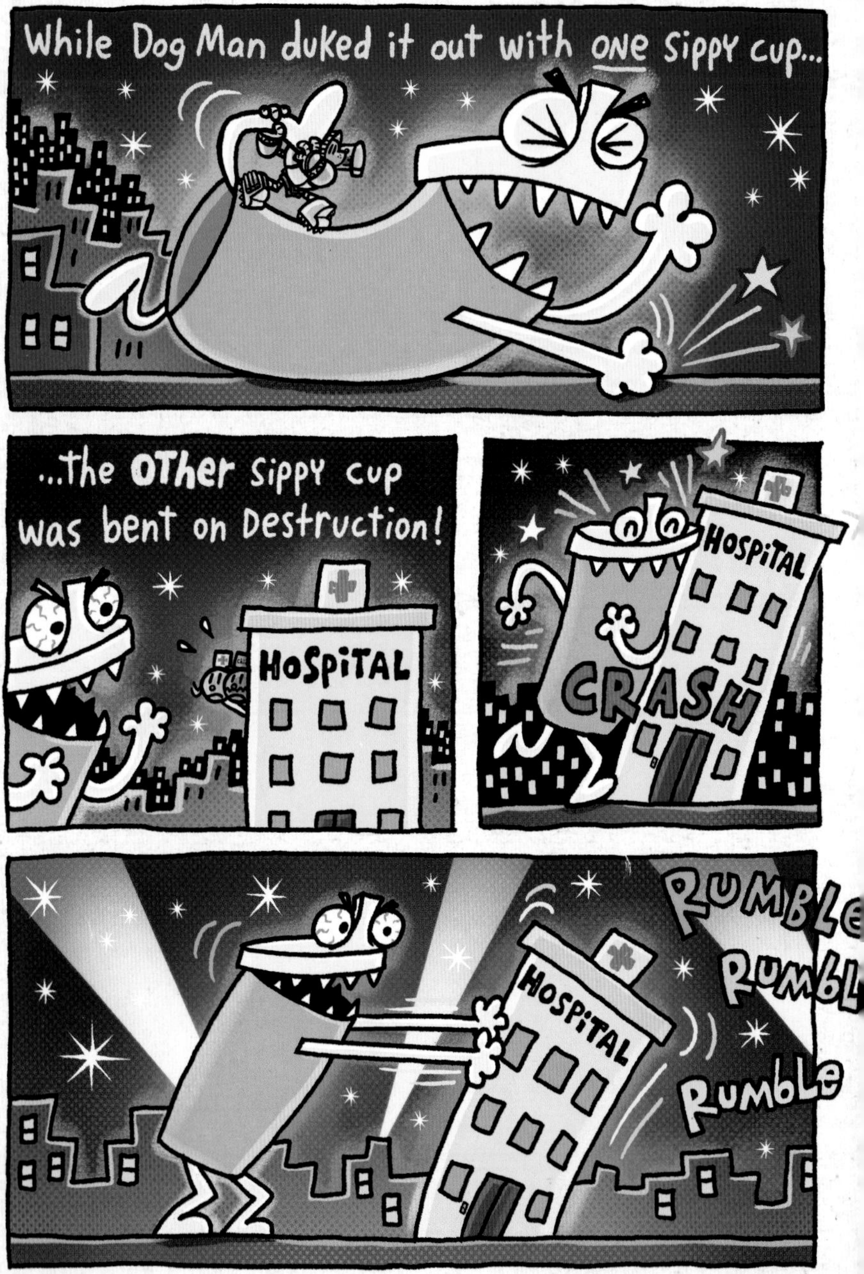
While Dog Man duked it out with ONE sippy cup...
...the OTHER sippy cup was bent on Destruction!
HOSPITAL
HOSPITAL
CRASH
HOSPITAL
RUMBLE
RUMBL
Rumble

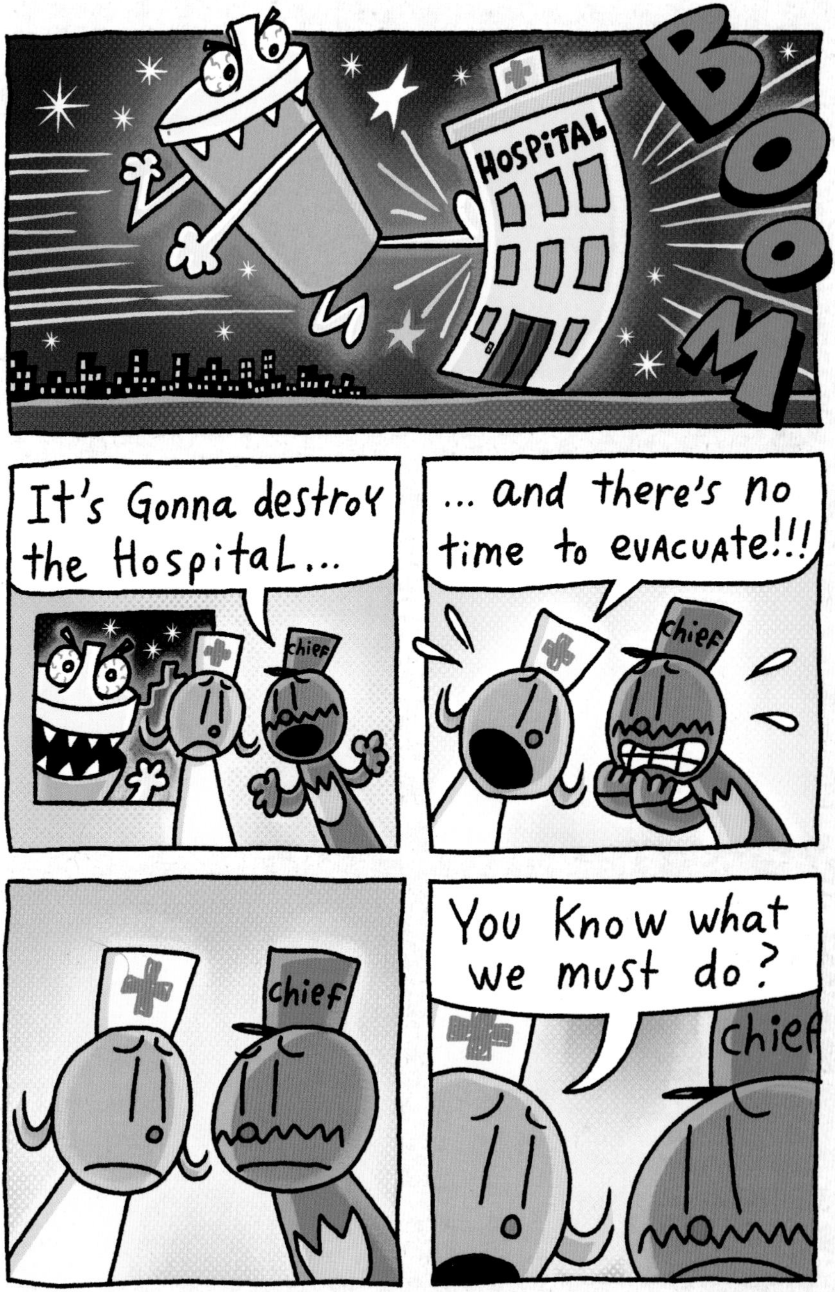
HOSPITAL
BOOOM
It's Gonna destroy the Hospital...
chief
... and there's no time to evacuate!!!
chief
chief
You know what we must do?
chief

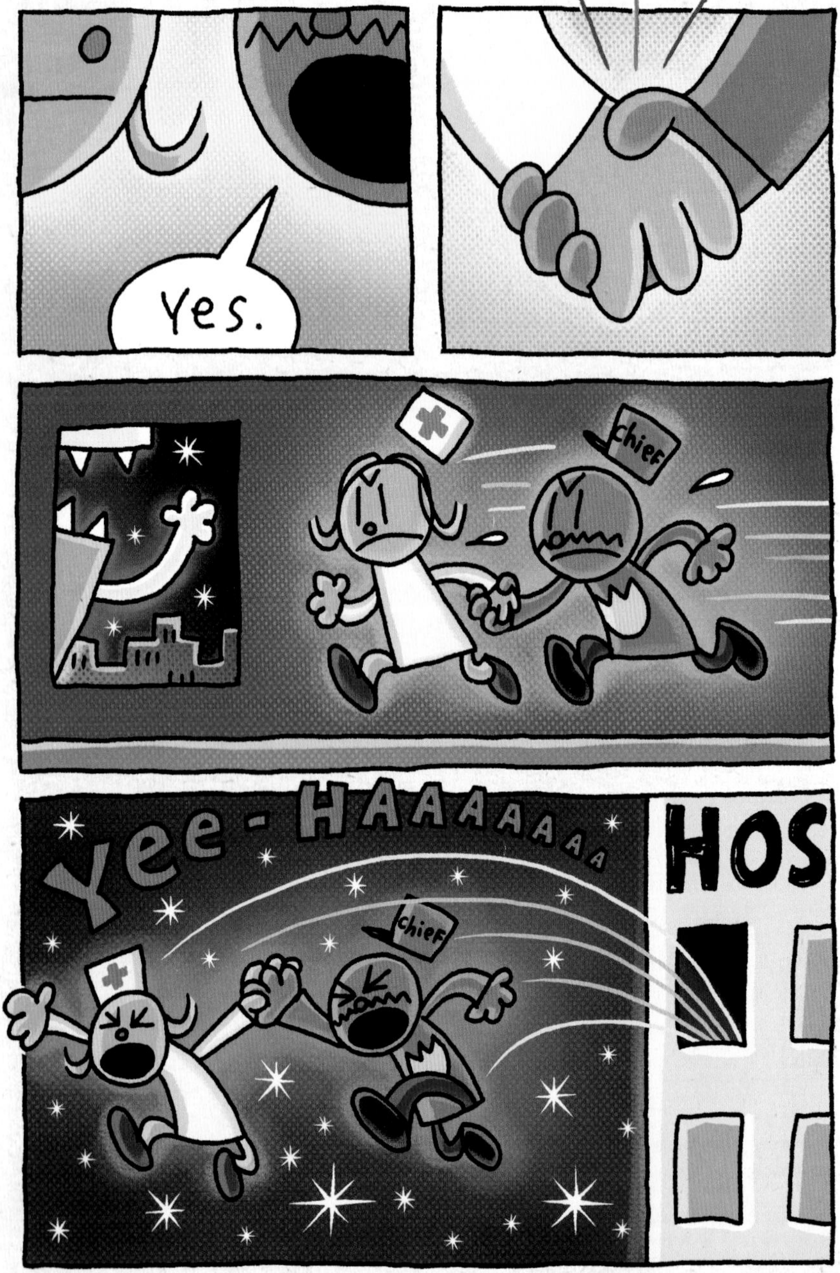
Yes.
chief
chief
YEE-HAAAAAAAA
HOS

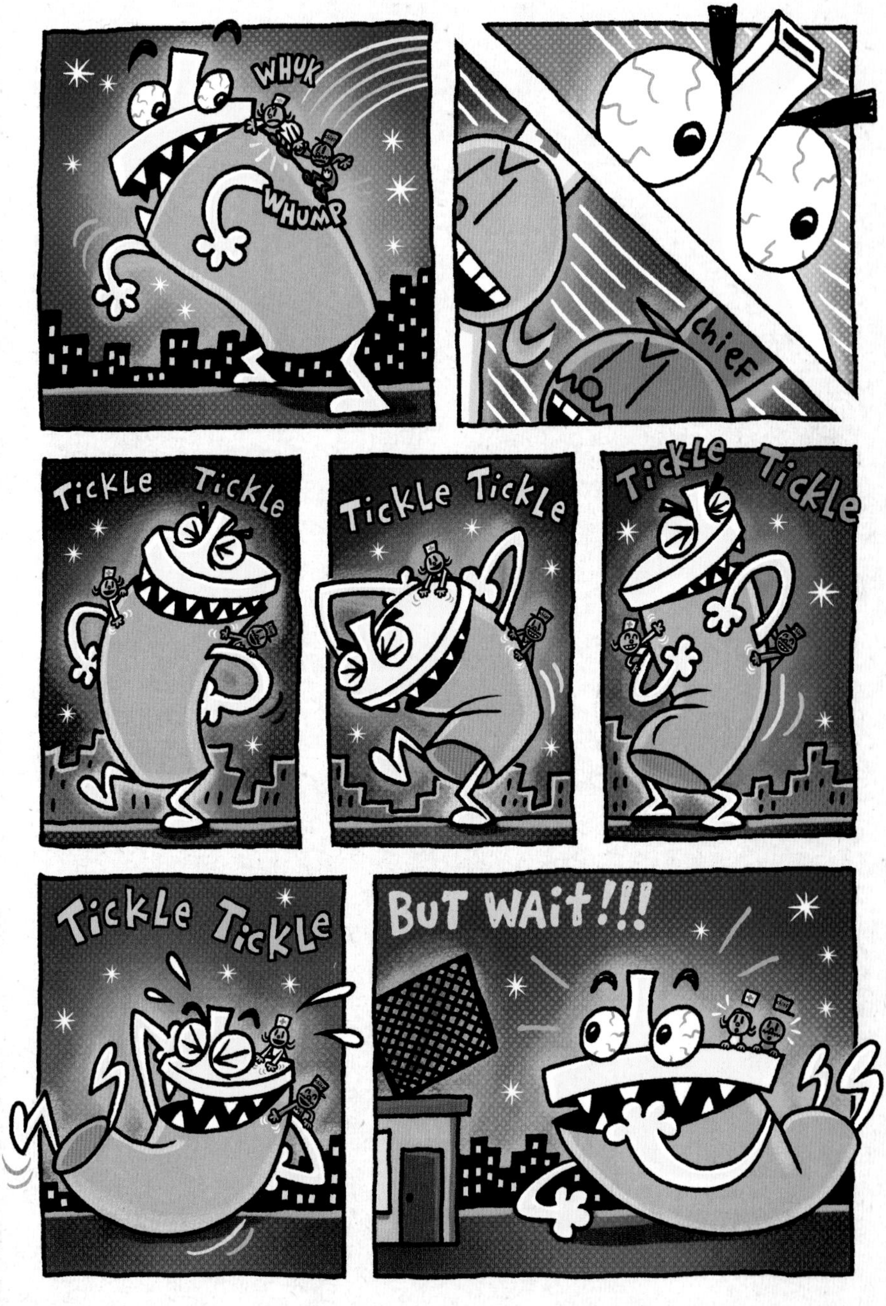
WHUK
WHUMP
CHIEF
Tickle Tickle
Tickle Tickle
Tickle Tickle
Tickle Tickle
BUT WAIT!!!

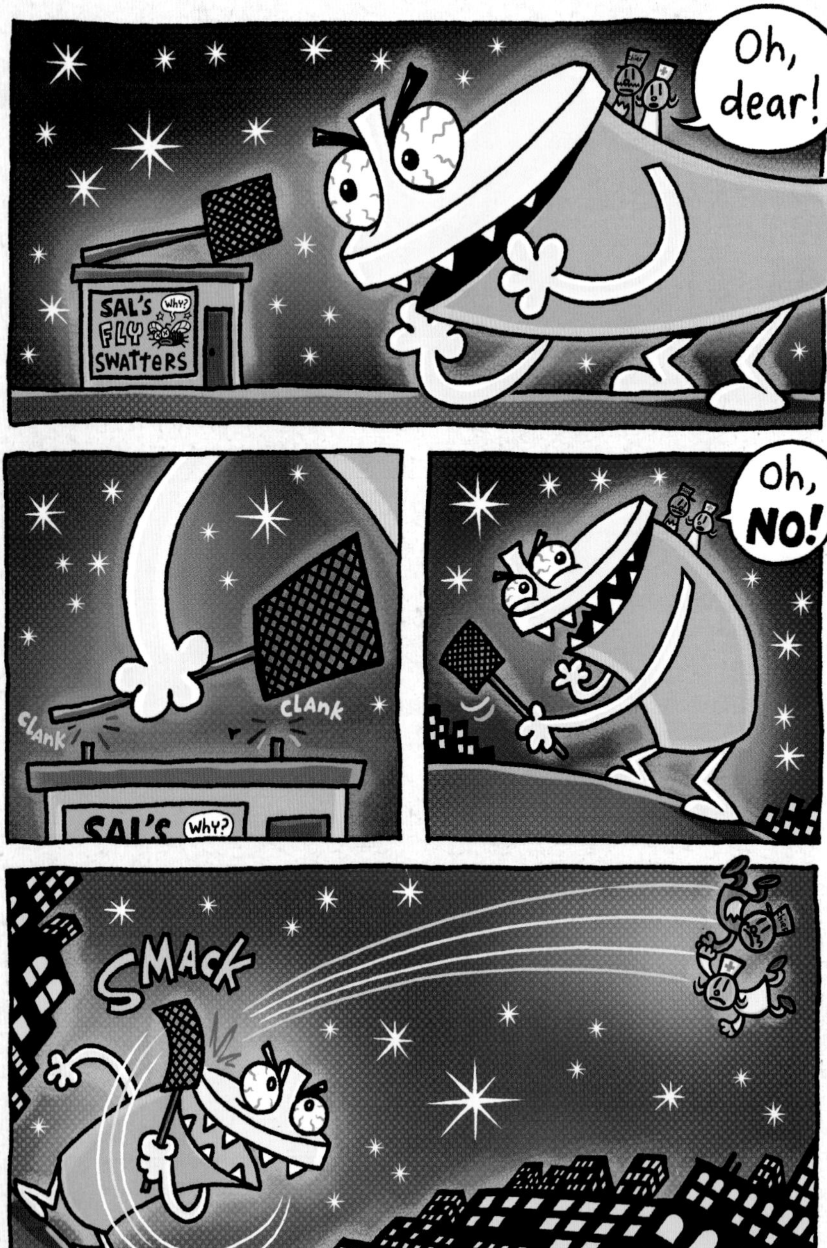
Oh, dear!
SAL'S FLY SWATTERS
WHY?
CLANK
CLANK
SAL'S
WHY?
Oh, NO!
SMACK

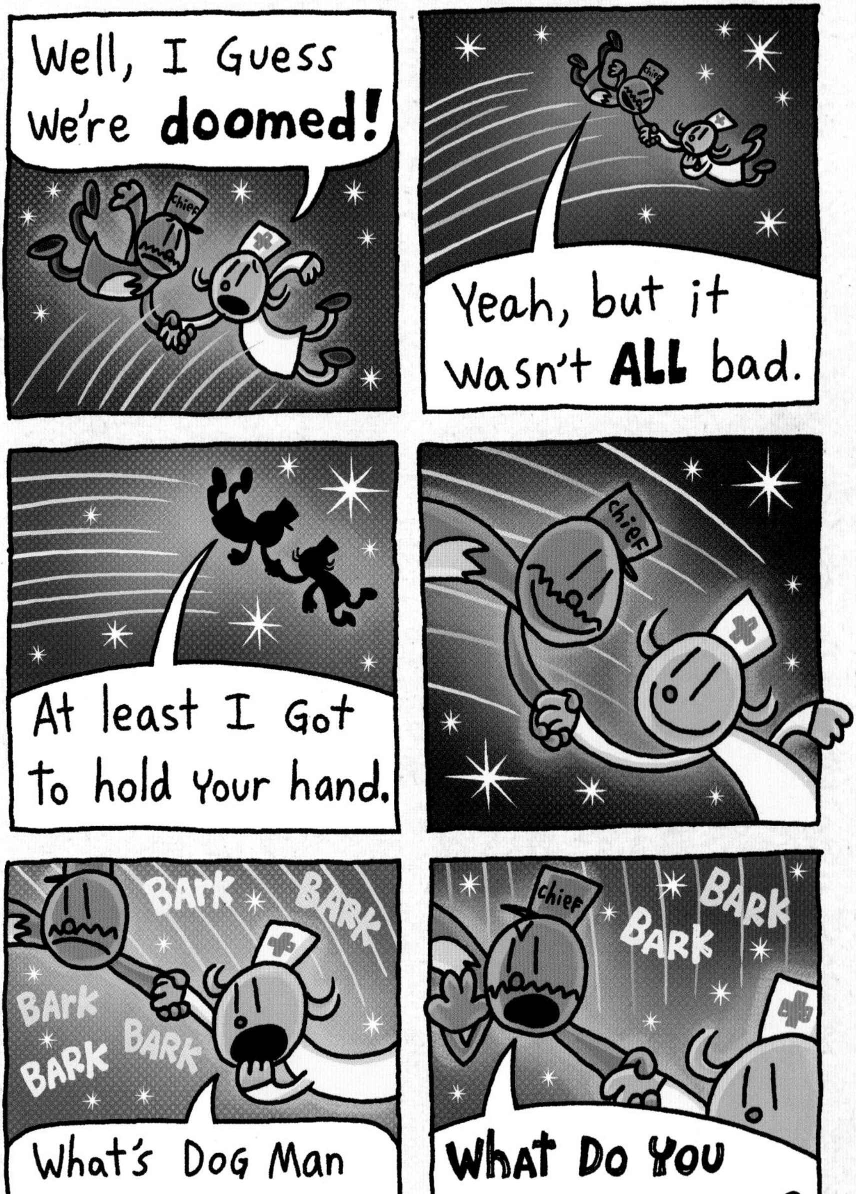
Well, I Guess we're doomed!
chief
Yeah, but it wasn't ALL bad.
At least I Got to hold your hand.
chief
BARK BARK
BARK BARK BARK
What's DoG Man barking about?
chief
BARK BARK
WHAT DO YOU WANT, DOG MAN?

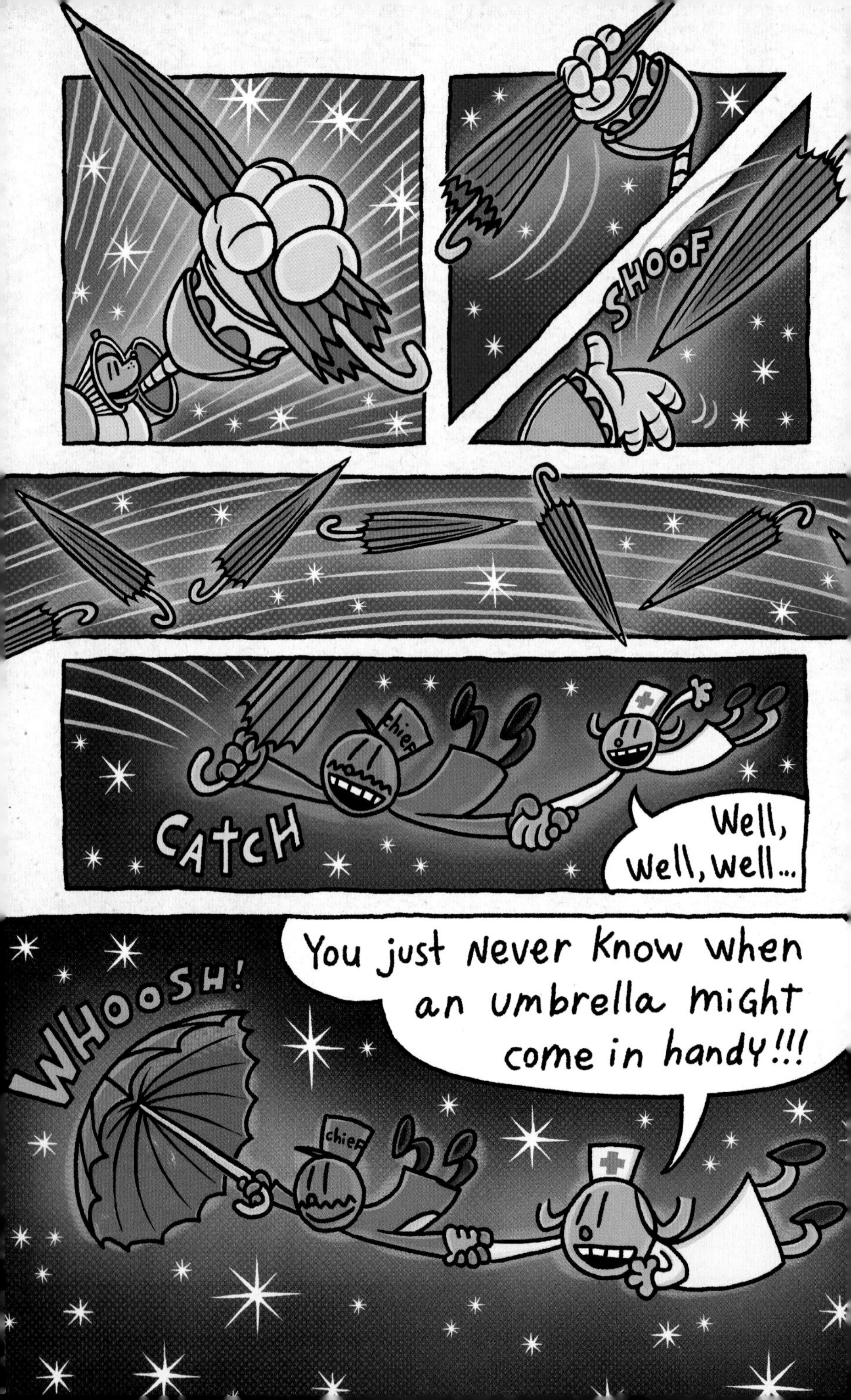
SHOOF
CATCH
Well, well, well...
WHOOSH!
You just never know when an umbrella might come in handy!!!

CHAPTER 13

The Most ROMANTIC CHAPTER Ever Written

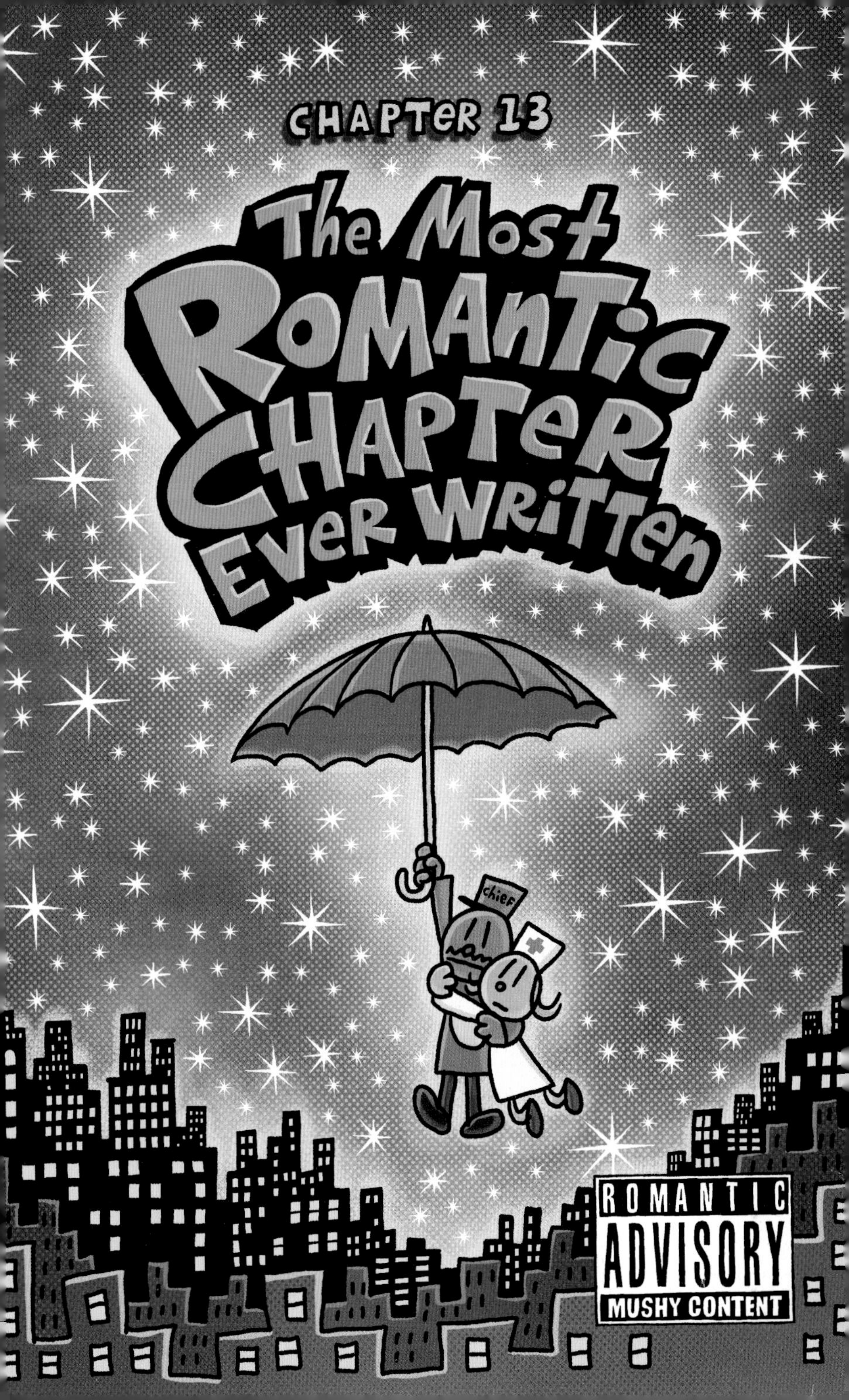
chief
ROMANTIC
ADVISORY
MUSHY CONTENT

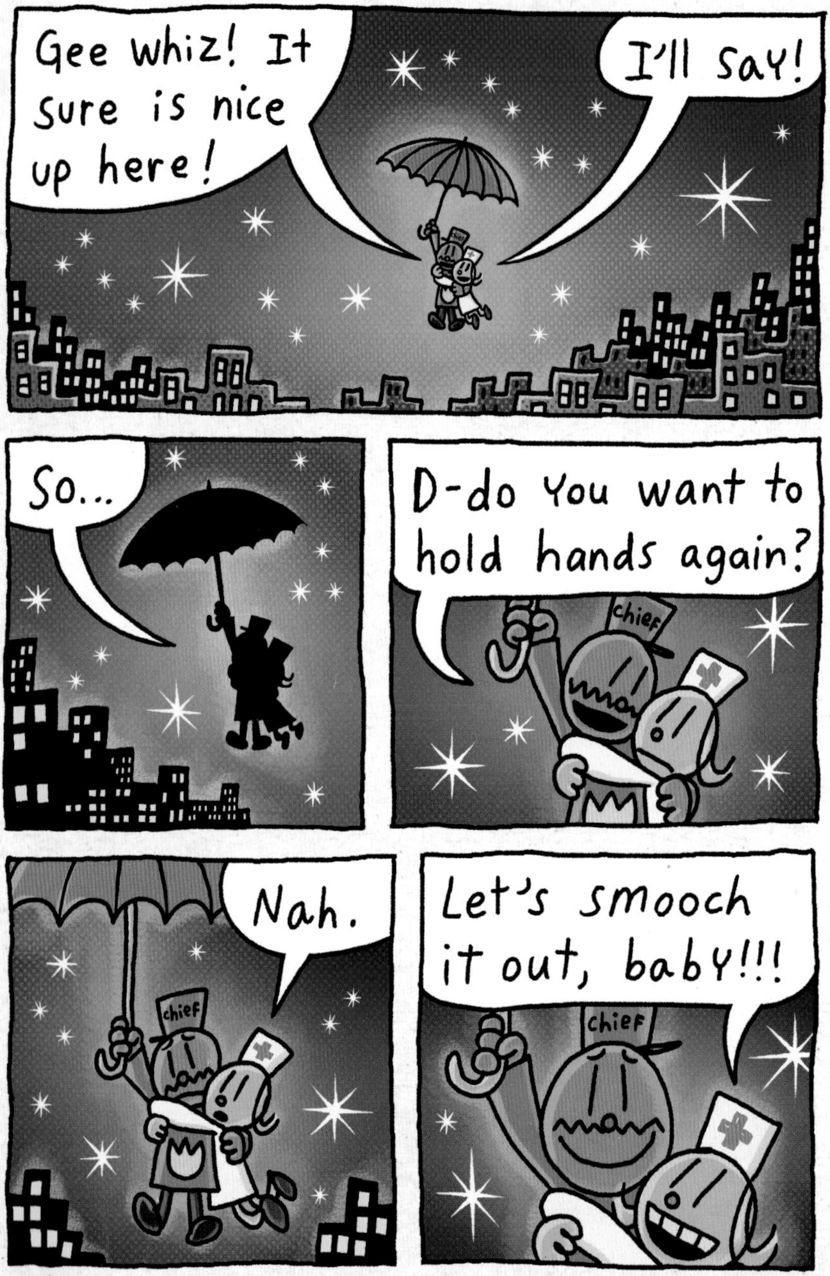
Gee whiz! It sure is nice up here!
I'll say!
So...
D-do you want to hold hands again?
Nah.
Let's smooch it out, baby!!!

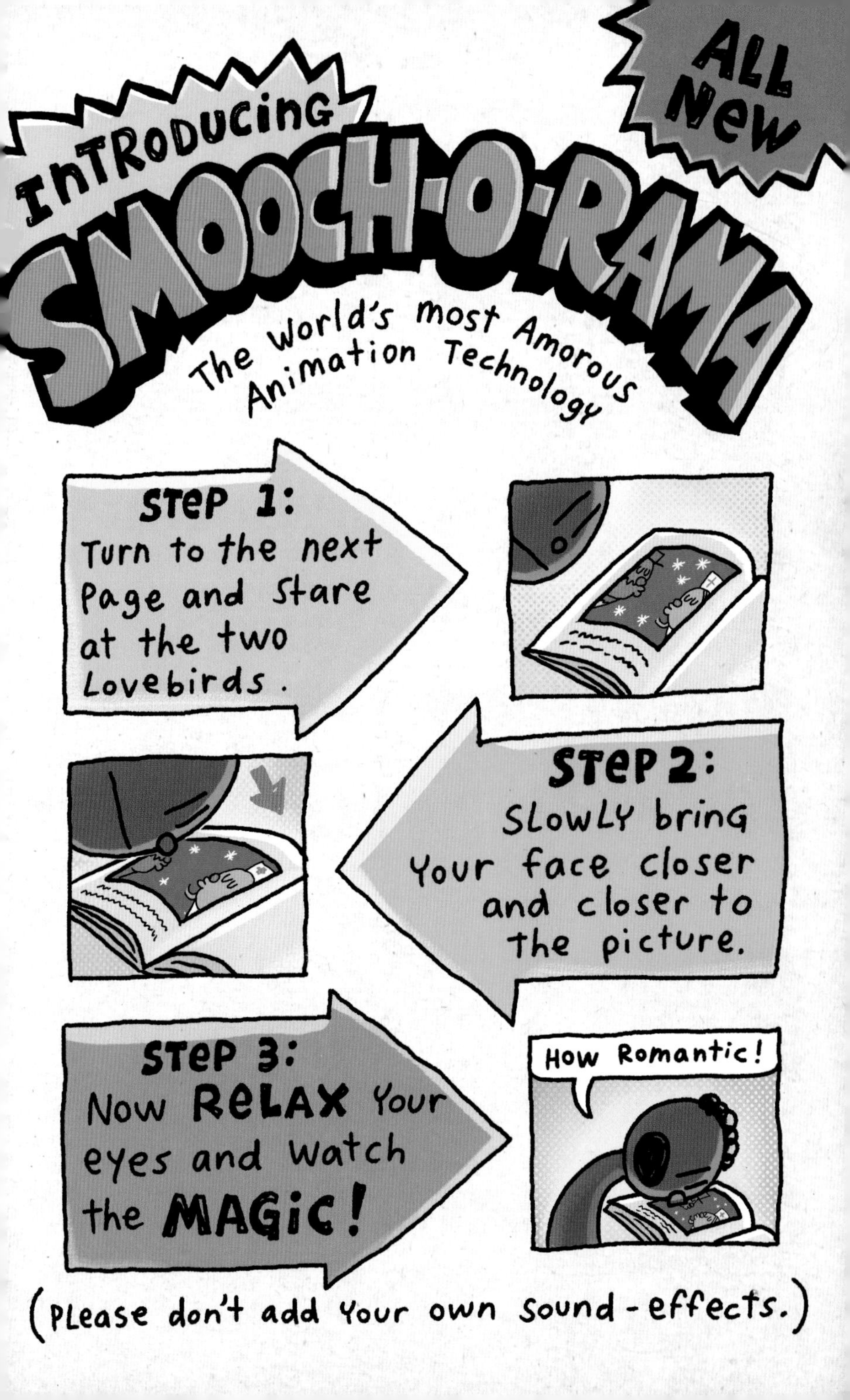
Introducing
All New
SMOOCH-O-RAMA
The World's most Amorous Animation Technology
STEP 1:
Turn to the next page and stare at the two Lovebirds.
STEP 2:
Slowly bring your face closer and closer to the picture.
STEP 3:
Now RELAX your eyes and watch the MAGIC!
How Romantic!
(Please don't add your own sound-effects.)

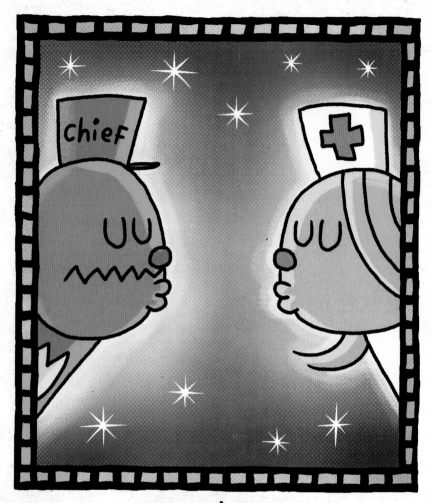

REMEMBER...

1. Stare at the image Above with both eyes.
2. SLOWLY bring Your face **CLOSE** to the page.
3. **RELAX** Your eyes (try to look "past" the image).
BONUS: You can make them kiss again and again
by slowly moving your head closer to
and farther away from the image.

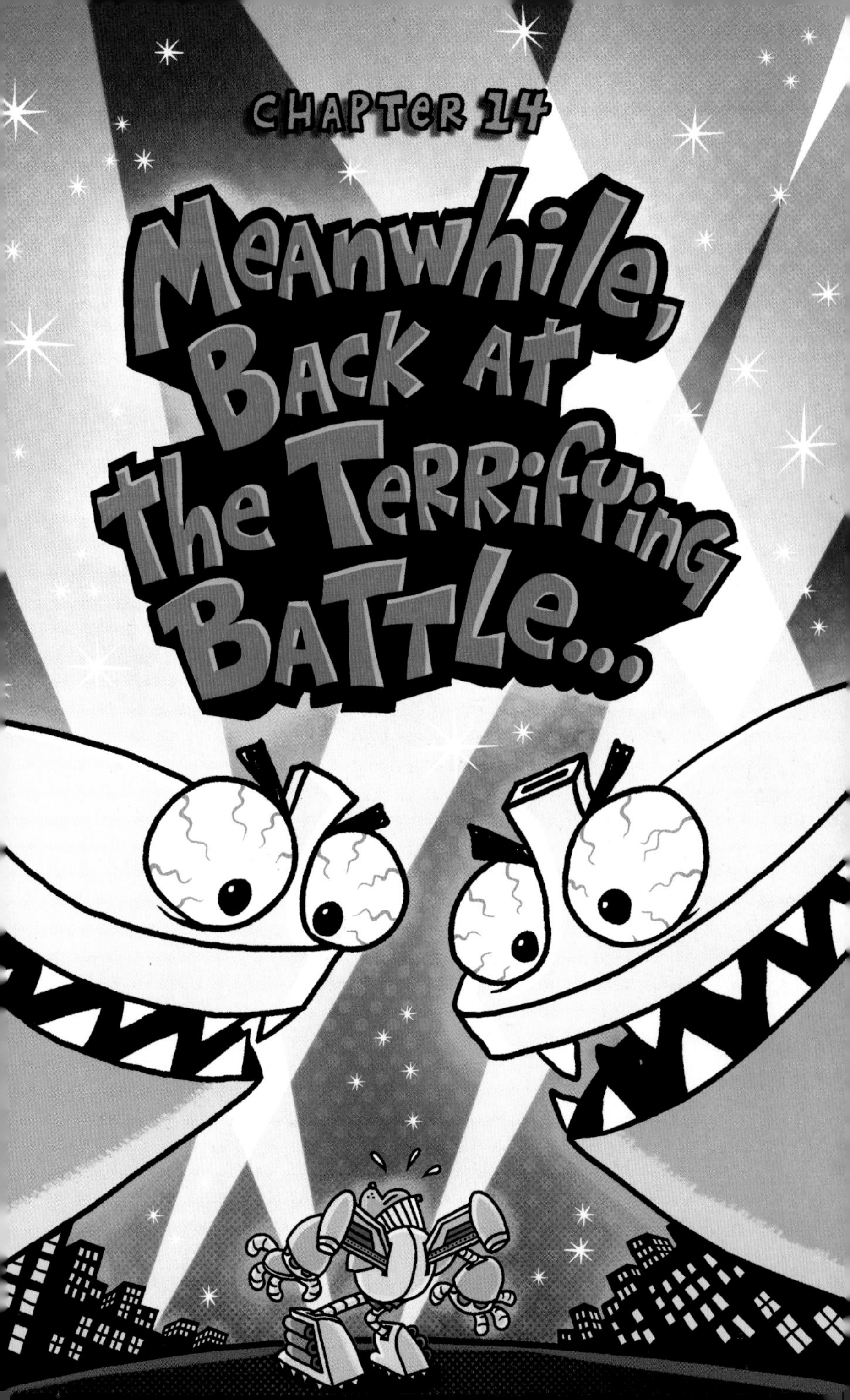
CHAPTER 14
Meanwhile, Back at the Terrifying Battle...

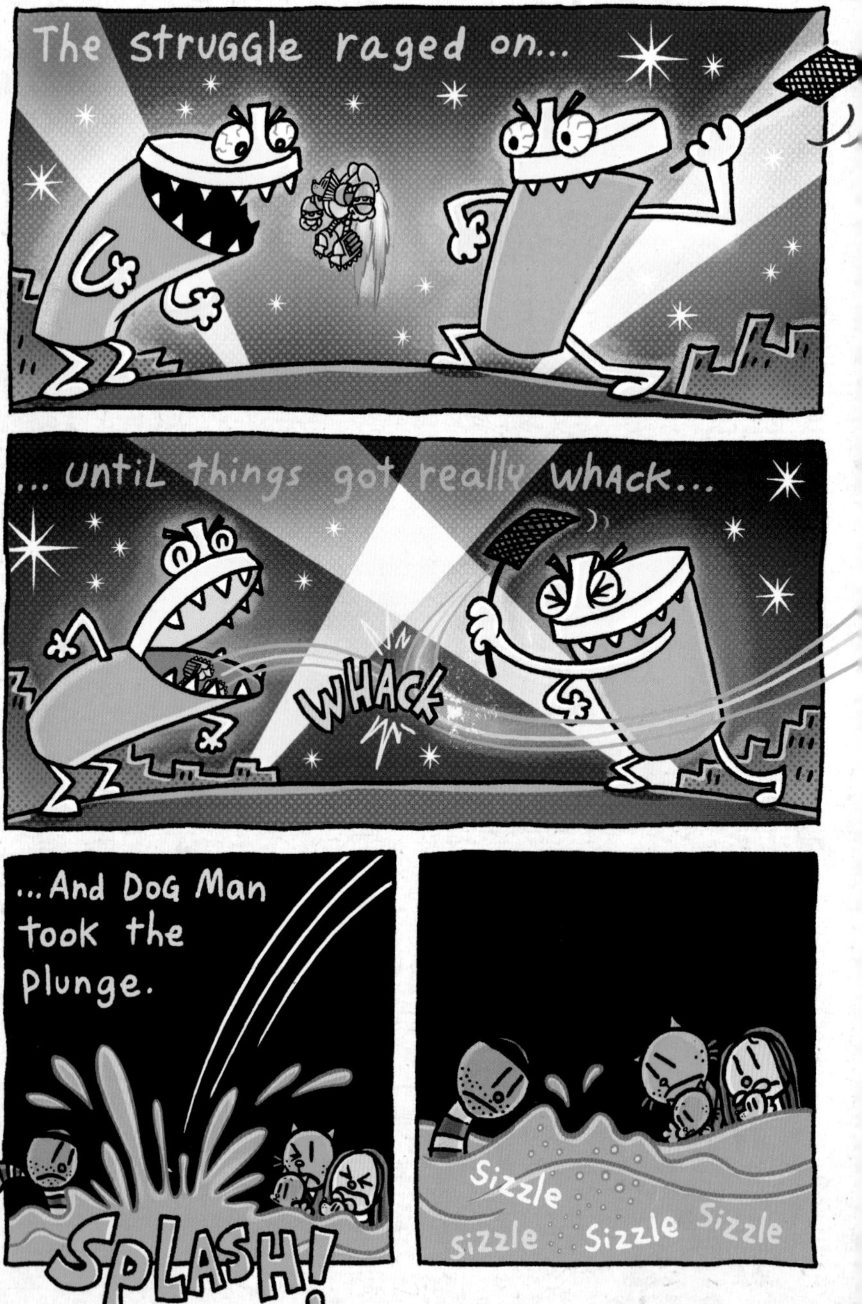
The struggle raged on...
... until things got really whack...
WHACK
...And Dog Man took the plunge.
SPLASH!
Sizzle
sizzle
Sizzle
Sizzle

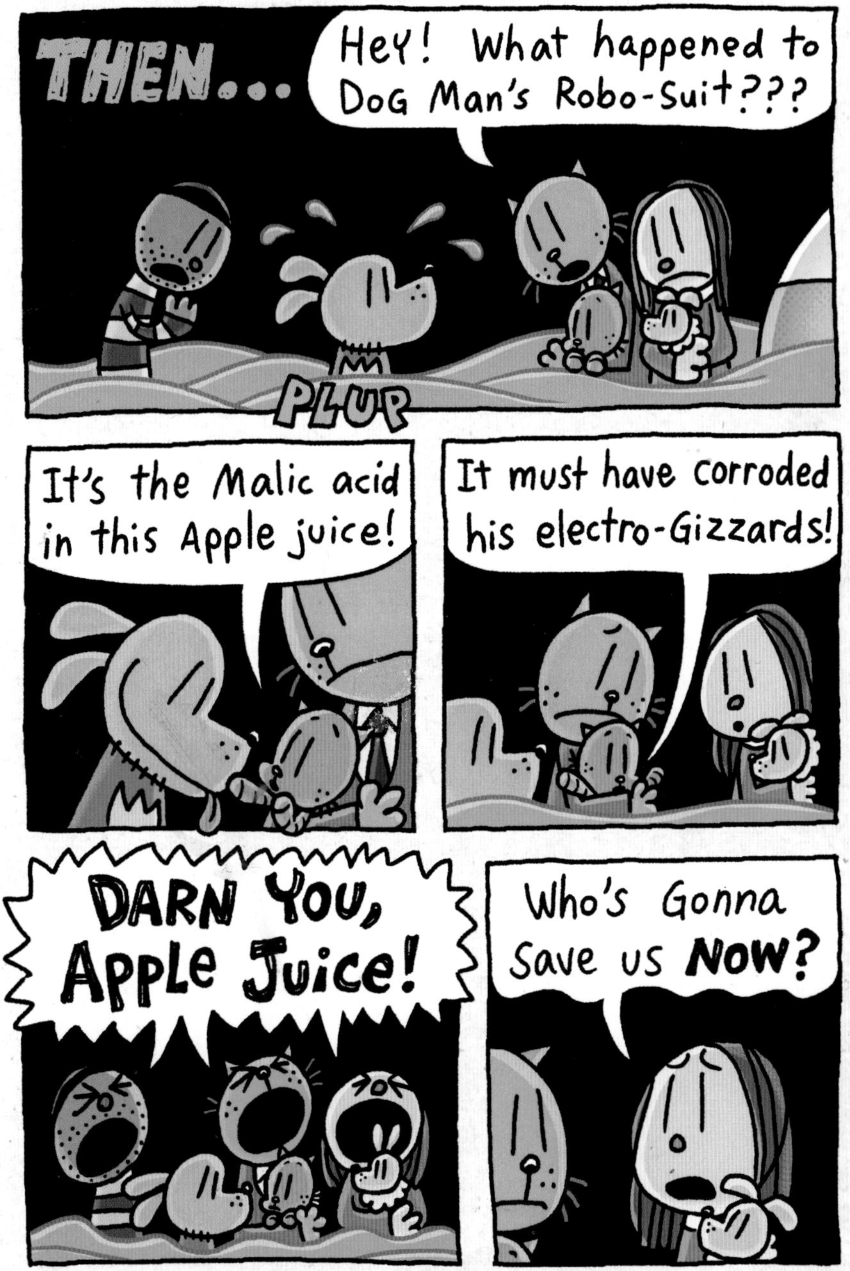
THEN...
Hey! What happened to Dog Man's Robo-Suit???
PLUP
It's the Malic acid in this Apple juice!
It must have corroded his electro-Gizzards!
DARN YOU, Apple Juice!
Who's Gonna Save us NOW?

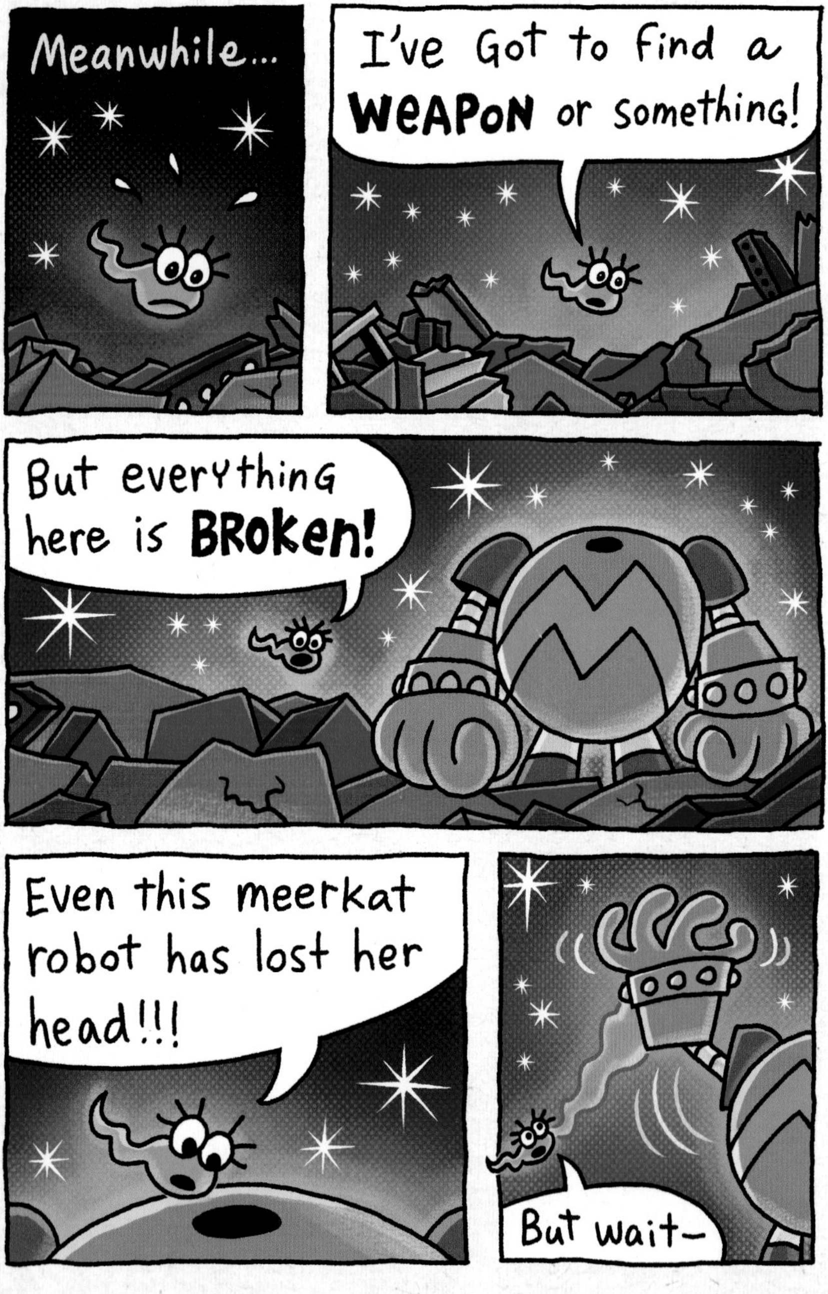
Meanwhile...
I've Got to find a WEAPON or something!
But everything here is BROKEN!
Even this meerkat robot has lost her head!!!
But wait–

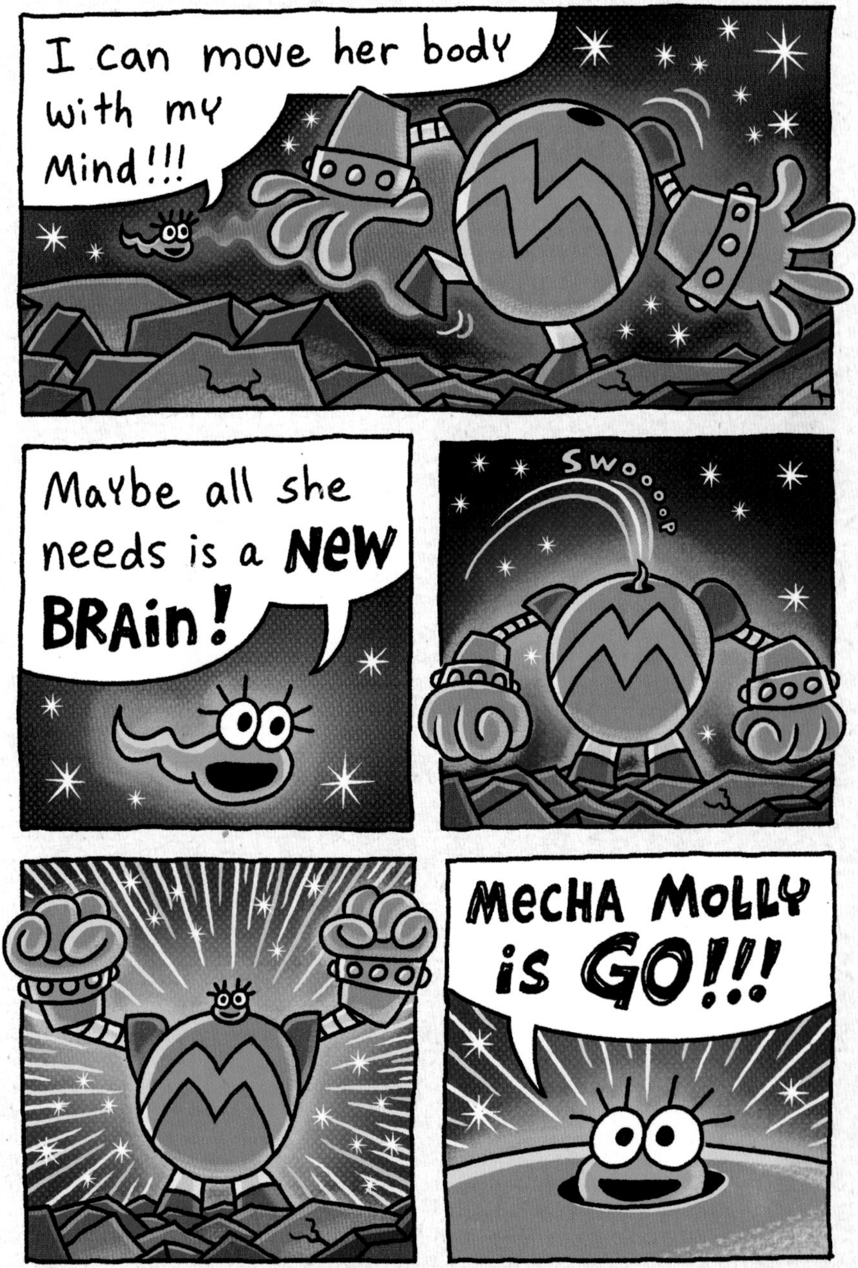
I can move her body with my Mind!!!
Maybe all she needs is a NEW BRAIN!
SWOOOOOP
MECHA MOLLY is GO!!!

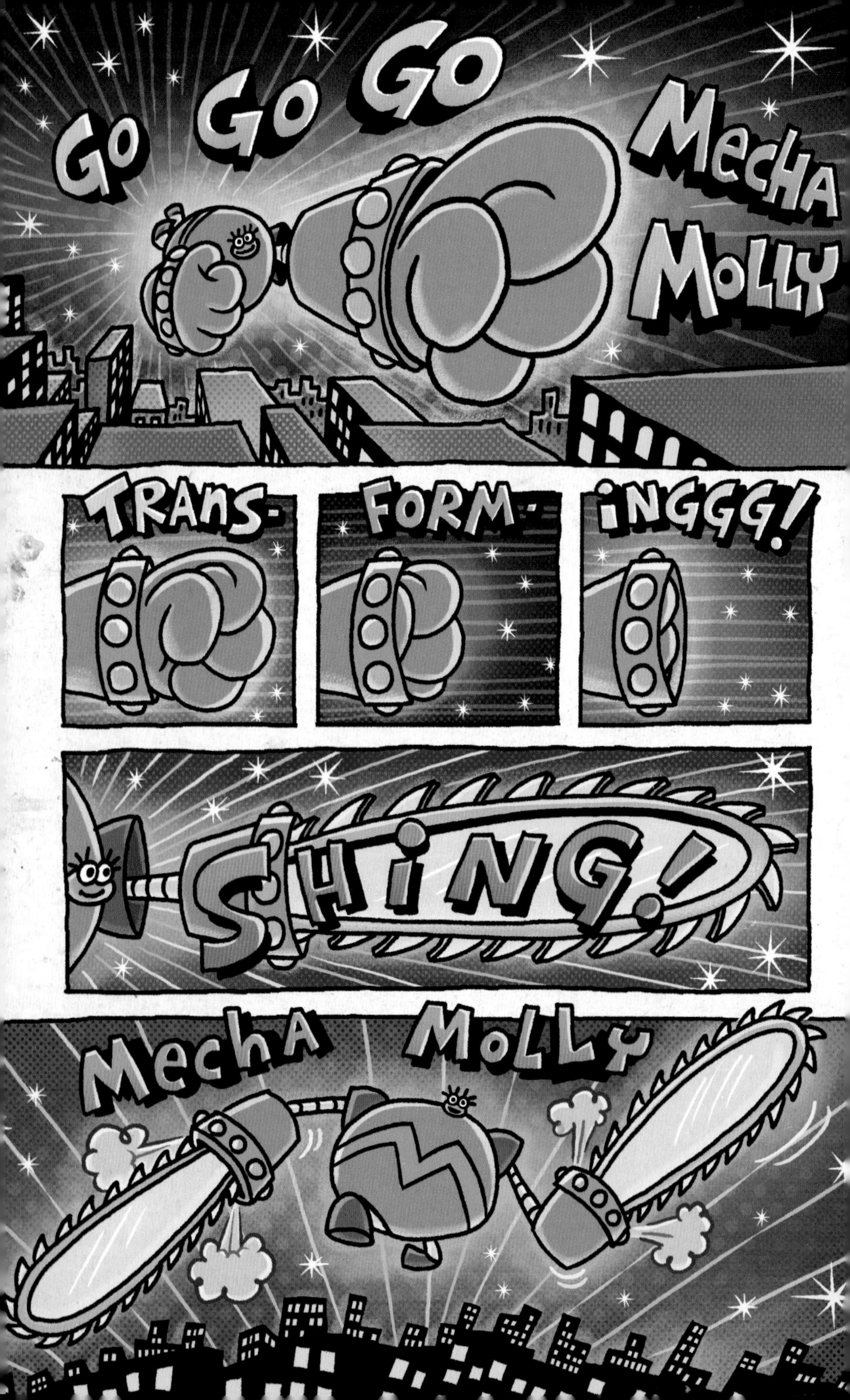
GO GO GO
Mecha Molly
TRANS-
FORM-
iNGGG!
SHiNG!
Mecha Molly

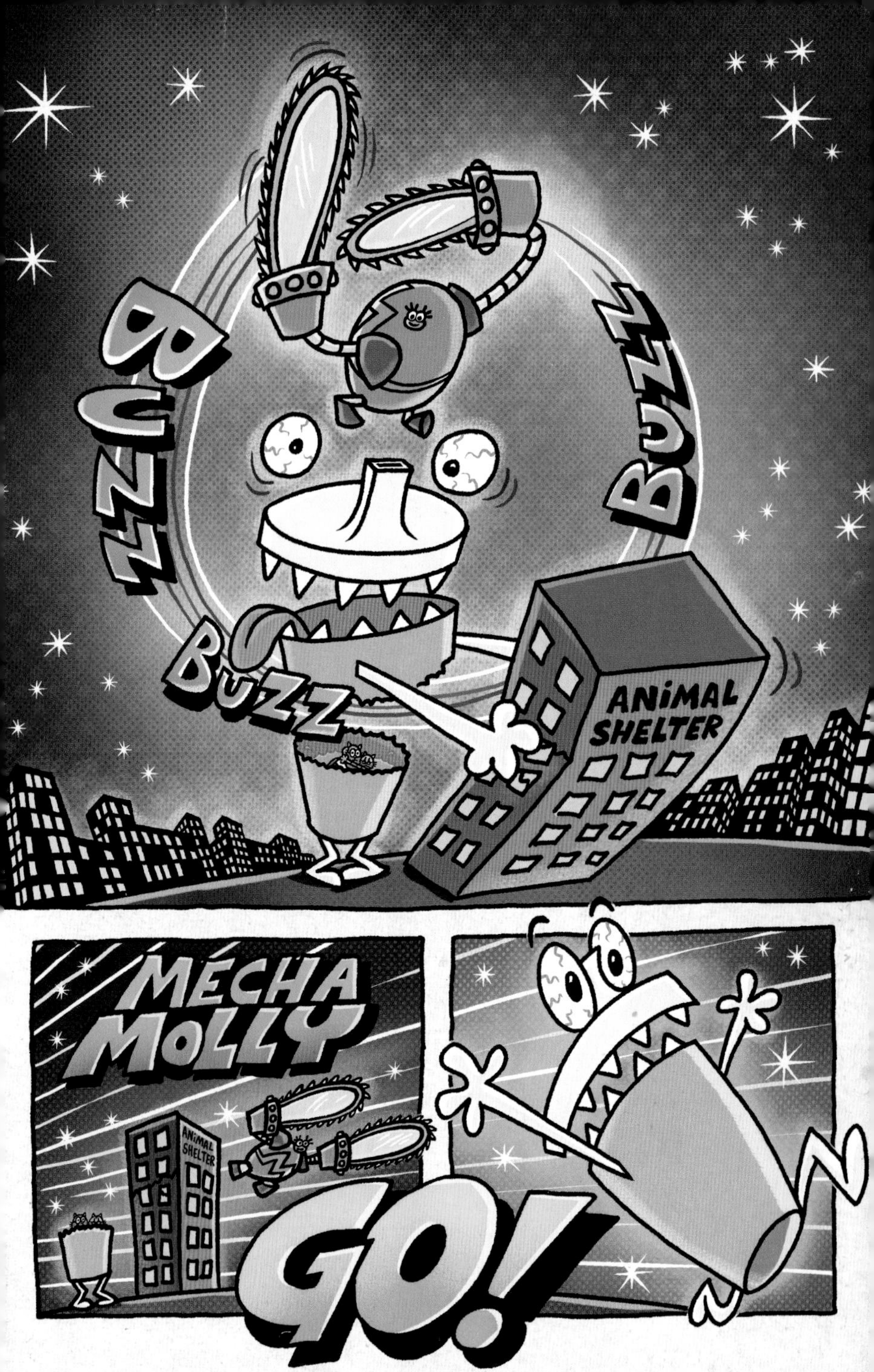
BUZZ
BUZZ
BUZZ
ANIMAL SHELTER
MÉCHA MOLLY
ANIMAL SHELTER
GO!

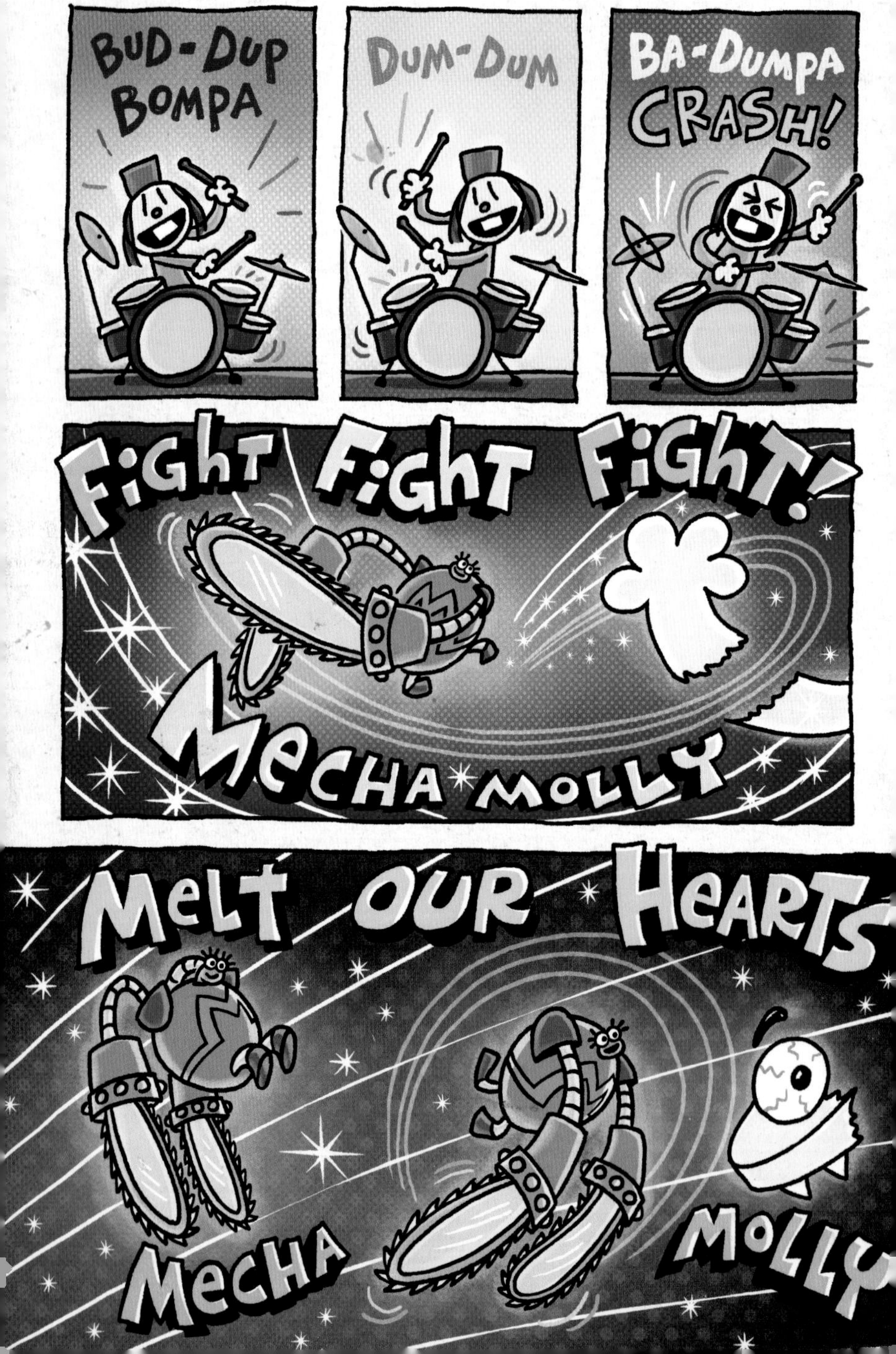
BUD-DUP BOMPA
DUM-DUM
BA-DUMPA CRASH!
FIGHT FIGHT FIGHT!
MECHA MOLLY
MELT OUR HEARTS
MECHA MOLLY

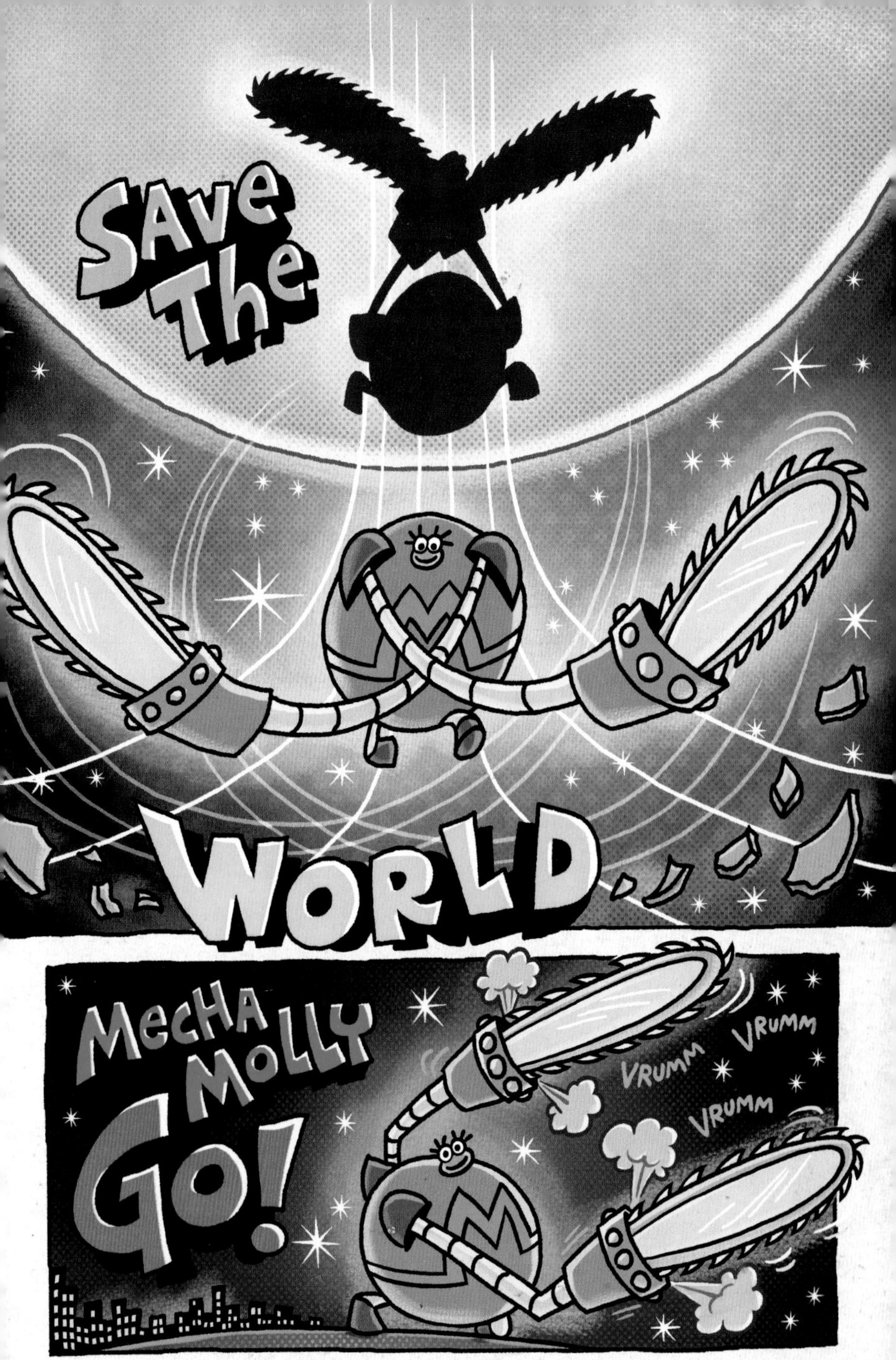
Save The
WORLD
Mecha Molly Go!
VRUMM
VRUMM
VRUMM

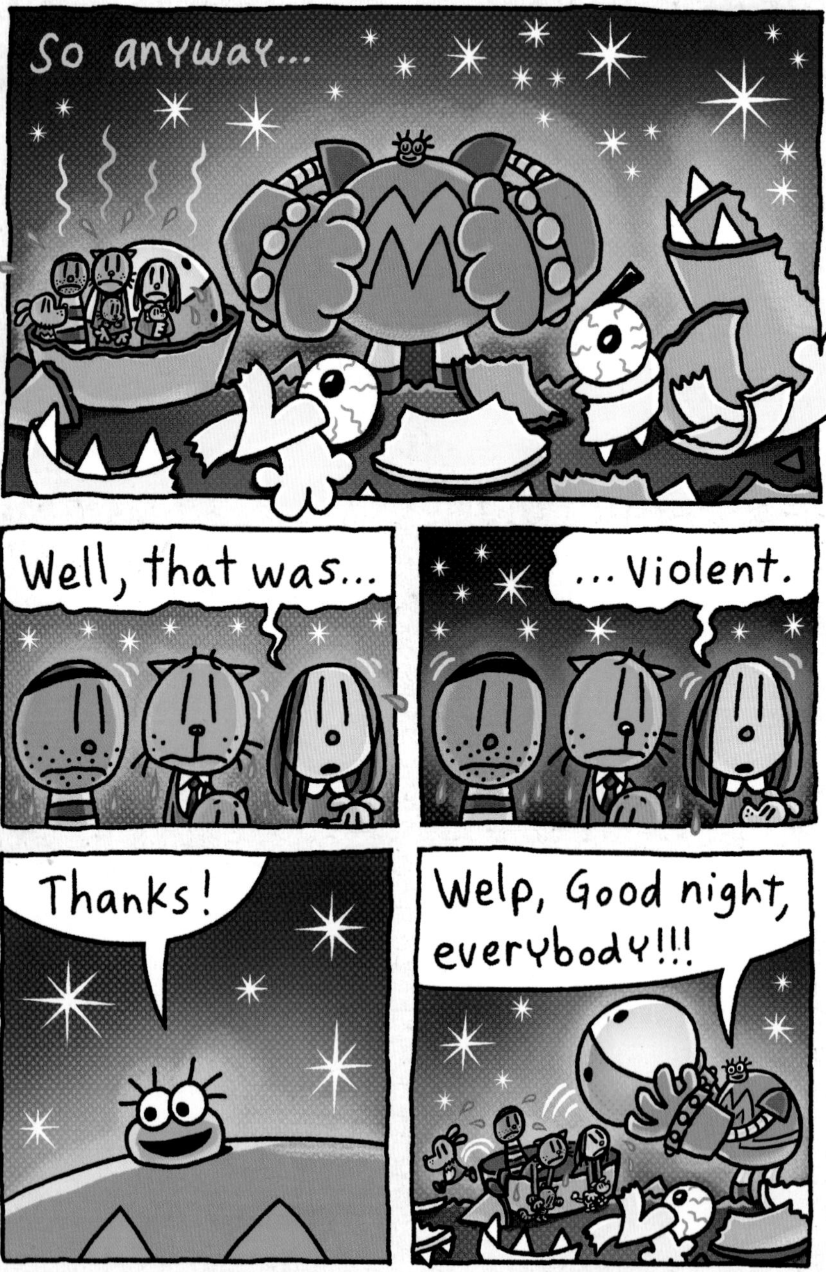
So anyway...
Well, that was...
...Violent.
Thanks!
Welp, Good night, everybody!!!

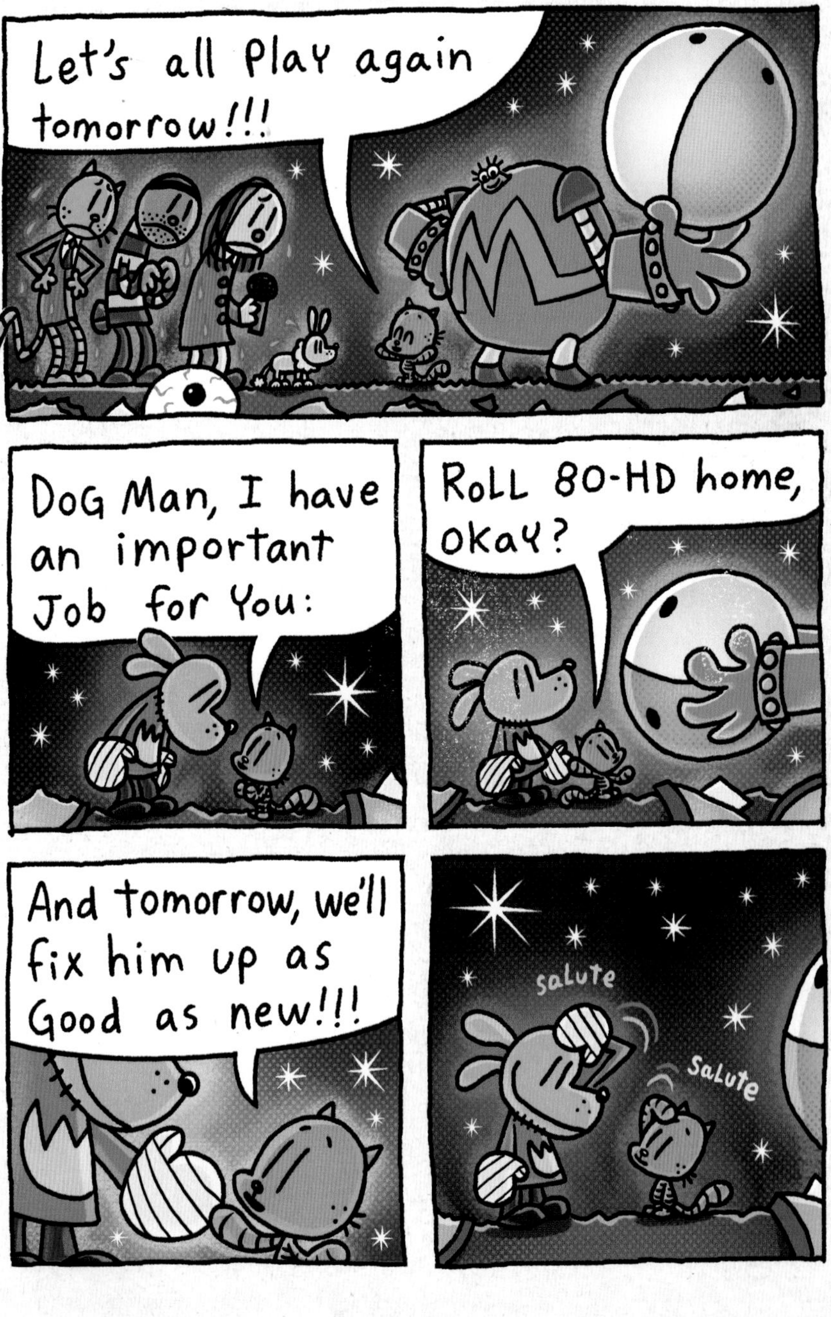
Let's all Play again tomorrow!!!
DoG Man, I have an important Job for You:
RoLL 80-HD home, OKaY?
And tomorrow, we'll fix him up as Good as new!!!
SaLute
SaLute

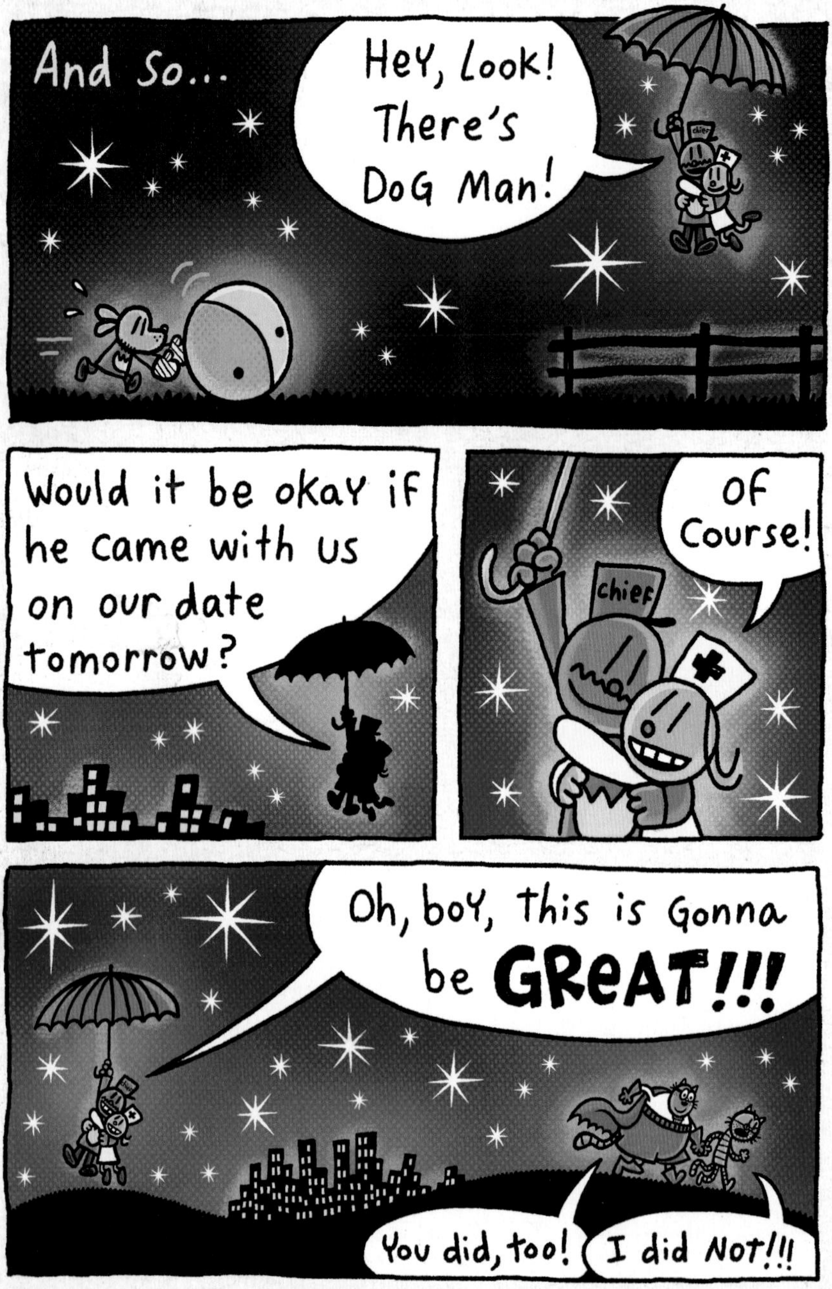
And so...
Hey, look! There's Dog Man!
Would it be okay if he came with us on our date tomorrow?
Of Course!
Oh, boy, this is gonna be GREAT!!!
You did, too!
I did NOT!!!

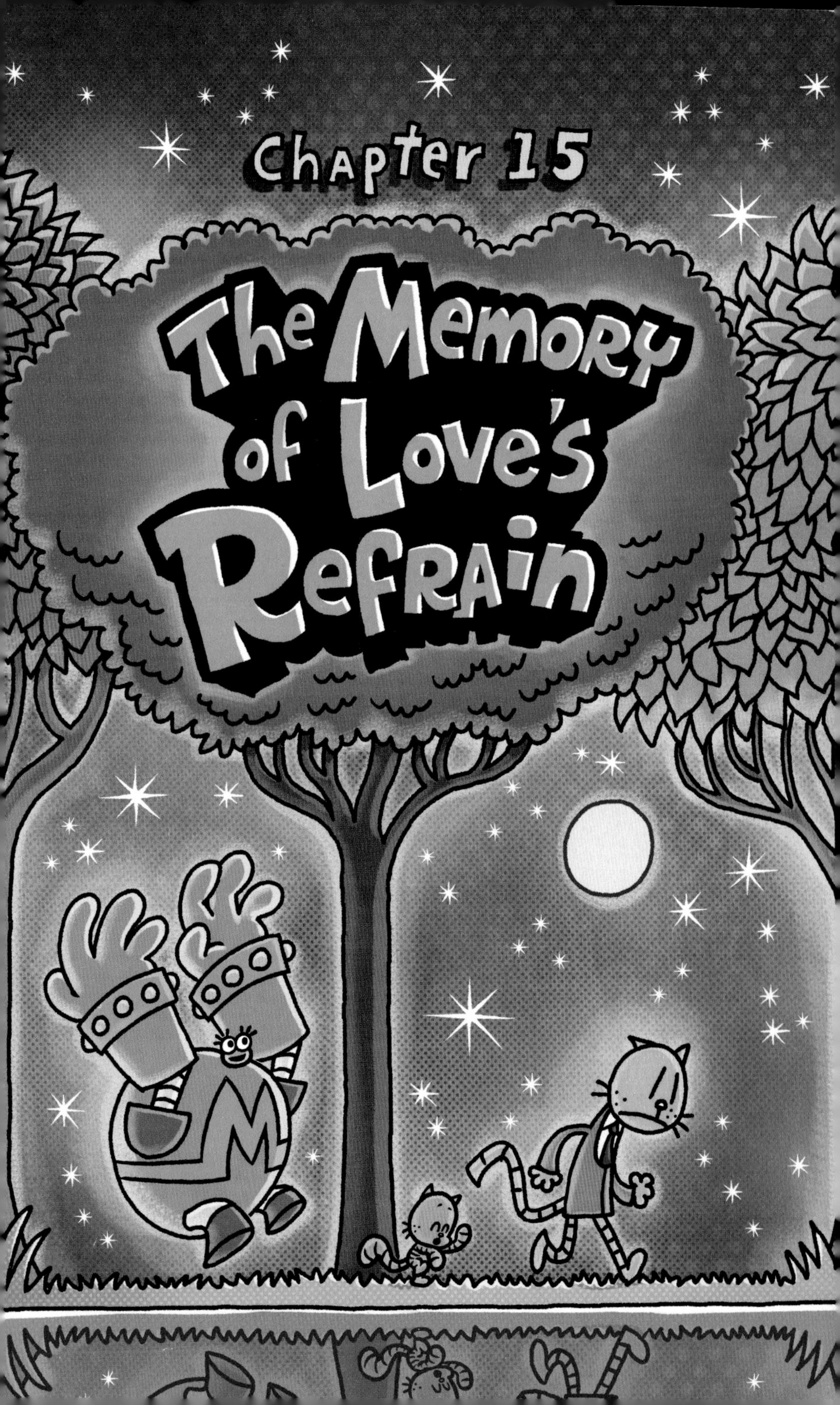
Chapter 15
The Memory of Love's Refrain

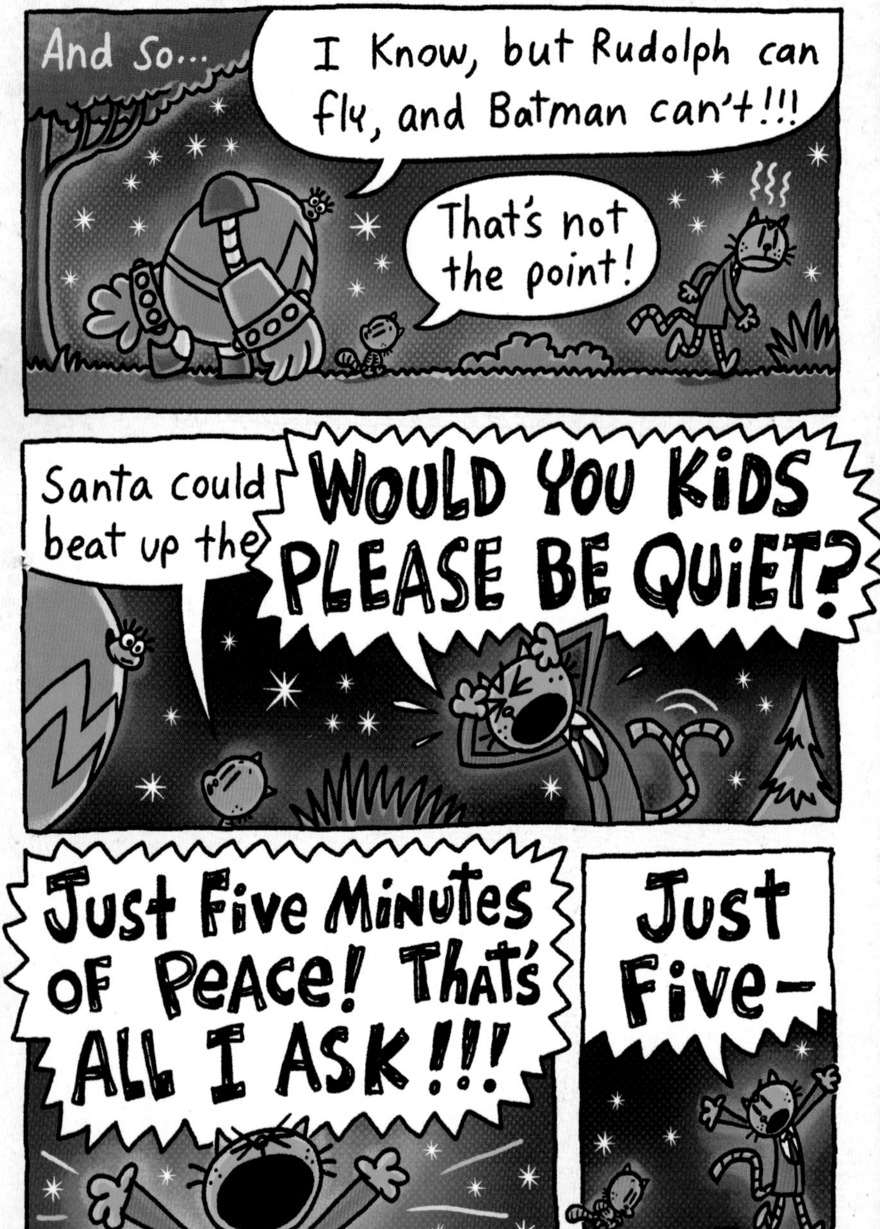

And So...
I Know, but Rudolph can fly, and Batman can't!!!
That's not the point!
Santa could beat up the
WOULD YOU KIDS PLEASE BE QUIET?
JUST FIVE MINUTES OF PEACE! THAT'S ALL I ASK!!!
JUST FIVE-

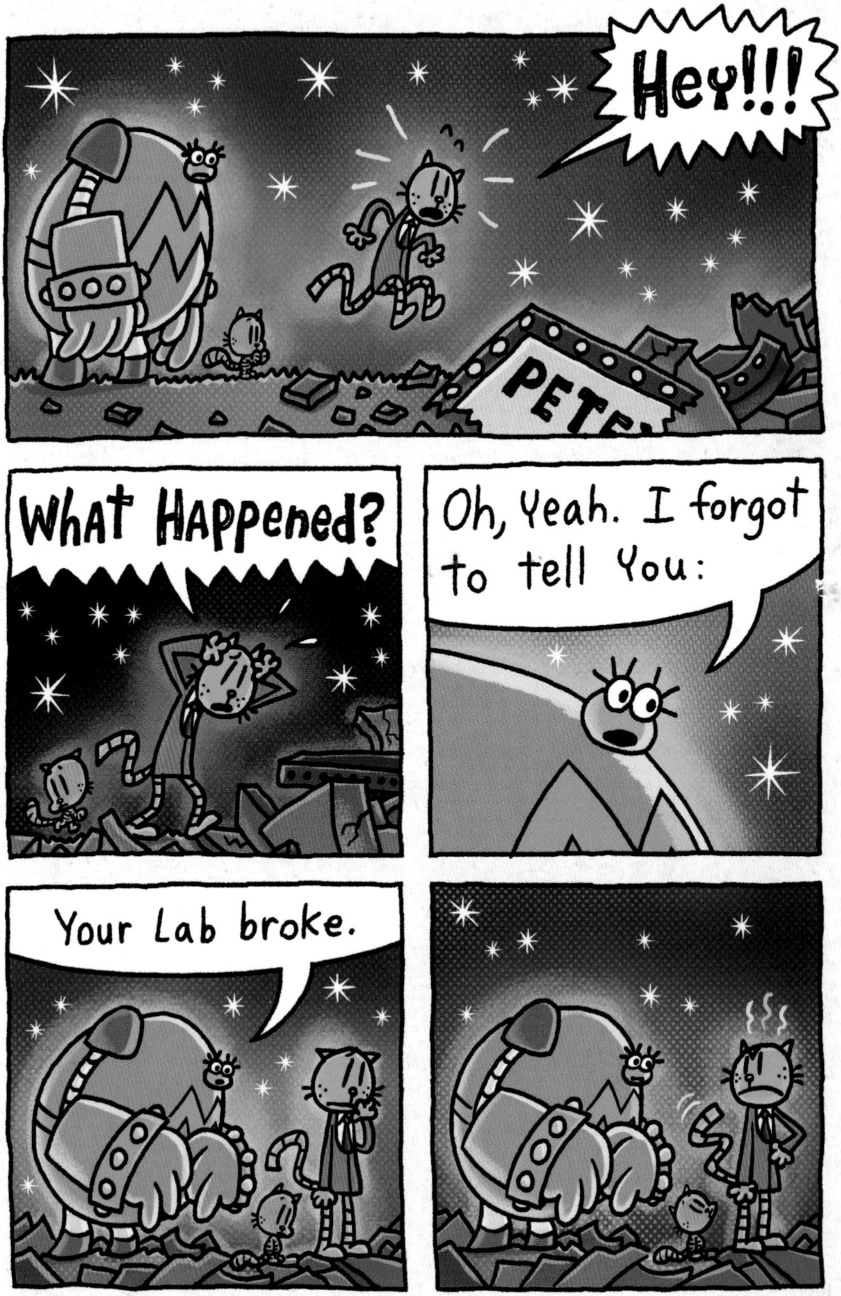

Hey!!!
PETE
WHAT HAPPENED?
Oh, Yeah. I forgot to tell You:
Your Lab broke.

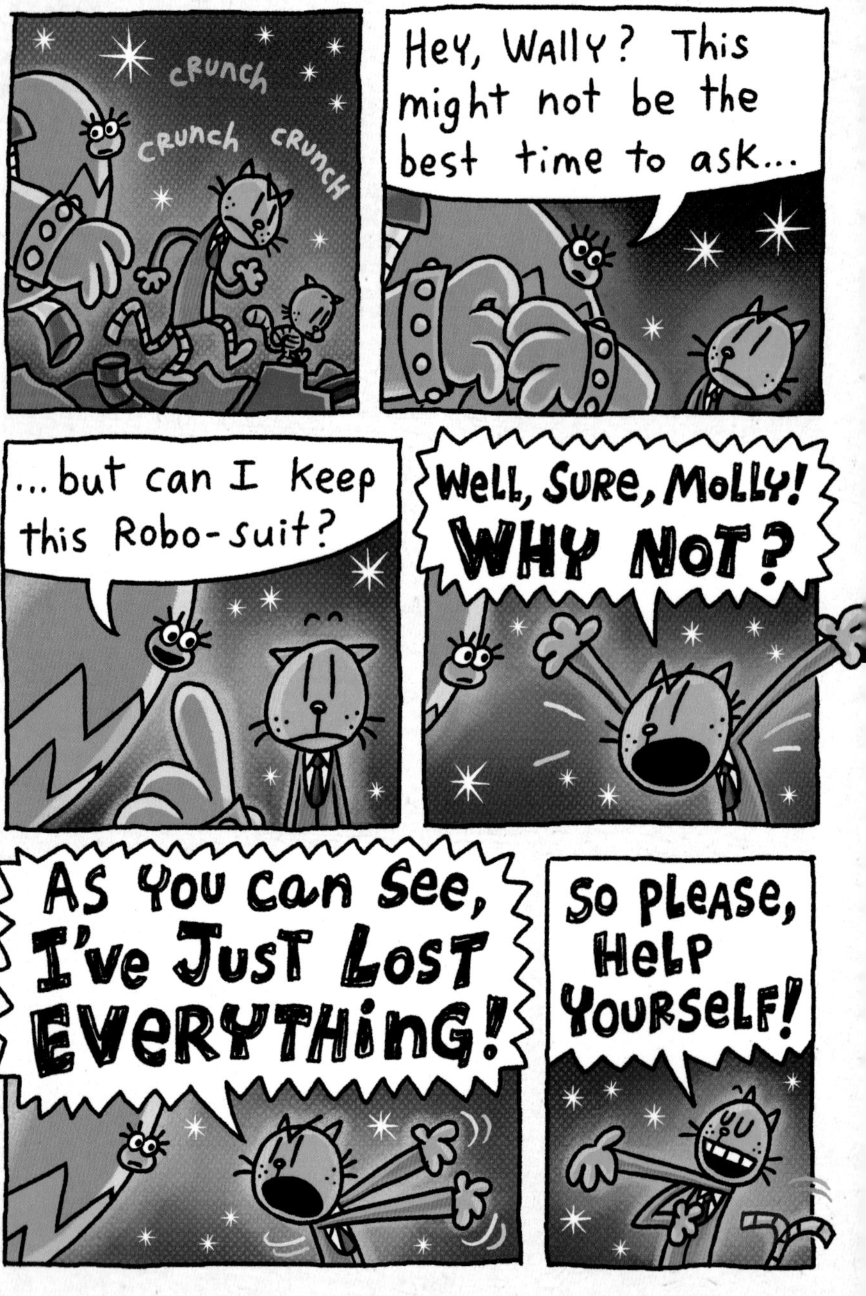
CRUNCH
CRUNCH
CRUNCH
Hey, Wally? This might not be the best time to ask...
...but can I keep this Robo-suit?
Well, sure, Molly! WHY NOT?
As you can see, I've just lost EVERYTHING!
So please, help yourself!

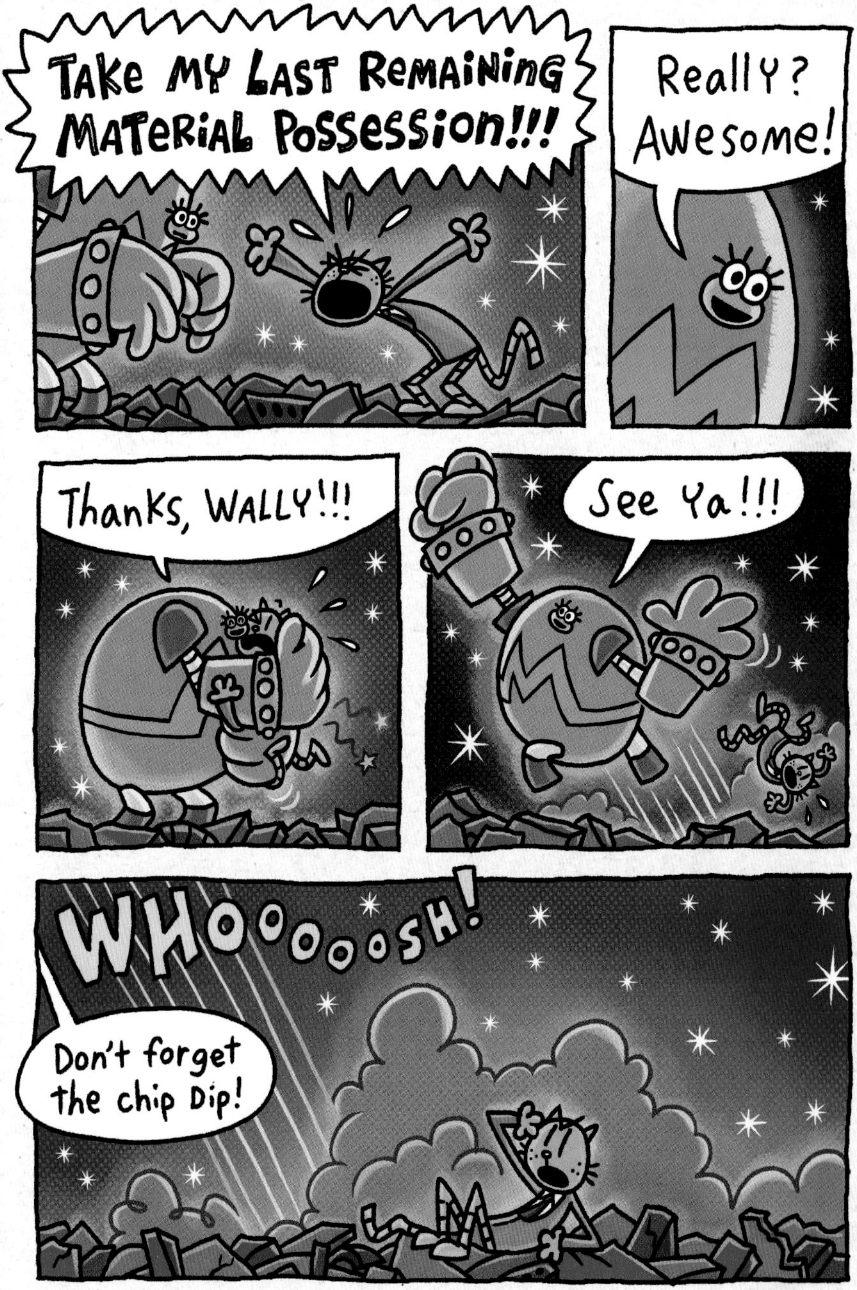
TAKE MY LAST REMAINING MATERIAL POSSESSION!!!
Really? Awesome!
Thanks, WALLY!!!
See Ya!!!
WHOOOOOOSH!
Don't forget the chip Dip!

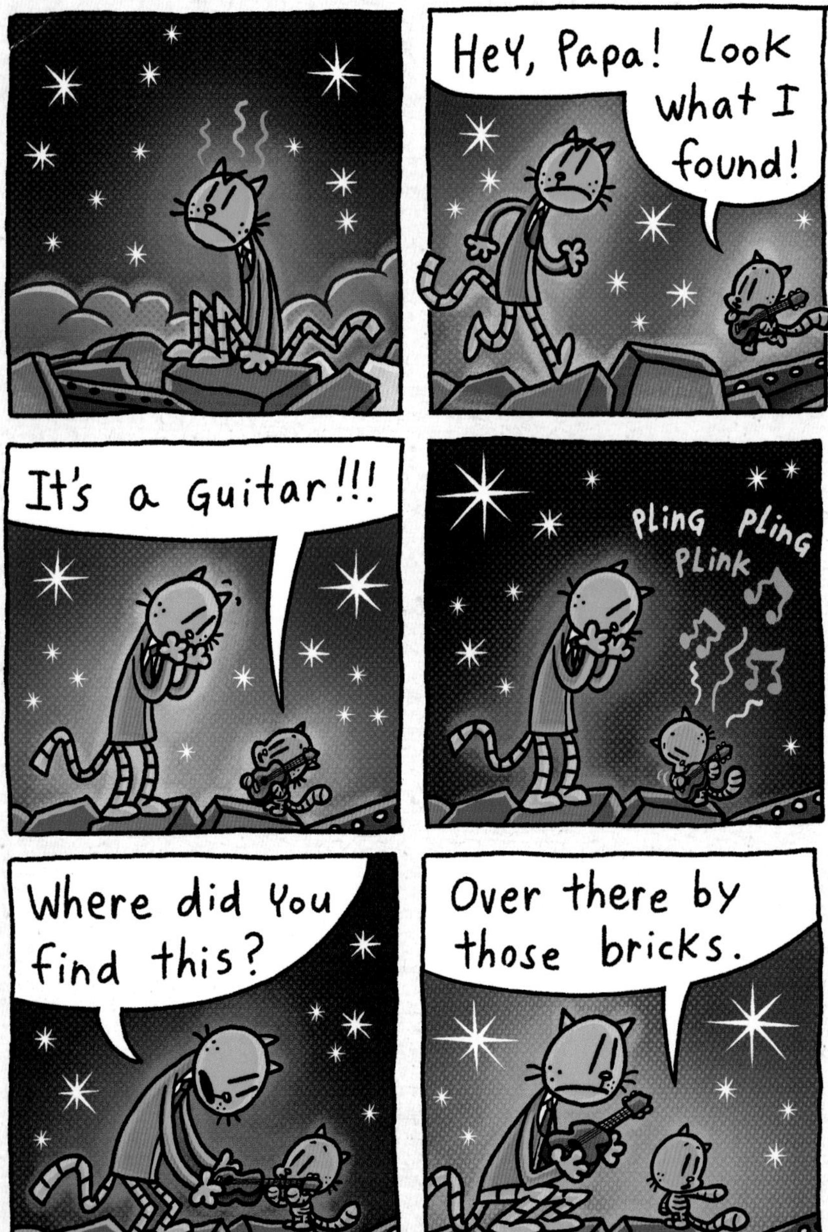
Hey, Papa! Look what I found!
It's a Guitar!!!
PLING PLING
PLINK
Where did you find this?
Over there by those bricks.

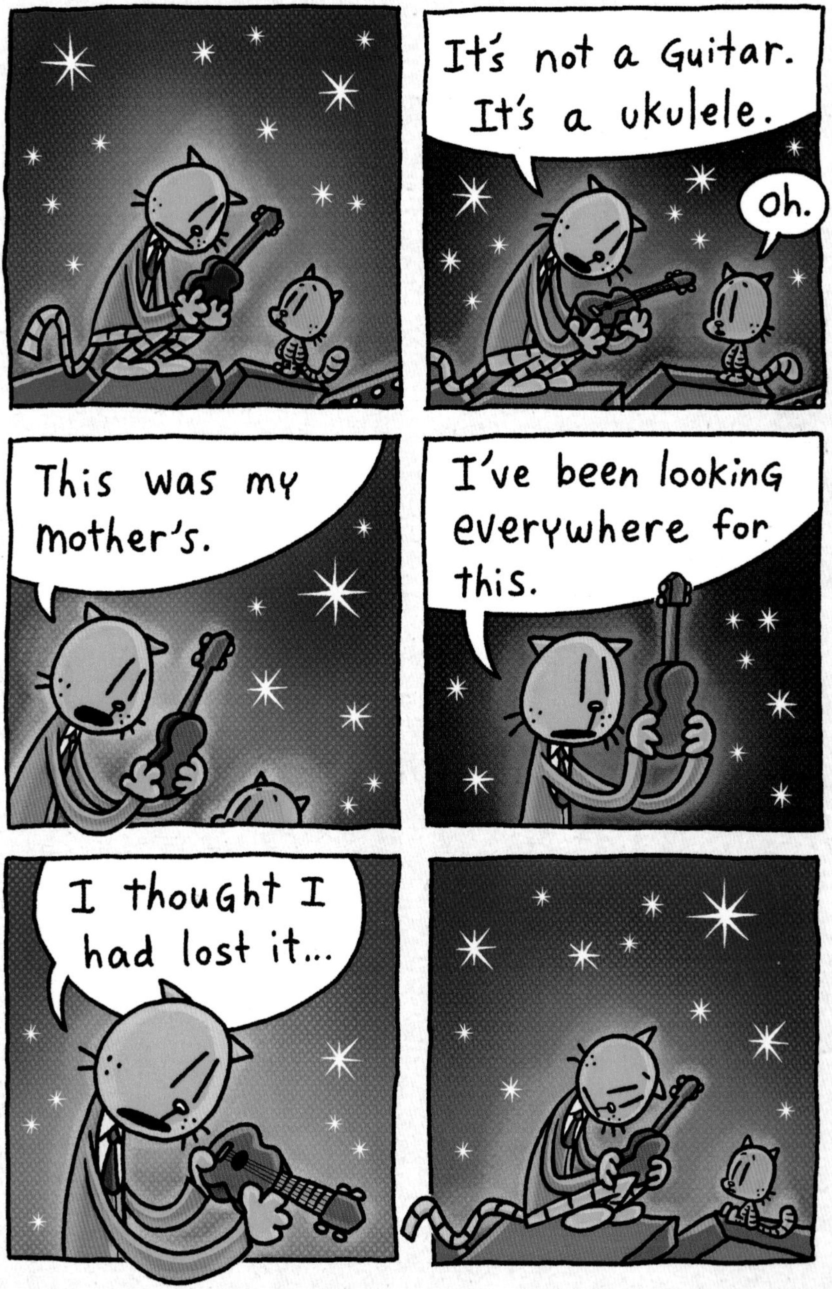

It's not a Guitar. It's a ukulele.
Oh.
This was my mother's.
I've been looking everywhere for this.
I thought I had lost it...

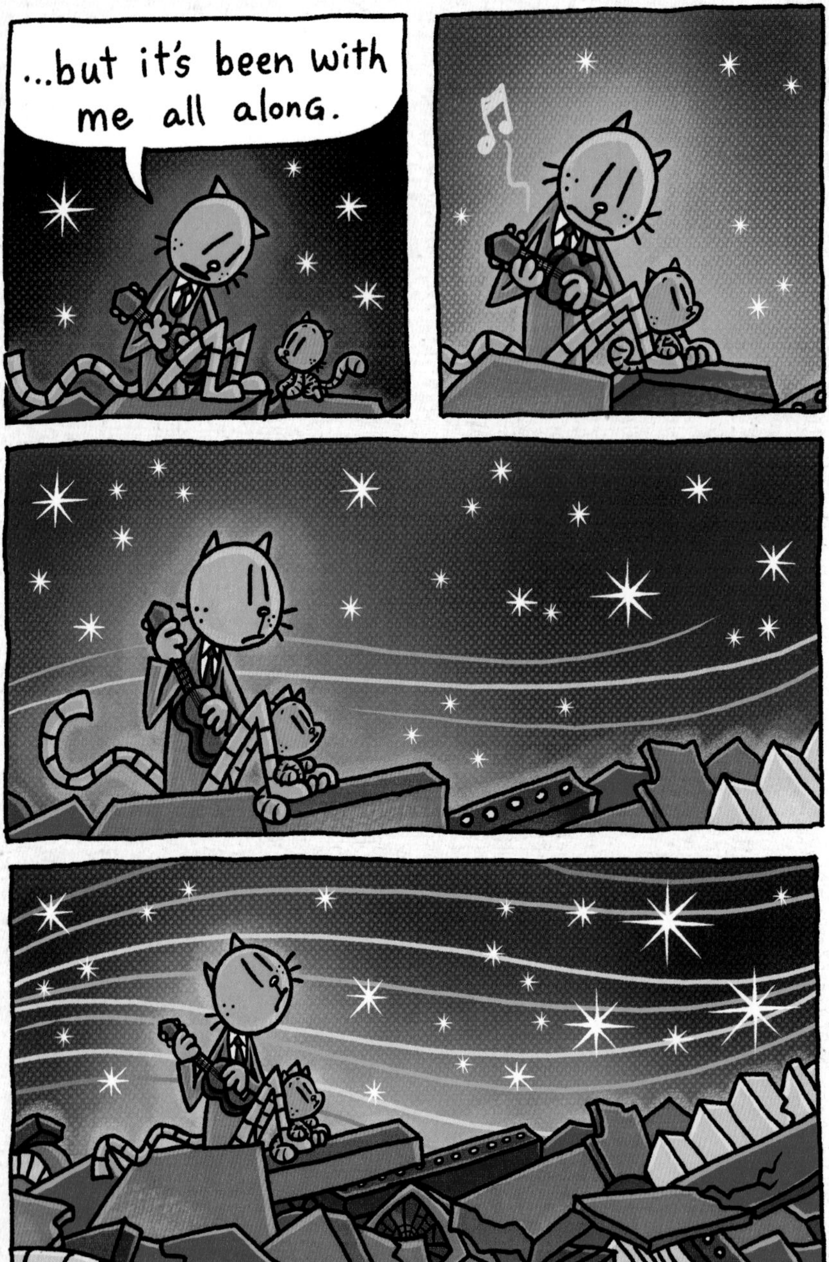
...but it's been with me all along.

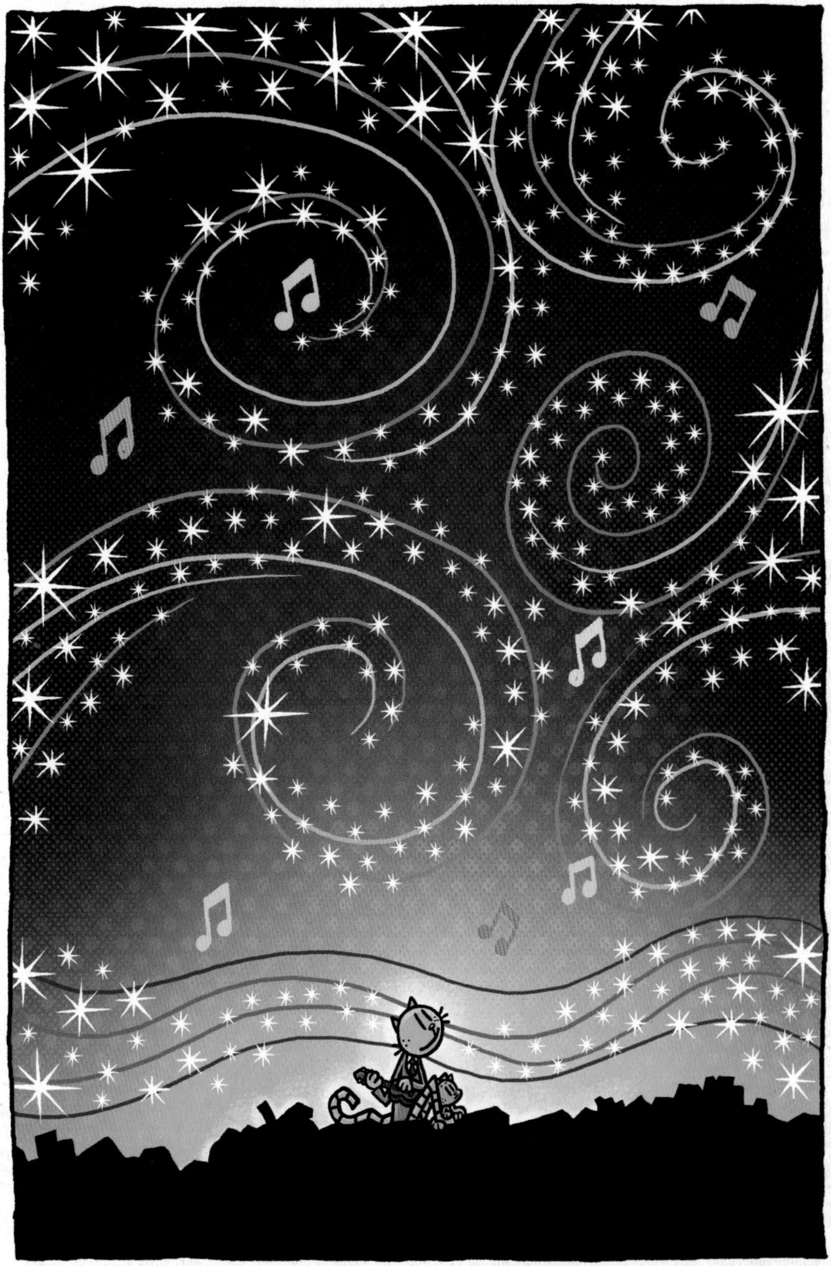

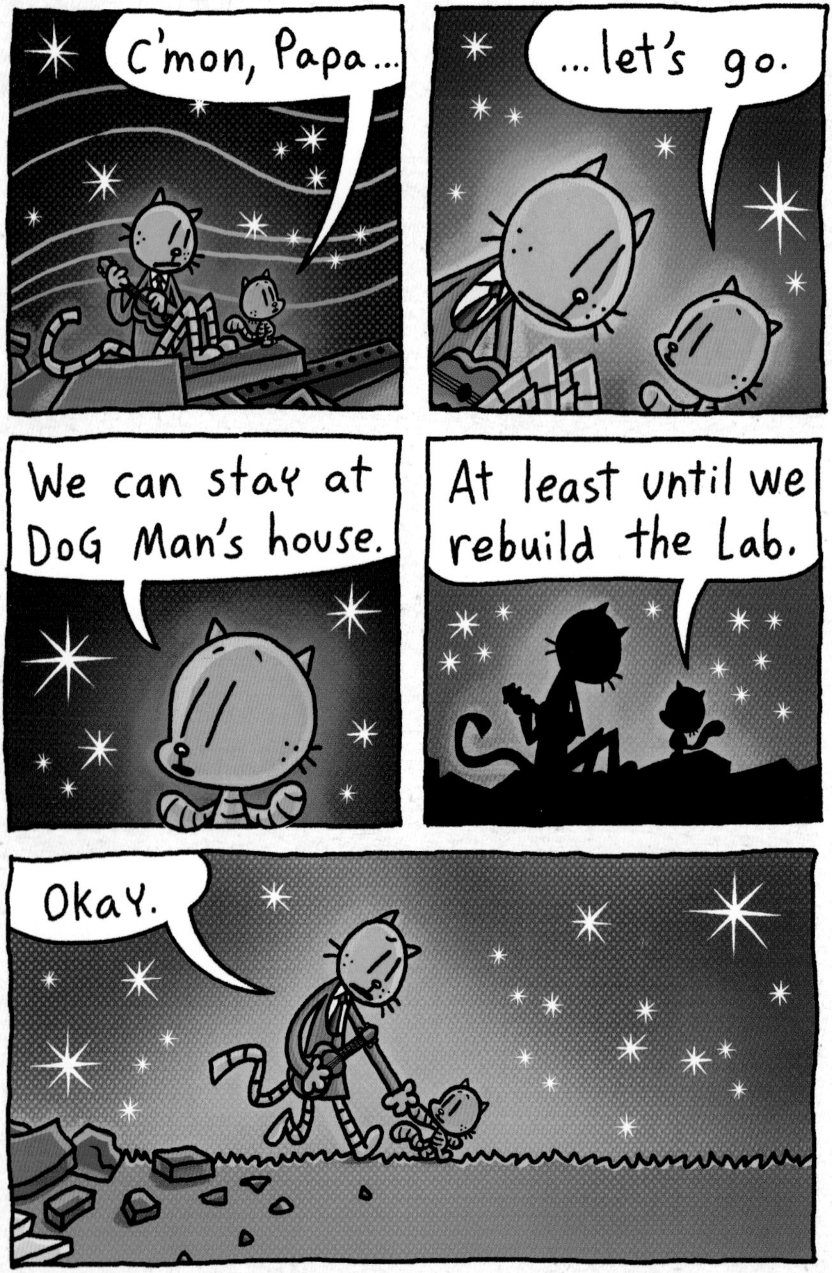
C'mon, Papa...
...let's go.
We can stay at DoG Man's house.
At least until we rebuild the Lab.
Okay.

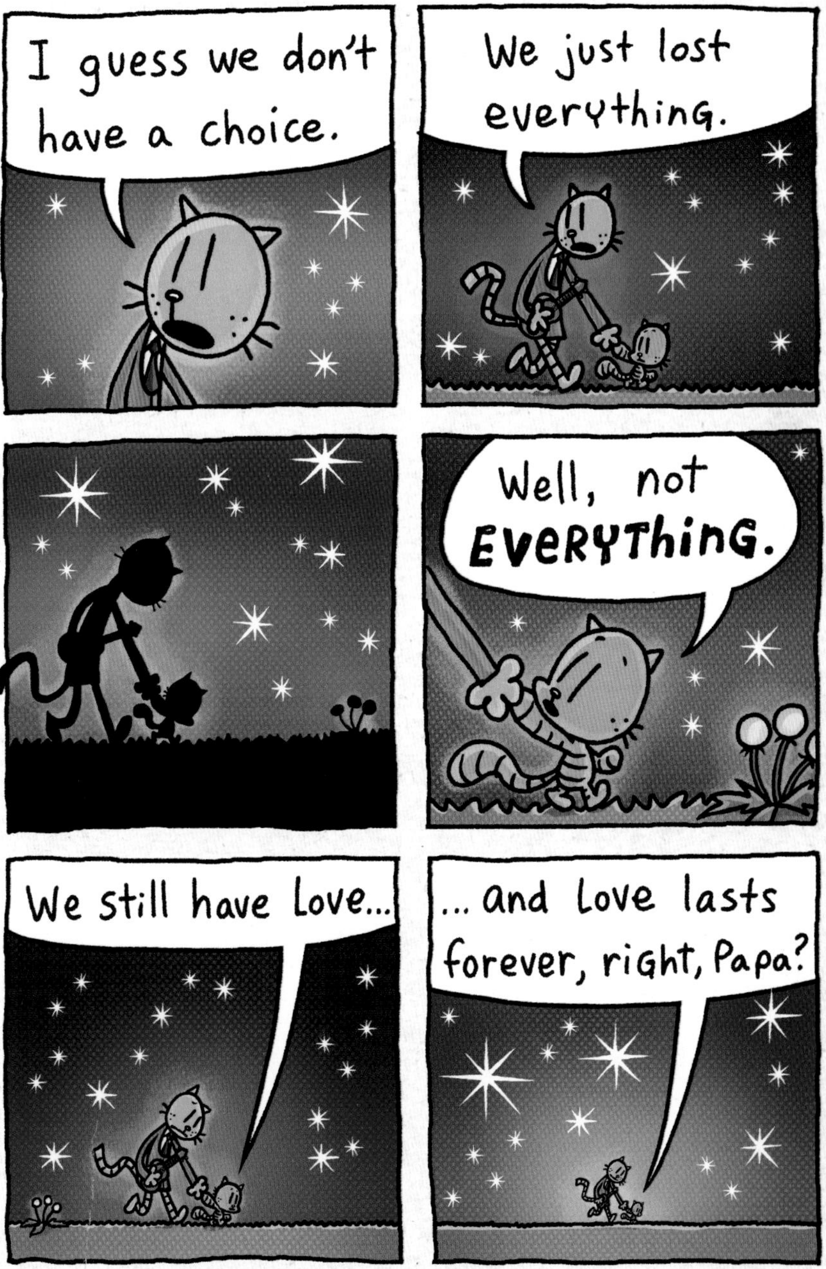
I guess we don't have a choice.
We just lost everything.
Well, not EVERYTHING.
We still have love...
... and love lasts forever, right, Papa?

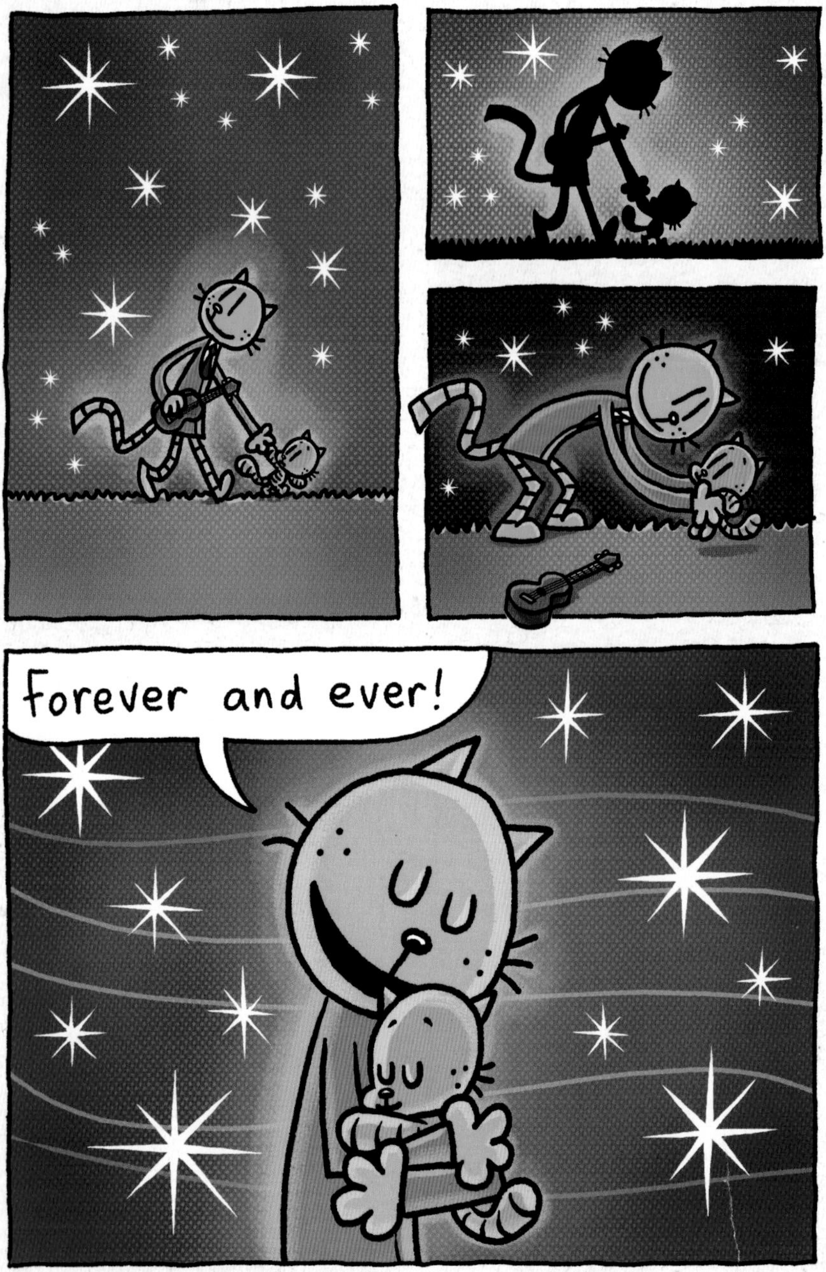
Forever and ever!

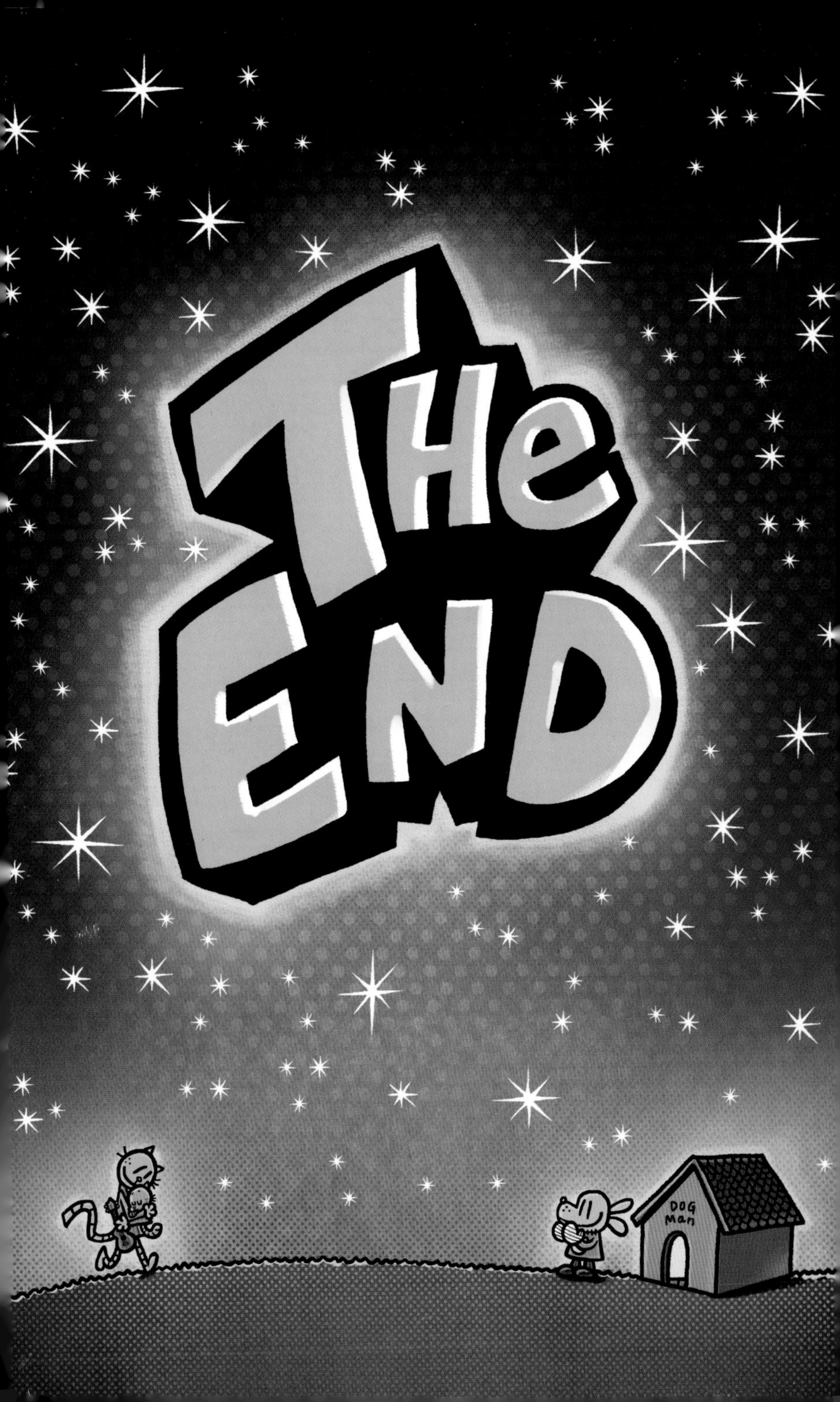
THE END
DOG Man

NOTES

by George and Harold

★ The musical interlude of Chief's dream (Chapter 1) is a parody of the song "The Greatest Love of ALL" by Michael Masser, with lyrics by Linda Creed.

★ Petey's red cardigan sweater and tie were based on the clothing often worn by beloved children's television host Mister Rogers.

★ On page 123, Petey is paraphrasing John 8:7 (NIV).

★ Petey's youthful "mistakes" and "bad choices" were chronicled in the graphic novel where he first appeared, *Super Diaper Baby 2: The Invasion of the Potty Snatchers*.

★ The title of Chapter 15 is the final line of the 1927 song "Stardust" by Hoagy Carmichael, with lyrics by Mitchell Parish.

★ This book was inspired by the two songs mentioned above, the quote on page 6, and the law of conservation of energy (a.k.a. the first law of thermodynamics).

HOW 2 DRAW MECHA MOLLY

in **22** Ridiculously easy steps!

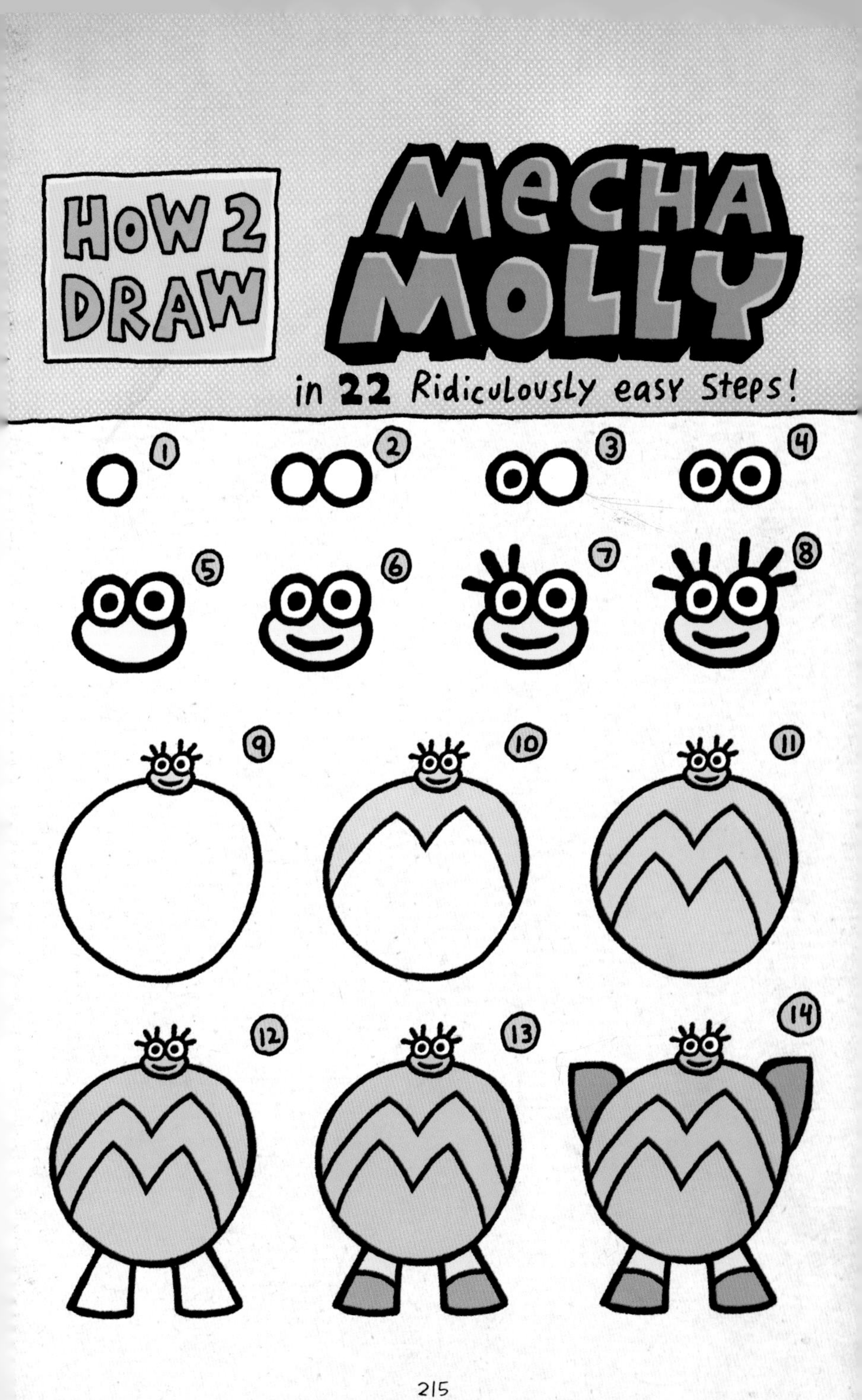
1
2
3
4
5
6
7
8
9
10
11
12
13
14

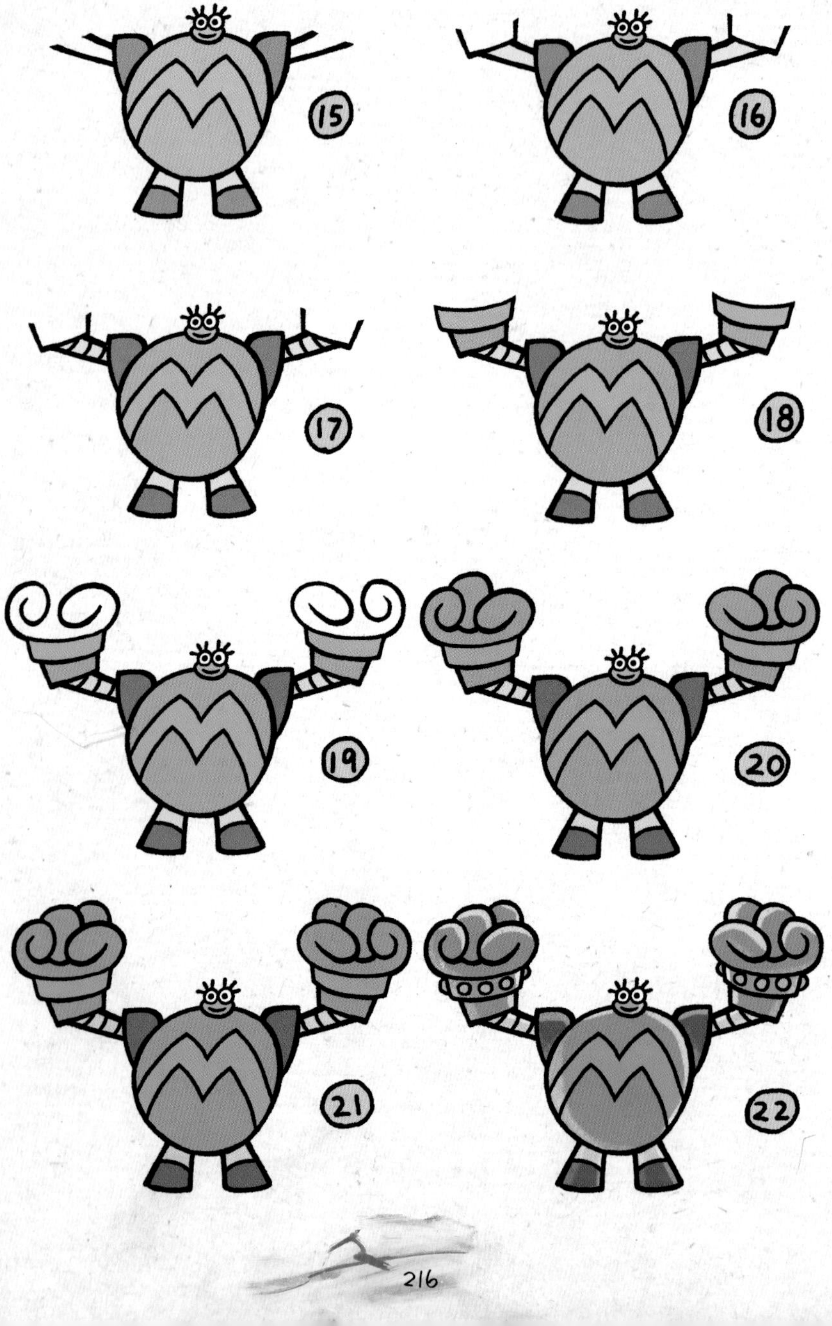
15
16
17
18
19
20
21
22

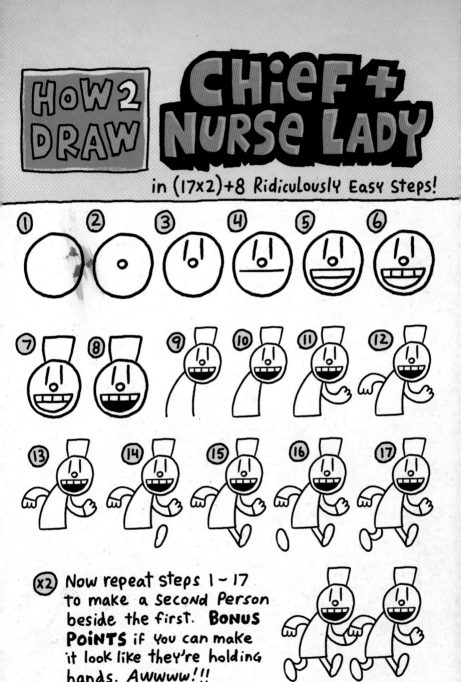

HOW 2 DRAW

CHIEF + NURSE LADY

in (17x2)+8 Ridiculously Easy Steps!

① ② ③ ④ ⑤ ⑥

⑦ ⑧ ⑨ ⑩ ⑪ ⑫

⑬ ⑭ ⑮ ⑯ ⑰

(x2) Now repeat steps 1 – 17 to make a second person beside the first. **BONUS POINTS** if you can make it look like they're holding hands. Awwww!!!

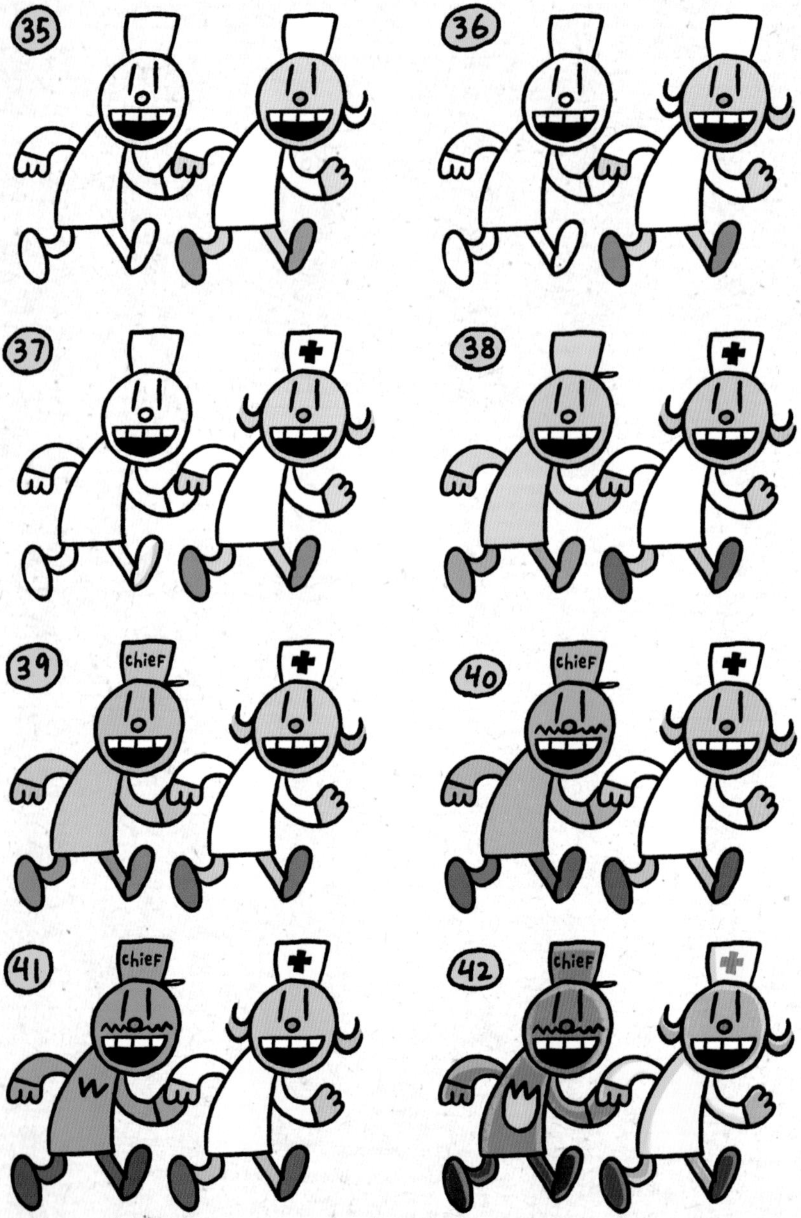
35
36
37
38
39
chief
40
chief
41
chief
W
42
chief

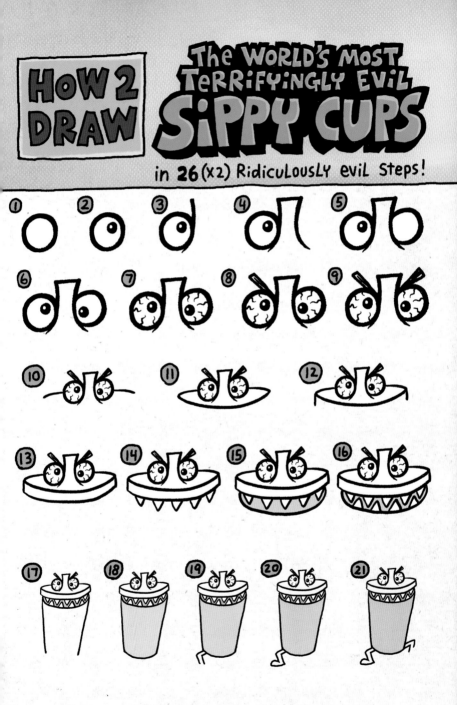

HOW 2 DRAW

The WORLD'S MOST TeRRiFYiNGLY EViL Sippy CUPS

in 26 (x2) RidicuLousLY eviL Steps!

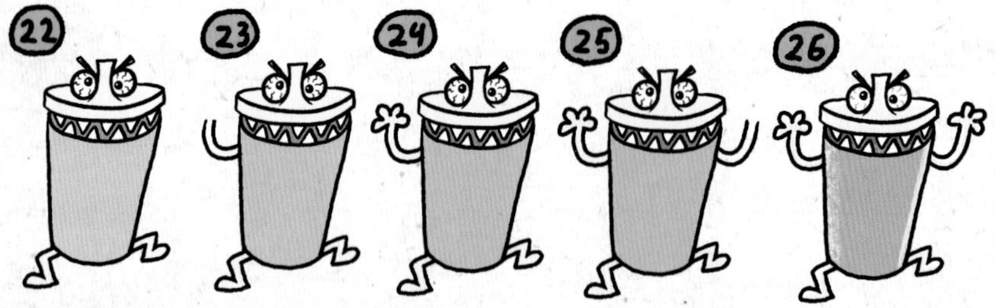
22
23
24
25
26

To draw the other Sippy Cup, Repeat Steps 1–9 on the previous page, then continue here

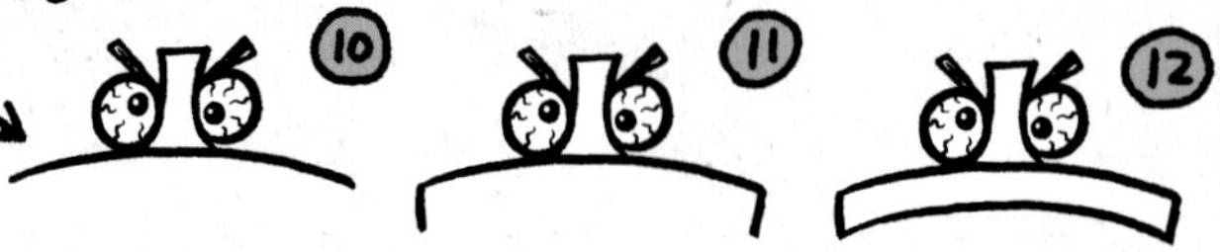
10
11
12

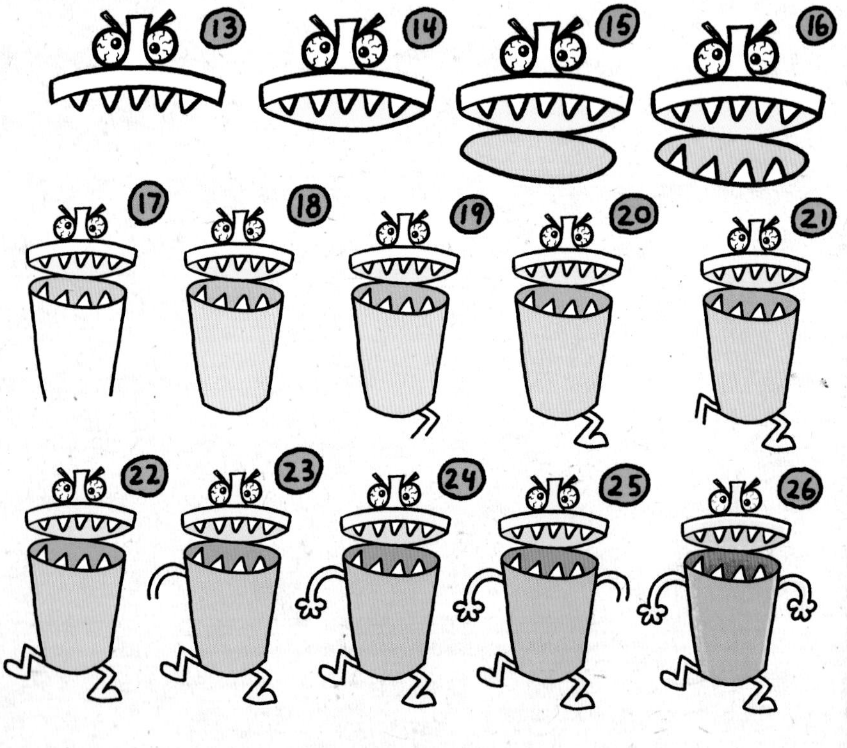
13
14
15
16
17
18
19
20
21
22
23
24
25
26

HOW 2 DRAW PETEY'S MOM

in **23** Ridiculously easy steps!

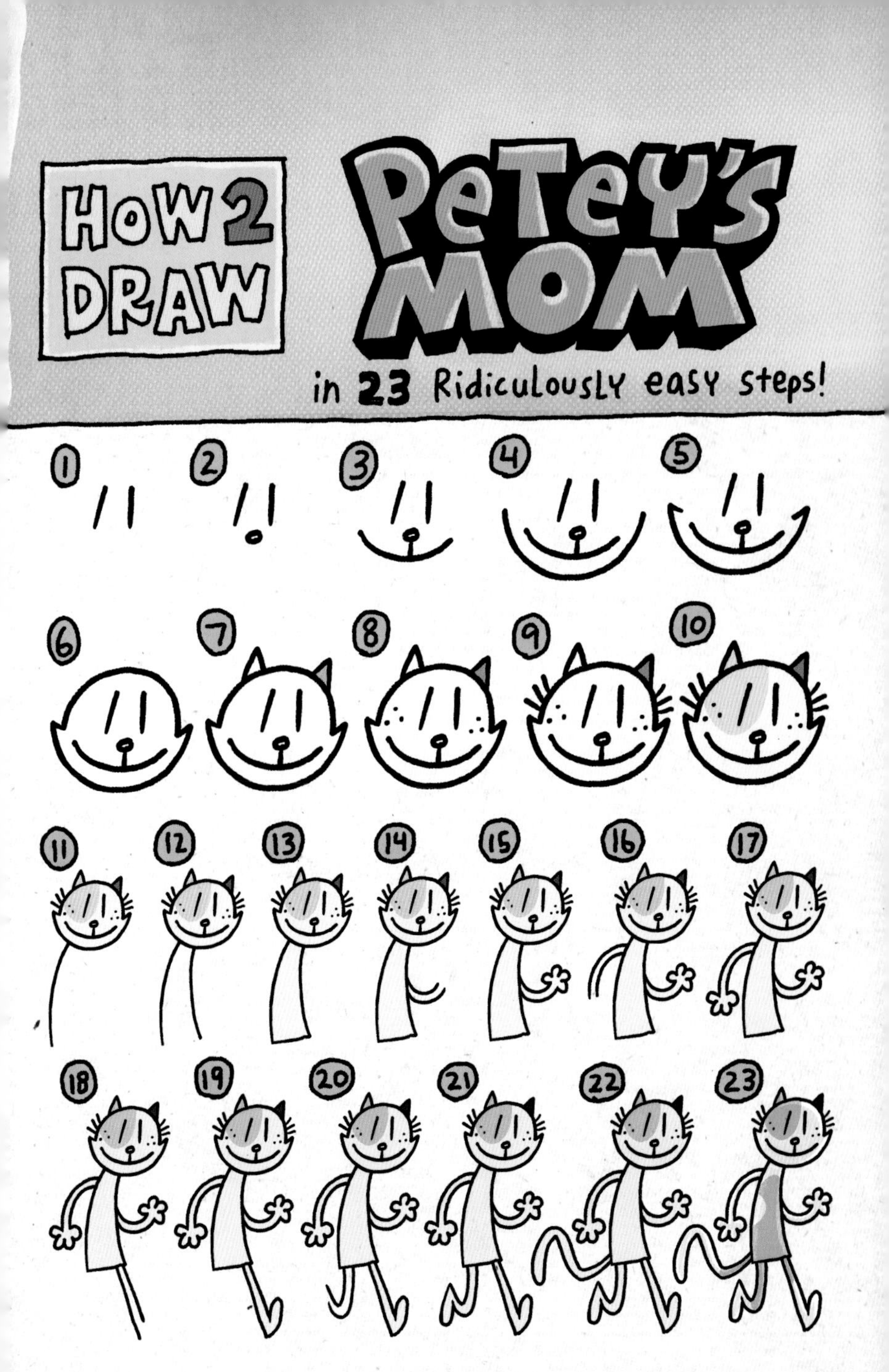
1
2
3
4
5
6
7
8
9
10
11
12
13
14
15
16
17
18
19
20
21
22
23

GET READING W

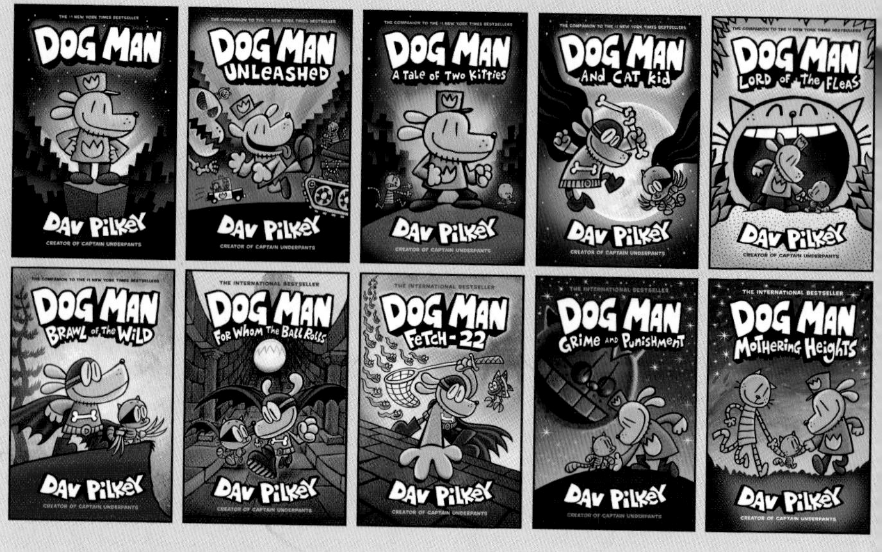

DOG MAN
DAV PILKEY
CREATOR OF CAPTAIN UNDERPANTS
DOG MAN UNLEASHED
DAV PILKEY
DOG MAN A Tale of Two Kitties
DAV PILKEY
DOG MAN AND CAT KID
DAV PILKEY
DOG MAN LORD OF THE FLEAS
DAV PILKEY
DOG MAN BRAWL of the WILD
DAV PILKEY
DOG MAN FOR WHOM THE BALL ROLLS
DAV PILKEY
DOG MAN FETCH-22
DAV PILKEY
DOG MAN GRIME AND PUNISHMENT
DAV PILKEY
DOG MAN MOTHERING HEIGHTS
DAV PILKEY

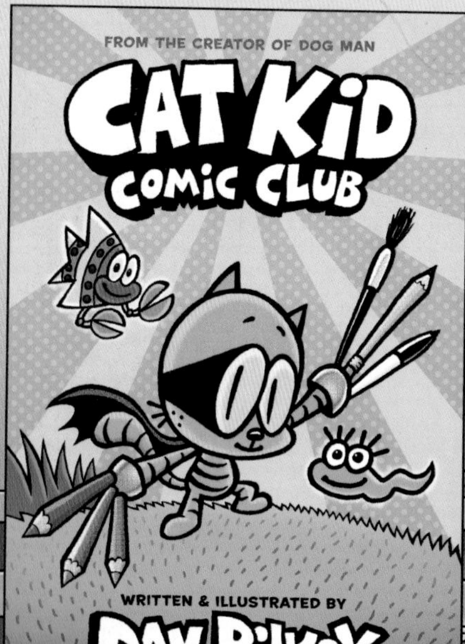

FROM THE CREATOR OF DOG MAN
CAT KID COMIC CLUB
WRITTEN & ILLUSTRATED BY
DAV PILKEY

★ "Irreverent, laugh-out-loud funny, and . . . downright moving."
— Publishers Weekly, starred review

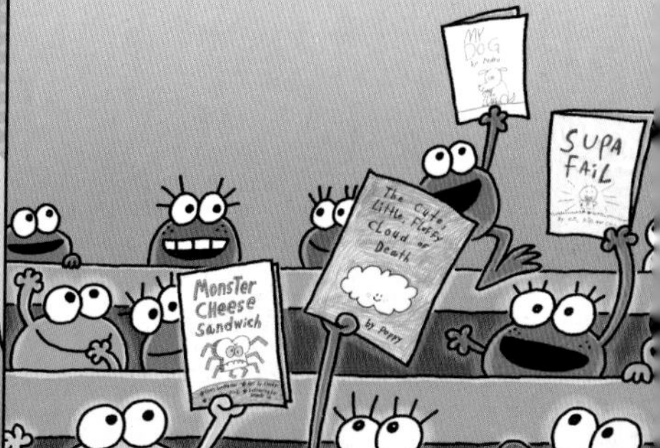

MY DOG
SUPA FAIL
The Cute, Little, Fluffy Cloud of Death
by Poppy
Monster Cheese Sandwich

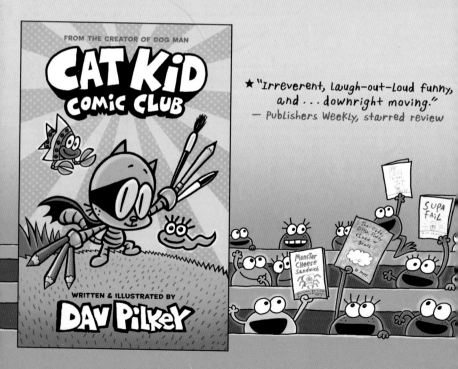

TH DAV PILKEY!

The Adventures of
Captain Underpants
Full Color
The First Epic Novel by
Dav Pilkey
Caldecott Honor Artist

Full Color
Captain Underpants
and the Attack of the Talking Toilets
The Second Epic Novel by
Dav Pilkey
Caldecott Honor Artist

Full Color
Captain Underpants
and the Invasion of the Incredibly Naughty Cafeteria Ladies from Outer Space (and the Subsequent Assault of the Equally Evil Lunchroom Zombie Nerds)
The Third Epic Novel by
Dav Pilkey
Caldecott Honor Artist

Full Color
Captain Underpants
and the Perilous Plot of Professor Poopypants
The Fourth Epic Novel by
Dav Pilkey
Caldecott Honor Artist

Full Color
Captain Underpants
and the Wrath of the Wicked Wedgie Woman
The Fifth Epic Novel by
Dav Pilkey
Caldecott Honor Artist

Full Color
Captain Underpants
and the Big, Bad Battle of the Bionic Booger Boy
Part 1: The Night of the Nasty Nostril Nuggets
The Sixth Epic Novel by
Dav Pilkey
Caldecott Honor Artist

Full Color
Captain Underpants
and the Big, Bad Battle of the Bionic Booger Boy
Part 2: The Revenge of the Ridiculous Robo-Boogers
The Seventh Epic Novel by
Dav Pilkey
Caldecott Honor Artist

Full Color
Captain Underpants
and the Preposterous Plight of the Purple Potty People
The Eighth Epic Novel by
Dav Pilkey
Caldecott Honor Artist

Full Color
Captain Underpants
and the Terrifying Re-Turn of Tippy Tinkletrousers
The Ninth Epic Novel by
Dav Pilkey
Caldecott Honor Artist

Full Color
Captain Underpants
and the Revolting Revenge of the Radioactive Robo-Boxers
The Tenth Epic Novel by
Dav Pilkey
Caldecott Honor Artist

Full Color
Captain Underpants
and the Tyrannical Retaliation of the Turbo Toilet 2000
The Eleventh Epic Novel by
Dav Pilkey
Caldecott Honor Artist

Full Color
Captain Underpants
and the Sensational Saga of Sir Stinks-A-Lot
The Twelfth Epic Novel by
Dav Pilkey
Caldecott Honor Artist

Dog Man
The Musical
Original Cast Recording

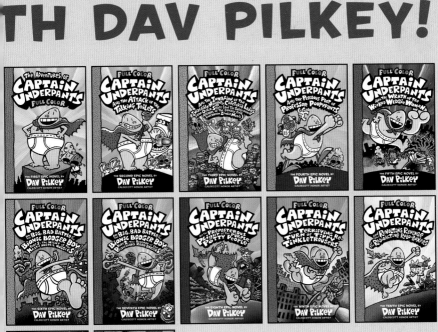

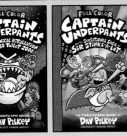

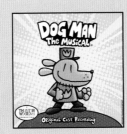

The epic musical adventure is now available from Broadway Records!

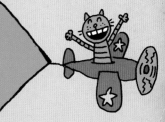

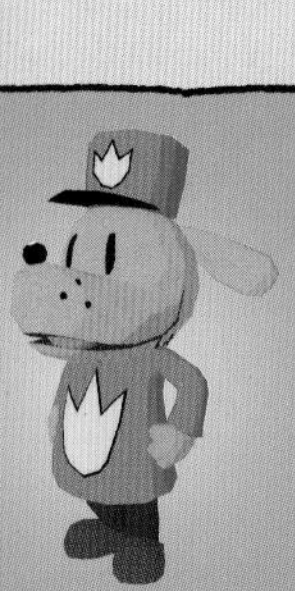

Meet all your favorite characters on the Dog Man Island in Home Base! Play games, make and share your own comics, and more at scholastic.com/homebase!

Download on the App Store

HOME BASE

SCHOLASTIC

GET IT ON Google Play

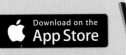

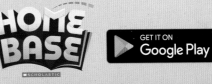

ABOUT THE
AUTHOR-ILLUSTRATOR

When Dav Pilkey was a kid, he was diagnosed with ADHD and dyslexia. Dav was so disruptive in class that his teachers made him sit out in the hallway every day. Luckily, Dav loved to draw and make up stories. He spent his time in the hallway creating his own original comic books — the very first adventures of Dog Man and Captain Underpants.

In college, Dav met a teacher who encouraged him to illustrate and write. He won a national competition in 1986 and the prize was the publication of his first book, WORLD WAR WON. He made many other books before being awarded the 1998 California Young Reader Medal for DOG BREATH, which was published in 1994, and in 1997 he won the Caldecott Honor for THE PAPERBOY.

THE ADVENTURES OF SUPER DIAPER BABY, published in 2002, was the first complete graphic novel spin-off from the Captain Underpants series and appeared at #6 on the USA Today bestseller list for all books, both adult and children's, and was also a New York Times bestseller. It was followed by THE ADVENTURES OF OOK AND GLUK: KUNG FU CAVEMEN FROM THE FUTURE and SUPER DIAPER BABY 2: THE INVASION OF THE POTTY SNATCHERS, both USA Today bestsellers. The unconventional style of these graphic novels is intended to encourage uninhibited creativity in kids.

His stories are semi-autobiographical and explore universal themes that celebrate friendship, tolerance, and the triumph of the good-hearted.

Dav loves to kayak in the Pacific Northwest with his wife.